WANDERER

ALSO BY THE AUTHOR

THE STARSTRUCK SAGA

Starstruck

Alienation

Traveler

Celestial

Starbound

Earthstuck

Inalienable

Dreadknot

AIX MARKS THE SPOT

OVER THE MOON

NOVELLAS AND SHORT STORIES

Miss Planet Earth (Pew! Pew! - The Quest for More Pew!)

The Horrible Habits of Humans (Pew! Pew! - Bite My Shiny Metal Pew!)

Miss Planet Earth and the Amulet of Beb Sha Na

Head over Heels (Starstruck Halloween Short)

Lasers and Tiaras (Starstruck Short)

Study Night at the Museum (Unbound: Stories of Transformation, Love, And Monsters)

BOOK NINE OF THE STARSTRUCK SAGA

WANDERER

S.E. ANDERSON

BOLIDE

WANDERER

Cover design by Sarah Anderson

First published in 2023 by Bolide Publishing Limited
Bolidepublishing.com

ISBN: 978-1-912996-38-4

TO CORA AND CRYSTAL
FOR KEEPING ME STEADY

PROLOGUE

BREAKING FREE FROM FACTORY-RELIGION: FROM WORSHIP TO REBELLION

I REFUSE TO BREAK A SWEAT OVER PEOPLE WHO don't deserve it. Salt can be a valuable resource and hella tasty to boot.

I won't be wasting it over the grunt patrolling beneath me. My hands clutch a bundle of pipes, my feet braced on an I-beam. A chill seeps into my back from the cement ceiling I'm pressed against, countered by the delicious burn of my muscles. I've stopped breathing. I can keep this up forever.

My body betrays me. Sweat beads on my brow and drips on the guard like the first raindrop before the storm. Ugh, what a waste. He stops, looks up, locks eyes with me. On instinct I release my toes, swinging down and wrapping my legs around his neck before he can even ask my star sign. Now, I squeeze.

WANDERER

The thought of how easily I could kill him bores me. One twist of my hips and his neck will snap. But while there's a surplus of utility closets in which to hide a body—they worship custodians religiously around here—they're interconnected through an AI with a sassy streak, who I've already failed to seduce.

The guard flops onto the floor with a thud, knocked out cold. No guilt pangs here. Even if this situation isn't of his own making—it's not his fault the only employment around here is as a nefarious criminal mastermind's lackey, and something's got to bring home the cheese—his mission was to keep me from doing what I must. However, life's a precious commodity, even more so than salt, and there would be nothing worse than wasting it.

I strip him, slipping his uniform over my infiniweave bodysuit. Keys. Stunner. Cap, which I pull low. My hip feels oddly light without Felling's weight sitting there. I pause, worried by her absence, before remembering where I set her for safekeeping. As much as I want her with me on these missions, she's literally a deadweight since she's been stuck in Miro's mind ball.

I can't allow myself to think about her. How I let her down, how I'm doing just that, again, right here and now, by not spending my every waking moment—and there are a lot of them—searching for a solution. But I can't move forward with all these loose ends dangling behind me. It's time to tie them up or cut them off.

I leave the guard sprawled on the floor behind me. He's seen my face, but the next guard won't be around for twenty minutes and I should be done in ten. Even if he wakes up before then, I've got his com badge. The guard's keycard moves me through the different sectors, and I weave easily through the steam tunnels. Security could really be tightened in a few key areas. How much I could make as a contractor? It would be nice to get paid to break into places for a change.

I need a challenge, and this mission just isn't cutting it. It's too easy: stars, the workers literally opened the front door for me, and invited me onto the factory floor in exchange for my help. Then again, everything's too easy, now that I've reversed my auto-lobotomy and have access to all my memories. Now, all that space and time lie open at my feet.

But being alone forces one to talk to oneself, and I don't particularly like who's answering. Then again, I don't need to like myself to live with myself. Maybe I've been putting up with my own crap for too long.

I miss them. Soul-searching is a lonely business. While I don't need anyone's help, it's nice to be lauded from time to time. This whole separation was about clearing out the old and making a clean slate. It's easier to distract myself with some self-appointed do-gooder crusading than putting the personal development work in on knowing myself. But just because I've forgotten about this job for fifteen thousand years doesn't mean it's not important. Easy, sure, but it eventually needs to get done.

I turn a corner and come face-to-face with another guard. Frash, got distracted by the soul-searching. I slam the stunner against his temple and he crumples like a rag doll. *Frashing boring.* Give me extra pairs of legs, give me poisoned darts, lasers, anything to make this infiltration even the slightest bit stimulating.

I take the guards' elevator up as far as it goes and slip into the accounting department. The bathroom is waiting for me, and I switch out of the guard's uniform, flushing it down the toilet. This of course clogs it, which sounds the alarm for the custodians, but I'm tiptoeing away as the office staff drop to their knees in eyes-seared-shut prayer.

"Clean us of our sins, oh crew," they chant. I chant along with them as the beloved custodial crew races past, mops held high. The second they've passed I'm back on my feet, in the administrative elevator, riding to the top of the tower.

Here comes the hard part. I mean, I *hope.*

The elevator sprays me with mistal-mist as the doors open on Trask's secretary. He looks up as I enter and frowns. My skin-tight bodysuit is the opposite of fashionable on this planet, where baggy clothes are the rage; a visual reminder to the people that they are trash, and the Divine Duster will one day brush them into his waste basket where he will recycle them for another life. The Divine Duster, guardian of the grime, who's sitting one office away. Not sure why they accept that their God incarnate runs their business, but that's partially why I'm here today.

"Do you… have an appointment?" The secretary averts his gaze. I must really be unsanctified. As Trask's secretary, he's effectively the High Priest of Hygiene.

"Can't remember," I say. "But he'll see me anyway."

I shove two fingers down my throat and vomit my breakfast all over his desk.

"What the Incinerator!" cries the secretary. Now him, I do feel sorry for. Breakfast had been full of beans and they have so many little arms.

"Call your custodians," I said. "I'll pray for your soul."

He drops to the floor, muttering a prayer.

I open the doors to the massive office of Trask Utility's CEO and God, Robert Trask. At the very tip of the glass tower, the walls are floor-to-ceiling glass, with a 270 degree view of the sprawling factory below. I could have jumped up here, but I had to make it a little bit challenging for myself, otherwise it's just cheating.

And there he is, at last: Robert Trask.

Wiped from my memory the last time I'd run the labyrinth; he'd once been a sort of nemesis of mine. Though I don't think he'd known about it. I'd spent months planning a rebellion with his workforce, who'd been run ragged by building the infinite utility closets this world required of them. A little investigating on my part revealed the religion was created by Trask in order to build an eager workforce to sell prefabs to neighboring star systems. His workers died off so quickly, none were the wiser. All was going well until Zander had his breakdown and we needed a bit of time to refocus but, as time travelers, no one would notice us missing—and no one did, for any of the fifteen thousand years that I was doing my own thing. The rebellion picked up as if I'd last sung with them yesterday, which, in their linear time, I had.

Trask wears an immaculate suit of navy blue, which covers his skin entirely, except for his face, which is also blue for other, indiscernible, reasons. He looks up at me as I enter, brows furrowing. He doesn't yell. I wish he would.

"Who are you?" He lifts an eyebrow.

Dull, dull, abysmally dull. Would it help if he screamed a little? It does feel better when I get recognized for my work, even slightly. I stride up to his desk and bat the lamp off, hoping for a reaction. He's probably pressed the panic button already. His guards might take a while.

So, I don't answer him, savoring the moment instead. His confusion. Dare I say, his fear? I slide onto the desk where the lamp once stood, my legs dangling over the parquet floor, leaning in. He smells like mistal root, too. I twist towards him and smile.

Still no reaction. *Fine.* I grab him by the tie, wrapping it twice around my wrist and pulling him over his papers and out of his seat. He gasps. Finally, his mask of composure breaks. He's gulping for air and I'm holding him here, close enough to smell his breakfast on his breath. I could do bicep curls, but he's too light for it to be fun.

"Remember me, Trask? I had an appointment with you."

He shakes his head—or tries to. It's not like he could answer verbally right now anyway.

"Really? This face doesn't ring any bells?" I sigh. "I have a message for you."

I drop him back in his seat. His eyes dart around the room, searching for his guards, but they're likely caught up in custodial worship all over the factory as my union friends wreak havoc with the plumbing.

Trask runs a hand over his neck. His face has returned to the mask of serenity. He's no fun.

"From… who?" His sentence comes out in a collapsing mishmash of vowels and vibrations.

"Whom."

"Excuse me?"

"You mean *whom*. I think. Grammar is tricky with translator chips. Anyway, I have a few here. The message is from a certain friend of mine, a man by the name of Mr. Sparegrout. Head of the Parasol Corporation. Heard of it?"

Trask's hands return to his desk. His papers are shuffled, and there's ink on his chest.

"Look, I don't have all day here." I raise my palm, a trickle of euphoria filling me as he flinches. I finally have his attention. "Sparegrout, about my height, fifty limbs? More eyes than your puny brain can process?"

Trask nods. "I've heard of him."

"He and Parasol need you off planet yesterday. You and your entire business: take to the stars, leave, and never set foot here again. Well, that's me paraphrasing. His actual words were '*Beat it.*'"

He throws back his head and laughs. Stars, I hate it when they laugh. I know it's a nervous reaction, but the lack of respect is… unpleasant.

"I can't do that," says Trask, hands folded neatly before him. "This factory relies exclusively on the extraction of Brathean oil which can only be found on this planet. No matter what Sparegrout's Beings' Rights group says, my people are happy here. They have a purpose, a faith. So you can tell that old coot, and his entire Parasol Corporation while you're at it, to shove their demands back where the suns don't shine. And if he sends another one of you to threaten me..."

I check my nails. There's blue soap under my index finger from when I jammed my uniform down the toilet. *Brathean oil, my lobe.* When you're the CEO-Godhead of a Factory-Religion you're not going to want to relocate your place of industry-worship. Building up a whole new workforce-believer base is time-consuming.

"You don't know who I am, do you?" I bat my eyelashes.

"Does it matter?" His foot rocks against the floor. I imagine his knee tapping the panic button repeatedly.

"My name," I say, sparks flying off my tongue, "is Blayde. So heed my words or this may be the last sunlight you see in a long, long time."

He blinks, frowns, furrows his brow, then it's right back to mask-ville. Rude.

"Listen, Blayde, or whoever you *think* you are. You're way out of your league. The Blayde of the ancient stories is not part of the business world. Face it, kiddo: that myth's outdated. There's no need for warriors when the battlefields are offices. The world has no more need for nation to go against nation: only corporation against corporation. So go use your fists against someone your own size. Trask Utility is bigger than even the Blayde of legend can fight. I am their *god*."

"Kiddo? Really?" There's so much wrong with his statement that I can't help but nitpick the small stuff. Just the kind of deluded mule who sucked all the fun out of this. "Trask, you're so nearsighted. Where there's a war, there are warriors. Sure, there may not be many like me out there anymore, who prefer the old ways to the new, and you may think you're one of them, but you're not even a blip on their radar. You know why empires last and businesses like yours don't? It's because we're not afraid to get our hands dirty. But just like empires, one pulled string and it could all come crashing—"

My poorly improvised spiel is interrupted by a poorly synthesized rendition of "Barely Beloved Sonata." Huh, hadn't heard that one in a while. Didn't think Trask'd be the type to put Hydran pop songs as his ringtone. I stare at him, and he stares at me, and I realize that the music isn't coming from him at all.

My shoe is vibrating.

"Are you going to get that?" Trask lifts an eyebrow.

I slip the shoe off, hold it up to my ear, sneering to cover up my dismay. Firstly, I had no idea my shoe was a phone. Secondly, how was it getting reception? And thirdly, since shoes don't have screens, it didn't have caller ID either.

"Who in the cosmos has this number?" I mutter.

Trask steeples his fingers, tapping them smugly against his lips. "I can't answer that."

"Then give me a second." I hold the shoe up to my ear again.

"Bl-Blayde?" a voice asks, stammering slightly. Now *there's* the fear I was hoping to get from Trask. It's not fun here, though.

"Who is this?" I hold up a finger to Trask. "How did you get this number?"

"You g-gave it to us?"

"When?"

"About five minutes ago. A note arrived with the number, and instructions to call you with the news."

"Who are you?" I slip off the desk. The parquet is cold against my almost-bare foot. "And what news?"

"Blayde, I am deeply sorry." The voice sounds… apologetic? "This is the Alliance Office of Sibling Liaison."

What in the Frash?— "Now that's new. How long have you had that?"

"Long enough to know that you do not like being bothered with useless information."

"So I take it this is important." My skin turns cold. This isn't the type of phone call I'm used to receiving.

The speaker crinkles as the stranger exhales. "Your brother is missing."

This must be a plot of some kind. "You're kidding me, right? He's *always* missing. That's the point. Incognito. And we're catching up soon. What kind of joke is this?"

"No joke, Ms. Blayde. Also, the note said to tell you that you are now thinking of the sequence 5, 7, 8, 4, 6, 92, pi, spaghetti. Apparently, that will help you understand that we are acting on your orders."

How could they—no, this couldn't be real. But they got the numbers right, down to pi-spaghetti. The incessant noise in my head finally has its use, as encryption software, I suppose. I have to concede to the fact that this could have been me, likely a future me, trying to lend a hand. If that's the case, then this is time-bindingly serious.

Zander's in trouble. Real trouble.

Still, who do these people think they are? "Omit the *Ms.* and explain yourself."

"Your brother and his concubine were on a rescue mission over Planet Rancor Gama." I cringe. I've known Sally long enough to know she wouldn't like that word. Maybe I *am* going soft. "He was told to rendezvous with us in a week, or try to make contact with us. It has now been two weeks and we've had no news. We are forced to presume him missing."

"And a note *from me* told you that I needed to know."

"It is not our place to question you, Blayde," says the voice. The tremor is still there, but slight. "We'll be waiting."

Across the desk, Trask is building a smile. His knee is still trying for that panic button. *Don't think I don't know, janitor-god.*

I frown. "You will?"

"You said you would come…?"

"I'd best listen to myself, then. I will be there in a minute. I have some business to complete first."

I sigh—I was so looking forward to seeing Trask get his comeuppance. I can, I suppose, stay here a little longer, step back in time to join my self-appointed allies. But the worry that's made its home in my chest has something to say about that. I won't be able to savor my victory. Zander needs me, and fast.

So, I toss my shoe-phone at Trask's face, relishing the satisfying snap of a nose breaking.

"I guess we'll have to wrap this up quicker than I'd hoped. You going to tell your people the truth?"

He lets out a jackal laugh. "Not a chance! You—"

I jump to his side, picking him up by the tie again. He's so busy clutching his nose he doesn't scream until I've shattered his window with a well-placed kick. I make sure the knot is secure before thrusting him out over the void of his creation. "So here; I have more power than you can imagine. If you do not leave this planet I will tear your world down for you, blah blah blah. Have fun with the union representatives."

Trask screams, but the sound is whipped away by the wind. Beneath him, a crowd roars: I'm right on schedule. Then—*kablooey*. Trask's screams turn to sobs as an explosion fills the air, the refinery silos crumble into nothing: concrete, cement, oil and flames being sucked into nothingness. Fifteen thousand years of planning all coming to fruition in an instant. Lovely.

And to think I'll be missing the riots… well, I *can* come back for those. Victory drinks will be on me.

"Did you get all that?" I say. He nods.

Finally the doors burst open, and in come six armed guards, weapons drawn. Both fantastic and terrible timing: they can't shoot me or I'll drop their precious leader, their Sanitizer Supreme, but I can't savor the ultimate fight scene. I toss Trask into the mass of guards, toppling a few of them, and recover my shoe as they try to sort themselves out.

"And the power of a word is a mighty thing," I say, hopping on one foot as I slip the shoe back on. I hate the sound of my voice, but I do like having the last word. "There goes the adoring love of your workforce. Already your stock is plummeting. Goodbye, Trask. I can't say it's been a pleasure meeting you."

The pallor of his face would be enough of a trophy, but I'm seized with worry—I've soured my own victory. Then again, the highs of rebellion never last as long as I want them to, even when I'm not distraught.

Zander's in danger. Zander's in danger.

I jump as the guards fire. At least the custodial staff will keep their jobs.

ONE

GALACTIC LOVE AND LOOT SPA'TACULAR

Sally

It's approximately two Alliance Standard weeks earlier on the Blayde timeline, if she were traveling with us in a strict progression of cause to event, though technically five hundred and twenty-seven years, two months, and two weeks earlier, if we consider the random location that Zander and I are enjoying our stay at this very moment—which is both happening and has already happened—so don't look too deeply into it.

It's two weeks earlier.

Get over it.

I DON'T RECOMMEND THE HOT FIRESLUG MASSAGE at the Qescids Villa of Ultimate Relaxation to the Max: it is not restful or relaxing, unless knowing what your kitchen appliances think about you is your personal form of stress relief. How that fireslug could tell that the mini fridge I had in my dorm during the single semester I'd given college a try found my clothing choices repulsive, I'll never know, but I left my session with more knots than I'd had going in.

"You look radiant, my star," said Zander as we met up afterwards, fluffy in his shwomp—a species of terry cloth robe bred exclusively for their docile softness. Mine was purring, the vibrations supposedly good for my bone density.

And he was right. I was radiant: as in, literally glowing.

I looked down at my skin. "Is this supposed to happen?"

He intertwined his fingers with mine and all at once I sank into his arms. Our shwomps purred in unison as I kissed him, deeply, soaking him in, letting go only to run my fingers through his soft, sweaty hair. He smelled of stardust and salt, skin still hot from his own fireslug massage.

I never wanted to break apart—we never needed to. Breathing was a habit, not a necessity. I could have his lips on mine until the end of time if I so wanted. A blink, and we were back in our hotel room, the shwomps in a cuddly pile on the floor as we no longer needed them on the bed—which, thankfully, wasn't the sentient kind.

For the first time I could remember, my life was bliss. I was on a vacation binge with the love of my life, all of space and time at our disposal. No worlds to save, no apocalypses to avert. No heroes or villains, only us. And whenever we needed a vacation from our vacation, we took one. All the missed moments and unfulfilled promises were within our grasp. The wait was worth every second, and we made every second worth it.

The wonderful thing about time travel is that you can go wherever you want without worrying about the whenever, because your now will always be waiting for you. Blayde would meet us one month from when she left Earth; but that month was almost six hundred years away from now, by my rough estimate.

We had surfed the lava waves of Vintra, so viscous they rolled like water down the volcano's steep slopes. We had been to planets made of sand and planets made of ice, water planets, fire planets, planets where the only way to travel was by kite, planets where the inhabitants were tall birds that walked on stilts to reach the sun. We'd seen stars that pulsed with rhythm, and planets held together by string-like threads of light. We'd seen stars being born, and watched galaxies die from a distance.

At each new planet we visited, I was amazed at the beauty that lay just beyond the boundaries of my imagination. Every place we went was more beautiful than the last, a kaleidoscope of colors and shapes so varied it seemed as if every day brought us somewhere different—although technically, to us, it did. We were two tiny specks on an infinite journey in an infinite universe, finding something incredible everywhere we went. The entire universe was ours for the taking—our playground, our promised land—and it was as grand and magnificent as we'd hoped.

And still, we had time.

I curled up next to Zander on our bed, his arms a warm cradle around me. My skin, while no longer literally radiant, still glowed the healthy peach color it had adopted sometime after Spa-World Number Three—the fourth spa we'd gone to; that was just its name. My body had filled out with well-built muscle. On the nightstand sat North West's bestselling novel, which I had bought while—accidentally—strolling through the future Vancouver airport, and had been too lovesick to realize it was 2040. I could sit up and read but I didn't want to move, my ear pressed against Zander's silent chest, listening instead to the rise and fall of his breath. Everything was perfect.

Except when Zander fell asleep. When he slowly started to sob.

The first time it had happened, I thought I was the one dreaming. But the tears in my hair were real. His silent sobs had echoed deep in my chest. I had woken him, and he remembered nothing. Every night since, he was ripped from his slumber with a grief that neither of us dared mention. Every morning, he'd smile and act like nothing had happened, like the agony he felt in the night was forgotten. We both knew it was because of the botched memory retrieval he'd attempted with

Blayde, all too aware that the endeavor had left him with much more than he'd bargained for.

But we weren't ready to dive into that, not yet. We were on vacation. We weren't thinking. We weren't worrying about Blayde's mission to find James a new body. We convinced ourselves it was a simple errand, as easy as shopping for new boots. When our vacation was over, we'd join them and find new adventures, as if James's physical death had never happened. As if all that was left of her wasn't confined to a barely functional crystal ball.

I could throw myself into loving Zander, wholly and fully, and supporting him through this difficult time. It was easier to think about his issues rather than deal with the loss of James. Selfish, I know, but being kept awake by his quiet sobs kept me from dreaming of that terrible moment when she collapsed into my arms, having given her life defending the universe, defending me.

No. Not her life. Her physical body. There is a difference.

I was sick and tired of losing the people I love. Losing my brother, John, had almost destroyed me; thinking I'd lost Matt and Zander had pushed me even closer to my own cliff. Losing people was part of life, it came with the territory: and since I had a very long life ahead of me, it sounded like I was going to have to get used to it sooner rather than later. But I wasn't going to accept it immediately.

I refused to believe James was dead. I refused to acknowledge every bad thought. I was on vacation, dammit.

"Right," said Zander, startling me. He was awake, and beaming, talking so close to my face that I could feel his breath with each word. "So, you know how the Wantraki and the Grathon had been at war for centuries?"

"I do now." I snuggled in closer. "Is that seriously what you're thinking about right now?"

The edges of his lips curled into a gentle smile that he reserved only for me. His eyes sparkled and he took my hands in his, speaking with his trademark enthusiasm.

"Well, legend has it they were to have one last peace conference, but neither party planned on relinquishing anything. By the middle of the conference they had nothing left but half a bottle of Wantraki Rum and some Grathon booze so strong it could not be named. It was not enough to give to the generals. So one of the colonels—nobody knows which side they were from—said it would be nice to mix both liquors and add juice from any fruit they could find. They still had a lot of peacemaking to talk over, *ironically*, and none of them could do it sober. So they used the juice of the only fruit they had on the planet: the lowly lemon."

"There are lemons this far from Earth?" I stoked my fingers through his hair as he talked, barely following. "I can see why this is a *legend*."

"They say the war ended that day with drunk men sobbing, hugging, and signing every paper slipped under their noses. And that's how the Nir'nil federation was born."

"Oh!" I straightened up. "You're hoping I'm going to ask to taste it. This is you asking for a drink."

He winked. "I'll order room service."

It took a lot of explaining on our hotel com panel, and once the poor server realized what Zander was after, he admitted that the drink had been outlawed over two centuries ago. We were forced to get dressed, hike down to the bar, then change into our bathing suits when we caught a rumor that the bartender at the swim-up bar could make us what we wanted if we greased his palms a little. Soon, we were standing waist-deep in something that wasn't exactly water, holding glasses that hummed in our hands, bright yellow smoke evaporating off their surface, a handful of soggy bills lighter. The Meegran bartender kept his back to us.

I clinked my glass against Zander's, rewarded with a crystal-clear ring. "Any particular way to drink it?"

"Bottoms up?"

I lifted my small glass, watching the emerald fungi bubble and foam as the alcohol fizzed in a steamy haze. If I didn't try it soon, it was literally going up in smoke. The closer I brought it to my nose, the more the high-pitched ringing in my ears started to sound like Tchaikovsky.

Then my head burst, like the crack of a million exploding watermelons in syncopation with the symphony. It was like consuming a full-blown supernova in one gulp.

"Woah," I gasped, putting down my glass in what I hoped was an alluring move. "Though, nothing like the Boltrii last week, mind you..."

"Nothing beats the Boltrii." Zander put his empty glass on the table and wrapped his arms around me once again. He must have been hearing the same music I was, because we started moving in time with it, dancing to our liquid pyrotechnic display.

To the Max, indeed, Qescids Villa of Ultimate Relaxation.

Zander nuzzled into my neck as we swayed, and I leaned into him, enjoying the gentle moment. The drink had made me dizzy, in the way a good kiss might. In the back of my comfortably muddled mind, I knew there must have been a reason Zander had his sudden craving.

"Wantraki and Grathon," I said. "You knew them. You were there, weren't you?"

His hands froze around my waist, the swaying slowing, but not stopping. "Maybe."

I pulled away, wanting to see his face, but his kept his nose hidden in my neck.

"You have a memory," I said. "Something came back?"

"How much do you know about the rest of this planet, Sally?" His breath was hot against my skin.

"Nothing more than what's posted in the lobby." I ran my hand down his back, smoothing his shwomp. It kept me from making nervous fists. "Jemmina. Entirely tropical rain forest biome. My type of atmosphere:

healthy, 80-20 Nitrogen-Oxygen, with a little wiggle room on those small particles. No inhabitants other than this resort: rest of the planet's surface is considered too dangerous. One of the largest and most expensive resorts of the Choo system."

"It wasn't always called that." Zander finally pulled away, my neck going cold. "Part of the resort is built on the ruins of an ancient civilization. They've displayed their excavations in the workout wing. I was taking a look around and… it just came back to me. I'd seen them before. I'd been *here* before. Stars, I worked the conference center here when the Wantraki and Grathon came for mediation. *I sliced the lemons.*"

"Zander, that's incredible!" I grasped him by the shoulders—he was shaking. "You remembered!"

"I have to go back," he said. "See if the treasure is still there."

I coughed. "The…" Maybe it was the lingering burn of the nameless drink, maybe the shock of Zander's casual utterance about treasure, but there was a fire in my belly that lit like an igniting star. "There's a treasure?"

"Sure, back then, whenever a truce was mediated, the leaders buried treasure together to demonstrate the value of their new accords surpassing material goods. Better together, all that. It must still be here."

Treasure hunting. Now *that* we hadn't done yet. I was smiling so hard, I couldn't feel my ears. "Do we leave now? Tonight?"

"Why wait?" He took my hand, gesturing to the jungle beyond the pool. "Think anyone will notice if we wander off?"

"Doubt it." I giggled. "We'll need to gather some supplies first, though. And probably get dressed. I'm not planning on walking through a jungle in a bikini."

"I'd like to see you try." Zander lifted an eyebrow and I felt like my insides had been replaced with that cocktail, fizzing and frothing away. Who knew it was possible for a person to look so hot that there was actually steam billowing off their body?

"Do you know where it's buried?" I brushed hair out of my face to distract from the sudden heat. "Can you find it again?"

"I think I can use some satellite maps to find the old conference center. From there…"

"That part hasn't unlocked yet, has it?"

He shook his head. Instead of dismay, my excitement grew. A true call to adventure. His smile stretched from ear to ear.

"Well then," I said, "I'll raid the complementary mini fridge and grab some water bottles from the fitness rooms. We'll bring the shwomps along for bedding?"

Which is how, three hours later, we found ourselves in the middle of a rainforest, with any trace of civilization long behind us and nothing but green vegetation before us, a satellite map to guide us, and the sense of mystery to push us along.

Now *this* is a vacation.

My shwomp snored gently on my back as we trudged through the undergrowth. It would have been easier with a machete of some kind, but those weren't available at the resort gift store. That, and the vegetation was too incredible to imagine slashing it back. Blue-leaved plants with red veins hung low over a trail made by centuries of large creatures trampling over it—or a centuries-old road far beneath—the only indication that this was a place to go at all. The plants grew and shrunk as if breathing, as if the entire leaf was a lung, the whole jungle a living creature.

As we walked, eight-winged, translucent dragonflies fluttered above us, examining the newcomers that had entered their world. They were not afraid of us, hovering right in front of our faces before dashing off when we got too close. They were friendly, but not *that* friendly.

I will never get tired of this.

Zander's arm reached for me, pulling me down, and I dropped to the forest floor. For a second, I thought things might get steamy but the vibe wasn't there. I crouched in silence, scanning the landscape, peering over Zander's shoulder—nothing. Not that I could possibly see anything more than a meter in any direction. I'd thought the jungle in Malaysia was thick, but this was a whole other story.

I knew better than to make a noise, so I poked him instead. Wordlessly, he pointed at a patch of red ferns straight ahead of us. I squinted—what was that? Oh, not ferns at all.

It was a moth. An elephant-sized moth. Its antennae twitched, but it was seemingly unaware of our presence.

Awesome.

"We're going to have to go around it," Zander whispered. "And give it a wide berth. I'm not looking forward to what it'll do if it finds us."

I nodded. "It's not as if we don't have a way of circumventing it completely?"

Zander shook his head. Did he *want* to tempt fate? Jumping around it would have been so easy, but he'd been avoiding that, lately. Oh well: new skills to add to the roster.

Keeping our own heads low made navigating the dense vegetation a challenge. The ground was soft with dead leaves. Were there snakes on this world?

And then—*crack*. A light, brittle snap seemed to echo through the forest. The tiniest of twigs breaking under my foot. The snap filled the air, only to be instantly drowned out by a howling siren, claiming the scene with a disheartening wail, and rendering my initial mistake entirely moot.

Only it wasn't the moth. The sound came from a giant, furry worm that had become firmly attached to Zander's arm, right up to the elbow. He twirled about madly, flailing his arms in a desperate attempt to dislodge the thing.

Our shwomps screamed back, drowning out all other sound. Mine tugged at my bag, trying to drag me away—I didn't even know they could do that. *My own bathrobe!*

Worse, the moth was now wide awake, its wings beating out a rhythm to rival any top-ten pop song, eclipsed only by that of the screaming worm and shwomps.

"RUN!" I screamed at Zander, not that he needed to be told. He sprinted to the trail, worm still clinging to his arm, shwomp bouncing on his back. I darted after him, still fighting against mine, and the wind generated by the moth's wings.

Could the moth fly through the dense trees? I didn't look back to check. My eyes were on Zander alone. I ran as fast as I could, leaping over the underbrush, desperate to get away from that… that *thing*. And the sound—the wailing of the furry things was enough to drown out the entire jungle around me, unless that too had suddenly gone silent.

"A little help?" Zander waved the worm in the air, still running. I jumped the extra few meters to catch up with him, arms extended, intending to tackle the thing off him. But when my hands wrapped around the fur, they found slime instead.

Glue. The worm's coat was laced with glue. Glue that had stuck to Zander's arm.

And just to make matters worse: yes, the moth could fly through the jungle. It was right behind us, its thunderous wings beating the air up a storm. It squawked, a terrible sound, like an eagle who'd just remembered he'd left the stove on. It was on us, it was going to eat us—

"Sally—*left!*" Zander's voice was loud enough to reach over the cacophony. I didn't think, I just ran. Left—and Zander took right, so fast and viciously, the worm flew from his arm, flew from my hand, the glue ripping off the top layer of skin, sending the worm soaring into the air.

And the moth just… swallowed it whole.

The critter's scream turned to a squeal and then—silence. Our shwomps went quiet. The thunder of the wings subsided as the creature returned to its nest, its belly full, its fury gone.

My hands were already healing, fresh skin covering the once-bloody palms like paint spilling over canvas. I gave them a shake for good measure, trying to forget the feeling of the squirming, hot, hairy glue that had covered them seconds earlier. If you need a way to make creepy-crawlies worse, make them *sticky* creepy-crawlies.

"You all right?" Zander marched through the jungle towards me. His arm was pink from the impromptu waxing session.

"Never better," I said, laughing. "That was… close?"

"Those weren't here last time." He frowned. "At least, I don't remember them."

I took a deep breath—this was going to take a while to get used to. There wasn't a handbook for recovering thousands of years of lost memory. I gave his bicep a reassuring squeeze. "Let's see what comes back when we get there?"

He nodded, reaching up to pat my hand before taking it in his own.

It wasn't easy to keep our hands clasped as we traipsed through the rainforest, and it slowed us down considerably, but the warmth was worth it. We walked for hours, until the sun was gone and darkness reached the rainforest floor. Thankfully the resort gift shop did have glow sticks—or an equivalent, I'm pretty sure it was a type of dried bioluminescent fish—in the shape of celebratory words, so I took RETIREMENT and Zander REGISCIDE, and we hiked on until those wore out.

Happy and exhausted, we made camp by laying our shwomps across tree limbs, snuggled up close, and let the rainforest sounds rock us to sleep, warm in each other's arms.

Waking up was far less pleasant, since I was now tied to a tree with thick ropes, and not in a sexy way.

TWO

ESCAPE FROM CONFERENCE ROOM A

Sally

IT'S EXTRAORDINARILY ROMANTIC TO BE SNATCHED away in the midst of your first, and possibly last, treasure hunt, I can tell you. At least it is for the first microsecond or so. Then the realization hits that you're dangling from a tree, and the excitement melts away faster than a milkshake on Venus.

I fumbled around the tree trunk until I found Zander's fingers and wrapped my hand around them. He squeezed back. We were about a meter off the ground, on opposite sides of the tree, ropes tight around our waists and ankles to keep us from slipping away. And I was granted the wrong side of the jungle, my view of the undergrowth resolutely inert.

"What's happening?" I whispered, just loud enough for him to hear. "Are you all right?"

"We're being robbed."

"Robbed?" *Shit.* "By who?"

"I'm not sure. They look like… tourists?"

I squirmed in my restraints. I needed to see what was going on.

"If you move a little closer, there's a knife in my back pocket," Zander continued. "We can use the blade to slice through our bindings..."

I rolled my eyes, glad he couldn't see the look on my face. "I'm sorry, I'm going to have to put my foot down on this one."

"What? Hold on, what are you—"

I grabbed his hand and in a blink we were on the ground, safely hidden behind some large ferns.

Zander lay on his back in some sort of shock. Rolling onto his belly and propping himself up so as to see through the underbrush, he muttered, "Where was the fun in that?"

"We got out of there, didn't we?" Things didn't need to be hard for the sake of it, jeez. "Anyway, if you want fun, go and get our bags back. That's challenging enough."

Three robbers circled our stuff: one human, one being with too much hair and too many arms—a Meegran—and one lizard-like person of a species I didn't know. The human was a cigar-smoking, mustache-wearing short man in a… cowboy hat? The lizard wore loose-fitting resort wear. And the Meegran—

"The bartender?" I gasped. "What's he doing here?"

And how had they gotten the drop on us? We should have woken up when they'd accosted us. The air smelled funny, sweet—had they drugged us? They were rummaging through our small assortment of things. A squeal—my shwomp was crying. My hands balled into fists. *Those bastards!*

The man spun around to face our tree, gun raised. "Where's the… oh, for frash sake!"

I braced for a fight, ready to strike at any moment. And then Zander did the unthinkable—he stood up.

"Are you kidding me right now?" I stared up at him.

"They have our map," he hissed. "We don't know where we're going."

"You!" The man pointed at Zander. "How did you get out? Bruno, find the other one!"

"She's with me," said Zander, pointing right at me. *Seriously, what the hell, man?* "And you need to learn how to tie better knots. We wriggled right out. Now, can you please return my map? You're interrupting a romantic escapade."

"We know all about the conferen*sssss*," said the lizard person.

"Yeah, cuz mister mixologist here can't keep his mouth shut despite my *very generous tip!*" Zander put his hands on his hips, glaring at the Meegran.

"Hands where I can see them," said the man. "You. Stand."

Was he talking to me? I got to my feet, gingerly, hands raised. Behind them, the bartender—*Bruno*, apparently— continued his search of the bags. Our shwomps whined.

"She ain't a peculiarly pretty piece, is she?" said the reptile. They were twice as tall as the man with the cigar, wearing a pink tank top with the resort logo on it. "Tomii, tell me she's ugly. Tomii!"

"She's hideous, doll," said the man—Tomii, I suppose. Zander tensed beside me.

"Don't you dare speak to her like that," he spat.

"What'cha gonna do about it?" The Lizard flicked their tongue like slurped spaghetti.

"Enough with the chitchat." Tomii waved his gun at Zander. "Where's the treasure?"

"Let her go free, and I'll take you to any treasure you want." Zander took a step forward, earning him a shot in the air. Shit, they weren't kidding. "Just leave her be. She has nothing to do with this."

"I have a different proposal for you." Tomii sneered, pointing the gun at my head. Wonderful. "You lead us to the treasure, or I blow her brains out. Deal?"

"Don't you dare hurt her!" Zander flew in front of me. "Don't you even touch a hair on her head!"

What was he playing at? The gun wasn't a problem. There were only three of them, not even military— Zander could have them on the ground in seconds, maybe a little longer if he wanted me to get some practice in. Instead he kept his mouth open in a pantomime of terror, though his eyes were bright, betraying the thrill of anticipation.

Okay, fine, I admit, it was a little hot.

"I won't." Tomii's lips curled in a snide smirk, as if the idea of having control over another sentient being filled him with a strange, twisted delight. "So long as you lead us to the treasure."

"Fine, anything you say." Zander sighed. "Just don't hurt her!"

Zander reached for my hand, leading me forward, keeping me close. The way his arm wrapped around my waist was both protective and strangely possessive. I feigned terror—it was better than keying them in to how confused I was right now. It would blow whatever Zander was planning.

"Their bags are clean," said the bartender. "Well, I say clean..."

He held up one of my laciest undergarments, and Zander's face went a scorching shade of scarlet. Now I was feeling a bit on the warm side, but not from shame. I loved that particular frill-ridden piece. It would be so easy to get that gun, to make them run…

"Good on you." Tomii turned to him, chuckling. "Shame to see that pretty thing be rendered useless, wouldn't it?"

He cocked the gun, holding it against the back of my head. He didn't shove it. He didn't have to. I wasn't moving now. The cold tip of the gun iced my spine, and I clenched my fists to stop myself from shaking on instinct. If Zander wasn't doing a good impression of being terrified before, it was impossible to tell now.

"Grab your bags," Tomii ordered. "Now. Do it."

I stepped away from the gun, making my way to our things on trembling legs. My duffle was a mess, and it had been so well folded. I grabbed my shwomp, draping it over my shoulders. It was freezing cold—poor thing was traumatized. I gave it a gentle pet down the lapel.

"Move," said Tomii.

Our satellite map now firmly in hand, Tomii led us through the jungle, the reptilian clinging to his arm. Our bartender took up the rear, his weapons aimed at us the entire time. He walked on two pairs of his back legs, using his other four hands to hold two guns, and a backpack. One hand was left empty and along for the ride, so it resorted to making little dolphin motions as we walked.

"What's in this for you?" Zander asked—not me, but the Meegran, who said nothing. What was Zander's plan here? Why were we holding back? "Seriously, you think the two of them will share the treasure with you?"

The Meegran's mandible chittered. "I'm the one who got them the info, didn't I?"

"You broke the bartender's vow of confidentiality in the process," said Zander.

"You were speaking so loud I couldn't help but overhear!" He laughed. "Did you want the whole world to know?"

He had a point there. We hadn't exactly been secretive about what we were planning. I'll blame that on the cocktail. Who else was in the jungle right now, trying to track down the lost treasure?

Zander sighed. It was useless trying to turn Bruno against the others, even if it was obvious their partnership wasn't going to last. Up ahead, Tomii and the reptilian were already making their own plans.

"You're getting me a brooch, Tomii!" said the reptilian. "Promise me?"

"Syrup, I'm getting you all the jewelry you'll ever want." He took a drag from his cigar, blowing the smoke in the air like a dirge. "Anything your heart desires, Sweewee."

"Why are you not shooting the long-haired human?" The reptilian—Sweewee? Was that their name or another term of endearment? "She'll steal my treasure."

"She won't," Tomii said. "The treasure is all yours, my dearest."

"You mean it?"

"I mean it." He dragged on his cigar again. "All the treasure you could ever want."

"You're the best, Tomii."

He shrugged. "All for my love of you, darling."

Zander glanced back at me, and I gave him an awkward smile. If he wasn't doing anything, that meant we weren't in any actual danger—slightly reassuring. So, we'd just keep following along, and playing the part of wide-eyed tourists.

Finally, we reached the conference center—or what was left of it. It didn't look like much, only a hill among others. But the satellite imagery didn't lie: there was something under the centuries of overgrowth. And, sure enough, when I squinted hard, it almost seemed like a pyramid was holding up the trees.

"Is this it?" whined Sweewee. They gripped Tomii's arm, claws digging into leather. "Is this where the treasure is?"

"Inside," said Tomii. "You—take the lead."

He waved his gun at Zander, and we stepped forward, only for Sweewee to *growl* at me, showing their sharp, needle-like teeth. I shuddered.

"Not *heeer*," Sweewee hissed. "She'll want the treasure for her ugly head."

What was it with the insults? I put my hands up, took a step back.

"Bruno, you stay here with the girl." Tomii stuffed out his cigar under his heel. "Prepare everything for our return."

Our bartender chittered his mandibles again but acquiesced with a nod, "She won't be a problem."

I stood firm as Zander led them towards the ancient structure, giving me a single glance back, the kind of half frown that said *sorry*. Sorry for what? Getting me into this mess? Leaving me outside, alone? Or for getting the treasure by himself? They turned the corner and were gone, disappearing behind the maybe-pyramid mound.

Meanwhile, Bruno the bartender scuttled around not quite sure what to do with himself. His presence was a constant reminder that we were dealing with ruthless criminals who weren't afraid to pull out their guns at any moment if things didn't go as they wanted them to.

Still aiming his gun at my gut, he dropped his backpack at his feet. He crouched, retrieving a flat blade from inside—a shovel, with a collapsible handle. He tossed it to me.

"Now dig," he ordered, indicating a patch of semi-clear ground.

I let the shovel land without catching it. "For what, dingus? Treasure's in there."

His lips curled into a smile, mandibles lifting. Now, trust me, you never want to see a Meegran smile like this. Most of those I've met keep a straight face for a reason: a smile would send any primate-based life-forms running for the hills.

"You're going to dig your own grave," he said. Ice shot up my spine, but I refused to shiver. "And then, you'll dig your friendo's grave, too."

I put my hands on my hips. "Or what? You'll shoot me?"

This seemed to catch him by surprise—at least three of his eight eyes twitched.

"Yes. That's the whole point."

"Well, I won't be digging a grave if I'm already dead, will I?" I crossed my arms over my chest. *Keep your cool, Sally Webber. He can't hurt you.* "And two guns? Don't you think that's a little redundant?"

From the way he bit his lip, he must have understood the flaw in his logic, but like any good minion, he didn't back down.

"Just shut up and dig."

I refused to move. "You realize what my guy said earlier was right, right? Did you see how they just left you out here without a second thought?"

"I already told you—shut up and dig."

"They never intended to share the treasure." I took a step forward, closer to the guns—they were shaking now. He was either terrified or furious. Both made men trigger-happy.

"Don't give them the chance to run off with it," I said, keeping my hands where he could see them. "Let's— "

A scream ripped through the air before I had the chance to finish my lackluster plan. We both turned towards the conference center, where the dragonflies and moths took flight—but silence had fallen again.

Bruno held up his gun.

"I'm not seeing any digging!"

My anger boiled over. "What are you going to do—wait, screw this." I wrapped my shwomp tight around my shoulders and raced towards the conference center, leaving Bruno shouting behind me. Around the bend, and then again, but finally I saw it: an opening in the mound. I darted through.

This most definitely had once been a conference center. In the dim light I could make out the emptiness within, the massive cement pillars that rose towards the ceiling, disappearing into darkness. At my feet, the rotten remains of synthetic carpeting. A wave of musty air greeted my nose, smelling of biomass and stale coffee. The only sound in the room was the breeze, and my own useless breathing.

Where was Zander? My chest tightened. I took a breath to process the feeling—I wasn't worried, no. Not for him. Then it hit me: this was the first time I was in an ancient construct deep underground, the first time since—

James isn't dead. You only saw her body die.

I slapped my chest to force it back into action and scanned the dark hall, my eyes adjusting quickly. The remnants of a boardroom table and chairs lay toppled in the corner, crumbled over the carpet. A disturbance in the dust led towards the massive staircase to my left—that's where they must have gone. I turned, only for a hand to grab my arm.

"Where do you think you're going?" asked Bruno, two guns suddenly at my head. Ah, that's why he had one hand empty. Well, I wasn't going to let him hold me back. I pulled back my fist and swung, hitting him in the root of his mandible.

He screamed as I was rewarded with a satisfying crunch. He let go, and I raced up the stairs and into the halls beyond.

I had no idea know how long it would take him to recover, so I didn't slow. I wasn't going to miss what was going down with the treasure, didn't want Zander alone —

The doors to conference room "weird birdlike symbol" were wide open. I dashed inside, impressed to see the chairs were still standing, as if waiting for someone to take the stage. Still, it was empty. I followed the trail of unsettled dust through the speakers' entrance, into the wings.

And there, a gaping hole waited for me in the middle of the corridor, the bottom lined with spikes. What kind of conference center was this?

I didn't waste any time, jumped over, and kept going.

"Run!" shouted Zander, as he rushed past me, grabbing my arm, Tomii close at his heels. I hadn't seen them coming, nor had I heard —

The massive boulder rolling behind us.

"Shit!" I fled as fast as I could. Why was this place booby-trapped? And where was Sweewee? I couldn't think, only run.

Even though I was going full pelt, the ball was gaining speed and quickly closing the gap between us. Someone was going to get smooshed.

"Round ball, square hall!" I said, "Lie down against the wall, make yourself flat!"

I didn't wait to see if anyone took my advice. I dove to the floor, flinging out my arms and legs so far they almost ripped out of their sockets. Just in time, as the cold stone brushed over my back, thunder threatening to burst my eardrums. But I wasn't turned to jelly today.

"You… you ok?" Zander asked.

I peeled myself off the ground. "I'm fine!" Zander sighed with relief.

"I'm all right too," said Tomii.

"Don't give a frash," said Zander.

No Sweewee in sight. Had they been the one to scream earlier? If so, Tomii didn't seem too torn up about it. And he'd lost his gun at some point, too. We were all on even ground now—well, as far as he knew.

"Move," said Tomii. "We must be getting close."

I expected Zander to retort, but he got up and marched back down the hallway from whence the boulder had come. If Tomii was worried about Bruno and how I'd joined them, he showed no sign of it. The man seemed so intent on the treasure that nothing else mattered.

"What happened to…" I asked, and Zander shook his head, jutting his chin towards Tomii.

"A pit," he replied. "We didn't know the corridor was booby-trapped until it was too late."

Behind the chute that dropped the boulder were large metal doors, and Zander swung them open, this time to reveal a single man, just… waiting there. Dressed in a tight, silvery skin suit with a black belt, he stood stock-still between two small doors.

"Welcome, travelers," he said. I struggled to keep my composure: a man—here? After all these centuries, behind booby traps? Either his lifespan was incredibly long, or this was a droid.

"Hey there," said Zander. "We're here to inspect the Peace Pot."

The man inclined his head. "Then you should already know which of these doors will lead you to the truth, and which will lead to pain and damnation."

"Sadly, that information was lost to history," said Zander, shaking his head.

"Then I will allow you these questions three to determine the door you require," they said, "but you must know—I always lie."

"Frash!" Zander threw his hands over his head. "I know this! Don't I? I should know this!"

"Excuse me," said Tomii, pushing forward, "but do you mean three questions per person, or for all of us combined?"

"Shared," said the man-droid. "You have two left."

"Leave the questions to me, all right?" said Zander. "Or you'll waste our only shot."

"Unless he's lying about that, too," I said. "He says he always lies. Which would mean, that's also a lie. Which is a paradox, because it would mean he's telling the truth. And if he's telling the truth…"

"I've got this," said Tomii. "What is two plus two?"

"Five," said the man-droid.

Tomii turned to us, smirking. "So tell me, which door is the right one?"

"The left one," said the man-droid.

Tomii slid his thumbs under his lapels, waggling his eyebrows. Without another word to us, he reached for the left door, giving us a smug wave. I took a step to follow him, and Zander threw out his hand to stop me. As the door closed behind Tomii, a scream filled the air.

The man-droid dropped his head into his hands, on the verge of mechanical tears. "I'm not programmed to do math."

My hands fell from my mouth, where they'd risen when I'd gasped. Tomii—dead? I'd never liked the man, but this was ridiculous. I mean, who puts death doors in their conference center?

"It's okay." Zander stepped up to him, rubbing his shoulder soothingly. "No one asked you if you wanted to be posted here for centuries, did they? You're just being a good droid, doing what you're told. But you need to take a break. This kind of job is degrading for your mental health."

"It's my one true purpose," he said. Did I imagine it, or was he… sniffling? "I cannot simply walk away."

"Well, if we claim the Peace Pot, then your job is over, right?" The droid nodded. "Great. Meet you on the way out. You can start making plans for your retirement!"

Zander and I took the door to the right.

The corridor beyond had a light at the end of the tunnel, both ominous and cool. I took Zander's hand and we walked towards the treasure we had fought so surprisingly hard for, our shwomps finally warming up. The walls here were soft and fluffy, too—*caterpillars*. The same gluey monstrosities were all over the corridor walls, sleeping.

At the end of the furry tunnel lay a simple, round room, and in the center, under a pool of artificial light, sat an empty altar. Zander rushed forward and picked up the small piece of paper that lay there.

"Just borrowing this for a minute." Zander frowned, handing me the paper. "Frash, I suppose I've been here more than once before."

It of course, was signed, in beautiful cursive:

Zander.

THREE

VENTI VISIONS OF THE BEYOND

Sally

"YOU ALREADY ROBBED THE PEACE POT?" I returned the paper to Zander. "There's no treasure?"

"There has to be a treasure," said Bruno, appearing out of the dark, all four hands holding guns now. Talk about overkill. And beside him—Sweewee. Arms crossed over their chest, laughing with their long lizard tongue.

"They've hidden it," said Sweewee.

"Where's the droid?" I spat. "What have you done to him?"

"He said something about taking up moth fishing." Sweewee shrugged. "Surprised to see me, asshole? After you left me for dead?"

"Tomii left you!" said Zander. "Look, I was just trying to see if I could jog old memories by coming back here, that's it. I wasn't intending on getting wrapped up in all your mess."

"Where's the treasure?" Bruno shoved two guns in each of our faces. "Where is it?"

"I have no idea." Zander dropped the paper back on the pedestal. "Nothing coming back to me, all right?"

"Then get on your knees," Bruno hissed. "And prepare to meet your maker."

"Oh, okay, let's make our peace." Zander let out a deep sigh. "Sally, up for that?"

I lifted an eyebrow. Still no insight on the endgame. "Sure, whatever. I'm going to die in a minute, so I don't know how that will change anything."

I bit my lip. I shouldn't be afraid. I had nothing to fear, not really. But the room, the familiarity of it, the dirt above me. Weight pushed down on my shoulders, my chest. This was the same kind of room where James died—No. Not dead. My breath hitched.

Zander dropped to his knees and lowering his head. Clearing his throat, he spoke, in a slow, light voice, incredibly calm.

"Oh great maker of the universe" he bellowed—why did he sound Irish?—"I can see how you'd be angry at me right now, and that you wish to punish me by ending this life of mine. Hey, that's cool. I've had a long run. I've got a beautiful, badass girlfriend, so thanks for that; she's made me incredibly happy. And these past few weeks have been fun, even when I had to force a T-rex to regurgitate Leo. I should have known they didn't have a gag reflex. I would also like to thank you for my victory over the Raalxai, the Azulians, the Deltazoids…

and, of course, for not letting me strangle myself with that water hose seventeen years ago. Still owe you for that one."

"Hold on." Bruno's guns shook slightly. "Did you say… your victory over the Raalxai?"

"I'm making peace here," Zander snapped. "It's kinda personal."

"You told us there was going to be treasure!" Sweewee growled. "You promised!"

"What's that?" Bruno waved his gun at Zander—whose arm was now covered in thick, black fur. He got to his feet, face pale, staring at the caterpillar that had wrapped itself around his elbow.

"Get it off me!" Zander squealed theatrically. "What is this thing? Somebody, get it off!"

Bruno pointed all four of his guns at Zander's arm, which he extended in terror as caterpillars wriggled higher. He looked over at me, the sheer terror in his face suddenly vanishing.

And he shook his arm.

The siren filled the cavern with terrible sound, bolstered by the other creatures awakening together. Incredibly off-key just to make everything worse. My hand pinched, then filled with warmth, but I didn't look to see what it was.

I seized Zander and we were off again, running through the tunnels, leaping over the pit of spikes, down the stairs, and out of the conference center. Light filled our eyes as we burst out, only to be met with a hoard of the giant moths, seemingly called to the cries of the caterpillars—the sound still ringing in my ears. We were hoisted into the air in the sticky, talon-like appendages of a moth. Zander's caterpillar, still shrieking, overtaken either by shock or some kind of survival technique, detached itself from Zander's arm. The moth lost all interest in us and dropped us like a hot potato the moment it caught a glimpse of its real treat plummeting down beside us. We screamed as the trees waved their branches to welcome us to our crash landing.

I grabbed for Zander—who was laughing even as he fell—and jumped us back in the hotel room where we belonged. I collapsed on the hard floor, eyes closed, trying to calm my overwhelmed senses. It was as if my feet were running, my face tingling with the phantom feeling of the air rushing against my cheeks.

"Now that," Zander said between laughs, "was an adventure."

"That was one stunt you pulled with the caterpillar." I slapped him lightly across the chest. The ceiling was shimmering. Probably due to the extreme release of adrenaline and endorphins. I needed a breather. "You had me going for a second."

"I did, did I?" He lifted an eyebrow, pushing himself up so he was leaning over me. "I really surprised you?"

"Had me terrified," I replied in mock falsetto. "Oh my, what shall I ever do without Zander around? Oh dearie, what was to become of me?"

"You were the one with two guns to your head. There were going to take my world away from me —"

"For about five seconds." I snickered.

He leaned in close and kissed me, all the excitement of the day fueled into his lips, a mixture of euphoria and relief setting my mind afire. I kissed him back, overwhelmed with pure bliss, focusing only on the here and now.

"You're hot," he said, pulling away. But he wasn't smiling. He was… flickering?

"You're not so bad yourself," I replied, and then promptly passed out.

The room was blinding white: pure illumination, no detail, no light source, and yet it glowed. The air was fresh with a clean crispness to it. There was no dust or dirt, no windows or even a door. I was wearing a white dress, white shoes. It hit me where I recognized this place from: every single movie ever where the character has…

"I'm dead?" I gasped, holding up my hands. They glowed a shimmering white. I had died before, but I didn't remember being dead.

"Ahem." The voice was faraway, yet like a whisper in my ear. It was familiar, but I couldn't quite place it.

I spun around, and there he was: younger than the last time I saw him, immaculate black hair and suit, standing tall in the middle of the room with his hands behind his back. He gave me a curt nod, but his expression did not change, his lips a fine line. The sight of him made my sleeping heart clench.

"Nimien?" My panic, oddly, wasn't rising: as if I had expected to see him here, though I didn't recall why. "What are you doing here?"

"Giving you your Luke moment." He smiled, only a small lift to the side of his lip as he met my gaze. "Good to see you, Sally."

"It's nice to see you too." I was surprised that I meant it. Why was I so calm? I wanted to race at him, to rip at his face—this was the Nimien who had tried to imprison me, who had altered time itself to make me his, not the older, wiser man who'd given his life to save ours at the Battle of the Labyrinth. This was wrong, all wrong. Why was I acting like it was the most natural thing in the world?

"What are you doing here? And what do you mean, 'Luke moment?'"

"I'm returning from beyond death itself to impart wisdom." His smile was forced. "I realize this must be unsettling—let me change the decor."

And just like that, I was in a Starbucks. I can't tell you which one, since it looked as generic as the white room at the end of the universe. All I can say is that Nimien was on the other side of the counter, wearing a jolly green apron emblazoned with the unthreatening name *David.*

"I'm dead, and you brought me to a Starbucks?" I wanted to leap over the bar and grab him by his tastefully embroidered nameplate, but I was unable to move.

"It's what your mind finds most soothing. Would you like a soy milk cappuccino?"

I clutched my hands into fists—at least I still had control over that.

"Get out of my head, Nimien," I spat. "You're not welcome in here."

"Excuse me, but I didn't *ask* to be here." He scooted down the line, expertly maneuvering the espresso machine. "I'm not really *here* in the first place. I'm an expression of your subconscious. You've been repressing me for a little too long."

Which explains why I didn't immediately destroy him like the parasite he was. "Go on, then. What do I want myself to know?"

"I thought I had a dying wish, didn't I?" His voice was sharp as the crack of a whip. "One I imparted to you as I lay on the ground of my lab, killed by my own son? Ring any bells?"

Oh. Right. I unclenched my fists, slipped them into my pockets. At least my subconscious had been kind enough to generate them in not-dead-after-all robes. "I remember."

"Why haven't you sought it out? It's not like you've not had any free time on your hands or anything…"

He foamed the milk in a separate pitcher, eyes low. Great, now my subconscious was being passive aggressive. I gritted my teeth.

"I'm in charge of what I do with my time." I didn't know if I was talking to Nimien, or myself. But even if it was myself, I obviously wanted me to play along for some reason. "Just because you're dead doesn't mean you can control me like you're doing right now. I needed a mental health break for a reason—obviously."

"Sally." He handed me my drink, no lid. "Go find the *Wanderer*. You'll be glad you did. I can promise you that."

"Nimien," I started, but it was too late. He had turned into a large bullfrog, hopping onto the counter where I was reaching for cinnamon. The frog was green, and had a large, puffed out chest, like in the fairy tales, with its mouth all puckered up.

"Rib-bit," it croaked, oh-so-slowly, glaring at me with those large frog eyes. Huge, green eyes with a hint of orange around the edges, pupils dilated like an animal in the dark.

"I fail to see the symbolism in this." Thanks, subconscious. Maybe I was better off with the manifestation of my trauma. "Right, brain, give me back Nimien. I need to talk to him."

The frog did not budge.

"Rallit." Its breath hit me in the face with the force of a sledgehammer, the pungent, earthy smell of a damp carpet. "Rallee."

"Shoo," I snapped. "Geddout of here. I need to talk to Nimien. I need my Luke moment."

"Raaaaallleeeeeeeeey," it croaked. "Ralleeeeeeey! Salleeeeee! Sally, wake up!"

I came awake like I came alive: all at once, and with gusto. I took a breath large then coughed it out, grabbing Zander's hand for support, his arm spookily too large.

We were still in the hotel room. My hand tingled, and when I lifted it off Zander's, I cringed: it was about the size of a toddler's. Zander held up a large, pustule-covered red thing—the artist formerly known as my hand.

"Why didn't you tell me the bartender bit you?" he said, brushing the hair out of my face, where it clung to my sweaty brow.

"Meegrans are poisonous? I hadn't noticed in the scramble to get out of there."

"Venomous."

"Semantics. I just had a Luke moment." I grabbed him by my good hand, and he hoisted me up to a seat, leaving my former hand on the floor beside me. I refused to look at it, betrayed. "You know, Luke Skywalker? *Star Wars.*"

"Sorry, I never finished it." He took a slow breath. "The tax stuff in the first film was too close to reality and not enough escapism for me."

Words stumbled out of my mouth like a drunkard out of a bar. I gulped and gulped, wondering why this was proving so tricky. After all, it was totally reasonable—I wasn't even asking for the moon! And if I had, who knows what he would have done? Probably broken all the laws of physics to make it happen, ethics be damned.

"Do you remember what Nimien said to me… before he died?" Zander remained silent, just holding me. "He told me that I would find my answers when I found the UPAF *Wanderer*. I think it's time."

"We can do that." His voice was dry. "What do you expect to find there?"

I shrugged. Sometimes that made me feel better, but sometimes it made me feel like an idiot. "I don't know. I don't even know what questions those are the answers to. All I know is I need to find it, or I'm going to end up back in Starbucks on a vision quest."

He furrowed his brows. "Is that your Luke moment? Wow, *Star Wars* takes a strange turn."

He helped me to my feet. I was still wearing my shwomp, the poor thing trembling slightly from… well, everything. I slipped it off and placed it on the bed next to Zander's, where they immediately wrapped around each other. As the adrenaline phased out of my system, as my hand slowly regrew, I wanted to do the same—wrap myself around Zander and cry out everything we'd just been through.

It was the first time in months I'd seen somebody die.

"It's time, isn't it?" Zander took a seat on the edge of the bed. "It's catching up with us. We've got to go back now, haven't we?"

I nodded. He sighed into the silent hotel room.

"Are you sure?" He reached for my hand—the good one—and I laced my fingers through his. "Just because I'm saying it doesn't mean it has to be so."

"I'm ready." I nodded, slowly. "We need to find the *Wanderer*. Then… it's time to go back."

It's time to see if Blayde succeeded. To see if we pop back into my correct time and James is waiting there for me, a beacon of health and hope. Blayde won't fail. She can't fail.

James. Isn't. Dead.

She didn't die because of me, no. She didn't truly die at all.

"I don't expect this search to be very difficult." Zander smiled, but it never reached his eyes. "Now that the Alliance mildly likes us, it's possible they'll be willing to give us the coordinates of the ship. We'll probably locate it in a matter of hours."

"And we'll finally know why Nimien's dying wish was for me to find it."

"We'll go to Pyrina tomorrow. After we get cleaned up, and a good night's sleep?"

It hit me then: this might be the last night in a long time it would be so easy. That we'd have a room to call our own, food just a com-tap away, a bath so expensive it vibrated the dirt right off your body. But this was my decision, my choice: vacations had to end sometime, and I wasn't going to traumatize any more bathrobes on my time off.

FOUR

THE JOYS OF OFFICE POLITICS AND BUREAUCRATIC WARFARE

Sally

"WHY DOES HIS PALACE LOOK LIKE VERSAILLES and the White House had a three-way with old *Star Trek* props?" I poked an ornate bronze statue of a wig-wearing reptilian that held up a light fixture. I couldn't help but snort at the absurdity of it all.

The Imperial Palace was as outrageously ostentatious as I'd expected. It was my first time to the Floating Islands—the bureaucratic black hole of the Alliance—but Zander knew his way around like he owned the place. I'd jumped us, with his help, to the second-greatest sitting room, where he dropped my duffel bag on a nearby quartz chair before we'd even fully materialized.

"It's a long story," he said. "Partly my fault. Good memories."

I stuffed my fingers into the depths of my pockets, feeling the fabric of my coat for what felt like an eternity. We'd barely escaped last time, and that was with a forced pardon. But a lot had changed since the last time we'd been on Pyrina. There was a new leader in this palace, one who I'd once drunk under the table.

I made my way to the window, staring out to the bay. It was a perfect day, the sky a crisp pink, no sign of the clouds of nanobots. Winged creatures skimmed the fiery red waves near the shore. It always felt like there was a permanent sunset on Pyrina, the sky constantly aflame.

I wondered, not for the first time, what the planet's real name was. With a translator in my head, all I ever processed was a close approximation of the essence of the word, but the word itself never hit my ears. It was absorbed, studied, and spat out in an understandable format before I even had a chance to hear it.

"What are *you* doing here?" The window shook as Dany slammed the double doors behind her. "Do you know what kind of security measures we have? You would have been shot on sight if anyone had seen you!"

She looked as radiant as the last time I'd seen her, her short blond hair shaved sheer on either side of her head, leaving room to display the inordinate number of golden earrings that dangled from her ears. Her crisp white uniform made her look larger than life, her shoes so black I'd expect to see straight to the other side of the universe if I stared close enough.

"Nice to see you too, your Imperial Majesty," said Zander. "Glad you found us first?"

"Unbelievable," Dany scoffed. "Every army in the near-universe would have turned on you in an instant. There are still measures *specifically* built for when you show up."

"Notice the distinct lack of lasers currently burning me to a crisp? Yeah, we dismantled them decades ago." Zander shrugged. "Sorry, Dany. Next time, we'll try the front door, if you'd rather have it that way."

"Not for another millennium at least." Dany's face was red. "Even after all you've done for us, I'm not allowed to be seen with you. My spin team thinks it'll set us back to the industrial revolution."

"Well, that hurts. Have you started dismantling your abusive power structures yet?"

"I've been emperor for less than a month! When would I have had the time?"

"Oh, I don't know, I think ending slavery would be my first priority."

"Systemic change takes time, Zander." Dany threw her hands up in the air. "We're still working out second contact protocol for the Aorians. Gods! Is this why you're here? To lecture me?"

I bit my lip. I thought Dany would have ended the horrible child-hire program the second she rose to power as well. I was naive to think the oppressive nature of the Alliance would change overnight with someone I liked at the helm. If the Alliance was still the enemy, would I be able to turn against my friends?

Not today. Not yet. They still had a chance to make a real difference. Dany could do so much good as empress. And they were actively working on a solution to meet with the Aorians, the lost colony of Humans from whom we'd 'rescued' Nimien, back when he was just Nim.

"Can't I come and visit my best friends every once in a while?" I stepped forward, my feet heavy, and my eyes caught the slightest upturn of her lips. I wanted to see the friend I had known there, not the regal being standing before me, the empress of a thousand skies. As if sensing my hesitation, she opened her arms, and I embraced her, feeling like an intruder in her world. She squeezed me back tightly, a warmth overcoming the weight of the distance between us.

"How's Marcy doing?" I asked. "Is she okay here? Can I see her?"

"I'm afraid she isn't available at the moment," Dany gave a long, drawn-out sigh. "She's busy with important tasks that can't be delayed, so I don't think she'll be joining us. I'm sorry, I know how much you want to see her."

"Important tasks?" Marcy exclaimed. "Since when did ranking neighborhoods by the quality of their foodie blogs become important to anyone?"

She had waltzed into the room like a model on a runway, dressed in an oversized cream-colored pantsuit with a glowing blue belt. I squealed in delight, and before I knew it I was hugging her tight, although I'm not sure if I crossed the room on foot or jumped to her side.

"It's helping me understand our people better." Dany struggled to be heard over my delighted shrieks. "I'm trying to show them we don't have to be distant figureheads. I want them to see how serious I am about making things better for our society."

"Well then, go out and show them yourself," huffed Marcy, "Instead of having me sit inside all day and only appear to them on the palace's social media."

"Dove, you're not supposed to be here," said Dany, eyes almost popping out of her head. Her forehead glistened with sweat.

"Where else am I meant to be? Seeing as how this palace is the only place I'm allowed to set foot." Marcy hugged me tighter still, as if I were her favorite teddy bear. "Sally, I'm so, so pleased to see you. Have my wife and her team made you feel welcome yet?"

"They can't just barge in here without warning," said Dany, "they could be *seen*!"

"I'm not barging," I said. "And if we don't have the front door, what other options do we have? You never pick up your phone."

"The roaming charges are terrible out here," said Marcy.

Dany licked her lips. "And I'm working on that. So, I take it this isn't a social call?"

Zander and I exchanged looks. We hadn't planned a speech, though maybe we should have.

Dany sighed again. "It never is. Well, spit it out. What do you need? Soldiers? Gold? Ships?"

"Just a single ship, if it isn't any trouble." I stepped away from Marcy's hug. Was Dany being sarcastic, or was any of that really on the table? "The *Wanderer*? I'm sorry, I don't know its classification or anything."

"The *Wanderer*?" Dany's brows drifted to her hairline. "You won't need fleet officials; no, you need to go to the archives."

"Oh! An air of mystery!" Zander leaned in, bracing his arms on his legs. "Do go on."

"You're not messing with me? You seriously don't know?" Dany blinked twice. "Everyone on this planet knows about the fate of the *Wanderer*. You don't want to go anywhere near it."

"Um, I don't," said Marcy, raising her hand. "It wasn't in the press packet."

"Oh, why's that?" Zander was entranced, his full attention on Dany. "Oh my stars, are there zombies?"

"Dany, can you give it to us straight?" I asked. "Stop trying to be so aloof. What happened to it?"

"It crashed. About five years ago." She frowned.

Oh. Great. So much for a mystery. Maybe we'd need an element of time travel to get to the heart of Nimien's secret.

"I don't have time for—Well, today's as good as any. Cethea, cancel my seventeen o'clock."

"Are you sure you want to do that, sire?" a voice squeaked from Dany's lapel. "The Minister of Sunrises has already had to reschedule three times with us."

"They have?" Dany pinched the bridge of her nose. "Fine. Tell them I'm running late. And—activate order 55-B." She turned to me now, forcing a smile. "Given this will neither be the first, nor the last time you two are going to ask for our help, and vice versa, I've taken the liberty of establishing an official liaison office with you."

I was still hung up on the fate of the ship; it took me a second to process what she was saying. Marcy beamed, holding her hands in front of her lips like the couple was about to reveal a prize on a game show.

Zander was as confused as I was. "You created an official what of the what now?"

"The Alliance Office for Sibling Liaison." Dany gave us a curt nod. "Paperwork's gone through, but you know how it is with HR—we didn't expect to have it up and running so quickly. People are being appointed. Their desks are being moved to their new locale. You two—three, counting Blayde—will be able to go through *there* as often as you want. My people will help you in getting what you need, provided you to give *us* a hand from time to time."

"Isn't it great?" said Marcy, "Now we can work together! And the populace will *have* to like you!"

Zander let out a groan that could have crumbled the palace to the ground. Sure, Dany didn't have time to abolish abusive systems, but had found enough to create a way to enforce *us*.

"Are you serious?" I said. "You never even asked us! You know our stance on the Alliance, you know how we feel about doing their dirty work."

"You are *literally* asking me for a favor right now," she said. Did she just get taller? "All I'm hoping for is for a little quid-pro-quo. Also—dirty work? What do you think I am?"

"An overlord," said Zander, and my heart clenched. If this was just my boyfriend and my best friend's wife having a spat, it would have been bad enough. But this could be explosive. "I don't want a relationship with strings attached, Danirshna."

"I'm trying to maintain a relationship, *Sand.*" Dany remained ramrod straight. "We can't pretend we don't know who we are anymore. We have responsibilities. I'm trying to find a solution that won't jeopardize our... *friendship*."

Marcy stepped closer to me. The heat drained from my face. I had been naive to think our relationship would be unaffected by her new status. We were different now, both of us, with opposing loyalties: her to Dany, and thus, the Alliance, me to Zander, the bane of their civilization. That animosity wasn't going to go away overnight because we'd once been drinking buddies on a small, distant planet.

"At the very least, the office will allow you to say hi whenever you want," said Marcy, her voice low.

"I can already come and go when I want," said Zander. He too appeared to be growing. "You call us friends, but you can't be seen with us?"

"*Yet*," said Dany, "And we're trying to fix that. *This office* will try to fix this. Usher in a new era of truth and transparency."

Zander nodded stiffly. "That remains to be seen."

"Then come," she said, waving to the door. "Let my people help you with your *Wanderer* problem. See the difference. Under new management and all."

Zander's gaze did not waver from Dany's face. Why was it always a pissing contest with these two?

"Let me get you the keys." Dany smiled.

"Won't need them," I said. "Just tell us where to find the room. And try to shake that minister off before dinner. We're taking you out."

"Sub-basement A, office 44B." Marcy slipped her arm through mine. "Mind if I join you?"

"Dove!" Dany cried, but it was too late. I'd already jumped, letting the sub-basement office pull me forward.

I could feel the tension radiating off Zander, his grip a smidge too tight. The same tension radiated off our new office as I opened my eyes to grey-green walls and a trio of frowns in tie-dye shirts and camouflage crocs. Marcy snorted.

"First of all, woah, that's awesome." She let go of my arm. "And secondly, no, I did not approve those outfits. We have an optimal uniform generator that's meant to come up with the ideal clothing for each department, and I'm not sure it understood the assignment."

"That's them?" The speaker was humanoid, but the resemblance with humans stopped there. Every inch of what would have been skin was covered in a rough, bone-like substance, cracking at every articulation. They were shorter than me by at least two heads, thin as the bone they were covered in.

"You know anyone else that can suddenly appear in a secure room?" a human replied with a scoff. She looked almost as if she could have come from Earth: dark black hair pulled back into a tight ponytail, a pair of spectacles balanced on a tiny nose.

"Not as scary as they tell you they are, are they?" the bone-person muttered. "Mom used to say they appear in pillars of flame. I'm not seeing any flame."

"I always though the girl would be taller." A human man sighed. "Not as plain, you know?"

"That's not Blayde," said the human woman. "That's the new one. The one they've been keeping out of the press, you know, the Terran female that broke into the Earth Agency."

"Then that's Blayde?" The man squinted at Marcy. "I can see it. Still, thought she would be more imposing."

Zander deflated. "You know that we can hear you, right?"

A collective gasp ran through the tiny room. The small team stared at us more intensely, a twinkle of fear in their wide eyes.

The office space was hexagonal, with three desks all facing the center, where we now stood. The desks were in different states of completion, seemingly building themselves out of thin air, like they were being eaten by termites but in reverse.

"I take it I have *you* to thank for the demotion?" The woman crossed her arms over her chest. "I was in line for a management position in the communications sector. Now I'm—what? I'm not doing PR for terrorists, even if they've been pardoned. This had better come with a pay increase."

Zander finally, *finally* looked at me, but it was only to give me a *look*. What did he want me to say? It wasn't my fault Dany had gone to such lengths in the very possibly wrong direction. I wasn't endorsing them by going along with it. Without his sister to balance him at work, his usual grin was fickle, and instead his lips drew a straight line.

"I hate to be *that* first lady." Marcy furrowed her brows. "But hello, I'm your boss. And they're here at my behest. Oh, nice, that's the first time I get to use behest in an actual sentence. Such a good word. *Behest*."

The trio gasped again, twice as loud as the last time, and for a second there wasn't enough air for us to breathe. In unison they folded in half, bowing so low I thought I'd missed out on a yoga cue.

"My liege," said the bone-person. Marcy waved them up.

"I will never get used to that," she muttered, before shaking her head and straightening again. "In any case, welcome to your new positions. I promise, they *do* come with a pay increase."

"We've already been briefed." The woman scoffed. She caught herself instantly. "We just don't understand it."

"Ahem." The man clasped his hands in front of him. "Our job is to assure the symbiotic relationship between our two parties. The Alliance scratches your backs, you scratch ours. Our office will be the only one in the entire universe with the means of contacting the legendary Siblings."

"Just drop your pants and get it over with," said the woman.

The man's eyes fell to the floor. Marcy snorted.

"Look, I don't know the details," I said. All these eyes were making my skin crawl. "I need some help finding a ship. Is that something you can do?"

"Of course." The woman blinked, oh-so-slowly, then made her way to her desk. "I believe I've been issued with a level of clearance, so we can, of course, process your request—is that all we're going to be doing for the rest of our lives?"

Though I understood her anger completely, I had no patience for it now. I could see how disoriented and confused these people were, but none of us asked for this. Dany obviously had some plans of her own. Marcy still had her arms crossed and lips pursed. I got the message loud and clear: she wasn't the mediator, they were.

Our new buffers.

"What's your name?" I asked, turning to the human.

"Klimpt." Her voice snapped like a whip. Somehow my translator poked my brain in a way that made me aware her pronouns were female. "Dhume Klimpt. New head of the Alliance Office for Sibling Liaison. At your service, apparently."

"May I call you Dhume?" I made myself smile, hoping it didn't look as forced as it felt. "My name is Sally Webber. If we're going to be working close together, I think it would be best for you all to call me Sally. And Zander, well..."

"You could call me Cosmo if you wanted to." He snickered. "Though I don't think you'd want code names here, that's all up to you."

"That's a magazine," said Marcy.

"Look, the point is I don't care. You can call me Zander or any of the names you grew up knowing me by, whether it be from a bedtime story or an Alliance history book. I would personally prefer Zander, but this is your world, your home. I understand if you don't trust me yet, but here, I'm trusting you. Help us find what we need. You can decide later if you want me to know your names, if you can trust me enough to know them."

The person covered in the bone-like skin took a step forward.

"Zander," she said with a nod, my translator catching her gender where I couldn't. "And Sally. My name is Marisha au Plinthea: information specialist. And I don't care what they say you've done; there are rumors spreading about how you stopped the plague of fear.

Rumors the higher-ups don't want us to know, so it's safe enough to assume they're true. Thank you, for everything."

"I'm Mondrin." The way he hunched made me believe this was a very big promotion for him. "I work—*worked*—Tech. I know everything there is to know about your hacks. I'm the guy they hired to install new protocols to stop you. Guess now I'm helping you. I'll be the one liaising with the rest of the Alliance. I get what we need from them, file reports back."

"We picked the best," said Marcy, a small smile drawing on her lips. "Well, the automated staff optimizer did. We just approved it and secured the funds."

"Good." Zander rubbed his palms together. "Now that we're all… acquainted. I need a ship tracked down. Who can get that for me?"

"What, no 'thank you'?" Marcy muttered under her breath.

"I can," said Marisha. "Well, it depends on the ship you're looking for. Is it a warship or a private vessel?"

As she spoke she moved over to a computer console, wiping her hand in front of the scanner. It immediately booted. The rest of the small group gathered behind Marisha's chair, as if unsure whether they should help or do work of their own. Most just watched Zander and me, their lips sealed.

"We're looking for the *Wanderer*," I said. "Location, crew log, something like that. Can you get that for us?"

If they weren't staring at us before, they were now. Every eye was on the two of us, every jaw hanging limp. Marisha's fingers froze over the keyboard.

"Have I said something wrong?" I was startled by their stares. I could feel Zander edging to move forward, as if he needed to protect me from something. Yet he did not move, and neither did I.

"You don't need me to look up anything." Marisha shook her head. "The *Wanderer* crashed on 9JQV Nope. It's one of the largest tragedies in Alliance history."

"We just heard. That's terrible." *Nope?* My brows furrowed. Was my translator malfunctioning? Not the right time to ask. "Were there any survivors?"

She glanced at both her colleagues in turn. "We don't know."

"An Alliance warship never goes down without capturing a gigantic amount of data," said Zander. "Did you not find anything during the search party?"

Mondrin stared at the floor again. "There was no search party."

I glanced at Zander, but he was too riveted to notice. "How come?"

"It's 9JQV *Nope*." Dhume spit the name as if it were a curse. "No one ever comes back from 9JQV Nope. That's just how it is."

My hands curled into fists but I forced them flat. "Someone needs to start giving me some answers." Seeing their wide eyes, I corrected myself quickly. "No!

Sorry. That's not a threat. I'm genuinely curious. Is the planet actually named 'Nope'?"

"9JQV Nope." Dhume's lips were a pencil thin line. I'm sure she would rather have been on the other side of the planet than speak to us. "Third planet in the QV system, 9J constellation. The first team sent out on exploration—back in the Era of the Great Expansion —was lost the second it hit the atmosphere. When the rescue team was sucked in too, it was clear this planet was bad news. It's been blacklisted ever since. Over fifty ships have crashed there, nonetheless—ours, and others—after ignoring the warnings. It's a danger to any ship that even assumes a standard orbit around it. With no distinguishing characteristics other than being a death trap to any ship that goes near it, Alliance astronomers thought it best to stick the name on. It's a shock that the *Wanderer* would even be in that system: their mission was meant to be light-years away."

"What makes it so dangerous?" I asked, at the same time as Zander said, "What classification is it?"

"Other than being the first ever Nope-class planet?" Dhume shook her head. "*Unclassified.* We can't even get a probe in close without it being sucked in, so we have to rely on the spectroscopic data. The atmosphere is breathable and oxygen-rich but seems to be infused with a thick, highly conductive element. The surface conditions are completely unknown; any crew that crashes there is considered lost in the line of duty."

"Could it be habitable?" I asked. "Is it out of the realm of possibility that the crew survived?"

"It's possible," said Marisha. "But highly improbable. The odds of surviving a crash there are infinitesimally small."

"But not zero," said Zander. "If there's a chance someone survived, we're going for a look-see."

"What?" I said, but he was already marching for the door. I grabbed his arm, pulling him back. "Hold your… horses? Hovercraft? What are you going on about?"

"Nimien's last wish was for you to find the *Wanderer*." Finally, there was that Zander smile back where it was supposed to be. "And he was kind of known as being the most intelligent being in the universe? He said you'll find your answers there. It's worth a look, at least."

"We have a search party?" Dhume asked, confused. "Marisha, stop me if I'm wrong, but they just said..."

"I heard it too." Marisha's hands rose to cover her mouth. "We have a search party. We actually have a search party."

Marcy nodded. It was incredible to see her poise in this room. She had fully embraced the mantle of first lady of the universe and she looked every inch the part. "Now this sounds like a superb mission of friendship. The ideal first mission to seal our union."

"I'm calling them some transport," Mondrin said, grabbing a phone off Marisha's desk.

"I guess they're going to be helpful, after all." Dhume grinned. "Marisha, make sure this doesn't leak until their return. All right? We need to keep this under wraps until we have good news."

I looked up at Zander in confusion. "Did we...?"

He shrugged. "I don't know." He shook his head. "But I think we're going to have to run another one of the Alliance's errands."

I sighed, leaning my head against his shoulder. "Well, I guess it's for the best." I took a deep breath. "If we do find people, we'll need a way of bringing them home."

"Let's just hope this doesn't become a habit." He frowned as he watched the team scramble through the tiny office under Marcy's proud watch. "Any idea what Nimien wanted us to find there?"

"I don't know, Zander," I replied, shaking my head. "But knowing Nimien, it won't be a picnic."

FIVE

LIGHTS, CAMERA, MISSION

Sally

TAKE IT FROM ME: DON'T VISIT ANY SPACE DOCKS if you have a fear of heights. So long as there's oxygen and gravity, nothing else matters to the station planners whose notion of "architecture" appears to be little more than flimsy grating and force fields to keep all the freaking air in. Sure, planets are gorgeous from above, but there's something about riding an elevator straight up as the horizon falls further and further away from you that makes you realize nothing matters and nothing ever will.

Zander took my hand, steadying my fidgeting fingers. His skin was warm against mine, hands soft from the multitude of anti-bacterial soaps we'd had to scrub with before this interstellar journey. The last time I'd seen him in a UPAF uniform, he'd grumbled far less about wearing one. Being on the *Traveler* had been a good excuse; now that we were working for—no, *with*—the Alliance, he was much less enthused by the idea of being dressed like this. I didn't care. I was just glad mine zipped all the way up this time. Marcy insisted. Kinda awesome being besties with the second most powerful woman this arm of the galaxy, the first of whom being her wife.

The elevator stopped with a lurch that almost sent me tumbling forward. The door sighed open, and there went my breath. I'd lived on a spaceship before, and yet nothing had been as sci-fi as this, standing in the hangar bay of interstellar warships. Well, I say standing: Zander was the only thing keeping me up, as my knees had completely given out beneath me.

We could have fit the city of New York in here, and parts of New Jersey too if they weren't embarrassed to be seen together. We had arrived at some mid-level, the ceiling extending up into darkness, the ground, well… there was nothing between the grated catwalk I would somehow have to walk on and Pyrina below. In the middle—*starships*. Three massive interstellar vehicles, large enough to hold crews of hundreds, if not thousands. The scale was nothing I could wrap my head around. We'd missed all this when we'd sneaked into Pyrina for the Presidential Ball; thank goodness Kork had been allocated a massive suitcase allowance.

I clutched Zander's hand. I was going to have to get over this fear of heights eventually, but in some strange way, it was all I had left of my brother.

"I see the clothes fit," Dhume said dryly. She held up the tablet and tapped it with her stylus without looking up. "Welcome to Voiddock Alpha-3."

Zander stepped onto the catwalk and I followed, keeping my eyes riveted on our liaison. No, I couldn't look down; I couldn't afford to see what awaited me if this catwalk were to fail. How was any of this safe?

We were not alone, either. Between us and our ship's gangplanks were strangers in uniform or in formal garb, each openly staring at us. There would be no tears shed if we failed in our mission.

Flash. I wasn't blinded for more than a blink, and already Dhume was ripping a polished lens out of someone's hands, slapping a slab of duct tape on the casing. The strap caught on the stranger's neck. He let out a garbled scream as she dragged him upwards. Add that to my list of Dhume details: deceptively long arms.

"Hey!" he shouted, reaching for the lens—camera?—but Dhume kept it high out of reach. Her face didn't even twitch. "I-I… I have a right…"

"You have the right to take whatever photographs you want," she said. "But your camera will be held in electronic stasis until we permit the release of those images. If you take the censor bar off, you will be arrested. You upload them, you will be arrested. Clear?" She turned to us, her lips in the straightest line I'd ever seen. "As far as first impressions go, you could do worse." She pressed her tablet against her chest. "Come."

She brushed past the photographer, who, looking up from where he'd been inspecting the camera, saw Zander—and put two and two together, I suppose, because the next thing that came out of his mouth was a bloodcurdling scream.

"And… 114 seconds before you scared someone shitless," said Dhume, tapping something on her tablet. "Marisha guessed fifty. She's buying drinks tonight."

Zander kept his head high as we followed Dhume down the catwalk, avoiding looking at the photographer's terror-stricken face. I'd never seen a man turn green faster than Bruce Banner Hulking out before.

Dhume smirked. "You understand why we're not allowing you to wander around here alone now?" she said, the closest thing to warmth in her voice I had heard from her so far.

"Of course." Zander clasped his hands behind his back, seemingly unperturbed. I still had to learn how to do that: I must look like I'm trying to hold in a fart.

The photographer had caught us hand in hand—what would the Alliance say when this news went public? If I'd known this would be the first impression their civilization at large would have of me, I would have done something nicer with my hair. I folded my hands like Zander's, pretending I wasn't currently doing the math of how far I would fall if this ended poorly.

"We'll be offering you transport to the 9JQV Prime system," said Dhume. "From there, you will be given your own shuttle and you will be on your own. You will be permitted no outside contact other than with the crew on the ship. While you're on this mission, the outside universe does not exist. Understood?"

We nodded. So much for a full search party—at least they were nice enough to give us a ride and a dinghy. And what a nice ride it was: the ship we were walking to was the very definition of a luxury vehicle. Sleek like a whale, it seemed like it had been carved out of a single block of marble. Built for speed—no, this aerodynamic shape in an environment without air… it was built to *look* like the very image of speed. All for show. Say what you want about the Alliance, their ship design was artistry. Focusing on the curve of the bow made it easier to avoid what was below my feet.

Did all these ships look the same, or was that just me? I felt a tug of familiarity—I missed the *Traveler*.

"If you run into trouble on the planet, our people will be incapable of assisting you. Is that clear?" We nodded again. "Good. When you retrieve the remnants of the *Wanderer*'s crew, you will escort them to the ship, and no place else. If there is no one to retrieve, you return directly to the ship. You will debrief your captain and him alone, and he will report back to us. Understood?"

"I'm getting the feeling this is all very *hush hush*." Zander glanced back over his shoulder. "What happens if I meet a telepath that gets the news out before I even open my mouth?"

Dhume spun around long enough to glare at him. "Please—Mister? Sir? *Frash it*—Zander, take this seriously."

"I *am* taking this seriously," he said, coolly. "I only ask because it's happened before. Telepaths are usually assholes. That kid on the playground who spreads gossip by screaming it at the top of their lungs. I want to be clear of all responsibility in a possible defamation lawsuit."

"Then don't run into any telepaths." Dhume shrugged. "And keep thinking about copyrighted material."

We approached the rim of the ship, to the side of the bow. A single door was open, waiting for us. Dhume handed Zander her tablet as we marched the last few meters.

"Sign here, here, and initial there." She tapped the screen with the tip of her nail. "And before you ask, yes, it is the contract we've had drawn up. I would say take your time to read it carefully, but time isn't something we have a lot of right now."

Zander frowned, his eyes a blur as they read through all the clauses. "Hold on. It says here that you have no obligation to get us off the planet?"

He handed me the tablet, but I was nowhere near as fast a reader as he was.

"You have your own method of transportation," she said. "If you spend too long on the surface without contacting us, we'll consider the contract null and void.

We are not your taxi service. We're being generous enough to take you there as it is."

"Who's doing who a favor here?" It was my turn to be indignant, cutting Zander off. "Do we at least have backup?"

"Backup? For the man who made a civilization fall from the confines of a jail cell?"

I turned to Zander. "You did what?"

"Only the once." He put his hands up defensively. "And it was all a huge misunderstanding. The Raalxai put me in jail for… it might have been littering? They gave me a book to read, then I—accidentally, I swear—threw up all over it—no fault of my own, the food was terrible. One thing led to another, and the next thing I know the prison is rubble and people are calling me their leader. Not a good month all in all."

"Look, we're on a strict schedule here." Dhume tapped the tablet screen again, making my hands shake. "Are you signing?"

I glanced at Zander—and he looked down at me. "You're the freelance hero, here."

With no objections, I signed, with as much grace as if I were accepting a UPS delivery.

"Everything's in order, then. I would wish you luck on your mission," said Dhume, "but then again, you never seemed to need luck before."

"I'll take it." Zander bowed at the waist, which seemed to surprise our liaison. She bowed too, a little stiffly, but still, it's the thought that counts. I bowed as well, though it didn't count as much.

"Thank you, Dhume," I said, as Zander stepped inside the ship. "Sorry for all the trouble we've caused."

"Just try to make it back in one piece," she said. "I can't fathom the paperwork it'll create if you blow up while on contract with us. Now, smile and enjoy your fanfare."

"Our…"

Thunder erupted from inside the ship. Shit, I'd let Zander go in there alone—had they recognized him, attacked him? Ignoring Dhume I leapt inside, fists raised for whatever good that would do, ready to defend my —

But the thunder was feet.

Uniformed soldiers lined the walls of the bright white corridor, hands behind their backs as they stomped their feet. Was this our fanfare? A welcome to the ship?

Zander turned back, smiling so slightly I almost missed it. I kept my face flat as I followed him down the corridors of soldiers, up to the bridge of our taxi.

Just like the first time I'd laid eyes on it, the bridge took my breath away. Sleek consoles wrapped around a floor-to-ceiling glass window to the stars, the captain's chair raised like a throne, the castle bringing itself to war. It gleamed like it was fresh off the manufacturing line, so spotless my eyes refused to accept it was real.

And there, standing tall at his station, was another reason for my breath to suddenly decide it was too good for my lungs.

Kork.

There was a twinkle in his eye as he caught my gaze, though his lips told another story—total neutrality. No smiling, bubbling James T. Kork today. No, today he was all captain. The admirals around him, each in their white-and-gold uniforms—a sharp contrast to the grayish-black the rest of us sported—kept their noses in the air as small orbs flittered around the room.

Eye-Bots. Cameras. Which meant…

Dany didn't just want us to be allies: she wanted us to be stars. We were on the *Traveler*, both the ship, and the show. We would be the next episode. I forced down my smile, hiding the spark of excitement that ignited in my belly. A propaganda ship: no one aboard it was versed in military protocol. Everyone was an actor and nothing more: except for Kork, the only Alliance captain I could call a friend.

Kork took a step forward, and the stomping applause stopped. Zander and I bowed, fully aware of the cameras on us, a gesture he returned.

"Terran Sally Webber." Kork's voice carried across the bridge. "It's a pleasure to meet you. Welcome aboard the *Traveler*."

Introducing me first? Ah, clever. I'm the ally, Zander's my contact. We're not directly linked to the Alliance this way.

"Captain," I replied. So, the footage from our last time here was not public record after all. Shame. "It's an honor to be aboard the *Traveler*. Let me introduce you to my partner—Zander."

Though the bridge was silent, it felt as if someone had increased the intensity of the hush. As if hundreds of people had gasped at once, holding their breath until there was none left for me.

"Honor, Captain Kork. Honor is what I feel right now." Zander's voice quivered. "Your ship is a shining star amidst a sea of darkness. May our presence here be a source of courage, not despair. I am deeply grateful for your kindness and generosity."

Kork nodded in appreciation. "It should be us thanking you, Mr. Zander. This mission is our most perilous yet. Without your help, we'd be doomed to lose our colleagues on the *Wanderer* forever. Our dear friends, comrades, and family members have been given a glimmer of hope because… because of you." He paused for a breath. "Is that good?"

"Um..." My brows came together against my will. "I mean, hope is inherently good, right?"

"And we're clear!"

The breath the crew had been holding spilled out in one large gust. Ranks were broken. Admirals dropped their snob. Kork's familiar smile filled his face like some great analogy.

"Back again for more?" Kork threw his arms wide. "And through the official channels this time, no less—guess I did something right!"

"Oh Captain, my captain!" I rushed forward, giving him a tight squeeze, audience be damned. Kork had saved my life, time and time again; I would never be tired of seeing the man. He swung me around in a bear hug, laughing.

"It's good to see you, Sally," he said, plopping me down. "How's freedom been treating you?"

"You have no idea. But how are you? The ball—"

A shadow crossed his face, but the smile was quick to chase it away.

"Let us just say, I owe my lifeblood to President Danirshna, and more." He turned to Zander now. "Don't think I forgot about you!"

The two embraced, seemingly trying to swing the other, laughing when they couldn't gain the upper hand. For a second, the rest of the ship melted away, leaving me and my friends in our own little universe.

"Hold on, where's Blayde?" said Kork as they finally gave up.

"Vacation time." Zander took a step back. "Where's the original crew?"

"Ah, where to start." Kork took a deep breath. "I forgot you missed the trials. Arrests were made. Crandle retired, she's working on her holo' deal. Xacrelf is getting a spin off. Ter is on paid leave and leaning towards a well-earned retirement. Most of the crew was recast; part of this mission is going to be devoted to screen tests."

He waved at the crew. All dressed in bright green *Crew-Crew* shirts, they were too busy talking with the producers—and avoiding Zander—to pay us any real attention. The eye-bots drifted through the air, lenses closed tight.

My heart dipped. I liked the original crew of the *Traveler*—sure, I'd never watched a single episode, but they were a kind bunch. Well, those who hadn't actively tried to kill me or start an interstellar war.

"So," Kork started, in a shrug-it-all-off tone, "we're taking you to Planet Nope. You know what's waiting for you there?"

"We're hoping a stranded crew wanting a way off the planet," I replied. "But other than that, it's all a mystery."

"Nope is exactly that." Kork nodded. "Ships get sucked in and never come out; no one knows what's under the cloud layer."

"Is there even a surface?" I asked.

"From what our astronomers can tell, yes. But how are you planning on getting the crew off the surface if—I mean, *when* you find them? We've no idea what that cloud layer is, but from what I understand, nothing can fly safely through it."

"But we can." Zander said. "We get in, scope the place, find the crew, and get out."

"Novalicious, hundo," came a voice. I spun around— fast enough to make me dizzy—and gawped into the beady eyes of the man behind me, who looked more out of place than I did. It was like someone had gotten their stickers mixed up between a *Star Trek* and a *Best of the 60s* retrospective and chucked them at him in frustration. While he wore the same uniform as the rest of the crew, there was nothing UPAF about him. His hair billowed out of his head like an avalanche, cascading down his back and chest in a huge bottle-green wave, with little red and blue stripes here and there like he'd grown a grassy ski jump out of his scalp, though overall the effect was of an out-of-date insect.

Kork chomped down on a sigh. "Sally, Zander, I'd like you to meet my new first mate: Spurlock Magnesar."

"Not *the* Spurlock Magnesar?" Zander swallowed audibly. "The musician who—"

"Far out, even the infamous Zander's heard of me?" Magnesar's face brightened, a flash of understated joy, like a tiny sparkler that had been reignited by someone's enthusiastic prodding. He made a zigzag motion with his hands, leaving a fist in the air, the last strum of a very silent air guitar. "Light-years, man. Light-years!"

I forced a smile. The man made absolutely no sense. I found myself, impossibly, missing Crandle.

"The Alliance believed that having a familiar face join the crew would be a real boost… to morale," said Kork. *To viewership* is what he probably meant. He gritted his teeth, forcing a smile. "Magnesar has won fifty-three Nova awards, so he was the… obvious hire."

"Anything to spread peace between stars through my music, man," said Magnesar. Not once did he make eye contact: no, every movement seemed to be targeted on a camera, his arms windmilling like they were playing an invisible instrument. Not a guitar, no, not unless guitars had six necks and a mouthpiece.

A shout broke him out of his trance-dance. The crew froze as one last actor took the stage, bursting out of the corridor like a meteor shower. At once, every uniform folded in the middle, bowing at the sight of—

"Marcy?"

Eyes turned to me, glaring. Oh shit, I'd said that last bit out loud. Marcy didn't meet my gaze, not exactly. Her lips a fine line, eyes twinkling under the thick pancake of asymmetrical makeup, dressed in an ornate, sculptural dress, like something one would wear to the Met gala rather than a ship undocking. She gave me a sideways wink that was unmistakable.

"Last minute change of plans," she proclaimed, hands on her hips. I recognized that pose: the I-don't-want-you-all-to-know-I'm-not-really-this-confident pose. "I'm to represent the president on this historic mission."

More murmurs filled the bridge, followed by loud sighs.

"Why can't they tell us this when we're drafting?" said one of the *Crew Crew*. "Right, back it up people, we're doing the ceremonial first bow again! Take two!"

Marcy strode to our side, head held high. Crew members of both sides whispered "*First Lady*" as she passed, and she gave them delicate waves. As she joined our little circle, her lips dropped to a frown.

"Marcy," I said. I wanted to hug her, but this wasn't the time or place. Not when cameras were around. Not when the producers were trying to usher us back out towards the corridor. "What are you doing here?"

"I came to be a part of this, silly. A ship-trip will be *much* more interesting than all the meet and greets I had planned for this week. Hello, Captain Kork, it's wonderful to see you again."

"You as well, First Lady," said Kork, bowing. "Welcome aboard."

"Outta Atmo'." Magnesar whistled. "You're the new Mrs. President, aren't you?"

"That's the gist of it," she said, grabbing my arm and spinning us on our heels.

"What's going on, Marce?" I said, as we walked towards the mouth of the bridge. "Why didn't you tell me you were coming?"

"Call it an impulsive diplomatic decision." Her massive grin was so fixed, I thought she was attempting ventriloquism. "Dany doesn't see it as necessary. I, however, disagree."

"Places, everyone," shouted one of the producers, before I could ask her anything more. Zander brushed up beside me and I took his hand. We looked every bit the power couple we were meant to be. Marcy readjusted her gown. Heads held high, we turned back towards the bridge. "And we're rolling in five, four, three—"

SIX

OR STARRY-EYED AND STARSIDE UP

Sally

THERE'S A UNIVERSE OF DIFFERENCE BETWEEN chaperoning ex-terrorists and giving them free run of your ship. The second we'd wrapped our introduction scenes—complete with confessional-style interviews—we were ushered to our quarters and locked in for the safety of the crew. Marcy wasn't given an adjoining room: probably best not to give said-terrorists access to the first lady. For some reason we'd been relegated to a tiny crew room, only large enough for the bunkbed that was taking up everything but the floor we now occupied.

"I'm worried about Marcy," I said, the second the lock latched in our room, at the same time as Zander said, "I don't think Marcy's allowed to be here."

"*Allowed*?" I bit my lip.

"She's the first lady. Dany would want her safe and out of sight. The opposite of heading to a Nope-class planet with cameras all over her face."

Marcy had been on my mind ever since we had arrived in Pyrina, and yet I had made zero attempt to reach out to her in private, not even for a quick chat. Guilt gnawed at my stomach. Here I was, able to travel through time and space, and yet, I was avoiding visiting her out of... what? A fear of being intrusive?

She could have needed me. Maybe she *did* need me.

"I'm going to find her," I declared.

Zander raised his eyebrows. "But how? We're locked—"

"Do you intentionally forget who we are?" I scoffed.

I didn't wait for an answer. I knew where to jump to: I had caught a glimpse of Marcy's lavish diplomatic suite before the Crew-Crew led Zander and me to our cramped bunks.

I knocked. I could have gone right inside, but I'm pretty sure that's considered rude.

Marcy opened the door. She had already changed out of her camera-ready clothes and into oversized sweats. Her lips were set in a tight line, her eyes dark with worry. But when she saw me, a small spark of light lit up in them.

"Sally," she said softly, "I wasn't expecting you."

I offered her a smile as I stepped inside. The room was large, but stale: unlike Kork's quarters, it didn't have a personal touch, just clean furniture and crisp sheets on the bed. The shutters were down on the wide window in preparation for our faster-than-light journey.

"You have quite the setup here," I said, marveling at an ornate light fixture.

"Yeah." Marcy let out a deep sigh before turning to face me again. She hesitated before speaking again. "Sorry for forcing you out of your room. I told them I didn't mind a bunk, but nobody listens."

Ah. That explained our bunk bed situation. The First Lady's comfort takes precedence.

"What's going on, Marce?" I wish I had pockets to stuff my hands into. "Does Dany know you're here?"

"Not exactly. But she won't notice me missing for a while; she hasn't slept in our room for weeks. By the time she figures out I'm no longer in the palace, we'll be celebrating a successful mission."

I stared at her, amazed she had pulled this off. A part of me was in awe of her dedication, the other half worried sick. I gave her hand a tight squeeze. Hopefully Kork would let us dip into his secret liquor cabinet tonight.

"It's okay, Sally." Marcy looked into my eyes with determination. "You know I can take care of myself."

I nodded, unable to speak. My heart ached for her. Dany had accepted the mantle of president-emperor only to force the Alliance to work with us: in a way, I was partially responsible for this strain on their relationship. And her being on this ship? With me, with Zander? It could fuel rumors across her domain. Her smile faded as if sensing my thoughts.

"We'll be fine," she said softly. "Dany just needs to... realize I'm missing, I suppose."

"Are you sure you're ok?" My voice trembled slightly. "I know it's been a long time since we've talked, and I don't want to push you into anything, I just—"

Marcy nodded again, and I could tell she was trying to put on a brave face. She opened her mouth like she was about to say something else, but then quickly shut it again.

"It's okay." She sighed and looked away. "I think I need some space right now."

My heart sank. What wasn't she telling me? Suddenly, I felt the distance between us: we were on the same ship, but it was as if we were galaxies apart.

"Of course," I murmured. "If you need me, you know where to find me."

She gave a small smile before turning away, closing the door behind me as I left.

Life on the *Traveler* was far less exciting now there wasn't death and conspiracy aboard. It was just another ship, a pristine one at that, and most places were off-limits to riffraff like us, so we wouldn't dirty their beautiful floor.

With the shutters down for warp, us confined to our quarters, and Marcy on her solo retreat, Zander and I spent the time going over the entire Planet Nope file, trying to establish a strategy for once we had reached the surface. Planets aren't exactly a small thing, and searching for a craft that went down years ago would be like looking for a needle in a haystack, or more accurately a better analogy in a dictionary of clichés.

We didn't even know what the surface conditions were like. The spectroscopic results showed rich nitrogen and oxygen content, so at the very least the air would be breathable, but that was as much as they could interpret, through the dense clouds. As for food, weather—we'd know when we got there.

Thankfully, the Alliance had calculated coordinates for where the missing ship would have landed, giving us a general idea of where to look. The plan, so far, was to break through the cloud layer there before finding a safe place to land. With jumping involved, it wasn't going to take long to search the surface in bite-sized quadrants.

"What are you hoping for?" asked Zander, as we wrapped up another day of hashing and rehashing the same idea.

"A stiff drink and a shwomp," I replied. Truth be told, I still didn't know. I just wanted to get it over with, so I wouldn't get any more weird Nimien dreams. I was done with him. I would much rather figure out what was happening with Marcy, and how I could be a better friend when it was obvious that she needed me.

Zander laughed. "I mean from the *Wanderer.*"

Why wouldn't he just let me play coy?

"I have no idea. Maybe I'll meet my future self again? Maybe I'll meet another past Nimien. Or maybe the ship's full of treasure and we'll be rich beyond our wildest dreams."

"Is that something we need right now?" He pulled a fistful of coins out of his pocket, dropping them on the table along with an assortment of dried flowers and a pen cap. "These things keep turning up. Maybe it's his old collection of Russian dolls or something more personal that he wants you to take care of now."

"I doubt it." I brushed the assorted currency off the 9JQV Nope file and closed it so that I didn't have to look at it anymore. "Seemed like he became a bit of a minimalist in his old age."

"Still, it's all *very* mysterious."

It was only after five days in our rooms that we were finally invited out, and it wasn't for dinner. No, true to their word, this ship would only bring us to our destination, not entertain us. So, within minutes of us reaching the mysterious planet, we were already filming the great departure scene.

All my body hair stood to attention as I stepped into the hangar bay. The last time I'd been here—when not secretly stuffed in a suitcase—I'd almost been murdered. Flashes came flooding back— the pain of the airlock, a hand wrapping around my lungs and squeezing. I didn't want to be here. Couldn't be here. Couldn't reach for Zander for support. Thankfully, the room was packed with people, squashing the threatening feeling for the time being.

"We need more makeup on row one," said a producer, waving over a long-armed floating orb. It hovered forward to the soldiers standing in tight formation beside our shuttle, makeup brushes spinning. So, this was to be an even bigger production than I'd been warned. I struggled to cram a neutral expression on my face.

"You two." The producer spun on his tiptoes, a graceful pirouette. "We need you here, and here."

He grabbed me by my shoulders, shoving me like a chair that needed to be out of the way for vacuuming. I smacked his hands away.

"Keep those off me or I'll break them off," I said, channeling my inner Blayde. If she couldn't be with us in person, at least I'd carry her in spirit.

The man seemed unperturbed, turning to Zander, who brushed him off and came to stand by me.

"Not if I break them first," Zander muttered under his breath, loud enough for the producer to hear. He backed away, face draining of color.

"Captain on deck!" a voice declared. *"Places! And—we're rolling."*

Hold on—where was Marcy? The whole excuse she'd made to come along was to represent Dany, so why was she kept out of the shot? Not being able to reach her these past days had left a sour taste in my mouth, but this…

Kork marched onto the deck, hands clasped behind his back, flanked by Magnesar. They stopped in front of us.

"Zander, Sally," said Kork. "You honor us with your courage, taking on this incredibly difficult rescue mission on your own. By doing so, you're demonstrating to the Alliance a new spirit of cooperation and friendship. May you return safely, so we may one day return the favor."

We bowed to each other, the soldiers stomping their feet in applause. So, I wouldn't have a real goodbye with Kork then. His eyes met mine as we rose, and I felt the sadness there, the worry. He knew this was a hopeless mission even more than we did. Was that why Marcy was excluded from this event? So, they could cut her out of the footage when this all went sideways?

"We will be swift," said Zander, placing a hand on his heart. "But we will be thorough. The true fate of the *Wanderer* and her crew will no longer be a mystery. Thank you for this… opportunity."

The stomps rang out again. An eye-bot flew in close to our faces, catching our expressions, our confidence. This was it.

Then, a throat cleared.

"Allow me." Magnesar stepped forward, waving his arms wide. "I have composed a song for this great event."

A murmur ran through the crowd— *uh oh*. This wasn't scripted, was it? Kork bit his lip, and, at a producer's behest, *stepped aside* for Magnesar to take center stage in the cargo deck.

Zander and I exchanged sidelong glances.

Magnesar pulled an instrument out of his uniform. Now, don't ask me what it was, because even if my life depended on it, I would have called it a frying pan. And he played it like a frying pan. Except for the whistling and tinkling.

He slapped the pan and the entire hangar bay cracked like a lightning strike. Every hair on my body stood on edge as his voice warbled out:

"Beyond that point lies the edge of reason, where dreams go to die and hopes commit treason…"

Was I supposed to like this? The entire hangar bay shook with the force of his enhanced voice. Fireworks exploded in my head.

"I've been reaching for the stars, pushing limits, going far. People say it can't be done, but I'll keep reaching for the sun…"

The producers waved to the assembled soldiers, and they stomped their feet along to the music. So maybe this was a bop and I just didn't have good taste.

"Omens are when man meets darkness, and then the darkness goes away, and then destiny will again hurry him, along one way… or another."

It sounded like a fever dream I once had, but it was getting pretty catchy, I admit. Not quite sure what it had to do with our departure. Hell, this was all a bit much just to borrow a shuttle from the Alliance, even without the rock-anthem-ballad thing.

The song swelled in pitch, slowly and beautifully.

"So goodbye, goodbye, I hope you find what you're looking for…" He took a deep breath, before belting out the high note of the song— *"wandereeeeeeeeeers!"*

good at it—hell, we'd almost gotten a manager, except he turned out to be a Jalagreen who was hoping for large audiences only to consume them. Fun times.

Needless to say, I could handle myself in micrograv' now. I flipped upside down, bracing my toes under the rail and using my free hands to clip Zander back into his seat. There. Now he had a better chance of waking up. His wounds were almost gone, so he was going to be back soon enough—but soon wasn't good enough if we were to save the hopper.

I had to get our power going if we had any chance of landing in one piece. I had seen Zander fly one of these enough; why hadn't I ever asked where the backup generator was? Did we even have one?

"Shit." I swore, if only to hear something other than the shuttle dying. The metal shook, quaking as the irregular pressure outside pulled and pushed against the thick walls, making low groaning noises like in a submarine horror movie.

I slammed my feet against the space-shield, propelling myself to the back of the shuttle, hitting the cargo door with a dull thud. The generator had to be back here somewhere, right? But when I tugged open the only panel available, all I found was a note saying "Replace service droid. Run bug checks for delusions of grandeur."

So, no backup generator, and no helpful droid either.

The only place I hadn't checked yet was under my feet. Figuratively, seeing as how my feet were currently propped against what had once been the ceiling. I shoved myself against the floor, which was now no longer straight below me but slightly off to the side. Who was lopsided, me or the shuttle? I didn't know, and I didn't care to know.

I ripped up the decorative carpet. *Fantastic, more grating!* I pulled up a panel and tossed it down the hopper. My body kept being tugged up to the ceiling, so I dug my nails into the remaining carpet, trying helplessly to keep myself anchored. And there, with a lovely, printed label—*Backup Generator*. Perfect.

I slammed my fist against the hatch, and it flew open, the panel spiraling across the cabin like a frisbee. A spaghetti dinner of wires waited for me, scrambled beyond recognition. Who was the joker with the label maker? The generator couldn't be —

"Sally!" Zander shouted from the cockpit. *Ah, finally, he joins the land of the living.* Switches flicked on and off—*click clack click clack click clack* —

"Over here! Backup generator's a mess!"

"Get it online! We're crashing!"

I opened my mouth to retort with something witty, but the shuttle lurched and took the words right out of my mouth. What the hell did he think I was doing back here, roasting a chicken? I plunged my hand inside the tangle, hoping beyond hope for something as recognizable as a switch, but it just kept going.

I had no idea how any of their technology worked.

"No switch!" I yelled back. "What do I do?"

"Plug the red wire into the back panel!"

"Which one?"

"The red one!"

"There are ten of those!" I shoved the wires around. In the growing darkness, it was impossible to make out more than shapes.

"Check them all!" He kept trying the switches, as if they'd suddenly decide to work on their own. The shuttle was still dark, silent as the tomb was about to become.

I did as he said, grabbing a fistful of wires and peeling the red ones from the bunch, stuffing them plug-first into the tiny outlet on the outside of the box. One after the other they failed, useless, until there were none left to test.

Sweat streamed down my brow, mixing with my watering eyes. We were still falling. How long until we reached the surface? Was there even a surface to crash on?

"Not working!" I said.

Click, click, click, click—a different switch, followed by a roar.

"I'm stuck!" Zander cried. "The seatbelt won't release!"

Do something, Sally, anything. My forehead was slick with sweat. I was out of options. I didn't know what I was doing, I was woefully unprepared for this—and who had I been to think I could waltz in and do what the Alliance's best people weren't even willing to try?

What the hell was I doing here?

"Sally." Zander's voice was the epitome of calm. "You've got this. I trust you."

His words were the jolt I needed to get my ass into gear. I grabbed the wires again, this time indiscriminately jamming them one after the other into the tiny plug. *Useless.* Tossing them to the side, I ran a hand over the small box—I hadn't missed it, there was no switch.

The shuttle flipped over entirely, turning the room upside down, my feet dangling a full meter above what was suddenly the new ground. I clung to the tiny box, nails digging into its airtight seal.

And Marcy fell out of the supply stack, crashing into the ceiling with a stifled scream.

"Marcy!" I shouted. I couldn't let go, not while we were still falling, not when I hadn't saved us. She groaned, her eyes slowly opening, then building wide, all in the space of a second.

What the hell was she doing here? She was supposed to be safe on the ship, not tumbling through the sky with me. This was Marcy we're talking about; she wasn't supposed to be—

"Sorry," she gasped.

The clouds parted, and the bright white replaced by—a city? It was so dark, all I could make out were glowing towers, pinks and blues, bright like neon, in the black, spread like paint by the fog. A futuristic city, by the colors of it.

A city. Here, under the clouds, in a world of fog and darkness.

Except—no, it couldn't be. As we fell further, the view became sharper, and it was clear these were not buildings at all. These were trees: either incredibly tall or uncomfortably close. Glowing trees, their leaves bright beacons in the mist. We were over a forest, not a city, a whole world of bioluminescence, glowing with life.

Glowing bright enough for me to see.

"Now!" Zander shouted.

His word rang in my ears as I wrenched my gaze away from the forest, away from Marcy, pulling myself higher, my fingers straining, letting go with one hand to reach up and grab one last red wire, stuffing it into the jack —

The shuttle lit up, whirring as it came back to life. The console burned brightly in the darkness. I breathed in relief. Zander's deft hands flicked switches and grabbed handles, and the shuttle spun back to its normal position, dumping me on the floor, Marcy falling on top of me, knocking all the wind from my lungs. I picked myself up, grabbed her, and raced to my chair, belting her in before gripping the hand rests. My knuckles were white.

We were still falling.

Not as fast, mind you; slow enough that I could walk on my own two feet instead of flinging myself around wildly. But still, *falling*. Crash-landing. Zander took long, measured breaths, adjusting his hands more than twice on the control panel, sweat smearing on the screens.

"What was that?" I was terrified.

"No idea," he muttered, staring straight ahead, eyes wide. "Electromagnetic pulse? Derzan, is that Marcy?"

"Hello," said Marcy, drearily. "Are we crashing?"

"That's probably what got the other ships, right?" Talking helped distract me from the panic. "There's one mystery solved."

He nodded; teeth still gritted. "Gives them good odds of survival: large ships have stronger backup generators."

"So then." I bit my lip. "Why are we still falling?"

He smiled the most awful, forced smile. "Because we seem to have lost an engine."

My stomach knotted itself into knots even a sailor wouldn't be able to undo. "Say what now?"

"What the hell? How can we have lost an engine?" Marcy squawked. "We're still flying!"

"We've got stabilizers." Zander's face stretched into a focused frown. "For guidance in the vacuum of space, but that's pretty much it. Nothing strong enough to break us out of this gravitational pull. We're in too deep."

"How screwed are we?" Marcy and I asked in unison.

"Jinx, you owe me a soda," she said.

"Well—"

Zander had no time to finish his sentence, nor did I to buy her a soda, because a tree appeared out of nowhere right in front of us; the shuttle, once a space-worthy vessel, crumpled instantly. Zander and Marcy disappeared with it, almost as if the tree had a personal vendetta against us. And me? Well, I went sailing through the windshield, the glass slicing my skin as I rocketed through the air, soaring through the branches of those eternally high trees.

There goes any hope of the Alliance ever lending us shuttles again, I thought as I flew, the wind blowing my hair back in billows, the coldness almost refreshing. Seconds later I crashed into the ground.

I didn't have any way of knowing, even as I opened my eyes on that mossy floor, just how much time had passed—or how much of me I'd just regrown. I opened my eyes to the dark world and the glowing, crisscrossing branches above. The forest was silent as the grave, an image I only now just got, as I felt a sense of death around me. Maybe my own.

I pushed myself up. The moss glowed turquoise where I pressed it with my hands, sending a shiver of childish glee through me—*sweet.*

A shuffle—the silence was broken. My chest clenched. I wasn't alone; someone was out there, in the dark.

"Who—"

I heard nothing as they drove a needle into my neck. My muscles relaxed, suddenly comfortable.

Maybe it would be okay if I took a little nap. It's important I catch up on my rest. I've been through so much.

I drifted off, back into the blackness, back where I belonged, back asleep as I deserved —

What felt like seconds later, my eyes fluttered open, but only for a minute or so—enough time for me to see a cross-hatched metal roof above me, close enough for my nose to brush against it.

Enough time for me to panic, before everything went black all over again.

SEVEN

ROCK DOWN TO BIOLUMINESCENT BOOGALOO

Zander

HAVE YOU EVER WOKEN UP TO THE GLORIOUS scent of roasted meat, only to realize that the smell was you? Disappointing in more ways than one, let me tell you. Not only are you denied a feast, but you have to deal with the fact that your clothes are on fire. Well, you're on fire.

"Fire?" I flew to my feet. Or, at least, tried to—unfortunately I seemed to have been impaled by a tree branch. Groovy, as the kids would say.

Assess the situation, Zander, I said to myself, in a voice sounding suspiciously like my sister's. All right, so, I have all my limbs. That's always a bonus. I patted out my arm, which was also on fire. I don't have an audience, so there's no cover story to think up on the spot. The only thing missing right now is —

"Sally!"

Stars, Sally was gone. I spun my head, left, right—the space-shield was shattered in two places: one where the tree limb had come through my chest, the other, in front of where Sally had been standing. She'd gone through. And we were…

"Warning: System Error. System Update: the system has crashed. Ship Update: The ship has crashed."

I grabbed the branch with both hands, hoisting myself forward to see through the damaged armored glass. Just as I feared—we were so far from the ground, I couldn't see it in the darkness. If Sally was down there, she most likely couldn't hear me.

A face flickered across my vision: Marcy. Marcy had been here. Marcy had been in the shuttle. And now she was… not in the shuttle. It was a small relief to think that wherever Sally was, she wasn't alone, that they had each other.

I just had to join them. I closed my eyes, trying to find her in the space between jumps, as Sally had been trying to teach me, but nothing. My memories of being able to do so on my own were trapped behind a fractured lock in my brain. I was stuck up here, and Sally was gone.

I didn't lose focus easily, but ever since Sally'd come into the equation, I'd found my weak spot. Was she hurt? Was she stuck, lost, pinned in a tree?

Get a hold of yourself, Blayde's voice said in my head. *Feelings dull the senses and reaction time. They make it harder to solve problems, not easier.*

I grabbed the branch tighter, pushing back this time. Frash, the seat was right behind me, pinning me in like a cocktail sandwich on a toothpick. I would have to jump.

At least I hadn't lost the ability to jump by sight in that mind-altering frash-up. I pulled forward again, chest squelching. I could just see—*there.*

And nothing.

Jumping was somehow off the table.

I clenched my teeth. No, my mortality wasn't back: I'd be dead already if that were the case. Something was scrambling my jumping, but I should still heal. I needed to. I squeezed my eyes tight, slipped my hand under the chair, and pulled the lever, dropping the back flat.

There came a terrible crunch, and the limb slid out of me—no, I was falling back, the shuttle dislodged—I was hurtling towards the ground.

My flailing arms caught a vine in the darkness, and I swung out of the way of the hopper's debris. I landed on safe, mossy dirt as the shuttle crashed a few feet away in a terrible crunch.

First, assess. I was alive, thc branch safely out of me, my chest filling itself with all those delightful organs. Our supplies would be in the wreck; I'd sort them out when I found Sally and Marce.

The forest floor teamed with bioluminescent life, thick and lush. Somehow, beneath kilometers of clouds, life thrived. Incredible—this wild universe was full of surprises.

"Puuuuuuurrrrrge!" a voice screamed. It occurred to me that it had been there for a while now. I had been too focused on my other problems to notice the one literally screaming in my ear.

A man burst out of the foliage. A *human* man. A *screaming* human man. I was so taken by surprise I did nothing as he sprung on me and grabbed me by the shoulders.

"Didn't you hear me?" he squeaked. "Purge! Run if you value your life!"

Now those are words I do not like to hear. Purges are never fun unless you're a librarian in a recently liberated society and finally get to burn books worth burning. There's only so many times you can recommend the over-printed biography of your not-so-great leader with a straight face.

"Purge?" I asked. "What purge?"

I was wrong, this wasn't a man: This was a *kid*. Not even through with puberty, poor guy, with a sprinkle of whiskers on his face, acne scars deep in his otherwise soft skin. His clothes were lush, silks and velvets ballooning around his joints, sewn smartly in what could only have been handmade high court clothing. He stared up at something behind me, his body trembling like a phone with bad news.

"They're coming! Run!" he screamed, before letting go of me and sprinting off in the direction he'd come as if said bad news was at his heels with a machete.

And for all I knew, it could have been. So, I did the most reasonable thing instinct roared at me to do: I took off after him.

The kid made a terrible ruckus, as if he'd never run a day in his life. His gait was awkward and irregular, and he breathed like he was about to drop the next heavy-breath album as he crashed through the ferns, bursts of light blossoming where he broke the lacy leaves, chin glued to his chest, hands covering his exposed neck.

What the frash was chasing him? Behind us was nothing but shadow. A large, impossible shadow. I wasn't going to stick around to figure out what it was. It was enough to send this kid running so hard his lungs were giving out.

Correction: it was chasing *us*. The shadow was gaining on us. It made no sound, no footsteps to give me the faintest of ideas of what it could be. The good news was I was gaining on the kid. I caught up seconds later, then politely slowed to match his pace. He didn't seem to notice me. The sweat dripping from his brow could have filled a few barrels if you could hold him still for that long.

The charge in the air grew sharper, making my hair stand on end—all my hair, even the top mop. Right, so we were being chased by a storm cloud. My nostrils flared with spark. There was no way for us to outrun it—but outwit it, maybe.

"Hold on!" I darted sideways and, grabbing the kid around the waist, threw the two of us off the high ground and into a dip. I put my hand over his mouth as he tried to scream, pulling us under the overhanging roots of one of the trees, holding us in the shadows until the fizzle of electricity was upon us, loud, beating inside my head—and until it was gone again, racing off somewhere I did not know or care to find out.

Finally I let go of the boy's mouth, and none too soon. He fell forward, propping himself up as he vomited on the leafy ground. I excused the lack of a thank you on the fact he was busy with a different kind of purge.

"What was that?" I stood and peered over the roots. There were no tracks on the ground where the creature had passed, the forest floor undisturbed. I ran through a list in my head of what it could have been, but nothing seemed to fit. I'd met beings of pure energy before, and they usually smelled like banana cream pie.

"*Sters*," the kid said, wiping the vomit off his mouth with the cuff of his frilly sleeve. How was this possible? This boy was as human as they came, like any you would see on any Alliance world, and yet the Alliance had no record of a human colony here. This planet had seemingly been isolated for its entire existence. It didn't add up.

"Shipwrecked?" I asked. A pretty straightforward question, but the kid frowned, as if he'd never heard the word before.

Right. Details didn't matter. The creature that had been chasing us might not be far away—we had to get out of here.

Sally—Sally was still missing. Had that thing gotten to her? I had to find her. Fast.

And Marcy… oh frash, I'd somehow lost her, too. Not that I even knew I was meant to be keeping an eye on her. Dany was going to kill me—over and over again.

"Are you safe to find your own way home?" I stood and offered my hand to the boy. But he remained crouched, shaking his head back and forth much too fast.

"Not going back," he muttered, in a strange, open-eyed trance sort of way.

I nodded. Connection was key if I was going to get any answers. "Running away?"

"Escaping." The boy ran his hands down his face, groaning. "And who are you, anyway? *Destiny awaits, alike for the free man—*"

I was polite enough to hide my groan. Didn't have time for this. Even if it was a relief to see a somewhat familiar face, Sally could be in danger even as we spoke.

And Marcy. I still couldn't wrap my head around the fact that the first lady of this arm of the galaxy was in this mess. What had she been doing on our shuttle? I should have checked, I always checked—

"Right," I said, peeling myself out of my spiral and forcing myself to stand and scan the horizon. Even with the light of the bioluminescent forest, it was impossible to see anything further than a few meters in the mist. I turned back to the boy. I couldn't in good conscience leave him here, not when danger was still right around the corner.

But every passing second put more distance between me and Sally and Marcy. I couldn't abandon them.

But I couldn't abandon him either.

"Where do you need to be?" I padded my frustration in the softest, warmest, cuddliest voice I could muster. Which failed miserably as he scrambled to his feet, eyes so wide I half-worried they'd pop out. But he wasn't looking at me, he was looking over my shoulder. I spun around and kicked myself internally. In the few seconds I'd been watching him, three beings had emerged from the mist—more *humans*. And armed, at that. Each one held an outdated Alliance gun of some kind, aimed at us—well, at me. The kid's eyes sparkled.

The man in the middle was the first to speak, gray hair shining blue in the glow of the forest flora. *"Destiny awaits, alike for the free man..."*

"... as well as he enslaved by another's might," the kid finished.

The man nodded, but kept his weapon right where it was, at a threatening height. The men flanking him did the same, their eyes on him—their superior officer? I kept my hands where he could see them; that at least gave them a false sense of control. The woman standing on the right handed the kid a canteen, and he took a deep swig, chugging hard. Water sloshed down the frills of his neckerchief.

The leader jutted his chin at me. "You weren't on the list."

"And I don't intend to be." I shrugged. "I was just on a walk, when all of a sudden—"

He grabbed my hand, tugging me to him. This was delicate—I could pull back, show him I wasn't someone to screw around with, but I needed to know what was going on if I wanted to find the others. I allowed him to examine my arm; he turned it this way and that as if he were estimating its net worth. He grunted.

"No scars," he muttered to the others. "Not a fighter."

"People do tend to misjudge me, on first impressions alone," I said, pulling back my arm, but keeping it where he could see it. "I take it by the scars you're one, though."

He nodded. "What were you doing in the forest?"

"Crashed. Looking for my girlfriend and her bestie."

"They crash with you?"

"Yes."

"How long ago?"

"Just now."

"During the purge?" He shook his head. "Then you'd best forget about them. They're gone."

Only now did he lower his gun, flicking the safety on with a swift movement of his thumb, slipping the weapon over his shoulder.

Frash this. I took a deep breath to keep myself from doing something stupid. "Great. Thanks for the ominous warnings."

"We're moving out," he said to the others, turning on his heels before I could utter a word. The kid joined them, a canteen in hand, and almost empty judging by the gentle slosh of water in the battered metal bottle. The others walked before and after him, as if escorting someone of great importance.

"What? No!" I didn't have time for this. At least the kid was in safe hands. I needed to peel off, but without any clear answers, I didn't know where to start. "If you know where they are, you have to tell me. They might need help."

"You crashed during a purge, you're not going to find them." The leader's voice was muffled. He didn't turn back. Sounded like he'd given his little speech thousands of times before. "You're going to have to mourn quickly, then move on; we have no use for anyone who gives less than 200% of what they've got."

"Good thing I'm not interested in your little military parade," I said. "If you run into a fireball of a woman and a space princess, let them know I'm looking for them."

The man stopped. He reached into his pocket, pulling out a bulky palm-screen device and tossed it in my direction.

"The circles are us, humans and such," he said. "Crosses are the Sters. Check the surroundings, if you don't believe me. Decide where you'd rather be: in this forest, alone and prey to them? Or with us. It's your choice."

I caught the gadget and switched it on. There's always more to learn about someone from their choice of gadget rather than its contents. In this case—Alliance coms, classic model, this one probably ten years old; not too out of date, but its dismal condition was the real giveaway. It looked like it had been used for years and years—no replacement parts and badly patched.

My metaphorical heart sank—he was right. There were no life signs, other than ours, for kilometers, except for a large pile of small circles off in the direction we were facing. If Sally and Marcy were in this forest, they would be there—otherwise, who knows? What if Sally was still dead? Was there something preventing her from healing? Something deep in the back of my head pondered, not for the first time, whether her immortality was temporary, if this death was the last. A shiver traveled up my body as I pushed the thought far, far away. Sally wouldn't have left without me, not if she had a say in the matter.

And if I'd let Marcy die… no, I couldn't bear that thought either. She might not see me very fondly after everything Sally and I had been through, but from my perspective, we were still friends; she was one of the closest I'd ever had, despite the years of distance on her end. I couldn't fail her.

I could have laughed. Yes, I'd allowed the First Lady of the Allied Empire to crash-land in the heart of darkness. At least now the Alliance was going to *have* to send a rescue team, if they even knew Marcy had joined us.

"You all right?" The kid was as white as a sheet, and yet there was still, somehow, a smile. I hadn't seen him come up to me. I'd assumed they'd all left me there. "You're shaking."

"What's the holdup?" The leader slid down an incline of leaves, throwing bursts of red and pink light into the air with every step. "We have a tight schedule."

"Sorry." The kid threw back a rough smile at me, then started walking up the hill once more, leaving me alone with the head honcho.

He held out his hand and I returned the coms. He slid it back into his pocket, turned and continued on his way without a word. I was right at his side a second later, my every muscle tense. I couldn't remain ignorant any longer. I was starting to feel fear in a way I couldn't process, a slow trickle that was filling me up.

"What is this place? What's happened to my friends?"

"They have either been captured or killed." He took a deep breath. "Your friends. Were they… symmetrical?"

"Yes?" This caught me off guard. Was it a trick question? "Why?"

"Then count yourself lucky: they'll survive the culling." He never once made eye contact as we walked. "They won't be harmed. Quite the opposite. But you're not going to see them again."

"Why?" Frash, I was going to lose it. I clenched my shaking hands. In the back of my head, I itched to throw him against a tree, to rip the answers out of him. I shook the thought away: I didn't like where it came from. "Where have these... Sters, right?... where have they taken them?"

"There's no telling," he said, like this was a daily occurrence in these parts. "They'll be at a processing facility now, but they could be anywhere on the planet by this time tomorrow."

"*Processing*?" My nails bit into the skin of my palms, and I wished for pain so I could feel anything but the absolute terror that was filling me now.

I'd let Sally down. I'd let Marcy down. They were lost, without me, in the hands of an unknown enemy, that was ready to do who knows what to them —

I closed my eyes, willing myself to find Sally in the ether—but nothing. Worse than nothing. I couldn't gather enough of my wits to even jump. My fists shook against my legs.

"Look, if you want answers, I'll take you to the place that has them all." The stranger patted my shoulder. "But these friends of yours? Consider them *gone*. You should be praying to whichever deity you pray to and thanking them for sparing you."

The soldiers arrived at a mound of leaves, reached down, and split it open, revealing a small opening to some kind of craft, the lights switching on as the doors slid open. They brushed away the other leaves, men in cam' suits and a woman in a tattered Alliance medical officer's uniform ushering in the kid. As the leaves tumbled, I recognized the craft to be a sturdy, well-built troop mover, with about a twenty-body capacity, more if you didn't bring any cargo.

But it was *old.* I knew from having seen the life signs on the coms device that its shields and stealth were out of commission, and just looking at the thing told me it should have been junked years upon years ago.

I glanced over at their leader, but he was far too busy kicking leaves back under the craft to hide the fact that we had ever been here.

"Your friends are gone," he said from the threshold of the mover. "Come with us."

Could I leave with them? No, Sally and Marcy were still out there, somewhere. But… Sally could still *jump.* Or should be able to. Just because I couldn't didn't mean she was planet bound. She had better than pinpoint accuracy, she could fold time-space to bring her to the exact atom where she wanted to be.

So, if she wasn't here it was either because she couldn't come, or because she didn't want to come. If she didn't want to, it meant she had a plan, and I needed to trust her, like she'd reminded me countless times before. She was capable, more than capable. But if she couldn't reach me…

Sometimes life revolves around a single choice. Follow these people with answers, follow the mission we'd chosen, or go after Sally. If she was held captive in a way that even she couldn't escape from, then the best chance I had of finding and freeing her was to get answers first.

I nodded and made my way forward, the split-second decision burning guilt in the pit of my stomach. The leader acknowledged me, turning away. Another soldier reached out to help me in.

Inside the mover, people wearing the oddest assortment of clothing I had ever seen sat with their backs against the walls, facing each other. Medics passed down the row to talk with each of them. Some looked as if they had just come out of a clothing catalog – others, a costume store, wearing strange ensembles like the one the teenager in the woods was sporting. I was ushered to the empty seat next to the door. A second later it slid shut, and I could feel us rising.

Some screamed as the back window displayed the tips of those impossibly high trees. Others gazed in shock. The man beside me, wearing a bright green tunic and a fedora, squeezed my hand and squeezed it tight. He was not the only one clutching a neighbor: others had grabbed a limb beside them and squeezed until their skin turned blue.

As we leveled off, the leader pulled out a clipboard and a pencil the size of my pinky. His men and his medics slid the curtains in the back closed and helped bring the focus back on him. Even the grip on my hand slackened.

"Everyone who can understand what I'm saying, please raise your hands now," he ordered. All hands flew up, except for that of an awkward boy close to the back who glanced around before lifting it slowly in the air.

The leader sighed, and quickly assigned someone to join the boy.

"Right. First things first, does anybody feel airsick? NoToes, get them sick bags. Were any of you injured in the run and need immediate medical care?"

One woman had a red gash across her cheek, deep enough to leave a scar. Another man had a pinprick of red on one of his arms, yet he received the same amount of attention as the woman. The medics hurried to wipe the blood away and sanitize the cut, injecting things into his arm that even I could not recognize.

"Good, that's taken care of," the leader continued. "For those who don't know me, I'm Major TrueFoot, and I'm assigned to your brigade. We'll be arriving at Party City in a few minutes, so try and relax. I know for most of you, this is your first flight. Do not feel ashamed if you have vomited; it will not reflect poorly upon you. Now, who here cannot read Pyrinian?"

Much to my surprise, most of the people in the shuttle raised their hands. TrueFoot sighed again.

"Right. You eight will stay on the ship to await further instruction. Those who can read, please disembark when we land and follow the signs. They will lead you to your clothes, food, and bunks. Once you've had time to get sufficiently acquainted with your new comrades, you will be called into what we call the schoolhouse, and we will try to answer anything else you need answering. Is that clear?"

We all nodded. The woman next to me locked eyes with me and gave a solemn nod. I smiled, trying to ease the mood. Her return smile revealed teeth filed to a point, the sharpness clashing with her close-fitting, brightly colored dress, which shimmered as she moved, making her look like a bird. A bird with nice sharp, nasty teeth.

Where was I? More importantly, where were Sally and Marcy?

And how the frash was I going to explain any of this to the President-Empress of the Alliance?

EIGHT

I'M ON THE WRONG SIDE OF GOTCHA DAY

Sally

ANYONE WHO LIKES WAKING UP IN AN UNFAMILIAR place, please raise your hand now, and you can swap places with me before I scream.

The second consciousness slammed into me, instinct bypassed all advice I had ever been given about being in a captive situation, and I sprang bolt upright. There went my chance to scope things out while people still thought I was asleep, but I had to be sure I wasn't in a freaking coffin. It was pointless, though; the room was so dark I could barely make out anything. My hand met the wall, cool to the touch, and I used it to pull myself up, scanning for a sign of anything that made sense.

Ok, so, we have walls, and floor by the feel of it—not the forest, then. The smell was rancid: like too many unwashed bodies in a damp basement. For a split second I thought I might be back in Miro's temple, before I remembered it had died when the universe hadn't. I breathed out, letting the memory of James wash over me, then fade.

I was wearing clean underclothes, of some soft material that molded tight around my skin, covering everything except the extremities—spacey long johns. I didn't remember them. They hadn't been part of the Alliance uniform I had crashed in. The realization sent shivers down my spine.

Somebody had *changed* my clothes.

"Zander?" I hissed, hoping, praying that he was here. No answer. I called again. No response.

I closed my eyes and took a deep breath, dipping my toes into the universe as I had so many times before, and felt… nothing.

No Universe. No Zander.

I tried not to panic: this had, after all, happened before in the bubble universes where I'd been cut off from our own infinity. I placed a hand on my chest, feeling nothing—ok, so I wasn't mortal.

I was just trapped.

Her face hit me in the memory banks like a notification ping. "Marcy!"

Shit, she was gone too. I ran my fingers through my hair, clutching it with my fists. She wasn't supposed to be anywhere near this mission. She shouldn't be anywhere near danger.

The only thing that stopped the panic attack in its tracks was something even more panic inducing. I stood there, frozen, realizing quite suddenly that there was something stuck to the back of my head. A bandage? I peeled it back, a clump of hair coming with it. The skin had already healed smooth, but my head became fuzzier as my fingers slid over a hard pimple. Guilt and shame shed off me in seconds, my hands shaking with the urge to fight. There was something inside my head, drugging me.

Terror filled me like an overstuffed suitcase at the mercy of a relentless packer, each additional fear crammed in, making it harder to contain. Alone, unjumpable, and sans-Zander—a terrible combination. If we'd been separated, how were we meant to find each other, even if —

Oh, shit. My phone. My phone was gone.

After carrying it across countless worlds, just to have it removed from my person—I shuddered. My situation was getting worse and worse. I needed something, anything, to give me an edge.

My eyes had taken advantage of all this terrible self-actualizing time to adjust to the dim lighting. I was in some kind of room, but not one I'd ever seen before. A room made of glass, with nothing but darkness outside. Shadows danced on the wall opposite me, trees in a storm. And right in front of me—more glass?

A glass room within a glass room. This was beyond weird.

"Zander!" I shouted, desperate. "Marcy!" I pulled my hands into fists to keep them from shaking, but that wasn't helping, so I forced them to work together and pull my hair up into a ponytail before I realized I didn't have an elastic and let it fall again. It ran like silk through my fingers. Someone had washed it. What had they done to me? And who were *they*?

"Hi!"

I looked down and—*hold up, is that a kid?* A tiny girl stood at my feet, looking up at me with the widest eyes I'd ever seen, hair pulled into pigtails. She must have been eight or nine. She didn't seem scared, just really, really smiley. I knelt in front of her, trying to reach her level, all while attempting to hide my total confusion.

"Hi there." I smiled right back. "My name is Sally. What's yours?"

"Trinkets!" she said—offering up no other information. Huh.

"Can you tell me where we are, Trinkets?" I hoped it would make her laugh. Instead, she threw her arms around my neck, almost knocking me over. I half-heartedly returned her hug, more confused than cuddly right now. "Where's your mom, kiddo?"

"Trinkets!" she said again. Was that her actual name?

This was eerie. Maybe this was another of those deep subconscious dreams I was prone to. I unhooked the girl from around my neck and stood up. She took off into the dark without saying goodbye.

Definitely not right.

Then, in the distance, a shadow *moved.*

WANDERER

A glowing blob flew towards me, and I staggered back. It came at me so fast I couldn't take in the scale of it. It was only when it froze right at the glass that I could make out its features, but it… it made no sense. An orb, a floating orb, filled with a swirling white fog—except the orb had legs. No—tentacles? Three glowing tentacles dangled from the orb, not touching the ground, which was—wowza, so far down from where I was standing.

Best not to be rude. I stood tall, not knowing where to look for a face. It made a series of whistles and clicks—was it trying to communicate? Could my translator handle an isolated species like this? There was no reason it shouldn't. I'd conversed with some strange creatures, and it hadn't let me down yet.

"Hi," I said, smiling without my teeth. "My name is Sally Webber. I'm a human, from Earth, and I seem to have crash—"

I didn't have time to finish before the air itself betrayed me and hoisted me off the floor.

Oh shit oh shit oh shit oh shit—

My legs dangled helplessly, arms pinwheeling, trying to fight whatever was lifting me. I was rising and rising and—

The air shook me like a rag doll in the hands of a baby. The invisible grip tightened around my torso and tossed me up and down and around and *shake shake shake shake I'm a coke can I'm going to burst I'm gonna puke —*

"*Nuuvi!*" A voice broke the silence. "Drop it right now! Remember what we practiced? Gentle flux, gentle!"

The pressure around my chest disappeared and I fell, slamming into the ground. I pushed myself up on trembling arms, my ears ringing like a million miniature car horns, each vying for attention in a sea of tiny traffic jams. I couldn't make out up from down, needed my eyes to stabilize, to focus—

"Please refrain from fluxing the animals," said a deeper voice. It hurt to hear them speak, like I was trying to make sense of a pressure that was building in my skull rather than sound. As if someone had filled my head with toxic rain. "They're delicate creatures. You understand?"

"My name is…" I hissed, trying to dismiss the pressure in my head. Like the most intense fit of brain fog my body had ever felt. "My name is Sally Webber. I crash-landed on your planet. There were people with me. Have you seen them?"

"She just turned twenty-seven yesterday," said the first voice, ignoring me completely. I pressed my palms against my temples—why did they sound so loud? "We're so proud of her. She has such control of her flux already."

"I can see that. It is remarkable at her age, indeed."

My vision cleared, slightly. Enough to make sense of the two other orb-tentacle beings in the outer glass room, much larger than the one that had—*fluxed* me?

They glowed like the forest had, light rings of pink between their gas pockets and their tentacles, blue down the extremities. Like an octopus of the deep, deep sea, except with a see-through head. It looked like it would be easy to pop.

But were they friend or foe? Did they just… not hear me? Were they ignorant or indifferent?

"Do you understand me?" I was on my knees before them, nothing but the glass between us. "Can you understand what I'm saying?"

If they did, they gave no sign of it—no facial expressions for me to go on, all tentacles limp, buoyed by an air current I couldn't feel.

"As you said, this is a fantastic opportunity to teach your offspring about responsibility," said the deeper voice. "Have you thought about which type she would prefer?"

The being drifted to the non-glass wall, and I saw—no. No, it couldn't be—there were more glass tanks like mine, and in the darkness, inside there were—

People.

We were… was this a prison?

"A finguy would be best," said the first voice. The two beings made their way around the room. "Just so long as it isn't a wawa. It has to be house trained, at least; there is no way my home will go through the mess of a wawa."

They stopped in front of my tank. "We have just the thing."

A giggle burst through the air—the girl, Trinkets. I spun to watch as she was lifted in the air like I'd been, though there wasn't any shaking this time.

"How old is it?" asked the first voice. "It seems small. I told you we're not interested in a wawa."

"Eight, but already housebroken. We find this is the best age for soul-bonding, as she is, developmentally, the same as your offspring. They will find a wonderful companion in this one."

I'd been right about her age, though how they would have the same years as on Earth, when their sun didn't even—no, that was my translator working overtime to convert without me having to. Powerful thing, and yet, it couldn't get these people's attention?

"Trinkets!" cried the child, and the air fizzled with something my mind was telling me was… levity?

"Adorable, but I'm not impressed."

They child landed delicately on her feet. "Again, again!"

"What about this one, then?" Another body rose into the air, this time from the tank beside us—a boy, limp. "Almost fifteen, mid-molt. Developing well. Almost no facial scarring from his molt."

The air rippled. "I would rather have a female. The males tend to be a little rough. I need a pet for my daughter, not a chore that makes her suffer."

Did she say *pet?* No, this couldn't be happening.

This wasn't a prison; this was a pet shop.

Which meant I was going to be…

Oh no. Oh no oh no oh no—

"Well, most of our females are adopted before their molt. Have you given any thought to owning a more exotic finguy? This one, for example, a true rarity: furry epidermis."

"I said pet, not chore." The air fizzled with electricity. "Furry finguy? What's the point? More suited for the deep north than for our longitude. The static makes their shedding stick everywhere."

"This one!"

I'd been so focused on the pair that I'd lost track of the small one that had shaken me. It was back now, lifting me again. I braced myself for the shaking—this time, so help me, I would throw up all over them. No one would want to clean up after a sickly pet, right?

"Yes, what about this one?" asked the parent. "It seems oddly calm. How old is it?"

"We're estimating mid-twenties," said the salesperson. "However, it was a stray, brought into our care this morning. We cannot sell it until we have had more time to observe its temperament, how it interacts with—"

"Doesn't look dangerous to me. We can purchase the training adjustor after all."

"Yes, but—" The salesperson stopped mid-sentence. The air fizzled around us. "Immediately, Granadam Vuzuk. As you say."

I drifted up and out of the tank, legs dangling weakly over the impossibly distant floor. I fought against the pressure, but there was nothing there to fight against, nothing to push. I was stuck.

The tentacles of the smaller creature wiggled excitedly. "Oh! It's so cute! *Thank you, thank you, thank you!*"

It plunked me into a box. Before I could see a thing, the top closed above me, the only light bleeding through the air holes on the lid.

"They only live to forty or fifty years, so this one's got another good ten or twenty before it starts getting health problems, if you treat if well enough. Some finguies live to be eighty or so, if well cared for."

Run, my head screamed. *Fight, get away. You can't stay here!*

Fight against what? Jump where? Already, my box was being carried out of the small room, much to the dismay of the youngsters in the pen.

"Trinkets!" shouted the girl.

"Tax returns!" called someone else, before we moved too far away for their voices to be heard.

"Make sure to dress it every day, it *will* get cold. It needs to eat at least three times a day. They also need grow lamps. Set them on a timer so you don't forget to simulate the diurnal cycle—"

I was right: I was in the process of becoming a pet. Okay, so that would make escape relatively easy. Kids get pets all the time, right? Not usually ones that know how to work doors. I'd wait until my new pet-mom went to sleep and slip out of the house. Easy peasy.

Deep breaths, Sally Webber. You will get out of this.

Whoever they were, they would never own me. I would be gone overnight. Whatever happened, no matter what the device in my head was feeding me, I was going to find Zander and Marcy and get us off this planet.

And then the bigger scale of things hit me. I was not the first to be sold. There were *humans* on this world. Humans—being sold as pets. Humans and other bipedal beings. Survivors of the *Wanderer*? Except, there were kids: where had the kids come from?

No, I don't need an anatomy lesson: I need a calendar.

"We need material adapted to its age and gender," said my new pet-mom's mom. "What accessories do you have to offer?"

"Can we buy a wet suit? Please, parent, please?"

The voices dimmed—they had left me alone. Maybe escape would be easier than I thought. I gathering my wits about me, then ran at the wall of the box, hoping to tip it over. It barely budged.

"Come on, come on!" I threw my shoulder as heavily as I could against the strange material, but to no avail.

The air holes! I ran at the corner of the box, kicking my legs up before gravity caught up, throwing myself at the ceiling, where I grabbed the edge of one hole with both hands, pulling myself up. But before I could do anything, the box rattled, and I was thrown back down. My head swam with a warm, wet feeling, thoroughly fogging my thoughts.

The air crackled with electricity, making my hair stand on end.

"She's a feisty one," said the salesperson. "You have been cleared for purchase. Congratulations on your new pod member."

So, yeah: a giant octopus had just bought me as a pet for their kid, and I couldn't do a damn thing about it. That's how my day was going.

"What do you recommend as a first covering?" the buyer asked.

"I wanna dress it!" said the kid. Nuuvi, I think they'd said their name was.

"Be very gentle, okay?" said the parent. "Maybe try touch instead of fluxing."

The box opened, a tentacle reaching in and wrapping around my torso, lifting me up. I screamed— but they didn't even flinch. Could they hear me at all? Before I could do anything, a dress was pulled over my head, tugged down my legs, and tied tightly around my waist with a big bow. My head went fuzzier still, as if scraping away the slate of anything I had been thinking about, leaving my mind pure darkness, stars flashing before my eyes. Vague black lines wrapped around my body like water clinging to my skin.

When I got to my new home, first thing I was gonna do was rip that *thing* from inside my head.

"Did I do it wrong?" The kid placed me delicately back in the box. "Parent, what just happened to it?"

"Don't worry, it's not painful to the animal," the salesman said in a tone flat, closing the lid above my head. "It stops them from doing something against their best interests, before they get a chance."

"Amazing technology, these training adjusters," their parent said, Granadam Vuzuk if I was following right.

"Now you're all set!" The salesperson oozed pride. I could physically feel it in the air around us. "Finguies are delicate creatures, so make sure to connect with the instructions and information through the Mist."

Being transported by telekinetically-carried box was by far the worst way I had ever traveled. It probably wouldn't have been so bad if the parent was the one *fluxing* me. Every few minutes I was thrown face forward on the floor. I fell to the other side of the box again, my shoulder colliding with the wall and sending a jolt through the implant on the back of my head. I returned to curl up in a ball in the middle of the box, hoping that would even it out, but my timing had been terrible—we were going down stairs. My head bounced mercilessly against the floor.

The box was set down, and I breathed in relief—our movement was smooth, and thankfully, silent. We must have been in their equivalent of a car. I squeezed my eyelids shut as tight as they could go, trying with all my might to get away, to jump, to throw my atoms into the universe and pull myself together anywhere but here. And at once—the pressure in my head. It was useless. My mind ripped from the cosmos, ripped away from everything, ripped away from Zander, from Marcy, from everyone I knew.

Had they been captured too? If so, why hadn't I seen them in the display pen? Were they lost? Still stuck in the crushed shuttle? If Zander wasn't here… he could be literally anywhere.

And Marcy… I bit my lip so hard I drew blood. The image of her strewn in the shuttle debris, her body limp, unbreathing…

What had she been doing there in the first place?

The box was picked back up again. This time the parent must have fluxed me, because the movement was smooth. And still—silent. It occurred to me that this whole time, I hadn't heard a single door open or close.

"Parent!" The air buzzed with excitement and small voices. I was put down on a smooth surface.

"Did you get it?" asked one of them "Did you bring a finguy?"

"Yes!" said the parent, and the air buzzed again. Physically buzzed: something they were doing was playing with the charge in the air. "But remember, this is Nuuvi's finguy. You must ask them if you want to play with it."

The box opened. Whatever space we were in glowed with soft pink light, still too dim to make out any detail. I looked straight up, to a round metal ceiling meters and meters above.

"It's so cute!" a voice exclaimed, and I was lifted out of the box again, drifting upwards in the air.

Six tentacled creatures hovered in a circle around me—three big, three small. No, seven: a tiny one drifted in and out from behind one of the larger ones. The pink glow came from them, not from any other lighting. Their house was as dark as the pet shop.

"It's so… big," said one of the other child-sized beings. "What binary did you pick?"

"Female," said Nuuvi, I think. It was hard to tell—they all looked exactly the same, except for the size. "Feel at the hair. The pretty hair."

My hair rose on my scalp, like I'd touched a plasma ball. They were affecting the electricity in the air. How? The space around me sounded like the loudest refrigerator in the world.

"Hi," I said, licking my dry lips. "I don't know if you can understand me, let alone hear me. But my name is Sally Webber, and I'm not supposed to be here. I crash-landed, and I was with someone—"

"It's flapping its mouth at us," said one of the children.

"It must like us!" said Nuuvi. "The mist says that's how the finguies communicate between each other."

"By the shape they make with their lip flaps?" said one of the adults. "Indeed, that is what the mist says. Remarkable."

They had… no concept of sound? So how were they speaking right now? They didn't seem to have eyes or ears or any of the sensory organs we did. They must…

My skin prickled with every word, like the air before the storm. Could they be communicating through… charge? They were interacting with something in the atmosphere to manipulate electricity. That must be how they influenced me and my body, whatever their fluxing was. My translator could pick up on it, but me, with my lame lip flaps and no electrical organ, I couldn't speak in a language they could even sense.

"We'll have to pick where you want its bed to go," said the parent.

The kid dropped me back into the box. If I wasn't what I was, that would have hurt. "In my room? Please, parent, please?"

"Of course, of course! Spax, get the purchases from the glider and bring them up to Nuuvi's room. Now."

"Of course, lord." A blue-rimmed octopod drifted above us, tentacles dragging behind it.

"I'll call her *Comfort Food*," said Nuuvi. "And we're going to do everything together..."

They picked me up with their tentacles this time, pulling me up to their gaseous bulb. I tried to ignore the sensation of their limbs around my body, the revulsion I felt all the way to my core. Bolts of small lightning fired in their inner mist.

I was going to get out of here, whatever it took. The second I was alone I would run away, back to the forest, back to the shuttle, where I'd find Zander and Marcy, and we'd leave, we'd leave together and run back home. I didn't care what was meant to be at the *Wanderer* anymore – I just wanted to go home.

The one thing I didn't take into account was their house being a fixture-less fishbowl.

NINE

PARTY ON, ZANDER: THE REBEL EDITION

Zander

EVERY SECOND IN THIS RUST BUCKET WAS TAKING me further in the wrong direction, far away from finding Sally. Or maybe closer to her. There was no way of knowing, and that was the problem.

I'd lost her before on other worlds, but it did nothing to dull the pain of separation. The knowledge that maybe this time would be the time we couldn't come back to each other. A planet is a big place, the universe an even bigger one; add time to the mix and you've given me another reason to want to gouge my eyes out.

I tried not to think about the Marcy problem. Dany would kill me a thousand times over for losing her in the woods of an alien planet, even if I'd only known she was with us for less than a Transnarian second.

Darkness still coated the window, so I couldn't gauge where we were or even how far we'd traveled. I could only guess at the speed, tuning in to the hum of the engine, counting seconds in my head before a choking propulsor sent me into rescue mode for a few instants and made me lose track. This flying death trap would be the end of me in more ways than one.

With a definite *clunk*, the engine choked and gave out for good. Thankfully, this time it was because we'd landed. The jolt jostled us and sent a few passengers screaming. It was a good landing, considering the state of the craft. I leaned back against my seat, closing my eyes, letting out a breath to calm myself. This wasn't like me.

The doors flew open, and more medics rushed in, taking the injured man out first. TrueFoot stood as they left, ushering us forward. The landing site was just as dark as the forest. His people waited outside, dressed in antiquated Alliance fatigues, lit up by the glow of old jugs filled with bioluminescent biomass held high like lanterns.

I waited for the others to leave, listening intently. Things *sounded* the same outside as inside: an eerie combo of hushed humans and mechanical silence. The squeak of boots on the polished floor, disjointed footsteps as unsteady feet slipped and tripped. Nothing more nefarious than a bowling alley, though those are dangerous in the dark of night. Any alley is.

I stood to leave but TrueFoot stepped in front of me before I could exit the craft, throwing out an arm to hold me back. The medics had already carted their patients away, and the civilians were being ushered off to somewhere else in the darkness. The teen I had met in the woods had disappeared from view.

"Where are they being taken?" I asked.

"Classrooms first," said TrueFoot. "They need to be briefed on the camp. Then they'll be assigned roles, given a new set of clothes, and given a tour. Satisfied?"

"I can't help but notice I'm not with them."

He nodded. "You're not an escapee. You're shipwrecked. You need a whole different debriefing." Debriefing—now those are words I liked to hear. "I'm taking you directly to General Provis. Follow me."

General Provis? Maybe it was because this was the first real name I'd heard since we'd crashed—none of this nickname mess—but it scratched at the back of my head with a soft familiarity. Maybe I already had an ally on this planet.

TrueFoot didn't turn around. I hopped out of the shuttle. My feet hit plastic—a roof? Artificial, though not Alliance regulation. I slid behind him, silent as the night. The floor was the least of my problems. He opened a door into the compound, the kind of glowing white pressure hatch you would see on the *Traveler*, except it wasn't attached to any walls. It led to a staircase, also without any walls, down to a hallway with doorknobs in the place of light fixtures.

I kept my head down as we dove into the maze of hallways, the shape confirming my gut feeling that whoever had designed this place had zero functionality in mind. It felt uncomfortably like a crashed ship that had grown walls and staircases at nature's whim. That and some intersections heralded with colorful banners that said "Captain Cake" and "It's The Birthday Exit."

First impressions told me we were at an army encampment, though a rugged one. More than once I'd had to squeeze past soldiers in patched uniforms marching in squished formations, shoulder to shoulder to bulkhead. For the first time since landing here, I was seeing non-humans. They all wore Alliance uniforms—some newer than others, and most decades out of date. Some from the space fleet, others from navy or… the army? You didn't see many Alliance infantrymen these days, but there were more than enough to go around right here. They paid no attention to me, too intent on what they were doing, ducking under the twisted statues that hung from the ceiling.

I gritted my teeth. These were the people who were supposed to help us? It looked like they were fighting a war—and losing. I wouldn't be surprised if their general didn't have time for me at all.

TrueFoot led me through the winding hallways, through outdoor sections hiding canvas tents and temporary wooden structures, all lit by the dim jug lanterns. I tried to hide my disappointment. But what was I expecting? Survivors, surviving: not an army with a procedurally-generated base with sometimes carpeted ceilings.

We ducked under a table bolted to the ceiling, with the most incredible cake suspended from it. Seven-tiered, it took up most of the hallway, a delectable chandelier. The space behind was dismal in comparison: a piece of the hull, battered all around but still intact enough to hold its shape. Its once shiny white exterior glimmered in the glow of the plants, smudged with scorch marks and clinging vines. Logs propped up one of the sides, closed crates stacked in neat rows underneath. The oldest section we'd been to yet.

TrueFoot held open a door flap. The hallway beyond was no longer the polished white it had once been. The ground was coated with a thick carpet of dirt, plants in jars strapped into the walls for light.

The last door was impressively intact, and TrueFoot knocked before sliding it open. My breath caught as I stepped in. For a second, I could imagine I was in space again. The compartment was furnished just as any high-ranking officer's would have been upon a UPAF vessel, though these quarters were fully utilitarian. Unlike the unsettling space outside, here, everything was correctly in its place. The room was sparse: made up like a war room, but with a cot jammed into the corner, a coarse blanket thrown haphazardly on top of it. A table sat in the middle, covered by a large hand-drawn map of the area. The other walls contained more maps from around the planet, with varying degrees of detail, some of them only a napkin with a crude street map hastily sketched upon them, while others were printed and inked in millimeter precision. Thankfully, no cake hung from the ceiling.

TrueFoot slipped into the compartment. "General Provis?"

Provis… Provis… now where had I heard that name before?

Across from us stood a tall, muscular man, with wispy chestnut brown hair pulled back into a high bun. He was hyper focused on one of the maps, jotting down notes upon it with a pencil stub. His black uniform—immaculate, even in this place—was much too large for him.

He turned as we entered, and for a second, recognition dawned as I took in his features. I had seen him before, though I couldn't place it. Neither the where nor the when, and if he knew who I was, he didn't say anything. His cheekbones were sharp, his jaw angular, and large, wide eyes that seemed never to blink. He stared at me, as if seeing right into me, knowing everything about me before I could even open my mouth. The stare was so intense, so deep, the sense of recognition returned tenfold.

I *knew* this man.

Odds were, he knew me too. I braced myself for his reaction: had I been an ally, an enemy? He nodded at TrueFoot, but his eyes were still riveted on me. He kept a stern frown, as if we had intruded upon something, but underneath the mask I could see he was startled by our arrival.

My arrival. Maybe.

"Who is this?" General Provis asked, finally pulling his gaze away and turning it on TrueFoot.

It was a soft relief that he didn't recognize me.

"Shipwrecked, sir." TrueFoot shuffled, making himself tall. "In the middle of the rescue zone."

Provis's eyes held true. "Was the mission a success?"

"Yes, sir." A tight smile drew itself on his lips. "We extracted fifteen souls, and all our men have returned uninjured. A *very* successful mission."

Provis drew a breath of relief. I could almost feel the joy radiating off TrueFoot. Stars, I was happy for them. Despite *still* not knowing what they were running from, a rescue mission of that size without a single loss was not an easy feat to pull off. They should be commended.

"You have done well, Major," said Provis. "Go and reward your men. I'll deal with the lost soul."

"Yes, sir." TrueFoot saluted and left, the room dimming as the door closed behind him. Provis rose to his feet and bowed lightly. I returned the greeting.

"Borelian whisky?" He turned away from me and lifted the bottle off his sidebar. I shook my head, though he didn't see it.

"No, sir," I replied instead.

"You may want it. It may be the last time you'll ever drink it. We don't have many reserves left. This bottle here has been sitting in my cabin for at least fifteen years. Was there when I inherited the post, and I only sipped it once, on the day it became mine. Let me introduce myself: I am General Provis, head of this encampment, unofficially known as Party City. And you are…?"

"Za—" Blayde's voice floated in my head, chiding me for giving him my true name so readily. I used to have hundreds of aliases in my arsenal, but Sally and Sally alone was on my mind now. I tried to push past her, but she blocked any other thought. "I'm, um, Luke Skywalker."

Provis furrowed his brows. "Well… of course you are." He met my gaze and saw right through me. Frash, was this man from Earth? "Any relation?"

"To whom?" I said, shrugging. No need to make enemies this early in the game. From my first impressions of this planet, they had more important things to worry about.

"Ah. That's disappointing."

Provis nodded slowly, and I noticed suddenly that he was *young*. Late twenties, maybe, already with his own command. A full-blown *General.*

Perhaps my past self knew his future self. That may explain why I couldn't put my finger on where I had seen him before. Or maybe it was just the soft frame of his face, which, in the moss light, reminded me of Sally.

Oh stars, one hour without her, and I was seeing her everywhere, wasn't I?

Provis collapsed in his chair, gesturing for me to take the seat across from him. I did, mulling over his disappointment. Maybe my new identity could be used to my advantage at some point.

"Well then, *Luke Skywalker*," he continued, "I would like to formally welcome you to Planet Nope. Known to the locals as Pure Hell."

From what I'd seen so far, I could understand that.

"That's going to require some more explanation." I leaned forward, showing the man he had my full attention. "What exactly is this place?"

"This?" He gestured to the maps on his wall. "Party City, home of the fourth infantry. We're situated on the planet's 54th quadrant, though that won't mean much to you."

"You're right, I've got nothing." I shook my head again. "Who are these Sters you're talking about? And … what's with all the ceiling cake?"

"How long since the crash?"

Good question. "An hour at most."

"That explains a lot." He glanced over his shoulder at the bottle of whisky, sighed, then turned back to stare me down. "You truly know nothing about this place? Any of this?"

"Only what I've inferred from the ride over." I crossed my hands on my lap. "You're rebels. You fight the Sters, a race that seems to have incredible power over you. The rest of the humans on this planet that I've seen have a terrible sense of fashion. A few can't read or write—some don't even speak the common language. So, I know a little bit more than nothing. Though not much more."

"You've not seen a Ster?"

"Not yet, no. Though I gather I heard one pass by me." I shuddered at the memory. "Well… *felt* it."

"Then consider yourself incredibly lucky. Ster isn't actually the name of their race: it's just what we've taken to calling them, short for what they really are."

"Monsters?" I suggested.

He laughed. "Not quite, though you'd be correct in many ways. No, here, Ster is short for *Masters*."

"Masters?" I felt my eyebrows coming together. "Masters of what? This planet?"

"Master of *us*."

"By us, you mean—"

"You, me, everyone on this planet who isn't one of them."

The office got cold. I could feel my every breath, the chill of the air over my lips. I said nothing, waiting.

"It's been this way since the first scout ship crashed on this planet," said Provis, "hundreds of years ago. They were greeted by a race of a monstrous size, with none of the humanoid markers of local groups. Survivors found themselves taken by force, and slowly… *domesticated* by the natives."

"Domesticated," I spat. "Enslaved?"

"The locals see it more as an adoption process."

I couldn't keep my laugh inside. *What?* Whatever I had been expecting, it had not been this. "They were made into *pets*?"

"I survived the crash of the *Wanderer*. Some days, I wish I hadn't." His face was unflinching—this was no laughing matter. "We came out of FTL at the wrong coordinates, got caught in Nope's gravitational pull, and ended up here, with no means of returning to orbit. I lived an entire year as *Pokii*, a native family's household 'finguy,' until I made contact with the rebels and orchestrated my escape. Since then, I've been working with them, trying to plan rescue missions, and ultimately, a way to win this war against the Sters. This base was built out of the ruins of one of their zoos; they created it based on the ship we crashed in. Do you follow?"

I nodded, saying nothing. My stomach churned like a malfunctioning washing machine. I had many questions, but only one remained on the surface, enveloping my mind and tugging at my heart. At least one had been answered: birthdays were the most common reason for warp malfunctions.

"You seem troubled," said Provis. *How the frash could I be anything else right now?* "Would you have that glass of whiskey?"

"My friends." My nails dug into my palms. "What's happened to them?"

"You weren't alone? You crashed here with someone else?"

"My partner, Sally," I said, though that somehow sounded wrong, not enough. Provis's face lit up, then fell, so quickly I almost thought I'd imagined it. It was uncanny: where had I seen him before? "And a friend, Marcy. We got separated. Does this mean they…"

His eyes grew wide, then he shook his head. "They survived the crash, unharmed?"

I nodded. No other option was allowed.

"And are they bipedal? Cute?" Again, with that question. I nodded again. I had a terrible, sinking feeling as to why they kept asking. "Then they'd be finguies, now. They would have been taken to a clinic, where they will most certainly be adopted within the next few days. They could even be at their new Sters' homes by now. They will be safe. Cared for. They'll have food and a soft bed. They'll even be loved. But—"

"Are you frashing kidding me?" My chair clattered behind me. I'd stood so quickly my mind hadn't yet caught up. It took everything not to rush out that door right now. "We need to set up a rescue mission. How are you still sitting there?"

"We simply don't have the manpower to mount a mission of that scale," said Provis. And he did look sorry, truly. Pity crossed his face, which was polite, I suppose. "Especially for so few."

Destroy this place. My thoughts were murky, dark, and not entirely mine. An oil slick over my mind. *Make them see "no" isn't acceptable. If he refuses to lead his men, I will.*

I shook the thoughts out of my head. No, I couldn't think like that. "They could escape, though, couldn't they? Like you did."

I gritted my teeth. If I couldn't jump, something must be stopping Sally, too. But even without jumping, she had other skills, things I had taught her over the past few months, things she had picked up herself as well as from her conspiracy-loving father and a mountain of

Hollywood films. Not very accurate, but useful nonetheless in creating her own personal database of survival skills. This is Sally we're talking about: she's relentless.

But Marcy? I, uh, didn't know about her. Maybe she would be a little more time sensitive.

"You can't." Provis hung his head. "They come up with new 'training' techniques every year. The latest on the line can stop even the *thought* of disobedience."

"But you got away!" I sputtered. Any thought of staying calm was gone now. "And the people you just rescued, they broke free!"

"In each of their cases, we had an inside man: something we don't have here. And without a Ster on the inside, we have no one to hold the door."

"The door?" I snorted. "You're kidding me."

"The Sters are unlike any lifeform in the Alliance," said Provis. "They aren't built like us. Their homes are impossible to navigate for humanoid species. Luckily, some Sters have joined the cause. They recognize us as intelligent beings and help in any way they can."

"Recognize…" I took a deep breath. "You… you can't even communicate with them? After all these years…?"

"Oh, we can understand *them* plenty. But they don't have organs for sight or sound. They communicate between each other using charges in the air, carried via *mist.* Our inside men contact us using a series of electrical pulses, a code invented by Sters and finguies together, perfectly encrypted so only our allies can read it."

"Get one of them on the line. We need to save them!"

His frown deepened. "Frankly, we don't have the resources for a tiny retrieval mission."

"Tiny?" I slammed my fist on the table, unable to restrain myself. "This is Sally we're talking about. My… my Sally. I can't let anything happen to her, I promised…"

"We couldn't even tell you where she is." Provis shook his head. "And… and even if we did, she's just *one* person."

My sleeping heart sank like a lead balloon filled with disappointment. Marcy. Marcy was out there too. And she had fewer skills to fall back on than Sally, if they were lucky enough to still be together. Which I wasn't entirely sure they were.

"The other woman. Marcy. She's the wife of the president."

Provis sighed through gritted teeth. "I'm sorry to tell you, we don't care much for Alliance politics here. One person's life is worth the same as anyone else's."

"So how many people's lives are worth the risk, in your eyes?" I snapped. "Five? Four? At what point is it not worth saving another's life?"

"I'm not willing to risk the lives of my men, and the position of this camp, for *two*. No matter who they are. No matter who's asking."

I could tell him who I was—the name often got *some* leeway, for good or for bad—but then I would find myself roped into a cause I didn't know and a war I was not prepared to fight. Was it worth the cost? For Sally? Of course it was—but there were other options before outing myself. Other ways of getting her back, even if it meant going it alone.

"Then I'd best be off," I said, rising to my feet.

"Off?" He raised an eyebrow. "Off where?"

"Back to where I crashed, for starters. If you're not going to help me, then there's no point in me wasting your time."

"You can't be serious," Provis scoffed. He reached for the bottle of whiskey, poured some into a glass, and pushed it towards me. When I didn't reach down and take it, he snatched it up and drank the contents in one gulp. "You can't possibly want to go back out there. After everything I just told you?"

"What you told me is that my friends are in danger. I can't let that happen. No force in the universe can stop me."

"I know how you must be feeling, but they're safe. Take refuge in that."

"Not when they might have, what did you call it… training technology in them?" I bent in a deep bow. "I have to go save them. Thank you for your hospitality."

I turned to the door, forcing myself to keep the pace, to not take off at a run. I needed to trace them back, find the processing facility, or whatever that was called…

"You'll never find where they've gone," he said. "They could be anywhere. *She* could be anywhere!"

"So," I said over my shoulder, "I'll search everywhere."

"We need you!" he said, making me stop. "If you want to help your friends, help *us*! Our goal is to liberate everyone under Ster control. Join us—think of all the good you'll be doing. All the lives you'll save. Not just theirs, but hundreds, thousands of men and women in the same situation as them!"

"You want me to play soldier until they're found? I don't have time to waste."

"No. Using time you'd otherwise be wasting on a pointless search. Think of your Sally—what would she want you to do?"

He was right—it was pointless to go alone, with no information whatsoever. I didn't even know where I was on a map right about then, or what direction to walk in to find our crash site—but I couldn't bear the thought of leaving Sally to fend for herself, under Ster domination, for anything longer than another second.

But I wasn't going to find her if I just ran off into the wilderness.

"I'm in," I said, turning around and holding out a hand to shake. Provis grunted as my hand crushed his, but I could tell he was pleased with himself. "The second you know where my friends are, you tell me, agreed?"

"Agreed.," He nodded curtly. "Welcome to the Fourth Infantry, Skywalker. Welcome to the cause."

TEN

A CEPHALOPOD CELEBRATION CONUNDRUM

Sally

IF THERE'S ONE CONSTANT I DIDN'T EXPECT IN THE universe, it was party hats. We may have been on a planet of creatures that didn't have sunlight or sound, had never heard of the Alliance, never had contact with anything outside of their atmosphere, that didn't even have heads for chrissakes, and yet, every single one came to Nuuvi's birthday with a nice pointy hat sitting smugly on top of their bulb.

I couldn't tell you how many days had passed since I'd arrived here. I hadn't seen the sun since the crash, and Nuuvi wasn't keeping up their promise to set my light on a timer. The little UV lamp over my sleeping bag turned on when they felt like it and turned off when I faked sleep long enough that they got bored.

Food was… equally fickle. Not a fan of kibble, let me tell you. It felt and tasted like I had been stung by a bee:

dry and empty and grainy on the teeth. Obviously, no one had asked the finguies what they wanted in their FinguyFood.

As impossible as it was to gauge time by Nuuvi's terrible UV lamp control—she was, admittedly, getting better at tucking me in for sleep— I had the lurking feeling my week was drawing to a close, and any minute now the *Traveler* would soar back to the Alliance to report us missing.

Maybe Zander was on board—highly unlikely, or he would have sent help, wouldn't he? Or maybe they were keeping him prisoner and forcing him to return?

Nah. My bestie's queen of the universe. Sorry, *First Lady*. They wouldn't leave her behind. Unless she'd already been saved.

I did what I had to do—I waited. I bided my time, memorizing the movements of my captors, the minute differences between the creatures, the colors of Nuuvi's family, and the blue highlights of their servants. Waiting for a single slipup so I could make my move.

Maybe today I would get my chance.

The guests trickled in through the eaves. I squinted at their blurry forms, wondering about the most likely cause of my current delirium. Lack of food? Sunlight? Sleep? Or was it the little nubbin in the back of my scalp that fed me that dull trickle of sedation 24/7—or whatever day/week arrangement we had here. My head ached dully from the ever-present tug of the neural control, the one I felt every time I thought of escape.

Which was constant now, and thus the ache was constant as well.

At first, my body was awash in a rainbow of emotions. My every movement became a struggle to control. But as with most things, you get used to it. And it seemed this planet had never met Pavlov. With a drug that was released every time I did something unbidden, I started to expect, and welcome, the fog. It was a funky tingle now, like eating a spoonful of pop rocks. I'd had some wild alien drugs in my short time as a space explorer, but none that got me borderline high off the thought of escape.

Well, it wasn't the only reason for the ache in my head: Nuuvi was obsessed with my hair. In preparation for their party, they had brushed it for hours, practicing their flux on the comb, which tugged my hair into knots worthy of Greek myths. And just because I no longer felt pain didn't mean I wasn't going to scream every time my head was ripped in one direction or another.

They couldn't hear a lick of it, or maybe they could and just didn't care. They talked over my yelps the entire time, telling me about their friends, both real and imaginary, and their parent's glorious job as governor of something-or-other. The high rank of their family meant they were all confined to the house in fear that rebel groups would try to hurt the pod in order to take control of the country. Nuuvi was, as any kid would be if they were locked in a fishbowl day in and day out, lonely.

Did I feel sorry for them? Hell, no. I currently had a bow tied around my neck and about half the hair I left home with, and that stuff doesn't grow back as fast as an amputated limb. I was dressed in a ballgown that closed with a sticky clasp all the way up the back, with the other half of my hair caught inside. But I stood politely as the guests arrived, if only for one very good reason —

They'd been asked to bring their finguies.

The second I heard that detail, hope swelled in my chest. I was not alone: there were others in the same situation as me, kept as pets by a gaseous-octopus child. I'd not had an opportunity to speak to any other humans since I had arrived in this place, and the prospect of having a normal conversation and gaining some insight on my situation was one I was rather looking forward to. If I could only meet another person like me, then perhaps we could figure a way out of this mess.

Maybe. Hopefully.

Not to mention a tiny possibility that Zander and Marcy were in the same boat I was. That they'd been adopted too. That they might come here as the pets of Nuuvi's friends. I didn't dare hope.

The inability to jump settled upon my shoulders. I couldn't stop thinking about Zander. Where was he? Was he all right? Was he eating well, was he sleeping at night? Could *he* jump?

Was he looking for me?

Of course he was. He always was. Our first trip together—did it count as our first date?—to Da-Duhui had been mostly a rescue mission. No. I didn't have to worry about Zander finding me. He *was* going to find me.

Unless I found him first.

And Marcy—were they together? Were they keeping each other stable, confident? Were they bonding? God, I hoped they were getting along. I *needed* my bestie to like my guy. She definitely had feelings about me dating a—what had she called him? —thousand-year old space hobo? Maybe this could be an unexpected way for them to hash things out.

I stood under Nuuvi, keeping my eyes on the guests, trying to keep the smell of their rancid food out of my nose. The floor was covered in birthday treats, meats from a thousand animals placed in concentric circles. I would have thrown up if I had anything substantial in my stomach. It was as if they ate every organ of every possible creature available on the market. If it had been cooked at all, it hadn't been long enough to warm even the outer membrane of meat. Guests picked at the floor food as more of them continued to arrive. They fluxed the meats, raw and dripping, straight up in between their tentacles. Thank God I didn't have to watch them chew.

"Look!" The floor fell out from under me as Nuuvi lifted me high into the air. If they had arms, it would have been my Simba moment. "My finguy!"

The guests let out sounds of admiration, based on what my translator interpreted for me. The air fizzled with excitement—literally. I was getting used to the way their emotions seemed to spread around them, but it was never enjoyable. Especially when you were the one floating in the middle of them.

"She's precious!" Nuuvi's friends repeated over and over again. "Absolutely dear! What did you name her?"

"Comfort Food," Nuuvi announced, proudly, and the other pint-sized guests did nothing to hold back their squeals of delight.

"Actually, it's Sally," I said. "Not that any of you would care."

"Oh look, she's trying to speak!" one of the guests said, their tentacles shaking. "Isn't that adorable?"

Cute as a button, sure thing. Thanks, pal.

"Nuuvi, can I introduce her to Leggy?" one of their child-sized creatures asked. "What if they could become friends?"

Leggy—my possible ally? I scanned the fishbowl room. Where had the creature hidden them?

"Dearest, are you sure Comfort Food is rcady to meet another finguy?" one of the adults from Nuuvi's pod asked tenderly. At least, I think it was one of their family members: they all looked the same to me. "Have you trained her well enough?"

"She's ready, Muf-parent." Nuuvi curled their tentacles under their body. "She'll be on her best behavior, I promise!"

"Have you been doing your exercises with her?"

"Of course." The tentacles curled tighter. I let out a snort of laughter, thankful no one could understand me. The extent of their training had been to throw brightly colored balls for me to bring back in the first hour of me being in their house. I hadn't gone along with it, and they had made no attempt since.

"You'll have to keep an eye on them, you know that. The males can get rather violent at play, and they're both rather young. You don't want Comfort Food to get hurt, do you?"

"I don't, Muf-parent. Comfort Food will be good, won't you, girl?"

Sure thing, Nuuvi dear. I'll play nice. We'll play nice. And then we'll be gone.

"You're sure?" asked the friend, reaching up to their party hat. "I've had Leggy since before his molt. If she hurts him…"

I took a deep breath. There went the chances of it being Zander. But still, if this finguy had been in the creatures' household for years, then they must know some juicy information.

"He won't hurt *her,* will he?" Nuuvi lowered me to the ground.

The friend's tentacles twitched, like a cat who wanted no more of your attention. "Do you think me a poor master?"

"No, of course not!"

"You're sure?" asked the friend, reaching up to their party hat and retrieved a *human being,* dressed in frilly eighteenth-century European court clothes, for lack of a better comparison. It took every ounce of self-control not to run to him. A human being, a man with soft brown hair and an easy demeanor, limp in his master's grasp. They lowered him to the ground with a tentacle, delicately placing him in front of me.

"Leggy, meet Comfort Food!" said the gas-octopod. "Comfort Food, this is your new friend Leggy. Go on, greet him!"

I didn't need her permission. Now that he stood right in front of me, I scanned the man over: he must have been my age, early twenties maybe, and glowing like a trust fund baby. His skin was clear, his smile white and perfect. He could have been a model.

But there was something weird with his eyes.

They stared at me intently, but… not entirely. Something was missing there, and I shuddered.

"I'm Sally," I said. If he was Alliance, he'd want me to bow, so I did. Then again, if he'd been with this monster since before puberty, maybe he didn't know much about Alliance tradition. I hadn't read anything about kids crashing here.

My stomach churned when he didn't reply. He tilted his head sideways, like a puppy, squinting. Unmoving.

"I came here as part of a rescue team," I continued. "We're here to get you home. But I crashed a week ago."

Still no reaction. Just a man, standing, staring. It was unnerving, bordering on inappropriate.

"What's your name?" I asked. He didn't answer. Was he no more able to understand me than Nuuvi was? It couldn't be; I had a translator. Language barriers didn't exist for me.

Unless… he never had a language to call his own.

"You have no idea what I'm saying, do you?" My voice was barely a whisper.

A look drew itself on his face, a look that made every one of my muscles tense. His shoulders forward, his chin jutting straight out, he stared at me with an intensity that could have lit my hair on fire. I felt slimy, I felt bare. I felt gross. My gut spoke to me more clearly than he had, telling me to *run.*

And he lunged at me.

Thankfully, after all this time living it up with Zander, I had a few moves of my own. I reacted on instinct, taking a step back to stabilize myself before he grabbed at my shoulders. I grabbed his first, dropping and flinging him over my head before sliding off to the side, poised for the next strike.

My head filled with heat—the implant. Thinking was becoming… fuzzy. I shook my head. I'd lived with brain fog for years, fought against it before I'd started treatment; I could handle it now.

Come on, faithful adrenaline. Get in on this.

"Wow, they're playing!" Nuuvi's friend said proudly. The air crackled with electricity. "How cute!"

Playing? I gritted my teeth and hopped back on my feet, hands in attack position. My head spun, and I took deep breaths to counter the dizziness. What had happened to him, what had turned his instincts sour like this? Why did he want to fight me? We didn't even know each other. We should have been on the same side, against the creatures. Instead he was something else entirely.

The creatures bobbed around us, just watching. I guess they were getting dinner and a show tonight. Had any others brought their humans along? How many people were carefully stashed under hats?

"Just think," said Nuuvi. "He's a male, she's a female…"

The friend trilled. "Mist around! They could be a matched pair!"

A matched pair? I almost threw up my kibble. For the sake of my sanity, I wasn't going to go there. Thankfully, the brain fog didn't let me.

"Stay away!" I shouted at Leggy. "Don't you dare come any closer!"

He wasn't listening. Not that he could understand me. I glared at him, trying to muster the Blayde look of death, but it was no use. He was excited.

He pushed himself to his feet and rushed at me again, arms outstretched, get this: *roaring*. I grabbed his extended wrist and twisted it back, using his own momentum against him. He screamed as I tossed him down and pinned him to the ground. My hands were slick with sweat as they struggled to restrain his flailing fists.

"No!" I said, digging my knee into the small of his back. Whatever the implant was meant to do to me, it was cracked fully open now; the heat that swirled in my brain made me long for a nap. I pushed my knee in deeper. "Do you understand that? *No!* Don't you dare try to attack me again! You understand?"

He whimpered. Maybe that was enough. Maybe *now* he understood me.

"Nuuvi, she's hurting him!"

A force slammed into me, throwing me off Leggy. I landed on the floor and slid, getting a face full of feast juices for my trouble.

Nuuvi's friend had just—fluxed me? I scrambled up as the creature dropped to the ground, running a tentacle delicately down Leggy's face. He was crying like a toddler.

What the hell?

"No, she wasn't!" Nuuvi drifted over to me, sounding indignant. "They were playing, Airell! She wouldn't hurt him!"

They grabbed me with a tentacle, lifting me off the ground. The other guests bobbed closer, intent on the drama, I'm sure. I tried my best not to squirm in the slimy grip.

"Aren't the females supposed to be weaker?" asked one of the adult-sized guests.

"Will nobody listen to me?" Nuuvi whimpered. "They were *playing*. That's it."

"That's what you get when you take in a rescue," said another, *tsk*'ing, which sounded more like a kettle reaching boil. "They always say to adopt, not shop, but you never know what happens when you bring in a mutt."

Don't think about it. I gritted my teeth harder. Soon there wouldn't be any enamel left.

This man had been born here. Raised here, by these… things. As a pet. He had no language, no culture, no connection.

That was what they were taking from us. By reducing us to finguies, they stripped us of our humanity. Everything that made us, us.

I had to get away from here. I had to get out.

But the only way out was… up.

Airell cradled Leggy in the crook of her tentacle. "She's wild, your finguy."

Leggy whimpered in the creature's grasp, snuggling into the suckers to dry his tears. He looked up at Airell with such… love in his eyes. Devotion. I suppose when all you know is one kind of love, it's the love you think you deserve. I clenched my fists.

"Yours attacked mine, not the other way around!" Nuuvi said. There was a tremor to their voice, like they too were on the verge of tears. "She was defending herself! You said he would behave!"

"He wasn't attacking!" Airell spat, clutching him tighter. "That's just how they play. Your finguy doesn't know how to behave."

"You'd better keep her in the other room while the guests are here," said the muf-parent, voice low. "Go on. It'll be better for everyone."

Nuuvi kept me tight in their tentacle, grumbling as they drifted over the partition to their room. The fishbowl house was set up like one of those Happy Meal plastic maze toys, with glass rooms and holes to drift between layers—impossible to navigate unless you could fly. They dropped me on my sleeping mat, none too gently.

"I can't believe Airell would try to embarrass me like that," they said, pushing their bulbous head against the glass, akin to a human slamming their head against the wall. "Leggy is *not* well trained."

"You're telling me," I muttered. I pulled my knees against my chest, hugging them tight. I'd been so excited about meeting another human, I hadn't thought about what would happen if they let me down.

I was alone here. Truly alone. In an inescapable house, run by monsters. Hell, now I was forced to watch them eat dinner, their feast sprawled on my glass ceiling.

"It's going to be okay, girl," said Nuuvi, patting me tenderly on the head with the very tip of their tentacle. "It wasn't your fault. I saw everything. You were just defending yourself."

I wish that meant something to me.

They drifted up and over the wall, through the maze of glass to the ceiling hole, leaving me alone in the room, my UV lamp my only company.

I wasn't going to let myself cry.

I crossed my legs and closed my eyes, concentrating. I had never believed in the power of meditation, and so far it had shown no results; but it was my only hope of escape. I had to jump away.

And yet, whatever I did, I couldn't. It was as if a sharp axe had sliced off all connection between me and the universe, stopping me from throwing myself into the nothing, stopping me from going anywhere.

Was I doing it wrong? I had never thought about trying to break down the process, and it was more difficult to do than I could have ever possibly envisioned.

I exhaled, trying to rid myself of any and every distraction. The dull ache became stronger as I emptied my mind, as if, being the last thing to remain, it clung to my brain for dear life. It became larger, encompassing all senses. I pushed it back. My only focus was the darkness.

But I couldn't find the universe. Try as I might to open my mind to its infinite expanse, I simply could not find it. I was reaching out to more darkness, a sheet before my eyes, just as it had been since we crash-landed on this planet. I pushed against it, but there was no change, no edging forward, only being forced back.

"Frash!" I still couldn't jump. I was still stuck.

As I broke down and allowed myself my little pity party, head swimming with artificial brain fog and a craving for brownies, a creature snuck into my room, uttering the words that would change my life forever:

"You… you can talk?"

ELEVEN

MIND GAMES AND MUSCLE GAINS

Zander

YOU CAN ONLY DO SO MANY PUSH-UPS BEFORE THE push-ups do you—*in*, that is. There's meant to be a limit. I'm sure I have one somewhere. For the time being, I made do with a random number and huffed and puffed as much as a Raglotian trying to bathe until I reached it and collapsed as dramatically as I could manage.

Boot camp is miserable enough the first time you do it. By the fifth, you start wishing you had vices to drown in. And by the time you lose count…

That single sip of whiskey was starting to sound like mana right now.

"Let me guess, you don't believe in push-ups?"

ShortThumb's face above me was all angles in the pink glow of the forest. Of all the boot camps on all the planets in all the wars I was roped into, she was one of the best drill sergeants I'd ever met. Well, of all the boot camps on all the planets in all the wars I was roped into that I could remember. After having been a pet finguy for two decades, she'd turned into the most ruthless swordswoman this side of Proxima Centauri, despite missing the top digit on both her thumbs, bobbed off for fashion's sake during her captivity.

"What do you want me to tell you?" I said, gasping for show.

"Look," she replied. "I am not someone who can come up with catchy slogans for an eight-minute workout. So, go for a good long one, and we'll look into the option of lunch."

Lunch was always an effective incentive. I rolled back over and gave the push-ups a good try. *Dull, dull, abysmally dull.* There were only so many times you could push away from the ground and fail to come up with some semblance of a plan that could hold together. Being alone with my thoughts was going to do me in before the push-ups ever did.

Already a week without Sally, and life was losing every drop of color. She had a way of making the world beautiful and strange just by being in it. Even in the midst of danger, it was fun, being with her. Without her, I was beginning to remember how dull the universe was the majority of the time.

I needed to save her. I needed to save Marcy.

I needed my sister.

I hadn't seen Blayde in longer than I could fathom. She'd wanted some time for soul-searching, but I could never formulate a foolproof plan without her assistance. She knew all the holes that could arise, and had solutions to solve them before they even happened. Without her, my mind functioned at half capacity.

Also, I missed her. So there was that.

"And—time." ShortThumb clapped once. "That's our morning. You're dismissed."

I pushed myself to my feet, brushing the soil from my fatigues, making a grand show of panting. Hopefully no one would notice the sweat-free brow in the dim light of the training pen. I hadn't seen the sun in the week I'd been here. Thankfully, no one ever looked too closely at me.

No matter where you were rescued from—shipwreck, pet hood—basic training was the first step before joining the rebel camp. My training began the morning after my meeting with Provis, and it hadn't stopped since. From knife skills to hand-to-hand combat to rifle accuracy, everything we could ever possibly use to defend ourselves was taught and perfected. Everything but blaster protocol: all our energy weapons were useless on this planet, prone to spontaneous combustion and more likely to destroy us than our targets.

Other than that, the training was incredibly efficient. I'd rank this boot camp a good nine out of a possible ten stars. Fat lot of good that would do when we took our pitchforks up against creatures capable of ripping us apart with their minds.

Our unit was made up of a dozen recent rescuees, and a captive-born who had just completed their integration course. All bipedal. Sters were not fans of non-human pets, but they were pretty bad at telling us apart, so a few other races got mixed into their system. Anybody with the wrong number of limbs who was lucky enough to survive the crash would have already found their place in one of the rebel camps.

The group moved as one, their shared anger towards the Sters driving them forward. Each of them had suffered at the hands of the enemy, and that suffering had forged a bond between them that I couldn't fully grasp. I was an outsider here, lacking the personal connection that fueled their thirst for vengeance. Their anger burned like a splinter, driving them ever forward towards their goal. It went beyond sharing a common enemy: these soldiers wore the horrors done to them on their bodies, on their faces, carried them in their names, so as to never forget.

I didn't have a history with the Sters to build on. I hadn't even seen one outside of crude drawings. My connection was empathetic rather than personal, and I knew better than to ask about their past experiences. I hadn't been given a new name. And I would not ask for one.

Heck, with a name like Skywalker, I'd fit right in.

"I fear that one day, I shall be afraid; that is the only fear I allow myself." My fellow recruit SharpTooth kicked the pile of leaves in front of him. They flew off in all

directions, some as large as his leg, crumpled black forms littering the air before fluttering back down, coating the glowing ferns that led us back to the mess hall.

HalfTongue's hands danced through the air. "That would be… General Laughry?"

They had been freed during the same rescue ops I was brought in with. We'd been placed in basic training together and not had a second of silence since. They had picked their own names. Neither had come from Alliance worlds, and they refused the nonsense words their Sters had imposed on them. SharpTooth had every one of his teeth filed to sharp points; HalfTongue, no description necessary. He didn't share how he lost his tongue, and nobody asked.

"You know your war heroes," said SharpTooth

"And you, your war quotes," signed HalfTongue.

"Holy Skylord, do you see that?"

SharpTooth darted off the path before we could answer, sending flashes of bioluminescent light into the air with every step, HalfTongue close at his heels. He pointed at a large silvery tarp.

Well, that was new.

I glanced back at ShortThumb, but she seemed as confused as I was. This wasn't part of the training.

We were far from the unsettling configuration of Party City; our training ground was meant to be difficult to reach, to teach us how to navigate the dark forest. Even so, we weren't encouraged to tread off the path.

The only person with a weapon was ShortThumb, and that was a stunner with questionable accuracy.

"It's a parachute," SharpTooth exclaimed, holding the fabric high. "One of ours!"

ShortThumb pushed past us. "There's no supply drop scheduled."

I followed them. Playing the role of an initiate wouldn't do us much good if there was actual trouble.

"There's a crate here," said SharpTooth, pulling the silvery parachute off and tossing it to the ground. "It's marked with the sign. It's one of ours." He beamed as ShortThumb approached.

She ran a hand over the wood, frowning as she walked around the crate. "It could just as easily be a trap. Unscheduled drops are unusual, but not impossible. We can't bring anything back to camp without knowing what it is."

The hair on the back of my neck was stiff. I'd seen this before: The enemy, dropping well- needed resources over a space they believed soldiers to be camping in, finding those who dared open the trove. Or, a frequent tactic, just giving their enemies the means to enjoy their vices: alcohol, tacos, slinkies—anything that would ruin the carefully crafted discipline.

Free presents usually had strings attached, and I didn't mean those from the parachute.

I ran my hand along the edge of the lid. It was made of crude wood, splintering at the touch. Nothing unusually hot or cold.

"You're not going to find the explosive by caressing it. It didn't work with Miro's doors, and it certainly won't work now."

The sound of Sally's voice made me stand bolt upright. I spun around, but—nothing. And no one else was reacting.

"Are you all right, Skywalker?" ShortThumb braced herself, one hand on the hilt of her stunner.

"Fine, just…" I shook myself out of my funk. "Does anyone have a knife?"

"What are you hoping to do, cadet?" ShortThumb pulled a knife out of her fatigues but didn't hand it to me.

"If this is a trap from the Sters hoping to find our location, then the crate will be rigged," I said. She nodded. Oh, maybe this *was* a test from the higher-ups. That made me breathe a little easier. Just concentrate and show them how it's done. "They're not very technologically advanced from what I can tell, so fancy pressure pads are out of their range. We're looking for a latch."

She flipped her knife, handing it to me by the hilt. I slid it between the lid and crate, taking it all the way around, but there wasn't a snag anywhere.

"At the very least, it's safe to open," I said, returning the knife to her.

Together, we lifted the crate lid, throwing it off to reveal —

A smiling face?

"Oh Gods, not again." ShortThumb sighed, lifting the life-sized doll out of the box and tossing it to the side. Beneath the inflatable doll were layers of bottles, protected by more folded latex.

HalfTongue laughed.

"Jackpot!" SharpTooth lifted one of the bottles up, examining it against a blue glowing fern. "We're going to live it up tonight!"

"Booze, for a camp full of soldiers?" Sally tittered. "I'd not be so quick to blow off any concern, hon."

Imaginary Sally was beginning to creep me out. Not that it wasn't nice seeing her—just that she turned out to be wearing nothing more than lacy lingerie, and was sitting seductively on the crate, pointing at the contents like some odd combination of pin-up and warning bells.

I forced myself still. What was wrong with me? Had I been poisoned? Something had slipped into my mind, creating this delirium.

I mean, I missed her—but not enough to start seeing her like *this*.

"I know," I hissed under my breath. I glanced into the crate to inspect it better. There was nothing out of the ordinary. Just bottles all the way down. ShortThumb turned to me, brows furrowed.

"What was that?" she asked.

"It seems… fine." I stared at the crate so as not to stare at Sally, who was swinging her feet against it. Loudly.

"This is definitely unusual." ShortThumb scratched her head. "We get deliveries from time to time, but nothing like this."

"*Tick, Tick, Tick*!" Sally said as she carried on banging her heels against the crate.

But her feet weren't making a noise.

And all at once it hit me: another way for the Sters to create mass damage without knowing where we were.

"Run!" I shouted, grabbing bottles and tossing them to the ground. Two rows, three rows down, and there it was, a small box I would have recognized anywhere. The old wind-up timepiece attached to it stared up at me with an angry glare.

Images flashed through my mind, a rapid fire of fear at the idea of this bomb going off, lighting the camp alight. The Sters would know our location. They would find us, capture us, exterminate us en masse, and that would be the end of it, that would be the end of any hope of finding Sally and Marcy —let alone a way for all of us to get off this planet.

I scanned it over, terror growing inside my chest. I couldn't disarm it, I didn't have the time, and this makeshift alien technology was unlike anything I had ever seen before. I had to get rid of it, destroy it—

"Get a move on!" Sally shouted in my ear.

I scooped up the bomb and ran.

Away from the camp, away from the rebels, from the only people I could trust on this poor excuse of a planet. My feet flew over the leafy ground, barely hitting the soil, no longer holding back for normality's sake. I was running, as fast as I could, unburdened by sore muscles, adrenaline pumping through every cell of my body, my head swimming with something close to panic.

Tick.

The clock stopped and I threw myself to the ground, covering the bomb with my body, squeezing my eyes shut so at least I wouldn't have to watch my body explode and recompose, not this time.

There was no boom.

No explosion. No organs ripping apart only to pull themselves back together in an achingly long process. Instead, there was silence.

I sat back up, confused, grabbing the box of explosives. The timer had run out, the ticking having finally stopped—but the bomb did not detonate.

A test.

It *was* a test.

"And you passed with flying colors," impossibly under-dressed Sally said with a slow clap, sitting on a stump facing me. She rolled her eyes as I stared at her. "Hey, you're the one doing the imagining here. Clothe me if it makes you more comfortable."

I blinked. "You're… I'm imagining you?"

"Your captive girlfriend appears to you in a way only you can see her, and hallucinations don't make the top of your *what the hell is happening* list?" She *tsk'd*. "I'm glad I came when I did. You're falling apart."

"I am not! I'm doing fine on my own."

"Then why do you think I'm here?"

"How should I know? I don't even know what you are yet!"

Her perfect teeth glowed blue in the plant-light. "I'm your conscience, honey. Or at least, an externalization of your subconscious mind. Somebody's been a bit of a mess lately. I'm here to fix that."

Of course she was. "Talking to myself is supposed to fix that?"

"Meh. It's worked before." She shrugged. "That little voice of Blayde's in your head sometimes? Yours truly. Rational decision maker, right here, in the flesh. Though not really in the flesh. You get it."

"You're my girlfriend, and you're me."

"I'm *just* you," she replied. "You only see me as your girlfriend because you want to."

"This is strange." If she was part of my own thought process… I concentrated, trying to shift my gaze, to change the way she appeared in my eyes, and there. Now she was comfortably clad in her shwomp.

"Don't think too hard about it." She pointed finger guns. "I'm here to help, not get in the way."

"As I said, I do fine on my own. You don't need to be here."

"And as a matter of fact, I do. And, technically, I am you, so you are doing fine on your own. Just with a little help from yourself. Now grab that bomb and smash it to bits."

"Why?"

"Just do it, all right?"

She pointed to her left at a large tree limb. I rolled my eyes, to which she only shrugged, pointing at the limb even more insistently. I picked it up, holding it like a baseball bat. She nodded.

And I swung it at the box.

It shattered, cogs and springs flying into the air, moss and dirt and mud and leaves springing to action and joining them in their dance, soaring up and up before crashing back down to the ground. I slammed the branch at the machine, again and again, each time with more force in the swing. My anger grew, flowing through me and out of me, through the branch into the fake bomb.

I screamed a scream I had been holding in for so long, a rage boiling inside me and through me until it enveloped me from head to toe.

The branch snapped in half, a large chunk of it flying off and crashing into a tree with such force that it stuck there. I stood in the small clearing, holding the destroyed branch. I breathed heavily, my body roiling as if it were the heart of a volcano.

"Better?" Sally asked.

"Not really."

She shrugged.

"Sometimes, there are things you can't do on your own," she asserted. "And this is not anything against you—everybody needs help. You're not all powerful, Zander. Grow the frash up."

"You're supposed to be me, aren't you? Do you have to be so rude?"

"Well, if no one else is going to tell you, I've got to. Do you feel hopeless?"

"I-I…" I stammered. "I think I do."

"Good." She smiled. "Time to put your trust in others again. You're going to find Sally, and you're going to find Marcy. You just need to be patient; help those who are helping you by making an effort. Remember, there's a lot more at stake than just her. Join their team and help them. Don't lead, help. Stars, being immortal has made you so…"

"Fearless?"

"Please!" She snorted. "You're *terrified*, even as we speak. No. Being immortal has made you brash. Foolish. Come on, grab the remains of that bomb and bring it back to camp. It's time you had an attitude check."

With that, she promptly walked away from me, as if determined to put as much distance as she could between us. My mind was reeling—my conscious mind, I suppose, seeing as how my subconscious was now exteriorized as my girlfriend, and seemed just fine.

Talking to myself now. I really was desperate.

I reached down and gathered the vestiges of the bomb, grabbing as many pieces as I could and stacking them on my arms until I had pretty much everything. Then I took off after Sally, trusting my subconscious knew the way back better than I did. I sure hadn't been paying attention to where I had been running.

Sally paused at the edge of Party City; her lips taut. There was no joy there, only concern. With a nod she indicated the general direction of the training facilities, an unspoken command to go on without her.

"Will I be seeing you again?" I asked, a sinking feeling in my gut.

"I'm not leaving until I fix you. Though hopefully, you'll clothe me in something a little more, well, tasteful, next time."

A pang of guilt gnawed at the back of my neck. "I would think the subconscious takes care of that, right?"

"We have a *lot* of work to do." She shook her head. "Now go. You've got places to be."

And with that, she faded into the recesses of my mind. I shuddered. Not a good sign that my own subconscious thought I needed fixing. I would have to convince it otherwise, and quickly.

I marched into camp, the silence tensing my muscles and putting me on edge. Party City was dark from the outside, lit up only by the glowing ivy that had crept up its aging I. Usually, this was a noisy place – had there been a real bomb? Had there been a Ster sighting? Were they gone or simply hiding?

Turns out, they were doing neither. As I approached the training area, voices filled the air—not fearful and whispering, but excited and cheerful. Finally, I turned the corner and found not only my fellow trainees, but practically the entire camp.

"Oh, there he is!" someone pointed out. Instantly, all heads turned to me, and the roar of applause rose all around me, a thunder that made the air tremble.

"What's this?" No one made any sign of hearing me. Instead, soldiers slapped me on the back, excitedly, hooting and shouting.

"ShortThumb?" I caught a glimpse of her between the strangers. "What's happened?"

"You've won!" She flashed me a wide, brilliant smile.

"Won what?"

"Provis wants to see you!"

She led me through the twisted hallways, past the reversed cake, then stood aside to let me enter alone, slapping me hard on the back for good measure. I stepped inside, arms still full of the broken shards of the false bomb. Provis sat at the war table, studying another hand-drawn map.

"Sir?" I cleared my throat. He jumped, his face breaking out into a smile when he realized it was me.

His brows furrowed and he pointed to my chest. "Why are you carrying that?"

"Haven't exactly had time to put it down."

"At what point did the… urm… device…?" He mimicked an explosion with his hands, complete with silent boom. It was all I could do not to laugh. He looked so young all of a sudden, far too young to be a general. The odd sense of familiarity hit me again. He could have been one of Sally's friends from back on Earth. I could see myself bar-hopping with him.

"After I realized it was a fake, I do know how to disarm these things. I just had to get something out."

"Yeah, I get that. Just put it anywhere. We have more important things to discuss." He gestured at the chair across from his desk. "Sit, Skywalker. I won't waste any time: you have just been promoted."

"I— I what?"

If there was any kind of protocol, Provis had just thrown it into the wind. One slipup on my part and now there was too much attention on me. I couldn't stay here much longer. The Alliance and the Siblings went together about as well as matter and antimatter.

"You don't have a plan," Sally said, leaning against the wall behind Provis. She was fully clothed this time, wearing a Pyrinian DriftBall t-shirt over silver infiniweave leggings. "Don't pretend you do."

She was trying to distract me. My own subconscious. I focused on Provis instead. "But—why? I've only been in boot camp for a week. You don't know me."

"I know enough about you to know you're the kind of man who puts the safety of others above his own," said Provis. "You're the kind of man who would give up his life for people he's known for all of a week. That's the kind of man I want leading my men."

"Sir, I don't know if that's wise." I swallowed. Hard. "I've never experienced the Sters the way the rest of you have. Your men will resent me. Most already do."

"You're speaking as if we're discussing whether or not to promote someone else." Provis leaned back in his chair.

"You know more than you let on, Skywalker. You are a leader. I have seen you on the training grounds; you fight in a way I have never seen before, both quick and efficient, but without urgency. Training is beneath you: You've fought before. Hell, you have led before. Haven't you?"

I nodded slowly.

"Where, *Luke Skywalker*?"

He was prodding. I tried to keep my face slack. Frash, he knew, didn't he?

"I'd rather not speak of it," I said, a little sharper than I was going for. Colors flashed somewhere in the back of my mind, images of battles and bloodlust and fear and terror and gore and —

"Control them," Sally ordered. "Let them flow: A trickle, not a current. You need to see your past, let the memories return. You don't have to—"

I plugged the dam and returned my focus to Provis, who watched me, one brow lifted, head tilted to the side. It was almost cute, like a big-eyed pocket-sized animal.

"Are you going to be all right?" he asked.

"Fine." I pulled my attention away from Fake-Sally. "My memories of the battlefield tend not to be ones I want to remember. Not great small talk."

"If this impacts the way you fight, I need to know now." His brows furrowed again. "I can't have you freezing up during an encounter."

"I can handle it." I kept my eyes riveted on him, trying not to glare at Sally, who threw her hands up into the air.

"Good. Because I have news for you, *Lieutenant* Skywalker." Provis's lips curled into the slightest smile. "We've found them."

"You've found Sally?" I leapt to my feet, all other emotions subsiding, leaving only relief. "Is she all right? Is she here…?"

"She's fine. A domestic finguy, as expected, but generally well-treated. She belongs to the governor's juvenile, so it's going to be tough to free her."

"This is incredible news," I said earnestly. *Sally was safe.* And if she was safe, Marcy couldn't be too far behind.

"In the meantime, I want you training our people." Provis handed me a piece of worn paper—a map. A circular building, set in a spiral of corridors like a turban shell. "Report to TrueFoot tomorrow at 0900. You will follow his instructions to the letter. He will be leaving for a rescue mission at a veterinarian clinic, and you'll be taking over his sessions while he's gone."

"Yes, sir."

"And, Zander?"

Zander. Good moment gone. He knew my name. Fear enveloped me like a cold, slimy amoeba. "Yes, sir?"

"Don't let anyone know who you are." He gripped me with his gaze, so intently that I forgot for a moment how to breathe. "Honestly, I don't like working with a known terrorist, but you've got abilities we need. You help free us—and eventually, get us off this planet—

and I promise to put in a good word with the president. Deal?"

Not that I needed one. "Who do you think sent me?"

"The Alliance cares so much for us, they sent *you?"* he scoffed. "I don't know if I should feel offended that they'd stoop so low, or that you think I'd fall for it."

"Do you want my help or not?" This was sweet coming from a man who supposedly wanted my skills. Oh stars, now that was going be a quanta to unpack. Better roll with it. "May I ask, how did you recognize me?"

"You're not exactly hiding." He barked a laugh. "Back in my day, we were trained to know the Alliance's most wanted a little more than they are now. Now, go."

Back in my day? He was barely older than Sally. Something didn't add up. I did as I was bid, though, grabbing the wreck of the broken bomb and slipping outside the crashed ship. Sally was waiting right outside, arms crossed in front of her chest.

"What was that back there?" she snapped, tapping her foot against the ground in a way I had never seen the real Sally do.

"What was what?"

She pursed her lips. "You know exactly what I mean."

"I really don't. Sorry."

She sighed, waving for us to begin walking. I followed her, still confused.

"By the way, you seem to get very confused, very easily," she said. "Stop waiting for answers and figure stuff out on your own, like you used to. Standing around being confused is a waste of time."

Me, standing around? No way was she my subconscious. I knew better. "Fine."

"And you can't keep repressing those memories!" She threw her hands up in this air, passing right through the upside-down cake. "There's a lot of important stuff in them!"

"Like what?"

"I can't just tell you, that would be missing the point!" She stuffed her hands under her armpits, grunting. "You're not whole without them. You need to start paying attention to them, instead of damming them up!"

"They were buried for a reason." Why was I arguing with myself? If these memories were supposed to come back, they would have, already. They would have all returned when I'd unblocked the mental dam in Nimien's journey-to-the-center-of-the-self. "We kept going back to Nimien *for a reason.* Maybe I'm not meant to have them."

"And you've grown since then," she said. "Look. You don't have to bring them all back at once. Let them trickle in. You need to know."

"Know what?"

"Who you are, Zander!" She prodded me firmly in the chest. I gasped as her fingers drew a sharp, stinging pain to the middle of my sternum. Frash, she *hurt.* "You're half of the man you were! Armies used to take one look at you and decide non-violence was tubular. What happened to the man who could put empires on their knees with a few choice words?"

"I decided I didn't want to be him anymore. At least—I think that's how it went."

"Exactly. That's an idea you've planted in your head, so you wouldn't have to deal with the past." She stepped in front of me, puffing out her chest. Her face redshifted faster than the most distant of galaxies. "Half of you is invisible. You hide by denying who you are to yourself, to the point that even you don't know who you are anymore."

"So what? It's easier like this."

She rolled her eyes. "Easier does not necessarily mean better."

"It keeps Sally safe."

"Is that why you told her you can't remember anything?" She tilted her head to the side. "Is that why you told her you're trying to recover your memories, when you haven't even tried to look at them?"

This was getting tedious. And where was I? I seemed to have wandered into a room with large chairs, rendered useless by their positioning on the ceiling. They looked comfortable enough if you could defy gravity.

"Zander," said Fake-Sally.

"Go away," I spat.

"I can't, I'm you." She glowered. "You need to pay attention to them. You can't hold them back forever."

"Watch me!"

With that final, defiant proclamation, I felt a surge of energy rush through me. I turned on my heel, heading for the door with a determination that surprised even me. I didn't know where I was going, or what I was going to do when I got there, but I couldn't stay here.

"Watch you?" Fake-Sally echoed. "Watch you do what, exactly? Pretend that you're not slowly coming apart at the seams? That you're not a walking, talking contradiction?"

The words struck me with all the subtlety of a supernova explosion. I blinked it out of my thoughts..

Fake-Sally didn't wait for an answer. She simply folded her arms, staring at me with a look that was half challenge, half pity. "Fine," she said, the word hanging in the air between. "But don't say I didn't warn you."

And with that, she vanished, her image dissipating like the last vestiges of a forgotten dream. I was left alone in the strange, upside-down room, my thoughts echoing in my head like a relentless drumbeat.

TWELVE

I NEVER SIGNED UP FOR AN ALIEN PLAYDATE

Sally

WHEN I DREAMED OF HAVING MY E.T. MOMENT AS a kid, I never expected to be on this side of the story.

I scrambled to my feet; there was a monster in my room. One of the creatures had made its way down here while my eyes were closed and was floating right in front of me. A smaller, more opaque little creature—though calling it little was relative, of course. Its head was still about the size of an exercise ball. I wondered, briefly, if I could ride on top of it like I'd just overly committed to a fitness routine at my office desk. The mere thought made my head swim with whatever goop they were pulsing into my brain.

"It's okay, Comfort Food," it said, drifting closer. The voice was squeakier than the others, like the charge it spoke into the air wasn't so finely tuned. "I swear I won't tell anybody. I'm really good at keeping secrets. I never told Muf-Parent about where Sib-Parent goes during the day. You can trust me."

I took a step back, cold rising up my spine as I collided with the wall. *Oh shit.* I was alone with a monster. A small one, but still big enough to swallow me whole if it wanted to. Despite the uncanny lack of eyes, it felt like it was looking right at me. Though I was probably projecting that.

I cleared my throat, still sore from shouting at the creep at the party. "You… you can hear me?"

The air in the room fizzled for a split second, and I could have sworn I heard the thing gasp. It sprung a good meter into the air, banging its bulb against the ceiling.

"You *can* talk!" It practically squealed. "Oh glow, a talking finguy!"

If I had a working heart, it would have skipped a beat. It had *heard* me. For the first time in days, someone had heard me, understood me. And it wasn't speaking to me as if I was a pet, but as if I was a magical being: a tad patronizing, but miles ahead of anything I'd experienced so far.

I took a step towards it. "You can… you can understand me?"

"You're a talking finguy!" It twirled around, tentacles flung wide. "Just like in the storybooks!"

I frowned. I didn't know what to say: a creature, speaking to me. For days, I'd wanted nothing more. But it couldn't have been the only one of its kind to understand me. If there were children, there had to be others. Which meant they weren't just treating us as pets: they were deliberately keeping us this way.

They knew we were intelligent.

My blood boiled. "All finguies can talk," I said, putting a delightful smile on my face. "If you're willing to listen."

It dipped in the air, hovering closer to me. It smelled like fish that had been left in the sun for too long. I shuddered. Even as a child, it was still at least two meters tall, towering over me without even trying.

"Then why am I the only one who can understand you?" it asked.

"Maybe you're special." Storybook tale indeed. "You have a special gift!"

"Whee!" The creature spun around oncc again. "I can talk to finguies!"

"My name is Sally," I said. "What's yours?"

"Sally? That's a silly name. I thought your name was Comfort Food?"

"That's what Nuuvi calls me. They can't hear me speak like you can. Only you know my real name."

"My name is Gluuk." It twirled again, tentacles almost brushing my knees. "Sally is so silly!"

Great, the one creature who could understand me, and it was a kid. Then again, if this truly was an innocent child, then maybe it could help me more than it knew. From the mouths of babes and all that.

"Gluuk, I need your help." I tried to cram as much meaning and intention into my little translator as I could. "I'm not supposed to be here. I have a family out there, you understand? I have a pod. And they're all very sad because I'm lost."

"But you're not lost," said Gluuk, "You're here, and Nuuvi's taking care of you. You have such nice food. It's so much better than out in the wild."

"I don't live in the wild, Gluuk." I took a deep breath. Okay, about to break this child's concept of the universe. I only wish it had Reese's Pieces rather than kibble and floor meat. "I'm from up there." I pointed, then realized they might not be able to see where I was indicating. "From… above the clouds. Me and all my friends. And I need to get back to them."

"There's nothing above the clouds!" The air fizzled again, this time sharper, a metallic scent filling my nose. "That's the realm of demons!"

"It's where I'm from, Gluuk." *Come on, kid, fulfill your destiny.* "Why would I lie to you? You're the only one who can hear me. The only one I can trust. I need to get out of here, find my pod, so we can all go home above the clouds. Can you help me?"

Gluuk didn't answer for a moment—for an excruciatingly long moment. For a second, I wondered if whatever luck that had granted it the power to understand me had dried up. Then, like a toy being stolen from an older sibling's room, I was yanked up into the air.

"I'll save you, Sally!" it said, flying shakily through the house, up, up, past the festivities and meat-soaked glass floor, up to the hole in the fishbowl. Gluuk's feeble childhood flux barely grasped me, and I almost slipped as we rushed past the screams of the guests calling its name.

But I was out! The fresh mossy air of the dark outside world filled my nostrils, cleansing them of the rotten stench of the house. I was wobbling through the sky, high above the glowing forest, but it was forest floor beneath me, not glass.

Where was Gluuk taking me?

I never had time to find out, as with one heavy spark and jolt, the grip of flux disappeared entirely, and I went tumbling to the forest floor I had been so excited to smell five seconds earlier. My life fell through my fingers as I plummeted through the damp air.

Oh—*shit.* The only way I was getting out of this house was in a body bag. Served me right for expecting any realism from a childhood classic. Gluuk was already flying behind me, its apologies reaching my ears despite the rush of wind.

I landed hard on moist soil, amid the pained cries of my alien overlords. I was surrounded by glowing pink plants, their light bouncing off the glistening white of the bone jutting out of my arm, making it look like a highlighter. My eyes teared up in frustration as I clutched my shattered skin. Whatever device was in my head was making me nauseous, when I shouldn't have felt a thing.

I threw up, hyperaware of the adrenaline running through my veins and the cold in my bones. I gripped the fresh plants with my intact arm like they were a plush toy. Screw it, I was out, but I couldn't run away, not when the entire birthday party was flying in on me.

I screamed.

It felt good to scream, scream with every molecule of air in my lungs, scream without caring that someone would try to shut me up. I screamed as if the world was ending. I screamed as if it was the last thing I was ever going to do.

I screamed as my head filled with warm and cozy soup. Ah, soup.

"Muf!" Nuuvi cried. "Muffy! Gluuk, what have you done?"

"It was an accident!" it said.

Come on, kid, tell them I can talk. Tell them I'm intelligent and I need a way home.

But Gluuk stayed silent. Maybe it thought it would only make things worse. Maybe it was just a terrified child who knew it had done a bad thing.

Nuuvi's glow descended upon me like a rain cloud. The moment I felt their pull, I was floating. Their light enveloped me, and I reached towards them with my free hand, almost without thinking. But I needed them to care. They had to care.

"She'll die if we don't take her to the vet!" Nuuvi was on the proverbial verge of tears, though through what eyes the tears would flow, I had no idea.

"Dearest, look," the muf-parent said to the frequently absent Lord something-or-other. "Comfort Food has hurt herself. And quite badly. I think she needs to go to the vet."

"Bah, it'll mend on its own," said another parent. "Just bind it up, it'll be fine. And if it isn't, I could take it out back, have Spax put it out of its misery."

I shuddered. The thought had never crossed my mind that I would be so easily disposable. I felt no pain; I felt nothing. Nothing but pure terror and a craving for nacho cheese. *Thanks, drugs.*

"No!" said Gluuk. The air fizzled, like hiccups and sobs. "I didn't mean to!"

"Sweet sensations!" the muf-parent shouted as Nuuvi sobbed louder and louder. Lord whatever expelled gas in an overly dramatic sigh.

"Fine, fine," they said, "Spax! Fetch the box! We're taking the finguy to the vet. We need to go."

I continued to make pained noises as the family shared fearful words. The blue-ringed being placed me gently in the carrying box and closed the lid. Darkness engulfed me, but excitement rose in my chest—I was close to being free. Soon I'd find Zander and Marcy, and escape this planet for good.

I was dying for a real toilet.

The carrying case bounced gently up and down. I waited, playing with my twisted arm to keep it from healing too fast, trying not to think too much about the shape of the bone. The little device in my head was pumping me full of delicious compliance drugs, which kept me uncomfortably giggly as I manhandled myself.

"We have an emergency," said Spax, dropping my box on a hard table-like surface, not caring for the finguy inside.

"And we have a line," said the clerk.

A split second elapsed, quite possibly one in which Spax made the identity of their boss known, after which the clerk's tone had a complete turnaround.

"Right this way, Distinguished-Hand," they said, taking the box off the table. I fought to keep my balance as it swung back and forth—no gentle fluxing here, no. Someone was in a hurry.

Slam—another hard table. The lid of my box flew off, and I was lifted into the air, placed on a cold, metal examination table with—oh God, were those wrist restraints?

I gripped my broken and bloodied arm, glaring up at the vet with my best Blayde fire in my eyes. They shooed away my undamaged hand and pulled the broken bone forward, making me cry out in shock. No bedside manner, seriously. Unlike my captors and their servants, this creature sported an entirely new color, glowing a pleasant green.

Not so pleasant now I associated it with *them*, though.

"This is a serious break," said the vet to Spax. "A complete snap. There should be small bone fragments floating around in the bloodstream – if they reach the heart, your finguy will die."

"What needs to be done?" asked Spax. "Lord Vuzuk will spare no expense for their child."

"The entire arm needs to come off to stop the fragments," said the vet. "Then I'll have to keep her under observation; if we miss even one shard of bone, she'll be dead before this day is done."

I stared at my arm. I'd never been to medical school, but I'm pretty sure that's not how bones work.

"This is the governor's family finguy, Nan," said Spax "Keep it alive, or you will face the consequences."

"I'll amputate right away." Before I could react, the vet shoved me down with their flux.

Spax's tentacles reached for me, then retracted. "Won't it hurt the finguy?"

The drugs had filled my brain completely by now. I was swimming in them, floating higher than a flux would ever take me. I would die for a plate of mozzarella sticks right about now.

"Finguies don't feel pain the way we do," said the vet, grabbing a large metal poker. "Don't worry. It will be as if nothing ever happened."

I had to get out of here. I struggled against the flux, but I couldn't go anywhere; its invisible force held me pressed against the table, completely immobile. A long, silver blade drifted into my field of vision—a scalpel. They were going to maim me, take my arm—

"No," I said. I was shaking, even under the pressure of the flux. My head rang like a gong with the implant forcing calm into my brain against my will. "Let me go!"

"She sure is a loud one, isn't she?" The vet cringed. "I can feel her in the mist. Has a lot of spirit. She'll do fine like this. So long as the governor's podling doesn't mind a damaged finguy."

"Doctor?" Another voice, too far out of view for me to see. I still couldn't turn my head. Couldn't see the extent of the damage. "We have a problem."

"What kind of problem?" The vet rose up. Small flickers of lightning raced in their gas. "I'm a little busy here. This is the *governor's* business."

"It seems to be some kind of… assault on the facility, sir," said the other. Even through my own panic, I could feel theirs fizzle through the air. "The south wall has shattered!"

"What?" The vet flew at them, their flux releasing me just lightly. Enough for me to turn my head, to see the charred stump of skin. I breathed—or rather, hissed.

"I think it may be some kind of… They're finguies, sir?"

The voices faded as they left, the vet following the other one who knows where, leaving Spax to guard me.

And no one to flux me down.

It was now or never.

I thrust my leg up into the air, grabbing Spax by the tentacle, swinging it like a vine to get to my real destination—their bulb. I swung a fist and punched—

Right *though* the thin membrane that kept their gas in. That kept their… thoughts in? Their minds?

With a resounding thump, the bulb popped, sending a cascade of sparks in all directions. The sound was that of a helium balloon deflating all at once, though in this case, it deflated slowly, like an exercise ball with a leak. The air filled with the smell of cinnamon-spice and pumpkins. I fell to the floor. Hell yeah: I had been listening in my badassery lessons.

I threw my fist back, forcing myself to take in the devastation in front of me. Holy… I hadn't known it would be so easy. Snapping out their lives was as easy as popping a balloon. There was a lot of gas in the bulb. My skin felt hot, and I threw my arms over my ears and took deep breaths.

Just like that, I'd killed them. It. If they refused to see us as people, I would do the same.

I'd… killed it. Something terrible and cruel, but still: it had been intentional.

I needed to run. I needed to go, not that I knew where. Much like Nuuvi's fishbowl home, it had no doors, only glass walls; unlike their home, however, the holes between rooms were wide enough for an entire operating team to comfortably squeeze through.

My footsteps hit the glass like thunder to my ears, louder than the tumult behind me, louder than the cries of all the temporary residents of this facility, louder than the shots outside. I wasn't listening, I was running, running down the hallway and into the lobby, where the bowl's edge had been blown open and dozens of uniformed *humanoids* were crashing in, weapons high, eyes burning with fury. They were a blur on my eyeballs, soaked through by whatever was being pumped into my head.

I threw myself back, confused whether I should run or hide. They were Alliance, but their uniforms were mismatched, patched, and torn. Were they friend or foe? I couldn't tell, but they were fighting the monsters that held me captive and soon overwhelmed them, like ants swarming a beetle or fans swarming the Beatles.

I hurried into the former waiting room, shading my eyes from the bright light and dust, fighting my way against the invading crowd, who made no attempt to stop me, too focused on bringing down the creatures inside the building. I rushed the wall of the broken fishbowl outside, soldiers there pushing other escapees like me towards—hopefully—our salvation.

I was free of the fishbowls, at last. Free of domestication. There was nothing but the neon forest between me and where I wanted to go.

Where was that?

I was running without thinking, before I noticed I was alone. The sick flow of the implant had been overpowered by adrenaline. I spun around and ran back but couldn't remember the path I had taken. Had I gone straight, had I taken turns? I was more turned around than a compass in a room full of magnets.

I closed my eyes, taking slow, deep breaths, trying to shut off my other senses, trying to focus on the one thing that mattered—finding my friends. If I could latch on, track them down, I could jump, I could join them…

The universe pulled back. I still couldn't reach it. So, it wasn't the fishbowls in my way—I truly had lost any ability to jump. I was stuck. I was… lost, as lost as a single sock in the Bermuda triangle.

I hadn't felt this lost since Da-Duhui, since I had fallen into the darkness. Or was it since Blayde abandoned me on Earth? No, that had been a different kind of lost. Now I was in Da'Duhui's Undercity again, panicking, my vision narrowing and my breathing more restricted. What had happened to me?

Had it never dawned on me how crazy this situation was? How bad it could be? I was lost on an alien planet with no way to find my friends, no way home. Zander and Marcy were gone. Blayde wasn't in this galaxy, maybe not even this era, and I was here. I was living, breathing in the glorious madness of space, alone.

I had to go. Now. I had to move forward. I had to keep going.

So, I walked.

The forest was silent, stretching on for miles. Nothing moved and there were no signs of animals. A fruity pine smell filled the air, stagnant and sweet. All that existed was the mist.

I wanted to pick a tree to sleep in, but I was still wired. My adrenaline had fought the compliance drugs but now their dull high was returning. Would they still work now I no longer desired escape, since I had already done it?

There was a new color, in the forest, a new kind of light. Off in the distance, off to my right. Dim, but white light all the same. White light for beings with no eyes? Had I stumbled upon the rebel camp on my own?

I began to run again, holding back nothing. The light was my salvation, I needed to reach it. It was so close I could feel it against my skin. My lips slid into a smile. I was there.

My heart sank at the sight of the tall, barbed metal fence stretching far into the horizon. Light poured from the other side, illuminating the forest like a beacon. This fortress had no dome like the other buildings on this planet; its light leaked directly into the night air, alone in the center of the forest.

As I turned to run, the air turned static around me, and I knew in my gut some kind of alarm had just been raised.

"Run!" somebody shouted from behind me, leaping over a bush.

I caught a quick glimpse of him through the poor lighting and did a double take: an Alliance uniform. A familiar Alliance uniform. It took me a second to place the face, seeing as how he was meant to be light-years away from this place. He looked just as he had on the *Traveler*, though far less sparkly and far more terrified.

"Magnesar?" I gasped.

"Sally *Webbah*! Novalicious! You're alive!" He looked over his shoulder. "I think we need to run, baby-cakes!"

And so I ran for my life for the second time today. Though I was starting to think I had hallucinated the first time. How in the universe had Kork's rockstar first mate ended up on this dumpster fire of a planet and made a better escape than me?

Magnesar was ripped away from me with an "*oomph*" of pain. Something then wrapped around my legs and pulled me in the opposite direction. I was soon dangling in the air, alongside Magnesar and other bundles of groaning people.

"They're not ours," said my octopod captor, shaking me in midair. I glared back at it as I swung back and forth like a pendulum, though I still wasn't sure if it could read my face.

"Most likely strays, helping to orchestrate the escape." Another creature drifted forward, bundles of wailing bipeds in its wake. "Not a rebel, judging by the clothes—probably a house pet who got loose. In any case, it looks like a healthy specimen. A female, too—she looks like a fighter." I snarled at him. No idea what had given him that impression. "Take them inside and get them cleaned up. If they're tagged, clear that up too."

"And the escapees?"

"Lower the rations and chuck them in solitary. Take the newbies to processing."

We fluxed upwards, a bouncing ball of groans and moans.

Now I knew for sure: I should never have gone towards the light.

INTERMISSION

SQUID IN THE MIDDLE: NAVIGATING YOUR NEW FIVE-FINGERED FRIEND

BHAMNO ADORED THEIR NEW PET.

The morning they had found it on their doorstep, they had been expecting a call from the governor to discuss the weapons deal. The situation had been poorly handled, leaving thousands of lives in the hands of a few unscrupulous figures. Instead, when their habitat had fizzled to announce the arrival of a visitor, they had lifted the cap and found an unlabeled package, with a little knot of cloven grass fastening it shut, as was traditional.

The finguy had to have been a gift from the Consortium, since they had always complained that Bhamno was too solitary and needed a companion to keep them from falling victim to the darkness of the job. They *were* in charge of all military developments for the nation, after all, no small challenge there, and didn't have time for relationships. Not that they wanted to build a pod any time soon. Adding more beings to their mist space sounded exhausting.

But everything changed once they received the finguy.

It was a stunning specimen. A female of the species, in absolute perfect form, so much so they could have entered them in finguy shows, if they had the time or the need. They never had an ego, a feat of which they were immensely proud. The creature was tame, perfectly obedient, following their every word to the letter as if it could *understand* them. As if it knew their language.

It *listened*. Actively.

It was not love at first sight. No, Bhamno's happiness at being gifted such a perfect finguy came later, after the initial shock of another mouth to feed—however small—wore off. The first time they had seen the little critter, they had wanted to tear it apart. Not the right time to give it to a zoo, and there was no possible way to return it, not if the Consortium truly was behind the gift.

The joy came when they realized how easy the finguy was to care for; almost as if all they had to do was feed it, and in exchange, the small creature gave them nothing but attention and devotion.

The finguy would sit on their bulb in silence as they went over their files and plans, conversing with the mist. Sometimes it would seem to be in the mist with them, almost as if it were trying to learn their world, to be able to know them better. It was like it, no, *she* cared; Bhamno liked that, being cared for. Or at least, the idea that something so mindless as a finguy could find something in them to love. An emotion so base, so worthless, and yet, so rewarding.

It gave them hope.

They named her Fast Weather; not that they ever needed to call her. She was never out of Bhamno's sight, and they liked that.

Eventually, they were so pleased that they bought the little creature an incredibly overpriced cushion—though they could not understand how anything could find the soft mushiness of the thing comfortable, actually putting your mass *down*—setting it up in the living room so the finguy could sleep by their side as they conversed bulb to bulb with the other military leaders of the nation.

The governor came over once, complaining about how their podling's finguy had been killed in a rebel raid and how they had to buy a new one. A younger one this time, they said. Neither finguy had shown their family anything but disdain, nothing like Bhamno's new pet. The small being would lie back on her cushion and smile as they lined up to compliment her beauty, noting her colorful hair, which fell in bright strands around her fern-shaped face. When she shook her head, it was almost like looking at the forest in spring.

Bhamno loved their pet. And the pet loved them. They decided, therefore, that since she was definitely going to be staying, they needed to purchase the everyday items they would need to display her to the world: a play-tower for her to climb in when they were out, for example, and a traveling box, for when she would accompany them to major locations. They'd need to buy nice clothing, for nice occasions. And maybe some of that really expensive finguy food, the stuff that came right from the butcher.

They needed a trip to the great finguy outlet. They said goodbye to Fast Weather, ordered the bubble to be pulled up front, and left for the town's lavish shopping center.

Bhamno lived in the larger city dome, as he had no family, making a habitat-dome quite a large and useless expense. The city was better: quicker to get around. It was all the habitat they needed.

They stopped at three finguy shops in the town center, taking the opportunity to ask about their fabulous pet. The multicolored hair, as they suspected, was incredibly rare—not altogether natural, probably from the (hush-hush) sky finguies, and not their land stock—yet none of the shops remembered selling one recently. Or ever, as a matter of fact. None of them had even laid eyes on such a finguy and had only heard about them in rumors. Bhamno left both proud and perplexed.

When they returned to their habitat, they were surprised that their butler had not lifted the cap. First, they were struck with anger—incompetence would not be tolerated— and then, fear: Had something gone wrong? Was Fast Weather hurt?

Bhamno rushed through their slot, drifting into their habitat, giving in to gravity—but there was no movement inside. No trickle of electricity from… anything. Their manservant's body lay on the ground—no charge. Dead, maybe. Bhamno's mists swirled—had somebody kidnapped Fast Weather?

Then—a spark. Something alive was in their habitat. Not in the parlor—*down.* In the study? They drifted through the down-hole, feeling around with their flux, reaching—

The pain to their bulb was sudden and considerable. They let out a spark of shock as they lost grip on their flux, their bulb a slave to the currents of the mist. The only thought in their head was worry for their sweet Fast Weather.

And then they felt it: just as they grappled with their flux, they barely made out the small form standing there, heavy weight in her hand. It had been the first time anything other than a smile had crossed her face, and she felt entirely different from the pet they had grown to love. She felt, well, terrifying. For the first time Bhamno realized that her perfect form was not the result of good breeding, but evidence of a pure hunter.

They had never been afraid of a finguy before. The air around her fizzled with electricity. She was alive, alive, alive—

"Kibble is a terrible substitute for a healthy diet," she said—she actually *spoke*—right into their brain.

And then the world was dark.

THIRTEEN

RUNNING IN CIRCLES IN THE ULTIMATE SWEATSHOP

Sally

BELIEVE ME WHEN I TELL YOU THAT THERE'S THE daily grind, and then there's the daily *grind.* When you're woken up every morning to run in a hamster wheel all day, you start to reflect on the nature of work, and wonder if seizing the means of production might be a tad too exhausting, and how that might be the whole *point* of the wheel. The morning charge zaps and you wake up and think, *Oh well, I've got another fourteen hours of running before I have to sleep again.* And you get up anyway.

I stood at the end of my sleeping mat for morning inspection, concealing my yawns in the elbow of my jumpsuit. The patches were faded, but they had held up for a few days now. My crunchy socks scratched my soles and my toes, an itch I was going to have to put up with for the rest of the day. It was another beautiful morning in the pit.

Our alien overlords drifted down from above, then along the row of people, the air tingling as they passed by. I shuddered, hating the feel of their touch. Sters: that was what we called them. Or so I was told by Marn, a woman of more muscle than flesh, who had the bedroll next to mine and sometimes exchanged a few hushed words with me when the Sters were out of reach. Not that they would ever understand what we were saying. Idle chitchat was something they did not tolerate, as though it was an infringement upon the buzz of their beloved mist, and they hated that.

From what I had gathered, we were on some kind of farm, and we were—much like a trained sheep dog but with opposable thumbs—the labor force. Many of the larger people were assigned to plowing fields or planting crops, while the smaller ones were given jobs such as milking a creature I had never seen—nobody should ever have seen it—sheering, feeding it, and so on.

Forever.

Every morning, jobs were doled out depending on muscle mass. The Sters were worse than my local gym, using their electrical current through muscle to determine the strongest of us, fluxing them out of our sleeping pit first for the harder jobs, moving down the ranks until only my group was left.

Team hamster wheel.

They fluxed us up, handed us our day's rations—a dry protein cracker and a glass of something that tasted like

Tang. And then we climbed into our wheels and started to run.

What's worse than having a dull, repetitive job, with high impact on your bones? Having a dull, repetitive job that is *useless.*

I was starting to be thankful for the drugs in my head. Now that the craving for escape was back, so were the highs of foggy brain juice! Highs that made me hungry for all sorts of things I wasn't likely to see for a while, but at least I felt something.

"It's illegal, you know," Marn had told me on my first day while she ran, pumping her arms dutifully by her sides.

"What is?" I was slow in the wheel, back then, struggling to keep from going around with it.

"The wheel." She made talking while running look easy. "They collect the sweat every few hours. Grab a sponge, squeeze it out into a bucket. It's a drug to them."

"A what now?"

"They inhale the steam." She pinched her fingers up to her lips, making me laugh. "I saw my former Sters doing it, once. They got caught, and I was sent here, so I wasn't wasted. But the animal control being who brought me here had no idea what this place is actually doing. Now we're… drug mules? Chemists? A mix of both. Yummy, yummy."

Our conversation had ended there, as a Ster rattled my wheel with their flux, forcing me to run faster.

Every day since then had been identical, with no sign of Magnesar anywhere. It was reaching the point where I wondered if I'd imagined him in the first place.

The wheel room was dark and sweaty and smelled of old shoes, despite the fact none of us wore any. Days passed like this. I ran, I slept — I schemed. Fruitlessly. There was simply no easy way of communicating with others, no way of seeing the outside of the two interlinked buildings I was kept in. Trying an impulsive solo escape was looking more and more promising than a well-planned and well-executed one. I had to try something, or I would be stuck here until further notice.

Except today: today, *he* was back.

Magnesar. The rockstar. Kork's new number one. And now—a runner like me?

He shuffled into the wheel room, clutching his ribs. He looked almost exactly the same as the last time I had seen him: except for the green hair, which had been sliced, no, hacked off, as if it had been clumsily done with a machete. He was greeted by everyone around him with a quiet nod. Anything more than that would have been noticed by the Sters.

Magnesar climbed into the empty wheel to my left and hesitantly started to run. It was the first time I had seen him in the light, without his magnificent hair, and I tried not to stare. He was not entirely human, though humanoid for sure. His skin was white, almost transparent like a frosted window. His irises were a pale grey, surrounded by a harsh face, each feature sharp, as if cut from granite.

"Sally Webber?" he asked slowly. "Light-years, girly girl. Light-years! OW!"

Of course, his words were met with a zap from our alien overlords. He glanced at me mournfully, then began running.

How had he gotten here? Or the greater question, how could I ask him? My mind wandered as I ran, the room filling back up with the thunder of feet on wood and the squeak of old gears. Magnesar was trapped here with me, and I had to take advantage of that.

I sifted through the mental list of tricks I'd picked up from the Siblings. Somewhere in the back of my head, I knew I could just run, make my way out fighting, letting nothing get in my way. There was no way I could free everyone, but if I could escape and find these mysterious rebels, maybe they could take this place down from the outside. But what was good for me could harm the rest of my fellow captives. I couldn't see myself winging it without someone caught on the sidelines getting hurt.

When the charge zapped, we stopped our wheels, taking our five-minute break: It was sponging time. We wiped off the sweat, handing it to the guard in exchange for a ladle of water poured haphazardly into our cups. And what a relief that water was. I gulped it down like a fish.

"Thank the suns you're alive." Magnesar slipped next to me, muttering into his cup as if he were drinking.

"Though I'm disappointed the galaxy will never hear the lament I composed for you."

I cringed, but when I looked into his eyes, all I saw was fire. Maybe he saw that in mine, too. He was so… sincere.

"Write it for someone else," I tried once again to channel my inner Blayde. "I'm not dying anytime soon."

"Novalicious," he replied, before we both got zapped for insubordination.

The rest of the day was a dreary carousel ride, going round and round without any purpose or direction. Each moment was just like the last, a repetitive loop of meaningless events that seemed to have no beginning or end. It was like being trapped in a never-ending game of musical chairs, except the chairs were all the same and the music was a broken record stuck on a single note. I couldn't shake the feeling that I was missing something important, but what that something was remained stubbornly out of reach.

Finally, the air zapped for lunch. We sat on the floor in front of our wheels, awaiting our protein patties. At least these were cooked to order and seemed fresh.

"How?" I muttered into the maybe-fresh meat, sitting down next to Magnesar and avoiding all eye contact.

"How what?" He crunched on the patty.

"How are you here?" I hissed. "You're supposed to be safe on the *Traveler*."

He nodded slowly, glancing from side to side. "Blayde is how."

"How did she… never mind." Of course, that woman would find us anywhere. With my time for questions being so limited, I couldn't dare ask him how the absolute heck she knew we were in trouble. "But why you?"

"The first lady is missing." His voice was low and gravelly, yet somehow, even whispered, it sounded strong and confident. "Only logical the first mate be the one to find her."

"I…" I stared at Magnesar. Was he serious? All that intensity I had seen in his eyes… maybe he wasn't the big hero I made him out to be. Maybe he was just the washed-up rockstar Zander knew him as.

Oh, frash.

But now I knew the most reassuring fact in all of history: Blayde was here. If she hadn't rescued me yet, that meant something more important was going down: maybe the rescue of Zander and Marce? It was mildly flattering: not being Blayde's priority meant she either thought I could handle myself, or that I wasn't worth rescuing in the first place. Hard to tell with her.

My heart fluttered; if she was back, she must have figured out how to save Felling. Which meant I could stop feeling guilty for letting her die on my watch, if she was no longer, you know, technically dead.

Before I could ask Magnesar anything else, the zap to announce the beginning of the afternoon work shift broke through our meal break. And back we were at the wheels.

By the time the day was over, my skin was sticky and raw, my breath stinging. I fell back on the smelly mat on the floor and my eyes shut instantly.

My eyes opened as quickly as they closed, and the new, same day began again.

Except it wasn't the same. Magnesar's alabaster skin did wonders for the bruises blossoming over his body. His lip was cut and swollen in at least two places, and an almost imperceptible limp accompanied his walk.

"What happened?" I asked as we marched single file into the wheel room. He shook his head—no. Oh, big brooding Rockstar over here. I wasn't going to be getting anything out of him unless it was through song.

He wasn't looking any better by the next day, quite possibly due to the shiner on the other eye or the scabs on his knuckles. He was being beaten—repeatedly. By whom, I didn't know. But it was another finguy, another one of us. The Sters didn't damage their livestock if they could help it. One of our own had taken it out on Magnesar's face, for no apparent reason other than to cause him pain.

His singing wasn't bad enough to warrant harm. Something bigger was going on here.

On the fifth day since Magnesar's return, we were eating our protein patties while trying to recover from the morning's run, when out of nowhere, Marn was thrown to the ground, screaming. A scrawny man was sitting atop her, desperately trying to wrestle the food from her hands, so ravenous he was foaming at the mouth.

Instincts kicked in and I lunged at him, crashing him away from Marn. I rolled across the ground and sprang to my feet with a shout. His face contorted in rage as he charged at me, like a wild beast.

The onlookers seemed to sense the gravity of the situation and formed a circle around us. Their presence stirred feelings of familiarity within me—was it not so long ago that I had dueled with Blayde and murdered her with a sword? The last time, I had been mortal and untrained. It was strange how that felt like a lifetime ago, yet life on this planet had made me into something new, something tougher.

I didn't like the person this planet was turning me into. But I was getting dang good in a fistfight. That and the brain goop was becoming a lovely little treat. I easily evaded his attack, delivering a punishing blow to his abdomen and follow it up with an uppercut to his nose. This left me open to land a bone-shattering chop above his kidney. He fell forward gasping for breath.

I had been so lost in the adrenaline of the fight that I'd forgotten the true enemy here. Before I could prepare my defense, I was lifted into the air, kicking and screaming against the invisible grasp of flux. And, for the first time since my capture, I was brought outside.

Darkness still covered the planet. The glowing forest was too far away to lend its light to us, making this patch of dead earth the only thing I could see. A strong wind blew across the complex, cold enough to reach my bones. My fists clenched.

Maybe it was time to run for it.

But the flux was too strong. I was brought into a small glass office and held out towards the Ster behind the desk, as a child would hold out the fat toad they'd just spent the last hour catching.

This was the first time I'd seen furniture in a Ster's space, other than at the vet's. What did they even have to put on tables? I hadn't seen them handle papers or tablets.

"What's this?"

The Ster behind the desk was the largest I'd ever seen: its bulb could rival a weather balloon. The air hummed around them, like an irregular heartbeat. My breath hitched in my throat. You could tell they were in charge around here—or, at least, it was them who reaped the benefits.

"I just broke up a fight in the wheel room, sir," the Ster holding me said, shaking me up and down a little.

"So?"

"So, this finguy tackled a male twice her size." Was it me, or did they sound—excited? "And didn't receive a single blow."

Sters didn't have eyes, so it was hard to tell if they were looking at you. But oh boy did I feel this one staring at me. My skin prickled—they were scanning me somehow.

"What do you want me to do with this?" they scoffed. "It's not as if we don't have enough fighters. You know very well that it's too small!"

"I swear, sir, this one's an exception," the overseer went on, dropping me on the desk. I could try to make a run for it now, it would be the best time for it—but there was a door between me and the yard, three meters' worth of a slippery glass wall I couldn't climb even if I did have shoes.

I opted for standing still, making myself as small as possible. Me, a fighting finguy? Whatever do you mean?

The larger Ster was done with this conversation. "What makes you think so?"

"I don't think so, I know so." The Ster who brought me in nodded vigorously. "This one's different. It's trained."

"Are you… are you sure?"

"Positive. Listen, boss, if I enter her in the…"

"It's your loss." The large Ster threw their tentacles in the air. A current ran through me, scanning me again—I shuddered. "The odds will be… well, it's your gamble. And if you break her, you owe me a fresh one. I take it this one is a runner?"

"Don't worry, sir, you won't be losing a runner tonight." I was lifted back off the table with a tentacle, like a cat who'd overstayed their welcome.

"See that I don't."

The Ster carried me back out into the yard, getting some distance between them and the bigger one before letting out a squeal of delight, or so I could only assume; it sounded like a puppy farting. They quickly pulled themself together, clutching me tight in their tentacle as they drifted away from the large building they'd been keeping me in.

"You're going to win!" Did they know that I could understand them? How much did they want me to hear? "And you're going to be called the Princess Punch, and you're going to take them down and surprise them all, and we're going to be rich, you're going to make me rich, oh yes, very rich…"

This was it. My only chance. I had to take it.

I took a breath, settled my gut, and plunged forward, sinking my teeth into the tentacle.

It tasted of rotting earth and sea. It tasted like my own guts. Everything in my stomach went flying, burning my mouth and cheeks. It was awful. I tasted that, too. I choked down my disgust and bit down until the cold blood touched my teeth. Then I bit down harder still.

The Ster roared, sparking. It shook me out, and I dropped the appendage, falling to the ground. I felt the wetness around my mouth, numbness in the deepest depths of my being. I wiped my mouth on the edge of my sleeve.

I barely had time to think between the time my feet hit the ground and starting sprinting. I ran, not knowing in which direction, just that I had to get away. The speed I had been holding back all week came back tenfold, the wind stinging my face as I pushed through the air.

They'd made me faster than I was before. Now, they could watch me run.

The buildings were behind me now, the fence ahead. The wall of chain links was ahead of me, waiting for me to climb it. There was no time to find a way under, no time to find a way through, so all that was left was up. I grabbed a link, ready to pull myself upwards, to salvation, to freedom, only to feel the sensations of hundreds of bees swarming through my veins. My blood rushed, alive, through my body, my fingers forming a fist around the metal.

My senses went haywire. There was nothing but shimmering, pulsating foggy colors, my nose smelling crisp barbecue, my hand stinging and vibrating.

I found myself on the ground, a few meters from the fence—had I been thrown back? The tingle continued around my veins, but I was no longer burning from the inside. As I blinked, my vision cleared, only to see the Ster who had grabbed me. Waiting.

A heavy knot in my stomach, a knot so heavy that I found myself laughing uncontrollably.

I did not have the strength left to escape.

They fluxed me into the air. I groaned, my body dangling as they carried me. Now, the Sters were going to punish me. Hurt me. Or at least, try to. I braced myself —

"This will be our little secret…" the creature murmured. They had wrapped a strip of plant around their bleeding tentacle but seemed oblivious to the pain now.

The Ster brought me back to the wheel room, saying nothing as they left me with the confused looks of the guards.

I was sweating. A normal reaction for someone who had just died of electrocution, one would think. I quickly sponged off, grabbed some water—no one tried to stop me—and returned to my post. Marn said nothing but raised her eyebrows inquisitively. I shrugged. I must have looked a sight.

"What happened to you?" she asked, hours later, as we settled into our sleep mats.

"Nothing, believe it or not. The guard who took me signed me up for something… a fight, I think they said, but there were no more details than that."

"Fight?" She sounded confused, but it was nowhere near what I felt.

"No details. But who was that guy that attacked you this morning? Why…"

"He's native," she explained, sadness creeping into her voice. "Born and raised as an animal. Can't speak, responds only to instinct. He was probably just hungry."

"What?" I said, almost too loud. "He's a…"

"More finguy than human. Pure animal state. He's not the only one here like that."

"That's horrible."

"Yeah, you're telling me." She shuddered. "Most of the people here were born on this planet. They find this crap normal. As for me…"

"Shipwrecked?" I asked. She nodded in response. "What ship?"

"The *Wanderer*," she replied. "You?"

"A shuttle – from the *Traveler*, but she never crashed. She's still up there, somewhere. Hold on, you're actually from the *Wanderer*?"

My mind had been filled with thoughts of escape since I got here. I had almost completely forgotten what had brought us here in the first place. The mission. My mission.

"Yeah, why? Do you know about…"

"All I know is I was told that ship holds some answers for me." I scooted closer to her. "You wouldn't be able to…"

"What exactly are you looking for? We were just a long-range survey ship. Nothing exciting."

"Were you carrying some kind of cargo…?"

"Nah, it was basic recon," she said. "Walda, Curtuk, John, and I—those were my team—we were completing basic training. We thought it was a drill, when the ship started malfunctioning… no one told us anything, we were nobodies. Heck, less than nobodies: 'Out of Alliance Draftees', you know."

"I don't, really."

"Aged out of the child-hire program," she explained. "We got lucky. We became foot soldiers. Not everyone gets rescued like we were."

My eyes went wide. "You were an abductee?"

"My father sold me to pay off his debts, so not exactly." She shrugged again, as if it were no big deal. "But the rest of the group all were."

"I'm sorry." I could not think of anything better than that to say. I would have to have a serious talk with Dany about ending those practices. The child-hire program disgusted me to no end. Is that what Nimien wanted me to see? Did he want me to stop the program, save those kids?

We drifted off to sleep, me swimming in complicated thoughts. What had Nimien sent us here to find? Was he trying to set me up as a savior to these people, or was there something more?

I wasn't a hero. I was barely one in training. I couldn't even run away from this farm.

And then I wasn't drifting off to sleep anymore—I was drifting up. Something was lifting me, fluxing me out of my bed.

I had an increasing suspicion that I wasn't going to get any sleep tonight.

FOURTEEN

A GOOD THUMPING FOR THE SOUL

Zander

THERE'S NO MORE SATISFYING WORKOUT THAN swinging a man over your shoulders. My last opponent landed on the ground, winded, surrounded by his groaning, exhausted peers. I hadn't broken a sweat.

"Need a sec," NoToes squawked, coughing as he tried to catch his breath.

TrueFoot glared at me, a wordless lecture about letting him have it easy, given his handicap. I shook my head *no*: if he had to fight, he had to be ready, with or without toes. I'm an equal opportunity kind of guy. Not to mention he had more potential than any other recruit under my supervision.

"I guess that's it for the day?" NoToes wiped his brow with the bottom of his shirt. "That is, unless you want to beat on us some more?"

"That's it," TrueFoot called from the opposite end of the training pit. "If it were up to me, I'd keep you all here until at least one of your blows landed, but the general said done by 1900, so we're done."

I grabbed my canteen, taking a big swig of water as my trainees filed out of the tent, muttering under their breaths. I pretended not to hear, distracted by the rotten stench of my own body. Great Derzan, I needed a shower. It must have been bad if I was the one noticing. Blayde would have pointed it out days ago, if she had been around, colorful insults piling on the shame.

Stars, I missed her.

"Lieutenant, you have a moment?"

I looked up at Provis. I didn't think he'd be interested in watching my training sessions: he wasn't that kind of General. Void, I think this was the first time I'd seen him outside of the confines of Party City.

"Sure, what's on your mind, General?" I put down the canteen as he approached. The angles of his face were harsher in the plant-light, removing the smooth edge of familiarity. Where had TrueFoot gone?

"Look, it's not that I want you to go easy on them." He ran a hand through his hair. The image of calm confidence was dissolving; something had him on edge. "But none of the rookies are going to learn anything if they only get a second of practice before you knock them down."

"They're lasting a little longer every time," I said. I was used to training with a person who anticipated my every move, who fought like I was a chess match that needed to be won in six moves or less. Ending it in fewer was my goal in every fight. "Maybe they'll make it to two seconds by next week. From what I hear, they could end up fighting something much faster than me on a battlefield."

Provis nodded, wetting his lips. "Even so. Maybe you should give them a fighting chance."

"I showed them the basic moves and how to counter them. They had a fighting chance—they just didn't do much fighting."

He shifted his weight, narrowing his eyes. So much for friendly conversation. What had him so uneasy?

"You think you're clever, don't you?" He raised an eyebrow.

"I don't think I'm *not* clever."

"What?"

I dropped my smile. "Sorry." So much for breaking the tension.

"Is this because of her?" He put a hand on my shoulder. I flinched at the unexpected touch.

"Because of whom?" But I knew exactly who he was talking about.

"The girl." The hand on my shoulder squeezed gently. "The girl you were looking for, the one who never made it to the rescue point. This, this whole… attitude, it's because of her, isn't it?"

I threw off the arm. "Leave her out of this."

He'd brought up the one thing I couldn't think about: Sally.

She had been at the vet, she had been seen breaking through the offensive line. But she hadn't reached the shuttle.

What had happened to her? Had the Sters caught her again? Or was she still out there, still running, lost and afraid?

And what about Marcy? There was no sign of her, anywhere. If I'd lost her, then all the progress we'd made with the Alliance would be lost. Dany would stop at nothing to flay me alive. Let's be honest, we had never been close in our time on Earth, not with both of us pretending not to know the other, trying to out-Terran the other. No, if I came back without Marcy, I'd never be allowed to show my face in Alliance space for the rest of eternity.

I couldn't stay here, training recruits against an enemy they couldn't fight. I needed to go after Sally and Marcy. The rebels just weren't ready, they would never be ready: hundreds of years of occupation were proof of that. Not when half of all humans on this planet were competing in pet shows. This wasn't a rebellion; it was barely survival.

I wasn't enough of an ass to say it out loud.

"Where did you learn to fight, anyway?" asked Provis, a gentle smile drawing on his face. A polite attempt to change the subject? "I've learned every Alliance-adopted form there is, yet I only recognize half the things you pull off on that mat. Where are you from, originally?"

"That's a long story." I dropped my gaze, avoiding his eyes. "You tend to pick up a few things beyond the rim."

"You... left Alliance space?" Provis let out a low whistle. "You must have some stories to tell."

Was he that starved for entertainment? Or just trying to get me to open up? Did I... did I have a fan? Either way, I didn't have the patience for this. He was standing far too close, his body almost touching mine.

"A while ago," I replied. "Got in a few fights. Brawls, mostly. I adapted."

I was a good liar. That was one thing I knew about myself. I told the stories people needed to hear. But nothing I had said so far seemed to faze him.

Finally, I met his gaze. His eyes were wide, sparkling. Familiar. He was... excited? He ran his fingers through his hair again. The air was too hot, this stranger too close. I didn't want to be here, didn't want to be a part of this anymore. I needed to breathe. I needed space. I needed —

"What aren't you telling me?" His breath was thick and syrupy on my nostrils.

I shook my head. "I've got nothing more to tell."

Provis studied me for a long, strained minute. He was shorter than me, yet right now, he stared down at me as if he were a Goliath. My mind was still focused on fighting, still working, planning, scheming, as I did when I was on an adrenaline high. Taking him in, weighing his weaknesses and strengths. He knew his technique, I could tell his patterns: he stood with confidence, alert, and ready for battle. His preferred arm was the right—his preferred leg, strangely, the left.

There was no question I could take him one-to-one. It would take seconds, less if I didn't hold back. I saw where this was going.

"How long?" he asked, as if reading my mind.

I shook my head. "How long what?"

"Have you been fighting." Provis slipped off his coat, tossing it onto a lone chair in the corner of the room. The muscles underneath were thick and ropy. "Have you been running, more likely."

"Long enough," I said, maybe a little too harshly. Provis's face was right in mine, inches away. I was too shocked to move. Why was he so close? Was he trying to prove something?

"Then let's have a go at it."

I should have seen it coming. "What, now?"

"Fight me. If you beat me, you teach those kids any way you see fit. I win, I call the shots. How does that sound? Doesn't matter. I'm your superior officer—we're doing this."

And now the boot drops. This is what he wants, what they all want—to see how they stand up against a story. All this talk about being happy to have me on their side when deep down they want to see if they can land a punch. "I was going to take a shower." I breathed through gritted teeth. "This is a waste of time."

He lifted his brow. "Afraid of a real challenge?"

"Just bored of not having one."

Finally, he stepped away, but it was to stand on the training mat, arms open wide: an invitation. I groaned internally; he was not going to let this go. And he was right: he was my commanding officer… while I played along, of course.

I turned, scanning him from head to toe. This was going to be ridiculous. Four moves, and I could see them all now. But still, there was something about him that made me wary: an unpredictable element that put me on edge.

One swift move and he could be out in a second – but I was above that, wasn't I?

"Jeez, would you listen to the man?"

Sally's voice was shrill in the night air, the girl herself—or the vision of her, rather—sitting backwards on the seat where Provis had tossed his coat. She brushed it lazily. This time, she was dressed like a Tax'ien cheerleader: long creamy-white hair that reached for the ceiling; thick layers of semi-transparent pants, paired with tight black boots running the length of her feet until they reached her midriff; free hand resting on her hip between sharp teeth that barely met. All three of her arms were bare. Not sure where the extra arm came from, but I suppose if she was Tax'ien, she had to be accurate.

Stars, not again. I ignored her, focusing instead on Provis. The instant I stepped on the mat, he began to circle, eyeing me down, weighing my weaknesses and strengths, same as I'd done to him.

A strike to the kidneys should do the trick.

"You've lost your edge, Zander." Sally let out a heavy sigh. "*Oh, how long will it take for me to pull him down?* This isn't some equation to solve, it's a fight. Raw and bloody and real. Now act like it."

The blow came out of nowhere, slamming into my cheekbone and sending my head spinning.

Frash. I had been paying too much attention to Sally. The blow was enough to make me lose my footing, and Provis flipped me on my back and pinned me down with his knee. An easy move and a beginner's mistake on my part.

"You treat it like a game, love." Sally leaned in front of me, her face obscuring my field of view. "Right now, you're letting him win, afraid to show your true self. You need to snap out of that."

"Have a better way of doing this I have yet to understand?" I muttered into the mat.

"What's that?" Provis asked. His satisfied smile was so wide it stretched across my full field of vision.

"Nice punch," I said. "Impressive."

He leapt up, chest puffed out. Score one for him. He wasn't going to get another. I rose to my feet, putting on a show of a slow recovery before taking up a defensive position.

"Fight like your life is on the line." The ghost of Sally's touch flickered on my cheek. "Trust me."

"But it isn't," I said under my breath. "It never is."

"Which is why you overthink things." She patted me on the back. "You win. You run the motions. You match, counter, deflect, as if you were making a sandwich. But you take nothing out of the experience. Pain is the best teacher. Start learning again."

"I can think clearly this way, it's better." I held up my fists to Provis. "I leave myself off the battlefield, I win every time."

"You don't learn from victories; you know that as well as I do," Sally retorted. "Stop thinking. Start learning."

I put her out of my mind as Provis advanced. The tips of my fingers quivered, twitching for a fight. I wasn't going to move first, so he did. I predicted the move, calculated three more, grabbed his leg as it came to me, and twisted. He fell flat on his face. I seized his arms, pinning them against his back. After a quick count to five I stood back up, offered a hand, which he promptly refused, and we were back to circling again.

And had I learned anything? No.

"One to one," said Provis. "We're tied."

"So it seems."

"Wow, so educational!" Sally laughed. "One move, the same you use every time!"

"One last go?" I asked, shaking her out of my head. "As you can probably tell, I desperately need that shower."

"Okay, so you're not listening to me." She rolled her eyes. "I am your subconscious, bud, I was just playing nice before. Get ready to hear."

All at once, my heart thumped against my chest like a jackhammer, sending surges of panic and rage through my veins. The icy tendrils of fear crept up my arms, while the searing burn from the punch on my cheek remained. I felt the tail end of the snap reverberate through my neck. The world spun under me. The world was red, and not just the blood in my eyeballs: red pulsing, the red of lava and fire, the red of blood. The world was on fire.

"What?" I gasped, a sound I could barely hear over the roar of blood echoing in my ears. My heart threatened to burst.

Sally waved from the sidelines. "Just switched those sensors back on." She grinned. "Enjoy the ride."

My mind reeled as it tried to comprehend the pain. Provis's first punch had been so good it would have knocked a man senseless, which was exactly what it was trying to do to me right now. There was the smell of hot metal, burning rubber, tears, stinging my throat.

"You okay there?" Provis asked. "You want to stop?"

"No, no, I'm fine."

I was beginning to seriously hate my subconscious. No matter how cute she looked right now. I had to get my act together. I needed to plan to predict, but my mind was foggy.

I saw the elbow quick enough, but did nothing to deflect it, knowing I could take it and use the opening to get him—but the pain that exploded in my sternum was like nothing I had experienced before. I gasped, but there was no air for me to breathe, nothing to stop the burn.

"Losing pain was never part of the equation," said Sally. "It has always been your warning system. With immortality, it had nothing to say: you thought you had nothing left to learn, so you stopped listening. Can you hear it now, Zander-boy?"

The blows came from every direction: up down, straight on, so quickly my mind couldn't keep up. The world was spinning, and I was lost, pushing away Provis's punches with a ferocity I hadn't felt in… well, ever, but nothing seemed to slow them down.

I was falling behind, responding rather than initiating. I needed to catch up, and would have to do it with burning lungs and sparks of pain. I dropped to the ground as Provis swung his arm, sliding through his legs, throwing back my elbow and jamming it into his kidneys. He muffled a cry of pain, spinning around and throwing blows ten times as fast. I had not accomplished much.

"You've done this a million times before, Zander!" Sally shouted. "Use the panic! Don't let it hold you back, channel it!"

I clamped my hand around the arm that suddenly lunged at me, but Provis broke free with a violent jerk and lunged his foot towards my hip. The kick crashed into my thigh with an explosive force, a searing fire spreading through my leg and up my spine. My vision blurred from the overwhelming pain, and nausea rose in my gut, threatening to spill out.

I gritted my teeth against it and threw myself forward, rolling around his leg and coming up behind him. He was already swinging at me with the other arm, but I managed to duck beneath it and grab his wrist, twisting it back and sending him stumbling to the ground.

Before I could even think of a follow-up move, he had scrambled to his feet and pivoted away from me, ready for another strike. His movements were agile, skillful—he had been trained well. I hesitated for a second before charging forward again, this time going for a shoulder throw as Provis swung his foot backwards towards me.

He was winning.

I could lose.

Losing could mean death.

As suddenly as the pain came, a jolt journeyed through my mind, a jolt of pure understanding. I knew what Provis felt, what he feared the second he began to fight.

I understood then—*I feared death.*

In that moment, I forgot my immortality, forgot the lack of consequence, and truly feared for the first time that I could remember. I was no longer fighting to win—I was fighting for my life.

I leapt into the air and kicked Provis square in the chest. He fell to the floor, winded, trying to push himself up, but he was struggling to catch his breath, arms failing. I pressed myself on him, using my body weight to pin him down, to end the fight.

"You win," he panted, slapping the mat. For some reason the air seemed stiller then.

"You okay?" I asked, but before I could move, he reached up, took my head in his hands and planted his lips squarely on mine.

My heart racing, the pain coursing through my face, I had no other choice but to feel the gentleness there, the eagerness, the heat that filled me. And for an instant I let it happen, basking in the rush of endorphins that flowed from his touch.

Oh. *Frash.*

I pulled away, gasping, flying to my feet. In an instant I was at the other side of the tent, head swimming, hands on my face. My skin was hot, sticky under my fingers.

"Zander, wait," Provis called. "I'm sorry, I—"

And then, I heard it, my ears picking up something other than my racing heartbeat. Thunder in the distance. Explosions.

"What was that?" I wiped the tingling feeling from my lips. Stopping the warmth from spreading any further.

My heart physically sank as I realized what was happening. As the sound of rolling thunder got louder—closer. As cries rose to fill the air. Provis must have understood as well, because he reached for the gun sitting on the table, flicking off the safety and holding it poised.

“Head to munitions and make sure our people are armed.” He marched out the door, head held high, years of training having prepared him for this exact moment. “We’re under attack.”

FIFTEEN

GOTTA FIGHT THEM ALL, THE SALLY EDITION

Sally

THEY SAY IF YOU FALL IN A DREAM, YOU WAKE up—so if you're lifted in reality, why doesn't that make you fall asleep?

My body went as stiff as a British upper lip. Fear rose in my throat, and I could no longer breathe, fighting the wave of shock running through me like a torrent. I couldn't fight it. I couldn't move. I felt like the first victim of a poltergeist movie, unable to do anything but shudder internally. How I had ever gotten a minute's sleep here, knowing I was surrounded by beings capable of lifting me whenever they felt like it, was beyond me.

I wasn't alone: in the darkness, I saw others, each rising through the air like little bubbles in a bubble bath. Four, five, maybe. At the top of the pit, the Sters waited for us, their dull glow the only light with which I could see.

Before I was thrown into a box, of course.

The flux cut and I was dropped onto the cold floor, lid slamming shut above me before I could catch my breath, plunging the interior back into darkness. I let my eyes adjust, listened to my breaths, the sound of an electric motor pushing up and down in my chest. The box was tight, barely larger than a coffin: not much room to move around in. Feeling around I managed to find a piece of cotton-like material, which felt a whole lot like a bathing suit.

Oh great. It was a leotard.

"Get dressed, you're up first," the Ster ordered. The same Ster I had bitten, if I were a betting woman. My ears rang with the electrical hum of their voice.

A leotard. It was so much nicer than the pants I was wearing now. Less fabric, but less blood, too—a nice trade-off? And it wasn't covered in my patented bile.

I did as I was told, trying not to think about what was waiting for me wherever we were going. Getting changed was a tall order, seeing how small the box was, but I managed in the end, ridding myself of the loose shirt and pants that belonged in a Victorian prison. I tossed the bundled farm clothes in a corner, hoping I would never see them again.

Finally, my box stopped moving—they'd put me down on something solid. The room around us must have been large, the charges echoing through it making it sound as though thousands of Sters were grouped together up there.

I sat up straight, wrapping my arms around my knees, waiting. My Tinkerbell moment, except barefoot and smelling like sewage. I was shaking so hard I could have been jelly.

An eternity later, the static snapped as if a breaker had tripped. A voice emerged from the hubbub, loud and clear —Too loud.

"People, people, calm down!" it said. "We'll start with an easy one, all right?" A spark filled the air—excitement? A cheer? "We have the reigning champion of the ring – The Flame!" More electrical cheer followed. "Who will be fighting the newest of the new—the, ahem, the—Princess Punch."

Not many cheers there. But a weight descended on my shoulders as the realization hit me.

First, that in whatever language these creatures were speaking, Princess Punch alliterated.

It also sounded terrible.

And second, and perhaps more troubling… this was a match. A fight.

Against another finguy.

I dropped my head into my hands. Shit. I should have known. Wherever life-forms are subjugated, there's illegal fighting. Dog fighting. Cock fighting. Heck, even Pokémon. And here, finguies playing by the Sters' rules—or lack of.

Suddenly, my box was lifted into the air—and rattled. They fluxed me around and around, until I bounced off the corners. I felt as if my life had been sucked into a vacuum cleaner. They wanted to rile me up, ready me for a fight.

And it was working. My mind was no longer murky. It was clear—well, as clear as the drugs in the back of my head allowed it to be—my legs were dry, and I had to get out.

I should have stayed out of its way this morning, just another animal on their farm. But I had showed my hand and now I was going to pay for it. I had gotten myself into this mess. I would have to get myself out.

I could fight and take down the opponent. I wasn't a warrior, I just had the unfair advantage of learning from my deadliest mistakes. I'd picked up a few things from Zander and Blayde. But if I won, I would be coming back here to fight again. Which led me to my bigger predicament: if I let myself get beaten to a pulp, only to have my wounds magically heal in front of their eyes—or whatever sense they used to see shit—then I would be in a world of hurt.

I couldn't win—but I couldn't get hurt, either. It was lose-lose.

My box was dropped on the ground, winding me. With a jolt it was turned on its side, and the lid fell off. A gentle breeze tickled my face, making my skin tingle. I shivered, not from the cold, but from the pungent scent of something rotting.

We were in a ring. A makeshift, circular ring, ten meters or so in diameter, cordoned off with a rough metal fence. I stood barefoot on a cold floor mat, goosebumps climbing up my skin. I finally looked down at my leotard, and with a shock saw it was a faded, pink color. Much too tight.

And when I looked up, I realized I was lucky. The man across from me had it even worse with his leotard: ripped, drenched, and black as the night. And absolutely way too tight in all the wrong places. I cringed for him.

Then he pounded his chest, roaring, and any empathy I had for him shot out the proverbial window. My adversary was a wall of pure muscle, and clearly capable of doling out a barrage of destruction.

The Flame. I had seen him in the sleeping pit before, one of the farm laborers. Despite his muscle, he was never on hamster-wheel crew: could I use that to my advantage? I had been running every day for seven days straight. I was exhausted, but my cardio was better than I'd ever had it on Earth. If he wasn't on wheel-crew, then maybe he was all muscle, no heart. Could I somehow wear him out?

A bell or a gong or something filled the air, sending the Sters into a frenzy. It was surreal, to be in a crowd so big, but to hear nothing. I could feel the rush of electricity, the knowledge of hooting and screaming coming through my translator. But the only sound to reach my eardrum was the roar of my opponent.

Screw it, let's find a third option. I turned on my heels and ran. The barrier was close, low; I could leap over it if I tried —

The shock that ran through my veins was like liquid fire injected straight into my heart. I gasped, falling to my knees, clutching my chest. Of course they wouldn't just let me run. I gritted my teeth against the electricity, pushed myself back to my feet. I guess there was no option three on the table. I was going to have to fight—but where was…

I didn't see the blur of his body until it was too late, and he'd already tackled me to the ground.

Instinct kicked in on the way down. I twisted my body, grabbing the man's broad shoulders and using his weight to continue his momentum and throw him over me. I slammed my feet against the ground, pushing myself up—only for him to grab at my wrist before I could move away, giving it a sharp tug strong enough to dislocate my shoulder.

I screamed in shock. The crowd fizzled for more. The static in the room was so strong my hair stood on end.

You call that a fight? Blayde's voice rang through my head. *You need to give them a show if you want to survive!*

I staggered back to my feet, touching the place where the socket had snapped. I could feel the nub of the bone through the skin. I locked eyes with Flame, who was watching me, scanning me, from across the ring. Without breaking eye contact, I shoved it back into place, then turned my scream into a shout of power, roaring at my opponent.

Not something I made a habit of. But the rush of adrenaline that followed was almost drug-like. The endorphins from having my shoulder back in place, the power of channeling a scream —

Come at me, bro.

He rushed forward once again, this time maneuvering to lift me into the air, bringing me up, up, up, then tossing me like I was nothing more than a rag doll, to fall on the ground with a crash. I rolled out of the way and back to my feet, keeping my eye on the target.

I roared and charged the man, throwing an arm out in a vain attempt to reach his gut. He was built like a powerhouse, his abs made of cement. He grinned, throwing a palm at my face—shoving my nose back up into my skull.

What a crunch. I was a human potato chip.

My head spun with shock. I fell to the ground, where he threw punch after punch after punch at the arms blocking my face, until my vision started to fizzle out.

I could, however, still see his dull, broad face above me, his empty, emotionless eyes. I saw in them the same expression I had seen that morning, in the so-called native, the human that was no longer human.

Flame was born and bred on this planet. Raised by Sters for one thing only. And he was not fighting for any other reason than he enjoyed it.

Maybe I didn't have to feel so bad about handing his ass to him.

I threw up my foot and hit him square in the groin. A low blow for a low game. He yelped and toppled forward, giving me the space I needed to hop to my feet. So much for trying to draw out the match. I didn't want to spend another second in this shithole.

If there was one thing I'd learned from Zander, it was how to throw a punch. And when you're not worried about pain, not worried about what's going to happen to your arm, you get a killer follow-through. With one strong swing across the face, I knocked him out. Flame tipped forward, out for the count.

The room went silent. Truly silent: no more fizzling, no more charge in the air.

I pushed myself to my feet, glancing around at the crowd. Every Ster on the compound must have been there, maybe even more. There were dozens of them, maybe a hundred, floating above us in silence, something I would have been proud of if I wasn't currently trapped.

The room erupted in a cheer, an electric roar of excitement. My hair stood on end as the audience gave me a standing ovation, hundreds of tentacles whipping the air into a hurricane.

I'd survived my first fight.

"Princess Punch wins!" One of the Sters drifted down into the ring. If I wasn't mistaken, there was a hint of unease in their voice. Maybe this was my chance. Maybe I could bite them, use them as —

No. Too many of them. I couldn't even get out of the ring; I wasn't going to get any further than that.

"But the night does not end here!" they continued, "Up next, the returning champion… Ravenous Roar!"

I braced myself, but no one was fluxing me out—was I meant to fight this guy too? Were they going to keep me in here until I collapsed? I held up my fists: maybe lightning did strike twice.

Then they dropped Magnesar into the ring, and my mind went blank.

I should have realized this was what he was being subjected to, night after night. He was wearing a tight blue leotard, his alabaster skin on full display, every mark and bruise like flowers on bone china.

And I was meant to add to them.

Magnesar looked crestfallen as he stepped towards me, his face paler than I'd ever seen it. He flexed his fists, frowning.

"Sorry, Sally cakes," he muttered under his breath, and the bell-thing rang. "I'm a lover, not a fighter."

We circled, sizing each other up. Unlike Flame, Magnesar was built for endurance, and it was obvious he could take a punch. Whatever he had endured as an interstellar Rockstar had prepared him to take shit for hours on end. Reigning champion and all. I also happened to like him and wasn't looking forward to picking a fight.

"We, um, should probably trade a few blows," he said.

I nodded, running my tongue over my crusty dry lips. "Just avoid the face?"

"Totally un-novalicious!" He snorted and rushed forward.

I blocked his flurry of blows, taking the shock in my forearms, unable to get a punch in edgewise. But, like a true gentleman, he kept his blows low, aiming for the abs. We were both breathing heavily by the time the bell rang out again.

"We get rounds?" I glanced up at the silent Sters. The air hummed, but nothing like the electricity of their cheers. Were they bored? Maybe booing? *Come on, give us a sign here!*

"Oh, you decimated The Flame too fast to know." Magnesar took a step back, rolling his head. There weren't any towels or water, so we just kept circling each other.

And then it hit me.

"We're talking," I said.

He raised an eyebrow. "So?"

"Look. Or listen, I guess." I made a big show of stretching as I spoke. "Feel that? They don't care. I don't think they can hear us."

"Frash, you're right," said Magnesar. A smile drew itself clumsily on his face. "So long— "

"No chatter!" shouted the MC. We were fluxed apart, thrown to opposite sides of the pit. There went that idea.

"Ah!" I screamed out of shock. The energy fizzled again.

But… the Sters couldn't understand us. They never could, else they would respond, right? Our translators would have gotten through to them. Except for Gluuk, who could understand me just fine, due to its weird chosen-one powers or whatever genetic abnormality allowed it to hear me.

So they knew we could talk, but didn't know what we were talking about. Hence chatter being forbidden. They must feel it, sense it in the way they sense their way around a room, sense it how they were watching this match right now.

The bell rang again. This time, we didn't hold back. We ran at each other, screaming, earning us an electrical cheer from the crowd. We swung punches at each other, ducking and weaving and putting on the very best of shows.

"We need to escape!" I screamed as I flung blows at his shoulder.

"I'd love to, Sally cakes. I could try to sing them all into a false sense of superiority?"

Did his race have some kind of magical singing powers? I didn't have time to find out.

"I'm sure—I can escape —my Ster—on our way—between here—and the pit."

I braced myself, taking Magnesar's punch to the kidneys. The crowd cheered again.

"The field generator," sang Magnesar, "is at the exact center of the farm!" He attempted a tackle, and I dodged out of the way. "If you can take it down, we can make a ru-un for it and get out of… haaaaarm's way."

My ears tingled at the terrible rhyme. Maybe it sounded better in whatever language he thought he was singing in.

I grabbed his arm, twisted it, and forced him back. Unfortunately, that meant we were back to circling, but the Sters hadn't stopped us: they really had no idea. We could scream whatever we wanted, so long as we screamed over each other.

I had to get closer so we could talk, and this was the only way. This time I ran at him, his eyes going wide as he took my assault and threw me over him. I sailed through the air, landing face-first in the dirt. He jumped on top of me, grabbing my neck in a tight headlock.

"But" —I hissed, and he slacked slightly — "the others?"

His grip slacked again. "You want to save—everyone?"

"We have to try."

I gasped, slapping the ground, attempting to forfeit. But that meant nothing to the Sters.

"Maybe we can use their flux against them," said Magnesar. "Have them float us to… heaven!"

His rhymes were getting more accurate, and yet, simultaneously, more obnoxious.

"What do you have in mind?"

"Bedrolls!"

The electricity in the air was rising— we had to do something, and fast. I took a deep breath and plunged against Magnesar's arm, letting him choke me more, more, more —

"What are you doing?" He tried to slacken his grip, but I was pushing too hard.

"Don't worry about me," I muttered. "I'll get over it."

I plunged into deep, dark nothing. My time in the ring was up: and so was my time on this farm.

Whatever it took.

SIXTEEN

THE BATTLE FOR PARTY CITY

Zander

WAR HAD COME TO OUR DOOR, LIKE THE RUDE houseguest that it was.

The sky was lighter than I'd seen since arriving, but not the comforting plant-light kind, no—this was the unnatural light of fire and smoke and burning flesh. It was a nightmarish assault on my senses like nothing before; the smell of sweat, steel, and oil; the roar of ships; the screams of men.

I took a giant gulp of air. My heavy footsteps echoed in the halls of Party City as I rushed to the armory, the chaos of war raging around me. It was a world I knew all too well, a place of familiar discomfort where chaos and brutality were my companions. But amidst the terror, I found a strange sense of relief. War had become my normality, and I had adapted to its rhythm of suffering and destruction. This is what I knew how to do. This is what I was good at. My body relaxed into the role.

Sally jogged alongside me, backwards, her gaudy apparel looking more than a little out of place. An irrepressible smirk spread across her entire face.

"Nonsense," she quipped, accurately responding to my internal musings. "The last time you led an army, your uniform had sequins."

"Go away! Can't you see I'm busy?"

"Oh, no, I think I'll hang about for a while." She beamed. "It's pretty obvious you can't do without me."

An explosion rang out to my left—too close. My heart threw itself into a frenzy, pounding so hard against my ribcage I worried it might break free. Sally laughed.

"Turn me back," I snapped. "Turn everything back off, or whatever. Turn it off."

"What, the pain?"

"Yes, the pain! We're under attack, and I can't fight like this, I…"

I had stopped running. My feet no longer listened to me. I was stuck in the middle of the path, soldiers rushing around me, but I couldn't lift a single frashing foot.

I had never asked for my subconscious to start lecturing me. Yet there it was, turning pain on and off in my mind as it pleased. How was I meant to do my job if my own mind was against me?

"Nothing's changed, Zander." Sally placed her hand on my chest, absorbing the pangs of my now-beating heart. "You're *you*. Now go and fight."

"But…"

"Now, Zander!" Her face was red with fury. "Fight like your men have to fight, *are* fighting, right now! Go!"

I clenched my fists, my body tense and coiled. Sweat beaded on my forehead, and the muscles in my neck ached as I spat out my words.

"I don't remember asking for your help!" My voice was tight from the pain. Every movement was agony. I couldn't fight, not like this…

"Yes, you can," she replied. I forgot she was in my head, once again. "Zander, they need you! Run!"

My feet finally got the memo, and I ran, almost crouched, hands over my ears to save them from the sound, that horrible noise, my pace jagged as I tried to find my way through the confusing maze of tents, so different by war-light.

The ground erupted beneath me. A shockwave pushed me off my feet and sent me flying into the air, only for me to tumble face-first to the ground. My hands covered my head instinctively as the world spun, the earth revolving around my body. Pieces of oversized confetti flew around me as the wall shattered.

I pushed myself back to my feet, overwhelmed by the loss of sensation in my legs. They shook so forcefully they had gone numb. I cursed myself. I had to keep going. My running became more jagged now, the straight line lost completely as I tried to make a mad dash for the artillery shed.

The Sters were bombing us. Somehow, they had found our base and brought their full force with them. I could imagine them, cradling the explosives in their tentacles as they drifted above us, dropping them at their leisure. Raining destruction from above as easily as a child squashing ants.

A red alert rang out inside my head. My muscles were burning, my lungs… on fire. I couldn't think, but I *needed* to. Sters didn't attack on foot—they didn't even have *feet.* What were our men shooting at?

The battle had become relentless, with neither side giving ground nor showing signs of tiring. The air around us hummed with sound—gunfire ringing out in all directions, interspersed with screams that echoed through the night.

I arrived at the site of the armory—or what was left of it. A ragged crater had replaced it, the edges still sizzling with the heat of destruction. The entire outside wall had been blasted away, revealing a world in shades of orange. I swore under my breath.

A weapon—I desperately needed something to defend myself with. I grabbed the closest thing, which appeared to have been, at some point, a lampshade, though I had never seen a lamp in the camp before. It was the only item of sufficient size nearby: everything else had been reduced to ash.

I took a deep breath and rushed at the sounds of fighting.

"Oh, for the love of Trud!" Fury ripped through ShortThumb's voice as she pulled at her cropped hair in frustration. She tossed her empty rifle to the ground. She had found refuge behind what was formerly a storage lean-to, the large strip of scrap metal from what was clearly once part of a ship formed a thick barrier between her and the oncoming army. I dove next to her.

"We can't win this fight!" she said. "There's too many of them!"

I peered through the gap between two pieces of bent sheet metal and saw that she was right. Soldiers had scattered and now cowered behind tents and piles of ammunition boxes, avoiding the spray of explosives coming from every angle.

"Trud?" I crouched beside her, picked up her rifle and handed it back.

"God of last resorts." She panted heavily, then laughed. "This is empty!"

"It's heavy. It's blunt. Makes for a good mace."

"And I suppose you can use a lampshade as a mace as well?"

"I could, I mean…" She was right: there wasn't much I could do with it. "It doesn't matter. I don't even know what we're up against."

"You haven't seen?" Her eyes went wide. "They sent… they sent *us,* Zander. Finguies. Battle finguies. Like rabid dogs, they are. It's not a pretty sight."

I tried to resist the urge to hyperventilate as I took a deep, shuddering breath to try to calm my racing heart. How could I have been so foolish? We had all convinced ourselves that the Sters wouldn't consider us a real threat, but what greater sign of our insignificance than sending our own people against us? A chill ran through me.

"What about weapons?" I couldn't think, only in terms of strategy. "How are they armed?"

"The foot soldiers have got loads of iron things. Clubs. Axes. Pointy, stabby things. Weapons more for clobberin' than for slicin'."

"We need helmets," I pointed out. "Or they'll crush our skulls like…"

The scrap metal barricade rang like a gong as a poker came flying down between us. A man dropped right into camp, wearing *our* uniform—the Sters had sent us *people*.

ShortThumb let out a squawk like a seagull, scrambling to her feet as the enemy finguy raised his weapon, aiming it at her face. I barely had time to get a grip on the soldier before he rolled, coming up and snarling in my face. ShortThumb was right: the man looked rabid, no humanity in his eyes, only bloodlust. I tried to push him away, but he wouldn't budge. His arms were rigid in my grasp.

With all the strength I could muster, I gave one final shove to the feral soldier, and he stumbled backwards, tripping over his own feet as he fell back into the pile of scrap metal from which we'd emerged seconds earlier.

He scrambled to his feet, brandishing the blunt iron above his head as he rushed towards us.

I slammed the lampshade over his head, kicking him square in the chest and ripping the poker from his grip, swinging it in a wide arc to slam into the rib cage of the soldier behind me, the cracking sound erupting into the air along with the distant gunfire. He collapsed to the ground; his breathing ragged.

I turned to the first man and slashed the poker across his legs. His screams filled my ears as he collapsed.

"Kill him, kill him!" ShortThumb was shouting. I reached down to pick up the iron club the second man had been carrying and tossed it to her.

"He's out of commission," I said. "We need to fight our way through this. Any idea how many troops they sent against us?"

"No way to tell." She hoisted the club with both hands, biting her lip. "Their eyes, they were… they were red."

I shuddered. "Probably just the lighting."

"No, they're definitely red." She crouched beside the finguy, picking his eye open. It didn't wake. "Trud. They're not entirely… us, are they? They're something…else…"

I put my hand on her shoulder. She was trembling. Frash.

"They're the enemy." I reached down to grab the metal helmet the soldier had been wearing. The Sters had truly made this race their own. They'd been *made* to fight us. ShortThumb was right: they weren't all that human anymore. They were something entirely different.

"Let's get out of here." ShortThumb grabbed the other free helmet, slamming it on her head. "There's too many of them. The Sters know we're set up here. We need to evac."

She was right. Outside the holes in the walls, Party City was on fire. There was nothing left to save. Nothing left to fight for but our lives. Tears filled my eyes as I watched our men being cut down one after another, hewn like blades of grass ripped away by a stormy wind. We were doomed.

"Right." I nodded. "Protocol. Yes. Find the meeting point. Run. Run!"

She took off, springing out the window and tearing off in the direction of the mountains. I wouldn't be following her. I still had work to do. The camp could not be saved, but our people could.

"Sally?" I shouted to the burning sky. "Now would be a good time to reverse what you did to me!"

No answer.

Frash me.

I shook my head and ran towards the gunfire.

Smoke and dust filled the air in the tumult of the fighting frenzy, making it hard to breathe. The noise was deafening. There were soldiers everywhere, of both camps, almost impossible to distinguish until it was too late. The enemy looked like us, fought like us. Their weapons were a mix of broken furniture and old guns—like ours.

The sense of doom descended on our camp. So many of us lost too soon. We had been overwhelmed, and we were losing ground fast. Our lines were thinning as more and more of our people fell victim to the enemy's relentless assault.

I grabbed my poker with both hands and swung in all directions, trying to protect what was left of my comrades while buying time for them to retreat. But it seemed our situation was hopeless; they had us outnumbered and outmatched in every way imaginable.

Amid the chaos, I spotted TrueFoot. His movements were supernatural, like he was possessed by some divine force that rendered him unstoppable as he punched and kicked his way through his opponents, dodging weapons with ease. It was like he had unleashed a wild, unstoppable force within himself and no blade or arrow could touch him. He fought on, relentlessly pushing toward our enemies' lines in an attempt to break them apart from within. Everywhere he went, our enemies were pushed back further still, until eventually their attack began to falter and weaken.

All it took was for a single enemy blade to find its mark. TrueFoot stumbled. For a moment, it seemed like he might be able to recover, but then he slumped to the ground, and I knew it was over.

I sprinted towards him, my heart pounding in my chest. The sounds of battle faded away as I drew closer, until all I could hear was the pounding of my own footsteps. The was so much blood, oh stars, so much blood. He looked up at me, motionless, and impossibly alive. I knelt by his side, not knowing what else to do.

"Listen, kid," TrueFoot wheezed, blood oozing from his mouth. He reached for my hand and squeezed it "This fight ain't over yet. You keep pushing, keep fighting. This is the finish line. Don't hold back. Don't..."

I could feel the tears welling up in my eyes as I watched him slip away. TrueFoot had given his life to save ours, a true hero until the end. Yet it was all for nothing. Our camp was overrun, and it felt like only a matter of time before we'd be completely wiped out. There was nothing left to do now but fight for our lives as long as we could.

I fell to the ground as a blow struck me across the back, my vertebrae crushed as the jagged iron weapon slammed into me with immense force. All the air left my lungs. The helmet rolled off, and cold sweat ran into my hair. I couldn't move; my feet were entirely limp, while my back seared with bright, hot pain, as intense as anything I had ever felt before. I was choking on the dirt, on the shock, on the pain. I crawled forward, but I was under so many feet, crushing me...

Everything seemed to slow down around me; time was slipping away from all of us now. A desperate cry filled my ears.

"Retreat!" Provis shouted, his fatigues aflame. "We do not have the manpower! For God's sake, retreat!"

He screamed, spiraling upward, bursting in front of me like a rocket in flight. Something was ripping him from the battlefield, pulling him towards the sky. There were Sters in the battle, and they wanted him.

And then I was screaming too, my vision going dark. I felt my heart pull apart, my skin ripping and bones snapping as something sharp sliced through my back, straight through to the other side. In that moment, everything stopped, everything slid to a halt, replaced instead by a pain so strong there were no words. I screamed with whatever air was left in my lungs, felt the blood in my windpipe as I gurgled.

This was the end.

"Get up."

A hand appeared in my field of vision, a gentle, clean, soft hand. I reached for it shakily and the fingers closed around mine, lifting me up until I stood again. The pain was still there, still burning like the heart of a star, but I owned it. It was my pain.

Sally said nothing. I understood, now, however much I despised her choice of timing. She nodded slowly.

I was shouting, screaming as I ripped the poker from my back, brandishing it in front of me with a newfound strength. I threw myself at the ravening hordes with an energy I had not felt in years, with a terror sprung from the pain racing through my body.

My skin burned as it sewed itself shut, every muscle grabbing and pulling to fix itself, stretching in impossible ways, yet I swung that poker at the monsters around me. They fell left and right, as I fought for something more than victory. I fought for my life.

The ground shook as if a giant had risen from the Earth. I screamed through gritted teeth and threw myself at the red-eyed beasts. Adrenaline coursed through me, blocking out the pain of my wounds as I swung my poker with a newfound strength.

My weapon connected with flesh and bone, shattering the feral man's skull in front of me. I felt its death on my skin, a cold chill that was both freeing and oddly comforting. Another one came for me, and I lunged forward, burying the poker deep in its chest. The force of my attack made it stumble back, giving me enough time to yank the poker out and swing again.

I could feel every blow reverberate through my body; each hit filled me with exhilaration and purpose like never before. I fought like a wild animal. This was to be my redemption—this was what would save me from certain death today.

"Retreat! Retreat!" somebody called out from behind me.

This battle could not have been won, and we were too few left, that much I knew. So I turned and ran, throwing myself into the motion as I raced to follow the voice, slicing this way and that to keep the ferals at bay. I had to protect the rebels. Save the survivors.

I reached the tree line and ran to the mountain pass as I'd done time and time again in our training. If anyone had made it to the shuttles, they were long gone—hopefully far from here, safe. As I ran away on shaky legs, numbness slowly started to creep in—first numbing my limbs; eventually numbing my mind too until there was nothing left.

ShortThumb nodded once she saw me, eyes bulging as she took in the mess that I was. I looked down to see that I was almost entirely painted red in blood. My shirt was ripped to shreds, exposing my chest. I pulled it off and used what was left of it to wipe off the rest of the viscera coating my arms.

Nobody said a word for the next hour.

Survivors trickled in slowly, each seeming to have escaped within less than an inch of their lives, some missing limbs. I administered first aid as best I could. Out of the one thousand people who had been established in the camp, barely a hundred of us made it to the pass. We were all that was left.

I sat on a bolder next to ShortThumb, who was being a little too obvious in trying to avoid looking at me. I recognized a few faces among those who had returned, but not many. Two or three who had trained under me had made it. And Provis…

He couldn't be dead. The Sters had snatched him for some reason or another. Everyone else they'd killed with impunity. He'd been the only one airlifted from the field—as if they'd come just for him.

Eventually, the night was silent again. The attackers had won, and they had won easily. We had lost men, infrastructure, any advantage in the war. We didn't even know if the shuttles had made it out.

Sally walked in front of me, poised and elegant. She wore a white dress, unblemished by the blood of the battlefield. She waved her hand at a crack between two rocks and was gone. I rose and followed her.

The crack was wider than I had initially thought and opened up into a large cavern on the other side. My eyes acclimated quickly to the dim light, but even so, the space was large enough that I could not see all the way to the end.

"I'm sorry for your loss," she said. "But that goes without saying, as I am you."

"Really, again with that? Gah, Sally—me —whatever! What is your problem?"

"Problem?" She tilted her head.

"Yeah, problem!" I threw my hands up into the air. "What a time to try and teach me a lesson!"

"You weren't listening before. Got your attention, though."

I shuddered. "I felt like I was dying."

"And you fought as if your life depended on it. You were more effective and discovered a tactic that would improve your performance in the future. I fail to see the problem."

"No, I fought like an animal in a trap. Without the time or space to apply strategy."

"We lost the camp. We lost the upper hand."

"You never had the upper hand," she snapped. "And it's not your fault; you're not responsible for protecting everyone in the camp."

"I could have tried!"

"You did try, Zander, but you can't save everyone. You just can't."

"I'm the only one here that can't die, that doesn't mind losing a limb. I don't have to worry about it slowing me down because it'll grow back! So what if I fight better when I'm fighting for my life; I'm fighting smarter if I'm not fighting selfishly. And who are you to tell me all this crap? You're supposed to be me, on my side!"

"Which is why I'm telling you that you need to learn how to accept not being a god."

"What now?" I sputtered. "I'm no god."

"Then how could you possibly hope to save everyone at once?" She rolled her eyes. "You're invincible, not omnipotent."

"I know that."

"Do you, though?" She shook her head. "Truth is, you learned to deal with that, once, way back when. You need to listen to your—"

"What?" I shouted. "That's what all this has been about? All these lectures, lessons, losses, just to get me to pay attention to those stupid memories?"

"Zander, no, It's…"

"Leave me be! I do not want to be the man I was. We hid those memories for a reason."

"You were all for getting them back, if I recall."

"And then I got a taste of what they were," I snapped. "That was enough for me."

I turned around and marched towards the crack in the stone, leaving her behind me. Yet there she was, poised between the exit and me.

"You can't repress them forever," she said. "Bottle them up, and they'll overflow."

I pushed right through her to the world outside, trying to put her out of my mind. The pain was gone; at least she did that right. I shook my head, as if I could shake her out. There was no way to tell if it was working or not, but she wasn't there when I opened my eyes.

When I did, however, I was greeted by incredulous glances from every single person before me. I froze, confused. They looked at me as if they were seeing a ghost.

"I found a cavern thing…" I started, but no one was listening, only staring.

"I saw it happen before my very eyes," ShortThumb said slowly. "It is him. It's the real one."

I took a step back, wishing I was still able to jump, jump away from the looks they were giving me.

"It's Zander," she said, almost looking proud. "It's really him. He's here to lead the way. He's here to save us all."

SEVENTEEN

THE GREAT ESCAPE, NOW WITH MORE ARTHROPODS

Sally

HERE'S A LIFE HACK FOR A BAD MENTAL HEALTH DAY: make a new friend, and vow revenge on your enemies. I tell you, I went to bed feeling like I was on cloud nine after the Sters returned us from Fight Club. Then again, I never wanted to see another cloud again in my life, so that's probably the worst image I could have come up with. Screw it, I was exhausted.

The next morning, I climbed out of my bedroll with a smile that stretched my cheeks to their breaking point. Marn noticed immediately.

"Where were you two last night?" Her eyes lit up as she gave me a wicked smile. "Have you found a way out?"

"No." I shook my head. Marn's eyes widened, and so did her smile.

"Oh, you lucky butt!" She giggled. If I'd had something to drink, it would have been the best moment for a spit take; instead, I just laughed up air.

"What?" I sputtered, then lowered my voice. "Us? No. No, no, no. We're not…"

Oh gosh. I hadn't even considered what others would think of our newfound friendship. Marn must have woken up to my empty bed, realized Magnesar wasn't there either, and put the wrong two and two together to get five. Had she not seen the dozen others missing? I took a deep breath.

"The Sters are making us fight," I said through gritted teeth. "We had no choice in the matter. Marn, don't. Stay calm."

"What?" Her hands flew to her mouth. "I only heard rumors… No, not you! But you'll… you'll be dead within the month."

I clenched my fists at my sides. "I have no intention of dying here. I don't even plan on being at the farm in a month."

I whispered our plan to her, throwing looks to the others near us, hoping they could hear every detail. Spreading the word was essential. If just one person missed the information, our rescue plan would fail.

I caught Magnesar's eye from across the room—the same marks on his face as any other morning, only now, I knew how he had gotten them—and some of them were my fault, oops. His confusion was evident, even under the mask of black and blue. I would have to find a good way to explain the lack of marks on my skin while we snuck in conversation on our hamster wheels.

And then I was fluxed up first.

No, this wasn't meant to happen; today was a big day for me, for us. If they were grabbing me so early, they knew. They must have heard our screaming match yesterday. Understood more than we gave them credit for. I cursed myself: I had gotten too bigheaded, hadn't I? Such a fool, thinking the Sters were the big dumb idiots I made them out to be…

But I wasn't the only one to be lifted, no. I recognized the faces that came up with me: the softer bodies, the smaller ones. And all at once a wave of relief washed over me: I wasn't found out. They were rewarding me for my work? How thoughtful: my alien overlord was afraid my fragile body was too roughed up from the night before to endure another day on the wheel.

"Be kind to that one," said one of the Sters—my Ster, I suppose we should say—to the one who corralled us out of the sleeping barn. "She'll make us rich!"

I gritted my teeth. Riches. My Ster didn't want to thank me, they just wanted to be sure their prize pony was going to be strong enough to perform more tricks tonight. That was what everything was about, wasn't it? Another constant of the universe: the powerless controlling the bottom of the ladder for their only taste of control.

I had a lot of time to think as I sat in front of my sewing machine. I wondered if the Ster population at large knew that their finguies' clothes were made by a finguy sweatshop. In any case, I had the chillest day since I'd arrived at the farm, even if it was hemming clown costumes for some other poor sod to wear.

"*Pssst*," said the woman next to me, never lifting her eyes from the sewing machine. "Tonight. Don't go to sleep. Pass it on."

I smiled as I whispered the words down the line. Our plan was spreading. The word was getting out. It was going to happen.

Blayde would be proud, I thought, rolling the idea over in my head, eyes set on the little needle moving up and down—getting mildly sidetracked by the confusing fact that they had sewing machines here. Made by finguies, for finguies, I suppose? But what would she say if I failed them all? If she were here, then getting out would be a cinch. But with me in charge… there were hundreds of ways tonight could fail miserably.

I took a deep breath and thought of Felling.

Thinking about her always… hurt. It felt like such a small word for the massive twist in my gut. The guilt of having let her down. Of failing her so terribly. After she'd given me some of the most pertinent advice of my life.

I couldn't do this alone.

I had my team. I had Magnesar and the other fighters. But tonight, the training wheels were off. Zander and Blayde weren't there to pick up my slack, to correct my course. This was my plan, and if I failed to execute it, the loss would be on me. Whatever it took, we were getting out of here.

And then? When everyone was safe? I was going to find Zander. I was going to find Marce.

But these people weren't going to be safe, not ever. Not if they stayed on this planet. This escape plan was about getting away from the farm: how would we escape the Sters forever?

This had to be what Nimien had sent us here for. He told me I would find my answers on this planet; had he wanted me to learn something by saving everyone?

Maybe he hoped I would learn how to lead. I just wish there'd been more midterms before the final.

If all went well, I could be out of here tonight. The thought itself was fuel to my mind, pushing me to work out the details down to the tiniest there was.

What would Zander do?

It would be reckless. But it could very well work.

My hands were so slick with anxious sweat by the end of the day that all my garments were stained. Thankfully, the Sters couldn't see. And, if Nim was right about me, no finguy would ever have to wear my shit work.

I crawled into bed, closed my eyes, and waited.

When the flux came, I relaxed into it. No need for them to sense my heightened resolve, though they might have assumed it was because of the fight anyway.

Pay no attention to the bedsheet tied to my ankle, no, that's not there at all.

I landed in the box. And, surprisingly, the lid didn't come down. The box drifted forward, and my Ster started… talking to me? My Ster carried our salvation out of the pit, too focused on their little fighter to even notice.

"There you are, my little party monster," said my Ster. Speaking to me, oh yes, directly to me. Once again, I panicked: how much did they understand? But they were in the habit of rambling to me when they were anxious, so I hoped this was all that was.

A monster. With anxiety.

Didn't make them any less of a monster.

"Tonight is going to be even better than the last," they continued, pulling me forward. My leg went taut, the blanket tugging. Good. "Xerg is planning on having you go up at the very end; you're such a hit, they're saving the best for last."

My leg went slack: whoever had just climbed the rope bedsheets had made it to the top of the pit. Now it was their turn to help the others. I untied the knot around my ankle, making a big show of changing into the leotard so the Ster couldn't tell the two actions apart.

The lack of a lid was just a bonus. I waited, watching as ceiling gave way to sky. The dark, the oppressive roof of clouds pressed down on us. I shivered in the cold night air, raising goosebumps on my exposed legs.

It was time. I clenched my fists.

I left Sally in the box that night.

I burst up at my Ster, and, before they could act, sank my teeth into their bulb.

There was no sound as they caught on the membrane. It was thin, like biting into an orange without peeling the rind. As my teeth tore into the flesh, the gas inside rushed at my face like a tidal wave, overwhelming me.

"Ah!" I cried. My eyes burned, the gas drying them out instantly. The air was cold and smelled strangely of… pumpkin spice latte? I wouldn't be having many of those when I got home.

I let go and fell to the ground, where my box waited for me, dropped the second I'd pierced the Ster. I hit the rim and bounced off, slamming into the rough gravel, my arms ripping as the rocks dug into every inch of exposed skin.

The Ster didn't scream. They made no sound—dead in an instant. They dropped to the ground like a hot air balloon that had run out of gas.

I would think about what I'd done later. I didn't have time for doubt, for second thoughts. All I could do now was run to the generator, run before any of the others noticed this Ster was gone, before the hordes of finguies currently climbing out of their pit were discovered. I pushed myself to my feet, scanning the darkness; already my eyes were adjusting, catching the edges of the buildings, my head aching with the fog of defiance.

The air went staticky—the alarm? Was it too late, or was I being paranoid? We didn't have much time; they would figure it out eventually. We might not know what senses the Sters had but it was enough to put up a fight. And boy, we would be putting up a fight.

No, the heat in the air was coming from the generator. At least, I hope that's what it was: a big, pointy glowing thing in the center of the farm? Could it be anything else? It hummed as I approached, warm like a toaster fire on a cold winter's night.

It didn't seem to have any cables. A collection of interconnected chambers spread out and out in a dance, interweaving with the environment.

I swore under my breath, mist forming around my mouth. I needed to stop assuming alien tech would be like mine. Especially on a planet where the aliens laughed by sparking the air. The air here was slightly conductive, after all: the generator just needed to produce the power, and their weird tech could transmit it practically anywhere.

Who cares? Destruction is destruction. I took a deep breath—this could hurt.

I opened the hatch to find about a million bugs.

Ok. This wasn't just going to hurt: It was gonna be gross, too.

Before I could think too hard about it, I jumped in, my mind screaming at me to stop. Instantly a surge of electricity went through me like I'd jumped into a vat of plasma. My skin was on fire—either for real or in my head, I didn't know; I couldn't even see. Every muscle seized as the little beasties crawled over me, drowning me whole. I squeezed my mouth shut tight, but their feet, their legs, they were crawling into my ears, into my nostrils—

And then the heat just… stopped.

The bugs were still moving, but I'd done what I'd intended: I'd shorted them out, or whatever. Outside, the forcefield that kept us all trapped would be coming down. I would have breathed out in relief if my nose wasn't currently stuffed with tiny electric bugs.

The thing with vats of bugs is that you can't swim in them. I mean, Scrooge McDuck already screwed us over with the swimming in money stuff, and bugs are another problem entirely. Every time you move your hands to wade through them, they get pissed.

I was still sinking. Just how deep did this generator go?

Something grabbed my hair—fingers? —and pulled, hard. I rose through the bugs, spitting and sputtering, my hands flailing… I reached up and seized the arm, and allowed it to pull me out, where I collapsed on the glass floor, reaching up to pull the critters from my nose.

"Light-years, Sally Cakes!" shouted Magnesar. "I was wrong to continue writing your lament! You're getting a power ballad!"

Magnesar sat on top of the generator. His bone-china face was even paler in the night light, spattered with worry. He jumped to his feet, pulling me up with him.

"Come on, we don't have much time!"

He took off at a run, holding me close to him, making sure I could keep up. I was slowly getting my senses back; the ringing in my ear was screams, shouts, pure unadulterated rage. More Ster bodies littered the ground, deflated like the one I'd brought down. No wonder the air smelled like a Starbucks in fall.

A planet-born tore at the throat of her Ster, chunks of membrane flying as the creature gurgled its last screams. I shuddered. There was no way of separating the finguies from the humans; if they'd never been treated like men, would they ever become them? Maybe they were an asset—their violence could be an aid, just as the fighting finguy had taken one Ster from the enemy's ranks. So long as they knew which side they were fighting for.

No. They couldn't keep being used. They were people, for goodness' sake: just because they were feral didn't mean they weren't human.

My gaze met that of the bloody man crouched over the Ster corpse, mouth dripping blue. I saw the emptiness there. I waved at him to follow, but would he? The Sters had taken everything from him.

The now-harmless gates had been thrown open, inert. We dashed for the exit, the sky lit up by the odd glow of the clouds. Magnesar's hand was still clenched in mine. We raced past the gate, into the glowing forest.

That light was the most beautiful thing I had ever seen. The hundreds of footsteps that thumped the forest floor beside me were music to me ears. I felt like laughing, crying; tears streamed down my face, doing both.

"Don't slow down, Sally cakes!" Magnesar tugged me forward. "They'll be after us!"

If there were any Sters left, sure. But it seemed the hundreds of angry prisoners had made quick work of them. Still, this wasn't a risk to take. We ran, fast as we could, our thighs screaming as we plunged deeper and deeper into the forest. Good thing we'd basically been marathon training for weeks. Magnesar seemed to know where we were meant to go, leading me forward.

"Sally?"

I leapt into the air as Marn emerged from behind a tree, her eyes bright and excited.

"Is that you?"

"Marn!" I screamed, rushing to her. Despite not knowing her beyond more than the few words we'd exchanged over protein bars, seeing her made my chest flutter. We wrapped each other in massive hugs.

"And me too, thank you very much, Marny-Marny-Mo-Marny," Magnesar chimed in. "Shall we get going?"

"Don't mind if we do," I said. "Which way?"

"That way," said Marn. "The rebel camp is supposedly based at the foot of that mountain over there."

"Hate to break your groove, but I can't see any mountains, Marny-Moe," muttered Magnesar.

"You'll just have to take my word for it. Let's do what we do best—let's run!"

She led us flying through the trees, but it wasn't as urgent as it had been. We were far enough away from the farm now that the Sters had—hopefully—given up. They couldn't follow, not when all of their stock had escaped. Not when their entire compound was down. Not when they couldn't even find their way out of the room full of ravenous finguies that they had trained to kill.

For the first time in weeks, the air was nothing but air. The electricity I'd felt there since I'd woken up in that awful pet shop was… gone. I could breathe again, and I did. Oh God, did I breathe. I let the wind whip through my hair, blessing every kilometer I put between me and that godforsaken place.

Eventually, the running stopped entirely, and we marched at a quick pace, until eventually the sky began to lighten. It felt like daytime, though there wasn't any evidence of that. Marn let out a long yawn, which was echoed by Magnesar, who fell against a tree, smiling.

"We made it," Marn said. "We frashing made it."

She tossed herself to the ground into the crunchy leaves, the sweat on her brow glistening. "I'm free," she chanted. "Free, free, free. I'm free. You're free. Free are we. You see?"

"Hey, that's one of mine," said Magnesar. "You a fan?"

She didn't answer, only sighing in relief. I sat down slowly, letting my own relief wash over me. The ordeal was finally over. Sanctuary was just a few more kilometers away. Zander was within reach. And even though I could think of no way off this iron maiden of a planet, just being with him again would make everything better. I smiled.

"Hey, Marn," I called, my eyes beginning to slip closed, weighed down by exhaustion. "How do you know about the rebel camp?"

"I was there, once," she explained. "Got lost. Got caught. Got stuck. But I know where camp is."

"You sure they haven't moved?"

"If they have, they'll leave us a way of finding them," she said. "Get some sleep. I'll keep watch, I still have adrenaline pumping. We'll get walking soon enough. We should be safe here."

"You sure?" asked Magnesar, his voice going cold. "I wouldn't think so…"

"Then we'll get going again." Marn pushed herself back to her feet. "We'll sleep when we're sure we're in the clear."

"Or I could sleep now"—Magnesar yawned— "and you shout if something attacks?" Marn extended an arm for him to take. He teetered slightly but was walking within minutes.

"I'll try to get our bearings," I offered, grabbing a low branch and pulling myself up the nearest tree. I climbed, rising slowly through the limbs, picturing Zander as he managed the same feat in less than half my time, grinning excitedly as he did so. I missed him so much that it hurt. And within a few hours, I would see him again, hold him again.

The view from the top of the tree was like something out of this universe. A glowing yawn of a forest extending for kilometers into the darkness, a haven of light, carried up into the mist. I scanned the treetops, squinting into the distance until… yes, those trees sloped closer, didn't they?

Mountains.

I swung myself back to the ground gently, sharing the good news with my fellow escapees. Soon, we were walking again, making a beeline in the direction I had pointed us.

We walked for hours, pausing every once in a while to rest, to make sure there was no sign of us being followed, and I would check on our position in relation to the mountains. We moved steadily along, with the mountains getting closer every time we stopped.

It was both a surprise and a relief when a uniformed man stepped into our path.

"Who are you?" he asked, casually enough, as his men stepped forward to surround us. I counted five, as well as the man who spoke.

"Please," Marn said hastily. "We just escaped a Ster compound. A farm. Please, we need help."

"You didn't answer me," the soldier said sternly. "Who are you?"

"I'm Marn Tavin. Assigned to the *Wanderer*. Crashed."

"And I'm a man who needs no introduction," said Magnesar, placing his hands on his hips. When he was met with nothing but silence, he frowned. "Come on, Spurlock Magnesar? I've been in the top charts longer than you've been alive! You living under a rock? Oh, right."

"Sally Webber," I said, stepping forward. "Came here on…"

"Hold on, *the* Sally Webber?" the man said. "From, um, was it the *Traveler*?"

"Yeah." I nodded. "Why? You've heard of me?"

"We've been told to keep an eye out for you." He smiled. "There's somebody here that's been dying to see you."

My heart leapt in my chest. He was here. He was actually here. I was going to see Zander in a matter of minutes. Absentmindedly, I brushed a strand of hair out of my face.

I was going to see Zander. I was going to see Zander.

"Follow us." The soldier turned to lead us towards the mountains. The trees fell away at the base, leaving the sharp cliff face completely smooth. It seemed as though we had reached a dead end.

Only we hadn't. The soldiers walked up to the wall of rock, took one step to the side and simply… disappeared. I shot Magnesar an inquisitive glance but couldn't seem to tear his eyes away. Marn took a cautious step forward, shooting us a sly smile before she too sidestepped, and was gone, just like the men.

Another one of the armed men followed close behind.

I made my way to where I had last seen her and smiled at the fissure in the rock that created a corridor sideways along the cliff face, hidden from the outside world by a simple optical illusion and a whole lotta dark. I sidestepped, squeezing through the thin slice of rock, walking carefully down the stretch of the cliff until the jagged path opened up into a larger one, a stretch of dirt that looked almost like a canyon of some kind, as if the trail had been carved away by water. It cut straight along the mountain side, sharp peaks of stone on each side, the sky open to the elements.

It was easier to maneuver now, the path wide enough for me to walk straight, though I sometimes had to turn sideways to avoid huge juts of rock fighting for the sky. I followed the uniformed man in front of me, avoiding the trails that spread out in every direction, a labyrinth of a hiding place.

Finally, the canyon opened onto a small clearing. Only a few tents were set up here. Jagged entrances to several caves lined the cliff face, each one covered in loose-hanging curtains to keep us from seeing inside. Ingenious little lanterns of colorful glowing moss in glass jars gave us enough light to see our way around.

"The commander wants to see you now," said my guard. "We've been searching a long time for you, Miss Webber."

I nodded, unable to contain my excitement, sheer anticipation pulsing through my body. I pushed my way forward to the tent, adjusting my horrid leotard as I went. No matter, not much could be done about that.

Zander, a commander? So soon? Well, that was no real shock to me. He was a leader, so it was only natural he'd take up a position to command. A military strategist beyond compare.

I threw open the tent flap, stepping hastily inside and peering at the figure at the desk, my smile fading quickly. The commander was not Zander. The feet on the desk swung back and forth quickly across the surface, as if acknowledging my presence before their owner could.

"At last, Sally blesses us with her presence," Blayde said, rolling her eyes. "Where in the universe did you leave my brother?"

EIGHTEEN

FROM SOME ANGLES, THE PATH TO SELF-DISCOVERY IS A WALK OF SHAME

Zander

I'M NEVER HERE TO MAKE FRIENDS. BUT A little friendliness would be nice from time to time.

I won't bore you with the list of campaigns I've been on—frash, I'd probably bore myself before I hit the halfway mark. But this was high on the list of worst ones, at least when it comes to ranking the marches. You'd think I was alone now by the way they were treating me. Nothing but dirty looks all around.

That's what you got for saving everyone's asses over, and over, again.

We were the survivors. The only ones from an entire camp, all of Party City. I didn't know everyone by name, but I did know the ones missing from our ranks: TrueFoot, SharpTooth, HalfTongue, Provis. People who *barely* had names. More people who would never escape this planet, and yet, those who remained were still speaking to each other. Already, they were making lists of the dead, remembering them, who they were and the things they had done, combining tears with laughter.

And then there was me. I'd been a survivor before, and would always be one, but I would never be one of them. Now that they'd seen the real me. Not now they'd recognized who—and what—I was.

The eternal survivor.

This had to be why I locked those memories away. Either I came from somewhere I could never return to, or I came from nowhere, and in the end, wasn't that the same thing? Never having a place to call home. Never having a people to call your own. Either there were survivors of my homeworld, or there were none.

Except my homeworld was Earth. *Canada.* No great story there. I was just one in a billion. A freak of nature. Destined to fit in everywhere, yet nowhere.

You see? This is what happens when I'm left to my own thoughts. I needed a friend. Or at least an AI who can pretend to be one.

I turned my eyes back to the trail to avoid the pointed looks from ShortThumb. She knew who I was, and the stories of what I could do. Blown out of proportion, of course. Still, in her eyes, I had caused the massacre by not having prevented it.

And, at this moment, I couldn't agree with her more.

"Don't you start with that," Sally snapped. "That kind of thinking will sour your mind."

"You can see why I don't want to remember," I muttered under my breath. Those glaring at me would have more reason to find me unstable. "Somewhere in there are the names of people I could have saved. The names of people I killed through inaction. That's not something I want to have available to me."

"Oh, please," she scoffed. "You know as well as I do that running from your problems isn't going to solve them. You've got to face them and *deal*."

"You keep telling me how hundreds of lifetimes' worth of memories is going to make me stronger. I still think it's too much. Not everything deserves to be faced. Some things are just trauma."

Sally shrugged. "Blayde's fine with it."

"Blayde's Blayde." My hands formed into fists, nails digging into the soft skin of my palm. Stars, I could die for a callus. "She's being held together by a precarious balance of chaos and caffeine. Though you're bound to be biased, you're my subconscious."

"You don't think I can be objective?" She lifted an eyebrow. "I'm just telling you what your conscious mind doesn't want you to hear. And if I'm saying it, it means deep down, you believe it. You may think Blayde is built differently. Let me tell you—you are the same."

I shook my head, digging the nails deeper. "She's better at handling the daily absurdity of our lives. But it doesn't mean she's stable. It just means she's learned how to fall."

"Who are you talking to?"

Thank the stars, ShortThumb was acknowledging me. Frash that it was for all the wrong reasons.

"Just myself. Tough night." I unclenched my fists, wiping my sweaty palms against each other.

ShortThumb nodded slowly. "Yeah."

We walked together in silence, Sally nowhere to be seen. I had to say something. When was she going to address the immortality in the room? But then again, ShortThumb was born and raised on this planet—I couldn't know what she had been told about me. Giant gas-powered cephalopod aliens sort of trump the teleporting immortal with fantastic hair when it comes to scary bedtime stories, at least on this planet.

"How much further to the other camp?" I asked. The silence was as uncomfortable as a porcupine at a balloon convention. At the very least I could make myself useful, put my mind to work on strategies.

"We'll make our way through the pass, and it's right there." She nodded straight ahead, where the lights of the distant misty plants seemed higher in the sky—a mountain? "Or at least, that's what's on the map."

"You've never been?"

"Never needed to." She shook her head. "Mountains are hard on our shuttles, as we can't go very high without risking our instruments fizzling out. That and we can't see the mountains in the dark. I've been at Party City since boot'."

I glanced back at the hundred or so survivors following our lead. "Will they have the resources to take us in?"

"If they don't, they'll radio the closest base and figure out how best to deal with us. We'll probably all go off to other quadrants, wherever we're needed most."

"Right."

"You'll end up in base camp."

I nodded. "What about you?"

"Who cares?" ShortThumb cut a sharp laugh, making the hair on the back of my neck tense. "I'm nothing compared to the greatest asset this rebellion has ever had. I suppose you really are as big an ass as the stories make you out to be."

I snorted harder than a Hardvari in heat. "Right. What did I do now?"

"You… everyone knows who you are, Zander. What's the point in denying it?"

"I'm not denying it."

"Yeah, well, Luke Skywalker was a stupid alias. Who has a name like that?" She crossed her arms over her chest, taking a deep breath. The blood there was dry. "You could have been helping us since day one, but no, you had to waste everyone's time going through basic like some kind of sad rescue."

"Not everyone would have accepted my help. Not if they knew who it was coming from."

"Hello?" She threw her arms wide, gesturing to the small train of survivors. "Have you seen how desperate we are?"

"Just because you're desperate doesn't mean you'll listen to the villains of your bedtime stories promising salvation."

"Please. We'll accept help from anyone at this point. Especially the man who stopped the entire Gavrouchian army in its tracks with just one word. Even if no one can agree on what the word was."

"The word was *stop*. Followed by a second: *please*. But I said it while leading an army three times as large as theirs, so I don't think what I said mattered. Plus, that whole ordeal has been blown way out of proportion."

"How so?"

"Have you met a Gavrouchian?"

"Um, no…"

"They'll tell you I was fifty feet tall and riding the wind itself. Truthfully, I showed up with my hair in rollers and a cape fresh from the hairdressers, riding a Scrimvor, when they declared war on us. I grabbed anybody I could find on the street on my way there. Gavrouchians tend to be spooked by loud noises and bright colors and such. I told them to stop, please, and they turned around and left. That's that."

"What were they fighting about?"

"Building permits. A local zoning commission had classified their asteroid as non-commercial. Turns out those get printed on *yellow* forms. So, that went over well."

ShortThumb's pace slowed. "So it's all lies."

"It's what I've been trying to tell you. I'm a story. And what's the value of a story in a world where your enemies cannot hear it?"

ShortThumb said nothing, avoiding my gaze. Even in the darkness I could see the faint light of the plants reflecting silver off her cheeks.

"I thought I could be more help if I was just a man." I took a deep breath. My words were coming out shaky, and I didn't know why. "I've been fighting for as long as I can remember. I have led armies and strategized defense plans for rebellions and revolutions—I just haven't stopped a war with a single word."

Sally's hand slid around my neck, weaving through the hairs there.

"You've neglected to tell her the war ended the second you stepped on the battlefield." She trailed her fingers up my scalp. "Who cares if they can't hear you? You don't even need to speak."

A shiver ran through my body: fear.

A taste of iron filled my mouth. Fire at the edge of my eyesight, sparks of memory dancing in front of my eyes. Blood, so much of it, of every color and —

And maybe that's exactly why I had those memories locked away.

Sally formed a fist with my hair and tugged, yanking my head backwards. I gritted my teeth.

"Just let me be," I hissed. "I don't want to know."

"Obviously you do." She pulled her hand free like it was covered in shit. "Or you wouldn't be splitting like this."

ShortThumb shot me a look, brows furrowed. I shook my head again. I had to get Sally—no, not Sally,

Sally—out of my head. I needed to be fully myself if I wanted to save the real one.

The mountain pass was indistinguishable from the rest of the forest. How our guides found their way through I would never know, but finally we reached our destination.

The hull of a beached ship.

I'd been around shipwrecks before, but none as feisty as this. Even in the darkness, the hull gleamed; somebody loved this ship, or why else go to the trouble of washing the junk? Sleek like the *Traveler*, it oozed grace, even with its nose shoved into the side of a mountain.

"The Sters harvested it when it went down," said ShortThumb, making me jump. "They think it's abandoned. We've been trying to get it spaceworthy ever since."

So this was it—the last step of the escape plan. If the clouds ever did part, this would be our ticket off this world.

But parting the darkness… that was the problem.

A door dropped unceremoniously from the hull, hitting the dart with a loud thump. A Drenovian soldier came rushing out, lantern held high.

"Oh stars, are you Party City?" They stopped in front of ShortThumb, eyes wide and unblinking as they examined us all. "When the coms went dark, we assumed the worst. Is this… everyone?"

There was a moment of silence, in which everything went unsaid. The sheer scale of the loss. None of us knew who was meant to speak first.

"I need to debrief General Staltz right away." ShortThumb stepped forward. "We have a man with us he'll certainly want to meet."

She reached back to grab my shoulder, instead punching me awkwardly in the chest. I brushed her off, stepping on her toes in the process.

"Staltz. Yes." The Drenovian swallowed, his throat turning neon for an instant. He didn't ask what a captain was doing heading our march, or why he didn't challenge her for speaking. He must have deduced, correctly, that she was all that was left. "Well, there's been a recent… change in leadership. A woman."

"A woman?" The smile that burst onto my face couldn't be contained. Instantly, it was as if a weight had lifted from my shoulders. A woman, a nameless woman, who had taken command? There could be only one.

Sally.

My skin pricked with anticipation. Of course she would rise through the ranks. Of course she would make a name for herself on this planet. What with her whip-fast intuition, her calm wisdom: she was the perfect choice as a leader. Sure, she was a little untested, but they would see her potential here as I had.

Unlike Party City, stepping into this ship's corridor was like stepping into space. The floor was so clean it sparkled, ready for televised glory. Either these soldiers had nothing better to do all day than scrub floors, or they really did have a full TV crew here. Maybe both. There were no facsimiles of cake hanging from the ceiling, no birthday banners making a permanent fixture. This was our ticket off this world, and it was ready and raring to go.

ShortThumb and I were shepherded away from the other survivors, up some stairs and down another spotless corridor. If this ship was laid out like the *Traveler*—which it increasingly seemed like it was—then we were heading to the bridge—no, the captain's quarters, via the side bridge. I was ready for the opulence of Kork's suite and was... thoroughly disappointed.

This war room was just that: a war room. All my excitement at potentially seeing Sally fell when I took in the woman studying maps at the far end of the room, her back to us—much too tall to be Sally, long black hair too natural to be Blayde's rainbow. The war room reminded me there was no joy to be found on this planet: this was strategy, battle plans covering every inch of space.

"Imperatrix?" The Drenovian cleared his throat, face bursting with neon green. The woman turned.

"Marcy?" I could barely say her name; the gasp that came out of my mouth stole it away. "What the void are you doing here?"

NINETEEN

WHEN TMI MEETS R&R

Sally

FINALLY. NOT THE WORD I WOULD HAVE USED. Right now, the only words in my head were a combination of "huh?" "what?" and "you've got to be shitting me," which makes *huwhshime*, which is as nonsensical as my current situation.

"Oh, you found Magnesar," said Blayde, waving at the pop star. "Glad you're all right, *Commander*. You can go back to composing that power ballad now. It may just be the most important thing you'll ever write."

She was dressed in army briefs, a scouting hat thrown on sideways for effect. The clothes showed no rank, no name, just a camouflage print, and an oversized portrait of a cat on her breast pocket, gazing into some impossible distance, whiskers aglitter. Her thick, black boots were the only serious addition to her outfit, made for marching. She was as stunning as always, more suited for a runway than for battle.

"What do you mean, *finally*?" I shoved her feet off the table and threw myself into the empty chair. Oh my God, a chair. I sat down into sturdy lumbar support for the first time in weeks. I could have cried. I sank completely into the bliss, distracted only by the sound of Magnesar slipping out of the door.

"Oh, come on, Sal," Blayde said, "you took much too long to get out of that farm."

"Wait, what?" I didn't have time for this. Well, realistically, I had all the time I ever wanted or needed, but I'd put up with too much shit just for there to be more now. "You knew that I was there? How? Why… and since when do you call me Sal?"

She raised her hand to stop me. "Girl. It's me you're talking to. I expected you to escape a wee bit faster: I assumed you had something worked out and didn't want to mess with your plan. And you see? You're here now, so it's all good."

I was seething. The blood in my veins was lucky to have all that skin to keep it from evaporating with all that heat.

"Magnesar and I were trapped in that shithole for *weeks*." I would have stood to confront her, but I was too damn tired. My lumbar was loving all this support. And hey, who was I to deny that? "And all this time, you just assumed I had a plan?"

She frowned. "You did, didn't you?"

"Of course I did," I lied. When she looked at me like that, I couldn't possibly tell her how useless I was. Not when she'd finally accepted me for who I was. And there was that word again—*finally*. I was so offended I didn't even want to think it. "It was complicated, you know, with not being able to jump on this stinking planet."

"Ah, well, it's important to have a variety of strengths for when the need arises." She smirked. "Something I learned from you, dear. Oh, before I forget: here."

The tiny monolith went sailing through the air. I caught it, the smooth surface so familiar in my hand. My phone.

"How…?"

"You left it on the *Traveler*." She winked. "Thought you might want some connection to the outside universe."

I wasn't used to this new Blayde yet. Old Blayde, I should say, seeing as how she was a composite of all her recovered memories. It was as if she had found clothes that actually fit her, rather than them gathering and pinching every time she moved. Now, she flowed with ease from one situation to another, so confident as to be relaxed.

It was unnerving. And a little cool.

That and being called *dear* by a woman with such demeanor made my face go hot.

"Why are you here, Blayde?" I slipped my phone into my… wait, I had no pockets. I was still in my leotard. Instead, I clutched it in my sweaty hands, its weight familiar and oddly comforting, even without a single bar of signal.

Blayde smiled. "Because you were in trouble. I do care about you, you know."

"How did you…?"

"The Alliance called me." She laughed, putting her feet back up on the desk. "Did you know we have a liaison now? Of course you do, it's all your fault. In any case, I came as soon as I could. Future me can be a little… pushy."

"Tell me about it," I muttered. If future Blayde was to current Blayde what current Blayde was to me, I could understand her dropping everything to answer her call. "How did you get here, anyway? I haven't been able to jump in or out or… anywhere, for that matter."

"By ship, of course." She grinned. "Our new friends at the—what's it called? – Office of Sibling Liaison? Needs a better name—they were very helpful. I got them to lend us the *Traveler* again. Well, actually, it was all Kork on that one—he insisted. They weren't too keen on a rescue mission to save the rescue party, but I promised I wouldn't be an idiot like my brother had been. That, and the first lady was missing, so they couldn't really go back to Pyrina without explaining to Dany how they lost her wife. Magnesar was all too happy to join: apparently, I've inspired his magnum opus. Did you hear? We're going to be a rock opera."

"So, the ship is still waiting for us, after all this time," I said, shaking my head. Thank goodness for Marcy stowing away. I leaned deeper into my chair, then threw my feet up on the desk beside Blayde—two could play that game. "Don't they have anything better to do?"

"Dany shouted something about trying to forge a new identity for her government. Right between 'what are you doing here?' and 'How come you all think you can just come and go in my hot tub as you please?' Anyway, your friend there has got something up her sleeve."

"Dany's good." I couldn't help but smile. I'd missed this. Blayde's presence only reinforced the feeling of freedom now filling my chest. Hope made flesh. That and speaking at a normal register was much better for my vocal cords. "I wouldn't be surprised if the Alliance actually does change."

"I would be," she said. "Ultimate power corrupts… ultimately. No matter how good the person. When lives are in your hands, you can't think in good or bad: only in us versus them."

Ah, well, that warm feeling was good. Amazing how quickly it chills when a literal time-lady starts dropping truths. "And this is coming from experience?"

"You bet it is, babe." She winked. "Been there, done that. And now I can remember it all, I can tell you it sucks balls. And yet, we always end up back in the same place."

I snorted. "You mean on an inescapable planet where the reigning life-forms think we're cute and want to play dress-up?"

"You know what I mean." She nudged her foot against mine on the tabletop. "Another insultingly stupid case of us versus them."

"Except this time they are actually evil."

Blayde took a deep breath. "Listen, kiddo: Once you've seen every possible conflict in the universe, you realize it's just small people trying to feel big and none of this shit matters in the grand scheme of things. Good, evil, it's all relative. It all sucks, but it's another constant in the universe."

"Kiddo?" I couldn't believe what I was hearing. I kicked my feet off the table, sitting bolt upright. "I have been a pet. A drug mule. A terrible wrestler. I'm no one's kiddo."

"It's unhealthy to hold a grudge." She stared at me across the table, unblinking. "Trust me, I know. Can't tell you how many I had to purge myself of, and it was not pretty."

"It's easy for you to say rise above it," I said. "You're one of the most powerful beings in existence right now. Maybe you don't care, but I do. I've seen what they're doing to us. And all this time, they *knew* we were sentient; I can't just let that slide."

"Freeing all these people from tyranny will be enough of a punch to these Sters' guts to last a few lifetimes."

"But it won't be *enough*. You said it yourself. We're small people. We have small squabbles, in the grand scheme of things. But to each of us? It's our entire existence. And it matters."

I leaned forward in my chair, catching her stare and refusing to break away, to even blink.

"Blayde, we need more than just escape. We need to be sure this can never happen again. And we need the Sters to pay for the lives they've stolen."

"I never took you for the vengeful type."

"I'm not talking about revenge. I'm talking about justice."

Blayde's brow furrowed. "Revenge is like scratching an itch, it feels good for a moment but it just gets worse. Justice is like using a salve, it may take longer but it actually solves the problem."

I gripped the armrests of my chair, still refusing to break my gaze. My entire body was shaking now: could I really take revenge against an entire species? I wanted to, deep in my gut; my body ached for the chance to inflict pain on those who had captured us, treated us like nothing, ignoring our sentience so they could take what they wanted from us. Literally our sweat and blood.

And all at once, I understood Zander more than ever before. I may only have been a finguy for a few weeks, but it was enough to make me furious, to make me want to fight for those whose voice had been taken from them—but was it my fight to fight? Was it wrong to take their battle from them?

My head was spinning. I was tired, hungry, and needed a nap. That and a few thousand philosophy classes. But who has time for philosophy when you're actively suffering?

"Fine, then. But what will justice be for these people?"

"We'd be actively scooping out the bottom tier of the Sters' entire social structure. The best revenge will be leaving them to clean up their own mess, don't you think?"

"So?" I crossed my arms over my chest, sneaking a pinch to keep myself from falling asleep. The exhaustion was settling in full force, now, and I hadn't yet mastered the act of letting it slide. "How do you plan on getting us off this rock? You know how to get around an impenetrable cloud barrier?"

"Well, it all begins a thousand years ago —"

I groaned. I was going to need something much stronger than a pinch to keep myself awake. "I don't need a history lesson. I need a ship. Oh, and a masseuse. Do you have one?"

"I'm trained in three hundred and seventy-two different forms of corporeal relief. Ask me nicely."

Get Zander back here right now, else I might fall for his sister. "Please, can you…?"

"You owe me a drink," she muttered, slapping the table. "And don't you dare fall asleep on me."

A minute later, I was wide awake, stuck on the table, and shaped like a pretzel. My ankles were the only thing keeping my head from falling on the floor.

"In order to forget the wheel, you become the wheel," said Blayde. "Anyway, are you ready for a little bit of Ster history?"

I take back what I said: this crush wasn't going to last long. I tried saying no, but my big toe was smooshing my larynx.

"So glad you're interested." She sat on the chair facing me. "Let's go back a thousand years, to when our alien overlords were swamp-dwelling polyps."

Maybe she was right: this terrible twist was definitely pulling something out of my back. I bit my lip and listened.

"The Sters were stuck in their dark and misty hidey-holes, too fragile for the harmful rays of their sun's light. They had the whole planet at their disposal when the sun set, but without the mist, they were fish out of water. The mist conducts their current, which allows them to communicate, share thoughts, and even *flux*, a limited telekinetic ability. It's also what renders them spiritually immortal—from mist to mist."

I almost choked right then and there. "They're immortal?" I croaked.

"In a way. Their mind is the part of the mist confined to their body. When their body dies, that mist is restored to the whole. Allowing them to basically… continue to exist. In the cloud."

"Oh my God," I gasped, then promptly choked on my own foot. "They… the mist is the *cloud*. That's why they never use paper or computers but still seem to know everything: all their information is stored around them."

"Precisely." Blayde dug her thumbs into my spine, releasing confusing happy sparks in my brain. Picture this: you're a part of a species whose entire existence revolves around mist. What's your end goal?"

"More mist?"

"And triangle triumphs." Her eyes sparkled with excitement. When was the last time I'd seen her this excited about… anything? "Unfortunately, it was near impossible to connect mist-pods across the planet when distances between marshes were more than a night's walk. That is, until a single ship crashed on this world."

I could see where this was going. Creatures who bent current to their will, meeting a ship that runs on their juices? The databanks of the Alliance would be picture books to them. Highly informative picture books…

And *astrogators*. The hyper-connected human at the heart of every Alliance ship, a person trained to think as the ship, to guide it through the dangerous process of warp. Connected directly to the machine through a conductive gel.

"The information on board that ship sparked a fire," she continued. "The first thing they learned was communication. They sent construction specs across the planet, a message heard by all, and soon the entire planet was connected. Connected with one purpose in mind: making this link permanent."

She walked out of my field of view, and her hands dug into my back. I almost cried out in pain before remembering I don't feel that shit. It was just intensely weird.

"The next thing they learned was protection. A ship capable of surviving the dangerous rays of space, thanks to brilliant engineering. Engineering that they slowly began to understand. They decided they would no longer have to be afraid of going outside their caves. Together, they decided to terraform their planet."

"Hold on: you're saying they created the cloud layer?" My eyes widened. I had not expected this.

And what had happened to the crew of that first ship? Every Ster I had met seemed to find it common knowledge that finguies were nothing more than pets, but if Gluuk was to be believed they had written about us in their old stories. Did they know where their technology came from? How much had been known, how much had been hidden? How does one even hide information when all knowledge is in the clouds?

"They built massive pumps that would alter the chemical composition of their atmosphere, spreading the mist and setting in motion the creation of permanent clouds, capable of blocking, or at least, absorbing, most of the sun's harmful rays. This would make their land habitable to them."

"So, they made the clouds," I said. "*The mist.*"

"They engineered attraction fields to catch even more wandering vessels, to pull them in, to find even more tech to take." Blayde's hands on my back, *in* my back, were the only things keeping me grounded. My body wanted to tremble and shake, to let the anger out; her hands shaped and guided it through and out of me.

I pulled my frown as low as it could go. "And you don't understand why I want revenge?"

"I do, and that's the problem. I should be over this. I feel for you Sally, I do. Hold on, we're going to try another shape —"

Before I could retort, she twisted me the other way around. Now, my feet were past my shoulders, though I wasn't quite sure how. I breathed deeply, feeling every loosened muscle in my back.

"How do you know all this, anyway?" I asked, in between deep, deep breaths. I was starting to wonder if the purpose of this massage was relaxation or summoning a demon.

"Some of it is from their natural history museum," she said. "The exhibits are self-aggrandizing, but they're incredibly informative for a species without a written language."

I bit my lip. "So, the fact we're sentient *is* common knowledge?"

"Not exactly." Her fingers were soft on my toes. "There seem to be different levels of knowledge. When I infiltrated the minister's household, he spoke of things his colleagues were privy to, which contradicted the displays in the museum. I believe the different colored tentacles represent a predisposition to access certain types of information, a genetic class system stratified by their ability to access the mist. Children seem to develop more as they grow, but they are limited by their sub-species. And since we're unable to connect, we're not seen as sentient. Intelligent, yes, but not sentient."

"Huh," was all I could say. Sneaking into a minister's home. I couldn't believe what I was hearing. So she'd been on this planet ages before making herself known. Why hadn't she sprung Zander? Shouldn't he be here?

"None of this tells us how we get out, though," I said, not ready for the emotional shit yet.

"Haven't I told you yet?" she said. "They're using an EM field to manipulate the clouds. A synthetic extension of their own flux. If they weren't so terrible, I would be impressed. But I'm not here to pass judgement."

I sure would. "Is that what's keeping us from jumping? It's scrambling us? So what's the plan? We build faraday cages around all the shuttles?"

"It doesn't have to be that difficult," she scoffed. "We simply turn off the field for a bit. Not too long, just enough to get us off this planet. Then it turns back on, and the Sters can go back to their day-to-day lives. Without an entire strata of their society, but they can deal."

"That…" My jaw dropped. It sounded so simple, coming from her. So very simple.

"Brilliance, I know," she snickered. "You in?"

"What are you planning? How do we shut this thing off?"

"Well, that's the tricky bit. For that, we need to break into Ster Capital and shut off one of the generators creating the field."

"Will that affect the entire field, or just a section?" I swallowed. This was a big planet: how many finguies were spread around the globe? We had to get every single one of them off. We needed ships, so many ships. How were we even going to get the word out?

"The whole thing, if we play our cards right." Her face appeared above mine, revealing a grin that lit up the entire room. "Though I can't look at any schematics, because you know, it's floating in the air around us right now."

"Ah."

"We'll use Marcy's army as a distraction," she added. "They'll get the Sters focused on the fight, letting us make our way through the city unnoticed. We bring down the field and use their device to proclaim our freedom in a way even they can understand. Then we get off this planet as fast as we can. The *Traveler* is waiting in orbit around a neighboring planet, and we jump as many as we can to the ship and get the rest to fly their shuttles there. Once the field is down, we can use time to our benefit, go back and reroute as many rescue vehicles as we need. We leave no-one behind."

"Hold on, did you say *Marcy's* army?"

I tried to drag myself to a seat, only to realize I was too pretzeled to move. Blayde pushed me back down on the table.

"Right. I'm telling you the story out of order." She pushed her thumb on my sternum, and I started to cry without knowing quite why. "Oh. That wasn't supposed to happen. You need to let go of some things, you know. Anyway, Marcy forced her way into a rebel camp, and now she's the head of the revolution. She's been unifying the camps: the hope of rescue… it's a powerful drug. The planet knows the Alliance is here for them. You were smart, taking her with you: a tangible representation of the Alliance's confidence in the mission's success."

"Yes… we were smart, weren't we?" I said between foreign sobs. Had that really been Marcy's plan, when she snuck into our shuttle? To force the Alliance's hand in the rescue? Then why hadn't she told us? "And… did you find Zander?"

"Finally, she asks!" Blayde laughed. "You've been so patient; I thought it would be the first question out of your lips. I just got word he's made it to Marcy's camp. I'll send him a message letting him know you got here safely. I'm sure he misses you oodles."

Now I knew where the tears were coming from, and they flowed even harder. Blayde brushed my hair from my face, shushing me sweetly.

"Have you… seen him?" I asked.

"Not yet. Not ready to discuss the Split."

"The what now?"

"The time we went our separate ways, which resulted in pretty terrible memory loss?" She shrugged. "Big split. Cosmic rift. You know, all that."

"So, how much of it is back?"

"All of it," she replied. Then, judging by her falling expression, she had seen *my* falling expression. "Everything came back at once."

"Oh," I said, feeling awkward. "It's just that…"

"What?"

"Well, Zander's memory's been taking a long time. Only a few memories returned, and even then, they were sparse."

"Oh." Her fingers paused. "I guess it's… different… for the both of us. Maybe it has something to do with us being pulled out of the machine too early."

"That's what we've been thinking." I took another deep breath. My tears had stopped, and I felt… drained. Empty. "And… what about Felling?"

"One problem at a time, Sally." Blayde's hands kneaded my back flab like bread dough. "Her mind is safe, but I haven't found a good body for her yet. Nothing's… worthy of her. But I'm not giving up. The second we're done here, I'm getting back to that."

I wanted Felling back now: it was hard to imagine she was still alive, after seeing her die. But I had to trust Blayde. She was the only one who could save her. That much was clear.

"And are you… are you ready to talk about Canada?"

To that, she nodded very, very slowly, solemnly, as if she were mourning the death of a long-lost friend. She seemed sad, all of a sudden. Old. Her eyes looked like they didn't match the rest of her body, having seen too much for her young frame.

"Are you going to be okay?" I extended a hand to squeeze hers. She did not refuse it. I didn't know the details, nothing more than the location, but it was enough.

"I managed to deal with it before." She shrugged. "I'll figure it out again."

"Zander still doesn't know." I shuddered. "At least, I don't think he does."

She nodded. "I don't know if he's ready for that. At least, not yet. Now, let's stop feeling sorry for ourselves and get back to work. We're going to war. Bathrobes are in the back."

"Great. Can you get this computer chip out of my brain first? I'd rather not save the planet while doped up on drugs. This thing's meant to keep me from escaping Sters, not a whole planet, so it'll probably short out when it realizes what we're going to do."

TWENTY

THE FIRST LADY'S FIRST STAND

Zander

MARCY, FIRST LADY OF THE ALLIANCE, WIFE OF the most powerful woman in this arm of the galaxy, and now, apparently, face of the finguy rebellion, looked worthy of her new title. Dressed in Alliance fatigues, she stood tall, her eyes focused, her face tight. This was not the Marcy I'd known on Earth, full of smiles and ready for fun. No, this Marcy was legion, this Marcy was battle ready, the pen in her hand the decisive direction for war.

This Marcy was also, if bellies are to be believed, *pregnant.*

How long had I been in Party City?

"Zander." I'd expected her expression to change at the sight of me, for better or worse. A little relief would have been nice: I sure couldn't hide mine at the sight of her. But she took me in with as much enthusiasm as if she were doing an inventory check of the food stores. "I was wondering where you'd gotten to."

"I thought you were with Sally." I was amazed I could form words right now. Marcy didn't answer, turning instead to ShortThumb, capping her pen before gesturing towards the few chairs in the room.

"You must be General Provis," said Marcy, bowing politely at ShortThumb. "Commander TrueFoot has spoken your praises. I am eternally sorry about Party City. We have no idea how the location reached Ster command, and we are taking every precaution to find out how this could have happened. The loss resonates through us all."

"Thank you… Imperatrix." ShortThumb bowed in return. "I'm sorry to say that General Provis was… taken during the battle. I am Captain ShortThumb, the highest-ranking officer of the survivors of Party City."

"Taken?" Marcy's eyes flicked to me. "By the Sters?"

"Lifted right off the field." I snapped my fingers. "Just like that, right in front of my eyes."

"And you couldn't stop them." Marcy's words were both a question and an accusation. I was getting tired of those.

"This planet has… grounded me," I explained. I collapsed into a seat, unable to hide the tremble in my knees any longer. "It's limited what I can bring to the table."

Now that I was finally sitting, I was starting to feel tired, and hungry at that. I caught a whiff of my pits and almost fell over with disgust. I should have taken that shower when I had the chance.

"Good." Marcy didn't look all that relieved, despite what her words were saying. "For the past weeks, I was under the impression Sally and you left me here, so it's nice to know you're as stuck as I am. Where is she, by the way?"

Sally. Past few *weeks.* The hair on my arms prickled with cold. Marcy was never meant to be on this planet; I'd imagined she was safely with Sally, somewhere… undetermined. Even though deep down I'd known Marcy wasn't at the extraction point, I couldn't think of her lost and alone on this world. And yet now I'd found her, and Sally was nowhere in sight. I took a deep breath.

"I thought she was with you," I said, sheepishly. Her face fell, mirroring mine.

Marcy nodded. Once. "Well… fuck."

"I'm sorry, I'm not sure I know who you are," said ShortThumb before I could say anything more. Her feet didn't touch the floor and swung back and forth like little pendulums. "I don't think I've ever heard the term Imperatrix before."

"Right, where are my manners?" Marcy finally let out one of her truly blinding smiles, one worthy of her title. "I'm Marcy Wong-Smith, First Lady of the Alliance, wife of Danirshna the third, high exalted President of the United Planetary Alliance, archaeon of the infinite stars and ruler of a thousand skies. Was lucky enough to get that shortened to Imperatrix."

"First Lady of the Alliance?" ShortThumb gasped. "They sent you to rescue us?"

"Well, they sent that dumbass." Marcy pointed at me. "I just tagged along for the ride. But it seems I have to do everything around here."

I was still too shocked by her presence to take that too personally. I crossed my arms over my chest, mostly to hide my stench.

"In any case," said Marcy, cozying into her seat, "with you here, this war will come to its conclusion swiftly. There's an end in sight."

I blinked. "Because you think I have a plan to stop a centuries-old war that I've been carrying in my pocket this whole time?"

"What?" Marcy laughed, though the smile didn't reach her eyes. Was she… mocking me? "You think we've been sitting on our hands all day, waiting for you to show up and rescue us? You misunderstand me, Zander. With you here, as in, *at this camp*. We've finally found you. You see, there's a certain woman who's been looking for you…"

"Sally?"

I sprang to my feet without a second's thought. My heart was racing—no, I didn't have a working heart, but my chest was still bursting.

Sally was safe. She was out there, fighting, being the incredible woman that she was.

"I told you; I have no idea where she is," Marcy said, "Zander, I was talking about your sister."

My breath caught in my throat. "Blayde?"

Since when was my voice so nasally? I couldn't think, couldn't breathe—my relief had been so short. Now, all I had was fear, seconded by confusion. I folded myself back into the chair. My knees couldn't keep me standing any longer.

How could Blayde be here? She didn't know we were on this mission, and even if she did, she'd have deduced that we were stuck, would have known better than to book a one-way ticket to awful-awful-land. Which meant if she was here… she was prepared.

Blayde was hope. Blayde was victory. I couldn't help but smile at the thought.

"You have another sister no one knows about?" Marcy snorted. "We received a strange letter yesterday, saying that the subjugation would end shortly, that we needed to find *you* so that it could be pulled off. It was signed by Blayde. She seemed certain you were somewhere on this planet, and apparently your help is *essential.* Something about a… Pineapple March."

I let out a sharp laugh, and not at Marcy's over-use of air quotes. No. Blayde was here, and she was throwing absolutely ludicrous battle plans at the wall and hoping they would stick. This would not end well.

But… she wasn't asking about Sally either. No one seemed worried about Sally in the slightest. I pulled together all my fear for her and clutched it in my fist. I couldn't be selfish. People came before a single person.

"Did Blayde shake a few neurons loose on her way here?"

"You tell me." Marcy lifted an eyebrow. "Did she?"

What a question. "No. I can see where she's going with this."

"Well, I can't," said ShortThumb. "What in Trod's name is a Pineapple?"

"It's a fruit," I explained. "From Earth. Sharp leaves, and a prickly skin. Tasty as heck, can completely hypnotize the Gavorkian army in a pinch. Anyway. Blayde needs us to create diversions on all fronts to divide the enemy."

Marcy frowned. "Are you sure about this?"

"I am, but if you want to be certain, just ask her in the reply letter. We need to coordinate our multi-pronged distraction before they come at us again."

ShortThumb snorted so hard I felt a drop on my cheek. "Excuse me?"

I gritted my teeth. Here we are coming at them with a perfect plan, and they're looking at me like I'm the evening entertainment. Trust me, I'm a one-man talent show, and my Jarkovian burlesque dancing is enough to make you weep, but this wasn't the kind of audience I wanted right now.

Provis's face lit up inside my mind. If *he* was here, they'd listen to me. He should have been the one to survive the attack: they needed him. They should have taken me instead.

"Last night's attack was just the first step," I said. "They understand now we're not ready for that kind of retaliation. They showed their hand, showed us they've figured out here the camps are, and that they can, and will, destroy us. They took one of our own."

"They know our locations?"

"How else could they have targeted the most remote camp? It's the one place that has a mountain in their way of their communications? They know how we're laid out. They know our camps. And they're going to strike again. We need to coordinate, and do so now, before it's too late."

"So, you want our divided army to attack on all fronts. Attack armies that are larger and more powerful than we are." Marcy leaned back in her seat. "I can't give that order. It's suicide."

"Not when you have another side to your attack." A smile crept up my face. "Not when my sister has a plan to infiltrate the government."

"You got all that from a *description* of her letter?"

"I got all that from Pineapple March, yes. The rest of the words were for your satisfaction alone."

"You're kidding me," said ShortThumb, shaking her head. "You have got to be kidding me."

"What does your sister plan to accomplish by infiltrating the government?" Marcy seemed a lot keener on what I was saying now, leaning closer in anticipation. "It's not like we can take them over from within. They can't understand a word we're saying, and our Ster accomplices are too few to take control. What is she planning?"

"May I see the note she sent?" I asked. "Maybe I can find out more from the words she used. You know, reading what was meant for *me*."

Marcy rose to her feet and lifted a map off the desk – only to reveal another map, and another, and soon she was holding what looked like fifty maps in one hand while scouring the desk's surface. She reached over to one of the maps hanging on the wall, lifted it up, and found the memo attached to the same clip. She pulled it out, unfolded it, and handed it to me.

"Here," she said. "Sorry 'bout that."

I took the sheet and unfolded it, feeling a strange sense of relief wash over me as I recognized my sister's scrawled words.

"You need the encryption key?" Marcy pulled up her maps to begin another search.

"Nah, got it." I scanned Blayde's words. I had long since gotten over the point where I needed one to read her cyphers.

To all lost souls out there,

Trust me when I say that the tyranny of your Sters is almost at an end. Your years of fighting will not dwindle to a forgotten cause – but rise to an unforgettable battle of epic proportions, from which we shall emerge victorious. Every piece is on the playing field. I just need your help finding one of them.

His name is Zander, and he is my brother. A few of you may know him from your annals of history: from myths, from legends, from whispers. Let's be honest, most of you know him from his wanted posters, or from the ill-advised charity calendar he did that sparked a religion. It was a whole thing.

He came here to find a ship, and I came here to find him. He's two Alliance units tall, or, in universal terms, one one-hundred-and-fifty-millionth of a light second. Well, approximately. Brown hair. Grayish-brown eyes. Light brown skin. Tends to grow back lost limbs.

When you find him, tell him we're going to attempt a Pineapple March. Tell him I've got a plan. He's just got to take the command on your end.

Because they're coming.

I saw them. They've grown themselves an army, ready to leave the cities and strike. We're going to war, whether we're ready or not. It's time to fight back.

You all must trust him. Trust us. We're going to help end this war. I understand you don't know us, but, for the most part, you know of us: and most of the stories are true. I promise that you'll be free within the next few days.

Be ready to give it your all.

Blayde

Blayde was *here*. It was going to be much easier to find Sally once we'd taken over the planet. If that was the only way to get her back, so be it. I'd led wars before. I would lead them again.

And the honorable cause was a distinct bonus.

"Gather your men." I rose to my feet, blood running hot. "Send the shuttles to each of the camps and tell them to prepare for war. Gather anything that can be used as a weapon. Get children and non-fighters to the safety of the mountains. Booby-trap all empty camps. Spread the word—we're going to take back our freedom. And we need to send a message to my sister. Just this." My hands clenched into fists. *"Pineapple Go."*

Marcy covered her mouth and politely let out a snort. "Dude. Calm your jets. This isn't how things happen here."

"How do things happen here?"

"With a lot less pomp and a lot more circumstance," she said, standing up. "Stop making speeches and tell me your plan. We don't need any more drama. Hold your horses or whatever spacey expression you guys use."

I rejected the urge to exhale loudly. Exhaling was rather useless after all.

"So. What does your sister intend to do with the government?"

"She doesn't say. But I can assume she found a weakness that she intends to take advantage of."

"Wow, this is eye opening." Marcy leaned back in her seat. "Look, Zander. Our past friendship on Earth says I should trust the two of you."

"And it's only because of said friendship that I'm not questioning your suitability as leader." I crossed my arms over my chest. "What are you even doing here, Marcy? Why did you join us in the shuttle?"

Her eyes narrowed. "I knew they couldn't leave with me here, so I came. Isn't that enough for you?"

"I don't think it's the whole story, no." I felt like an ass for this, but I gestured at her belly. "Did you know? When you climbed on the shuttle, did you know you were with child? Does Dany know?"

Both Marcy's and ShortThumb's eyes went wide at this.

"*With child?*" ShortThumb snorted again. "What century are you from?"

Marcy raised a hand to calm her. "I agree, that's borderline creepy AF, Zander. None of that is any of your business."

"It is if you're leading this rebellion."

"You need to stop that," Sally snapped, standing at my left elbow, dressed in a long Myrish gown. Which was strange, seeing as how I had never been to Myra. "You don't listen to me, do you? I told you, you are not responsible for these people. You need to learn how to step back."

Not now. Not now. Not now.

"Zander." Marcy stood, fingertips digging into the table. "I'm willing to trust you and your sister on this plan. You have more experience, I'll give you that. Your reputation puts you on the winning side of history. But it sounds like you're sending my people into a last stand, and I can't have that. I need a concrete plan, not something that sounds like the Trader Joe's special of the month. One that gets us off world alive, rather than as disembodied souls. I will follow your advice, but you will let me lead my people, do you understand?"

I nodded. This was not the Marcy I had seen at Sally's welcome home party. Maybe this Marcy was ready to lead. It seemed she had picked up much more than a fetus during her months on Pyrina.

"Clear as a vacuum," I said. "We need *your people* to create a large-scale distraction on all fronts to allow Blayde to run her plan. This will serve to divide the Ster army so that no unit will have to face the full brunt of a Ster battalion at once." Sally leaned over the table, observing as if she were actually here. I shook her out of my vision. I couldn't have her distracting me. I pointed out locations on the map. "We start attacks here, here, and here. Followed by a second wave in these parts. This will convince the Sters we are retaliating for Party City, and that we're dumb enough to throw our entire force behind this act of revenge."

"Isn't that exactly what we're doing?"

"Well, they don't know about Blayde's secret plan."

"*I* don't even know about Blayde's secret plan!" Marcy slammed her fist on the table. "Zander, you had better be right about this."

"You said it yourself, *Imperatrix,* I always end up on the winning side of history."

We stared at each other; her eyes boring into mine. When had she become such a force? When we'd been on Earth, she had been this happy-go-lucky woman, someone who always had a smile to offer and a shoulder to cry on, even on the darkest days—not a war plan.

And then, the strangest thing happened: Spurlock Magnesar sprang into the tent.

I wouldn't have recognized him if not for his voice, because of course he flung himself inside singing his auto-song-ography, but he looked nothing like the man who'd sung us off the *Traveler* mere weeks ago. His gorgeous hair had been shorn down almost to the scalp, and under his secondhand uniform, he was skin and bones. But the smile that now radiated from his face couldn't be anybody else's.

"Oh I surfed a supernova two light-years and a few, but I never met anybody as nuclear as you," he wailed, throwing his

hands out wide to slide across the floor like a surfer. "Great Lady Empress Wife, how are you?"

"Magnesar," said Marcy, smiling a smile so forced it could power a small generator if only we could figure out how to harness the energy of desperation. "What are you doing here?"

"I came to save you!" he said. "Well, that was the intended plan. I accompanied the novalicious Blayde on a mission to find you. Thought the Alliance could do with a new power ballad about a royal rescue. I got a little sidetracked, but not to worry, it's given me more material. Now, the plan is a full rock-opera about the operation! Mankind reduced to domesticated status, banding together to rise up. I think I'll end Act I with the fierce Sally Webber ceasing the means of production and leading the rebellion—unless we're going with a four-act structure, in which case..."

I sprang to his side faster than I thought I could move without jumping. "You have news from Sally?"

"News?" Magnesar clamped his hand on my shoulder. "Hundo, we lived an adventure together! She rescued me from the clutches of the Sters!"

Marcy let out a heady sigh. "Thank God. Where is she now?"

I thought I had been the one to ask, but my mouth was dry. Sally was safe. The real Sally. Out of the corner of my eye, the Sally created by my subconscious trickled and faded away—for now. My inner heart leapt inside my chest, propelling me a whole foot into the air.

"With Blayde, over at camp Underpass. They're planning how to bring down the cloud generators so we can fly out of here, *ratatatat*, beyond our cage of sky!"

He made a soaring motion with his hand and ShortThumb snorted. Magnesar seemed undeterred, rattling off a few bars of a victory anthem he said we hadn't earned yet.

Oh, my stars, Sally was safe. Sally was with Blayde. Sally was…

"I need to go to her," I said. Now that I knew where she was I couldn't go another second without seeing her.

"I'm as glad as you are that she's safe." Marcy shook her head. "But we need you here, Zander."

"Except you don't. Isn't that what you spent this past hour trying to tell me?"

"Uh, Zander, this is getting way too petty for me," said ShortThumb, dropping her eyes to the floor. "Tomorrow I'm either going to be free or dead. Either way, I won't have to deal with the Sters ever again. I can't focus on anything but that right now." She glanced over at Magnesar. "Though I have to say, an anthem could help us right now. Bring our spirits up."

She was, unfortunately, right. Heat rose in my cheeks. As much as I was desperate to see Sally, the real one, we were at war. I was letting her distract me, pull my focus from what was really important: saving everyone.

And then it hit me.

Music had saved the universe once in my recent memory: maybe it could do it again. And this time, it only needed to save a planet.

"Sters can't hear us speak, can they?" I asked, watching Magnesar strum to the beat of an invisible instrument. It was either a guitar or a squid he was trying to force into the oven.

"They feel it, but they can't hear it," said Marcy. "Our translators have no way of generating the charges they communicate with."

"Well then, I think we may have found our secret weapon."

Magnesar wrestled with the imaginary instrument in his arms, while the three of us exchanged knowing glances. It was time for the first officer of the *Traveler* to be the star he claimed to be.

TWENTY-ONE

PIXAR MOVIES SAVE MY LIFE AGAIN

Sally

WE WERE DRESSED HEAD TO TOE IN BLACK, DESPITE the fact it wouldn't blend into anything when Sters were involved. It didn't matter. Our little hopper was painted black too. It just felt cooler. Blayde flew us towards the glowing orbs of the Ster city, the bright blues and pinks of a million floaty octopus creatures combining to create a gentle sunrise on a planet that saw none. Thousands of glass domes gently rippled over the landscape, twisting and distorting the forest behind.

It was the first time I'd seen their civilization up close.

It was magnificent.

I hated myself for thinking that.

"What does the facility look like?" I asked, transfixed by the city. Blayde made a muffled "*Idunno*" noise beside me. We had to find them visually, since the exact location was locked in a mist we couldn't access with our puny brains.

"It makes clouds. What would a cloud factory look like?"

I had been asking myself that question since we'd first constructed the plan. The only things I could conjure up were cooling towers, the memory of long car drives and puffy white steam dancing in my mind. In less than a day, if we could pull this off, we were free. We were going to topple the Sters and get every human off this planet safe and sound, as promised.

If this was what Nimien had sent us to find, then I suppose his last act was a kindness for the universe.

If it wasn't, then what was I missing?

Blayde flew over the valley, closer and closer to the city, but still no sign of any cloud factories. They would be hard to pick out of the dark landscape in any case. Instead, glowing blots of red blossomed in the far distance. I swallowed.

"The attacks have begun," I said. Blayde didn't reply.

The city filled our windshield now, terrible and beautiful all at once. Millions of Sters frozen in place, transfixed by the noise that filled their air. *Our* noise. They had spent so much time ignoring us that now we were making ourselves heard, it was overwhelming.

I couldn't feel sorry for them even if I tried.

We flew past the city. Nada.

"It should be easier to find a cloud farm than this." I gestured at the landscape. "You'd need space. Big open fields. No forest."

"Ah," said Blayde. "Good point. We go where there's no glow. Brilliant, Sally."

I smiled, letting myself take full credit where credit might not have been due. I liked this new-ish Blayde, this Blayde who threw out compliments quicker than insults. I knew she'd had good reason to wipe her mind, but her more complete new-self regained whatever assurance she'd lost in the process.

But in other ways, she was just the same as she had always been: she gave no warning as she jerked hard to the left. I grabbed my seatbelt with both hands as I was almost flung into the door.

"Watch your flying!" I shouted.

"A flux! They're onto us!"

Oh shit. I couldn't help fly the ship. I couldn't do anything except grip the seat and hold on tight as Blayde swerved again, moving us out of the way of another invisible hand. I clenched my guts to keep anything from rising back up. This was bad. If we were grabbed now, in the middle of the city, the multi-pronged assault would be useless. The rebels would —

And then I saw it.

A patch of darkness.

A hint of steam.

A dense patch of clouds.

"Over there!" I shouted, pointing. "It's over there!"

Blayde floored it. We spiraled out of the grip, then accelerated forward full throttle, pushing me hard into the seat. I gritted my teeth as she shot towards the potential cloud farm, tears streaming straight from my eyes into the ratty headrest.

"Sally, do you remember when we ditched the ship in Malaysia?"

"Yeah." I didn't like where this was going. "Why?"

"Because we have to do the same thing now. Except, sans jumping."

I clenched my teeth tighter. "See you on the other side."

The good thing about falling in pitch darkness is you can't see how far you have to fall. Well, good thing for someone like me who hates heights with vengeance. This was the second time I'd fallen on this planet, only this time I didn't have the sweet forest to cushion my landing.

I was out for longer than I'd like to admit.

But when I awoke, feeling the ecstasy of my bones knitting together, I knew I wasn't alone. Blayde stood above me, offering me a hand in the darkness.

"Good find," she said, pulling me to my feet. "Now let's shut this place down."

One perk of being a race of flying aliens: no one is ever worried about falling in pits. The entire complex sprawled out before us, glowing eerily in the plant-light. The pits were dozens of meters wide, perfectly circular, as if someone had buried a handful of nuclear cooling towers. This was just the beginning of the complex: dozens of vents sprawled out behind it, bellowing out glowing white vapor. *The mist.* This was more than just a place to control the clouds: this was where they were produced.

And in the very center, through the mist, an imposing control tower. It was, as most towers are, tower-like and tall. The mist lifted into the sky until it merged with the clouds and disappeared, completely engulfed.

I let out a long, low whistle, unable to keep it in.

"You said it," said Blayde. "Though you shouldn't have. They probably know we're here now."

As if the Sters could sense anything through so much mist rolling up from the earth. Either way, we ran. Blayde took the lead, dashing between the pits, and racing towards the control tower.

But when we reached the base, nothing waited for us. Leave it to those flying aliens to build their doors impossibly high.

"Well." I gestured at the sincere lack of doors. "Any suggestions?"

Blayde said nothing, only smiled. It was unsettling to see her without her regular pencil-thin lips: as much as I liked the new look, it was a little much. Like she was in on a secret no one else knew and she wasn't intending on sharing.

"I think we need a ride," she finally replied, as if it was the most logical option in the world.

"Right. And how do you suggest we get one?"

"You're not going to like it."

"Do I ever?"

"Remember Area 51?"

I took a deep breath. Of course I remembered Area 51. I also remembered the first of many betrayals against James and felt ashamed all over again. Blayde didn't seem the least bit fazed, though. I pinched the bridge of my nose. In that instance, we'd played bewildered, lost tourists who'd gotten in so much trouble with the guards they accidentally killed Zander and unwittingly brought us into their base, like some kind of regenerating Trojan horse. I doubted Blayde would want to take our pantomime *that* far.

It sorta warmed my heart that we had these shared cherished moments, though.

"Let me guess," I replied, "We're lost, misbehaving finguies?"

"Exactly. Now be cute."

She reached down and turned off the scrambler at her hip. The buzz died, leaving us with the hum of the dark hills.

The air shimmered. The glow of a Ster? The light moved through the mist, ever closer. I shuddered, taking a step closer to Blayde. I never wanted to be within their grasp again.

"Wait. What do regular finguies do?" asked Blayde.

"I don't know, I wasn't a very good one."

"Me neither, all I did was sleep."

The mist parted to reveal a Ster—a blue one. Here we go again.

"Oh, hello there," it said, cooing electrically. It didn't seem bothered by the tingle in the air. Which meant that part of our diversion was gone. Shit. "What do we have here?"

"I like long walks," said Blayde, before giving me a playful push. "I don't like the cold."

What the heck was she going on about? "Give me treats, gimme ball." I tried to channel my best Galli, missing my family dog with every fiber of my being.

"You poor things!" said the Ster. "Are you lost?"

"Rub my belly and destroy the autocracy," Blayde continued, pushing me once again. I pushed her back, for whatever good that would do us.

"This won't do." Instantly, I felt my feet kick off from the ground—I was being fluxed again, hopefully for the very last time. "Let's get you safe."

Blayde hummed cheerfully as we rose through the air. The Ster was bringing us up to the tower—how kind of it. I gritted my teeth and refused to look down. Why was it always heights?

"Is that… are you humming the weird song Magnesar wrote for us when they sent us off?" I asked.

"*Wandereeeeers*!" Blayde grinned wider. "What? It's really catchy. Magnesar made me listen to the recording on the way over. A few dozen times."

The Ster fluxed us up, up, over the edge of the tower, and I couldn't help but gasp.

The second we drifted through the guard tower, I dropped unceremoniously on the glass floor. I rolled over; with an *oomph* and a hiss, Blayde had already subdued the guard, having zapped it square on the top of its head.

"Jeez, you could have warned me," I muttered, pushing myself up. It was hard to see: the only light came from the glowing gas inside the guard's bulb.

"And you should have seen it coming," she said with a shrug. "Oh, will you look at this?"

She zapped the bulb again, and the creature rose into the air, with Blayde clinging to it like a backpack. With another zap, it lifted a tentacle.

"No way," I said, "We are not Ratatouille-ing this."

"Either my translator's malfunctioning, or your solution is to eat this creature with summer veggies." Blayde wrapped her legs tighter around the creature. Was it conscious? Or was it dead, animated only by her taser? Either way, I felt sick to my stomach. "In any case, hold on tight. I've never had to drive this thing before, and it won't be smooth. I can promise you one thing, though."

"Let me guess, it will be fun?"

"You know me so well," she said, as I gripped a slimy tentacle and she zapped us into the air.

The flying wasn't graceful. To call it comfortable would be an insult to design everywhere. But it was efficient at navigating the impossible ups and downs of Ster architecture.

Blayde drove us into the entrails of the cloud factory, her stretching and pulling what had once been the brainstem of the creature, me clinging on for dear life, trying not to think of the ethical ramifications of our actions. We're saving humanity, I told myself, over and over again.

But it didn't wash away the stench of Ster corpse.

When we reached the bottom of the tower, dark corridors spread out like the spokes of a wheel. Blade spun us in a full circle, making me clutch the corpse even harder. Eww.

"Gotta love a species that never learned to use proper signage." She groaned. "What's the Earth saying for picking at random? *You do the boogie-woogie and you turn yourself around?*"

"There's gotta be a better way to distinguish the right path," I said. "You can't… I don't know, connect with the creature's mind?"

Blayde looked down at the deflated bulb she sat on, then back at me. "Too late for that. He's at one with the clouds now."

"Then maybe… I don't know, we should listen for machinery or something?"

A grin spread on her face. "Brilliant, Sally. If all these steam tunnels lead to cloud production, they'd make a massive amount of noise, but the control would be the one place to have light machinery."

This side of Blayde was truly unsettling. The more she complimented me, the more I wondered what was hanging over my head. Did she know something about me that I didn't? Or maybe she was just being patronizing for patronizing's sake. Either way, she'd again assumed genius where there wasn't any: that wasn't what I was going to say.

"This way," she said, and I had no choice but to follow as I was clinging to our only means of transportation.

This was the right decision: the hallway led us to, of all things, a tiny internal forest. Dozens of terrariums occupied the small room, filled with glowing plants. If this was a computer, it wasn't like anything I'd ever seen before.

"Right, this is going to be a steep learning curve." Blayde brought us towards a display of glass cases. "Maybe if I do… this?"

She made the corpse lift a tentacle, then dropped it sloppily on one of the terrariums. The air filled with ice again, though not listening this time: Icy hots. Probably not the right move.

"Great," said Blayde. "What are you playing at, Universe? You owe me one! Come on!"

I didn't have time to think. Three Sters burst through the door, the air charged around them. If the guard's mind had been absorbed by the cloud, they'd know exactly what we were. If it hadn't…

"Guard Spraxis, what is the meaning of this?" asked the one taking point. "This is not your quadrant!"

Blayde and I looked at each other. They didn't know, but the second we opened our mouths, we'd be done for, and it wasn't like we could communicate with them.

Could we?

Blayde shrugged, as if thinking the same as me, and poked at the creature's crown. A wail went through the air.

"What is it, Guard Spraxis?" cried the supervisor. "Are you in pain?"

Blayde poked another corner. This time, Spraxis's corpse let out what could only qualify as a moan. And a slightly sexy one at that.

"This is not the time for that, Guard Spraxis," said the supervisor, the voice low. The room fizzled. Oh dear. We'd found a sweet spot.

Blayde lifted her eyebrows and poked it again. And again. And again. The moans filled the air, with different levels of intensity. The two backup guards gingerly hovered back out of the room.

"What good is this doing?" I whispered.

"Shh, we're getting it hot and bothered." She made a tentacle swing on another terrarium. "All we need to do is screw this thing up."

"Well, it seems like you're definitely screwing something."

Spraxis's corpse continued to wail in a somewhat suggestive manner. I'd been so focused on the awful sound I hadn't noticed the alarm was off. But how would we know if we'd managed to shut off the clouds?

"Oh, Guard Spraxis," said the supervisor, as the door swung shut behind it. "I didn't know you felt this strongly about us."

Blayde jammed her finger into the brain over and over again. The sounds became more intense. I dropped to the floor, if only to use my arms for something more important than clinging on: blocking my ears.

But me dropping from Spraxis's corpse was apparently part of the seduction, as the supervisor rushed at Spraxis, intertwining its tentacles in a tight embrace. How Blayde was keeping herself from vomiting was completely beyond me.

"Oh, Guard Spraxis!" it said, "Will you make me the happiest supervisor on the sphere and give yourself to me?"

I glanced around the control room—anything but look at the scene unfolding behind me. The computers were unlike any control system I'd ever seen. I couldn't interact with the terrariums, whatever they were: no tentacles, no flux.

Well, except the one controlling the force field at the farm. I suppose I'd already tried suppressing that. I hopped off our ride, staring at the trap door on the floor. This was not going to be pleasant.

"Don't give me that face, Sally," said Blayde, still astride the corpse, continuing to press on alternate parts of Spraxis's brain as the supervisor made out with it. Though calling it making out was generous on my part. "What's on your mind?"

"The farm," I said, swallowing hard. "I had to short out the bugs."

"What bu—"

I threw open the trap door to reveal what I'd feared: a million creepy crawlies, doing whatever bugs do. How this generated anything I didn't know, but I knew what shut them off, and I wasn't going through that again.

"So, what are you waiting for?" said Blayde. "Short them out!"

"I can't." The memory of their billions of little legs crawling over my skin… my breath hitched. It was too much. I couldn't physically move. "I've done it before. You do it."

"I'm a bit busy," she said.

"Just knock it out and be done with it!"

"It's our only bargaining chip!"

I bit my lip. Throwing myself into a pit of bugs would be better than watching whatever that was. I jumped, only to stop at the top of my arc.

The moans stopped abruptly.

A Ster had fluxed me right out of the air.

A familiar Ster.

"Comfort Food?" said my former owner's parent. "Is that really you?"

TWENTY-TWO

LET THE MUSIC MOVE YOU (AND THE MONSTERS OUT OF THE WAY)

Zander

IN MANY PARTS OF THE GALAXY, MY VERY presence was enough to end a war. My reputation had a terrible habit of preceding me, and when it didn't, something about my face or my smell scattered the armies and their media teams. But not on this particular world; their hostile physiology meant even my face went unseen and my shouts unheard. So, instead of making an impressive appearance that could have saved them all—or simply following Blayde's excellent plan—I was relegated to being the "man behind the mask.".

Or, worse yet, the man-who-kinda-just-stood-behind-the-mask.

"I'm useless here." I waited at Marcy's side as we surveilled the battle from behind a dozen screens. "I need to be out there."

"You're a stronger asset at my side." Marcy took a deep breath, pinching the bridge of her nose between two fingers. "Your experience is invaluable."

Not the glowing thanks and respect I was hoping for, but it was something.

If only Provis were here. Provis should be leading us into war.

"Listen to yourself," said the Sally of my subconscious. The Myrish birds on her shoulders cawed in unison. She still hadn't given up the gown: I think she liked it. Did that mean *I* liked it? "You need to allow yourself to step back. To put your trust in others. Take a glance at your memories; let them guide you through this next part."

"Isn't that exactly what I'm doing? Blayde has her memories back, and she thinks this is a good idea. I'm trusting her." I was getting tired of speaking under my breath, but Fake-Sally still refused to respond to me otherwise. Besides, I *had* learned to put my trust in others: if Provis was leading the charge, I would have followed him into battle. Anywhere.

"Because *she* assumes you have yours back too, and that you know what you can handle." Sally shook her head. "I'm *you*. Why don't you trust me?"

"It's *because* you're me that I don't trust you." I tried to focus on Marcy. She cringed as explosions lit up a screen—Camp Spooky was no more. "Now go, I've got work to do."

Sally shook her head. "You're going to regret this."

"You see if I don't."

The Sally of my subconscious was gone, again.

But maybe she was right, in some small way: maybe I was spreading myself too thin trying to save everyone. Maybe I should focus on saving just one. They knew the plan, and they knew what to do: they didn't need me anymore.

"Who were you talking to?" Marcy glanced back at me. "Please don't tell me I'm losing you, too."

"No, I'm here. But I mean it when I say I'm no use to you in this room."

She turned back to the screens. The image quality was terrible, and limited by the few working cameras, but one thing was clear: an enemy that could lift you up from the battlefield without even touching you was not going to go down easily. Rifles were only good enough if the creatures were distracted, shaking somebody else around while you shot at them.

It *was* working. Just not fast enough.

"When do we unleash Magnesar?" I asked.

Marcy took a deep breath. "Not yet. We don't have enough sound systems set up. It's a little hard to do in the middle of a war."

She watched the screens in silence again. I couldn't bear it anymore.

"You don't need me here, Marcy," I insisted. "I need to go out there."

"No. You stay."

"But why?"

"Because that's an order!" She spun around, brandishing her finger in my face. "You're too dangerous out there, Zander. I've heard the stories. Read the histories. You may represent the Alliance at the moment but I can't have you off leash."

"*Leash*?" I spat. "I don't work for you! We're meant to be working *with* you!"

"Exactly, we work together now. Do you know how hard that is to sell? We need this operation to go perfectly."

"You're only thinking of the story." I stepped forward, but she didn't pull back her finger. "Aren't you? Of how this is going to be spun for the masses?"

"It's crossed my mind."

"And you need to show them that I'm under your control."

"It would be nice."

I wanted nothing more than to storm out of the tent that instant, remind her who exactly was in control. But there were lives on the line, people that needed to get off this nightmare world. I gave a sharp nod.

"Isn't this what Dany has been doing to *you*?" I asked, softening my voice slightly. "The leash is exactly why you're here. Why are you doing the same to me?"

Marcy sighed. Her eyes were fixed on the screens, as if the words hadn't made her flinch. "It's not the same, Zander. Dany was trying to keep me safe. I'm trying to keep everyone else safe."

I opened my mouth, ready to protest, but she held up her hand, stopping me mid-sentence. "Do you have any idea how hard it's been to get this many people coordinated? How much worse it would be if they were all scattered? We can't win this battle without everyone working together. That includes you. You need to stay here and do what I tell you, or else we won't be able to do our part in this. Do you understand?"

I agreed reluctantly. We were fighting an uphill battle against an enemy that had superior power, but I hated being stuck in the room while everyone else was out there risking their lives for something bigger than themselves.

Marcy seemed to sense my unease and placed a hand on my shoulder comfortingly. "We will find a way through this, Zander," she said softly, her voice full of determination and strength. "But for now, stay here and help us from inside."

I exhaled slowly and nodded again, pushing down my own doubts and fears as best as I could. Marcy gave an understanding smile before turning back towards the screens with renewed vigor—as though ready to take on whatever came our way with courage and strength of heart.

Who they needed was Provis. And I was going to save him.

Then again, I didn't know where to go for that, either.

"Tell you what," I said. "You want the press to think I was at your side the entire time? Fine. I'll say I was behind you all the way. But if you won't let me help on the battlefield, let me do you one better: the heroic rescue mission."

She lifted her eyebrow. "Provis?"

"And all other prisoners of war." My lip twitched as I forced back my smile. "He's not the only one who was taken by the Sters, I'm sure. Let me lead a dramatic rescue and get them all out."

"The hope was that he would bring the troops and reinvigorate the fight, but no one knows where he is. Unless you know something I don't?"

"No, but I'm really good at finding people." I made myself tall, a soldier at attention. Her attention. "What do you say?"

She glanced at the chaos on the screens: at Magnesar in the corner, busy composing his anthem; at her generals around the maps, moving the lines like waves at the beach. Then, back at me.

"Fine." She closed her eyes for an instant. "But you're not going alone. Take Captain ShortThumb."

"I wouldn't have gone with anyone else," I said, gesturing to the captain, whose eyes went wide in surprise. "Looking forward to hearing Magnesar sing."

"Likewise," Marcy replied, and turned back to her screens.

ShortThumb followed me out of the tent, glancing anxiously over her shoulder. "Where are we going?"

"To save Provis," I said.

"We are?" She looked back at the tent once more, then ahead. The camp was a ghost town: everyone had been mobilized to the fronts. "But… how?"

"Still working that out."

"You don't have a plan?"

"I rarely do, but things have a tendency to sort themselves out."

We reached the hangar bay—fancy name for a parking lot. The best ships had been allotted to those who needed them most: this was our last hurrah, after all. It would all be for nothing if we didn't give it our everything. Said everything did not include the one hopper left, a ratty ship that must have been stapled together from three ships from different generations. It would have to do. No one asked if we were meant to be there, no one even glanced our way as we stepped into our commandeered craft. Another day, I might have reprimanded them for their inattention, but that was the least of our problems. With that, the two of us took to the sky.

So there we were, flying above a world that was so much bigger than ourselves. ShortThumb leaned as far as she dared out of the window, protected by our low-level shield, which barely managed to keep the air out. She turned to me.

"Ok. I'm going to ask this again... but... how exactly are we meant to find Provis? Is the plan coming together?"

I gritted my teeth, my eyes scanning the dark horizon.

"I assume the Sters took him for a reason." My palms were sweaty against the controls, leaving sticky, wet smears along the switches. Thankfully, ShortThumb was looking anywhere but. "Probably to squeeze him for information. Seeing as Sters don't seem to think we're all that intelligent, they'd take him where they keep all their finguies: a military base of some kind."

"There's a large one to the north of the city," she said, never removing her eyes from the landscape. "It's surrounded by fences, something Sters don't have a particular need for unless they're dealing with us. We theorized that's where they were experimenting on finguies, though we never managed to infiltrate it."

I nodded "Perfect. That's where we'll head first."

We aimlessly meandered in the sky for what felt like a comically indefinite period, while our eyes scanned the earth below, like detectives on a quest for a needle in a haystack. Finally, my eyes were met with a sight that sent a chill down my spine—a massive camp, situated between two peaks like an eagle's nest. The perimeter of the camp was lined with electrified fences and patrolled by a battalion of Sters, their horrific luminescence shining in the night like neon ghosts.

Without a word, we gently guided our hopper towards a nearby clearing, and worked our way delicately through the trees until we had reached a vantage point overlooking the camp. It was clear from the layout that this was no ordinary prison; massive opaque buildings filled the space inside the fence, with more Sters than I'd ever seen before.

"Shit," ShortThumb swore under her breath. "This place is better guarded than Provis's secret booze fridge."

I nodded grimly, my stomach churning with dread. With fences like that, this was a finguy testing base, no doubt about it—and Provis was somewhere inside, trapped in the middle of this nest of Sters. We were running out of time; we had to find a way in, and fast.

But how? The fence surrounding the camp was easily four times taller than either of us, and evidently shielded. Even with the element of surprise, no one, let alone two measly humans, stood a chance against an army of Sters.

"We need a plan," I said finally, turning away from the base and back to ShortThumb. She nodded, her eyes already scanning the clearing for anything that might help us.

"You've done this millions of times before," said Fake-Sally, crouching beside me in the underbrush. I glared up at her.

"I thought I left you behind at the camp," I growled.

"What's that?" ShortThumb whipped her head my way. I bit my lip.

"It's how I deal with my self-doubt," I explained. "I talk to it like it's an externalized version of myself."

"Huh. Practical. I should try that too. Your sense of fashion is dreadful!"

I couldn't have asked for anyone better to accompany me on this rescue mission. My heart fell: well, no. Sally could have been here. The real one.

I couldn't wait for the two of them to meet.

"Wow, you are really falling off target," said Fake-Sally. "Focus. I'm telling you, there is a wealth of knowledge just waiting for you..."

I shook her out of my head, though the pressure in my temples refused to leave with her. I could do this. I had enough recent memories to get myself through this.

"Right," I said, trying to drown her out. "The thing with force shields is they tend to be unidirectional. This being a finguy camp, they're probably more focused on keeping finguies in than civilians out, yes?"

I rose gingerly to my feet, and without thinking, threw myself towards the perimeter. I could run through it, I could.

I hadn't counted on them using *two* shields.

I was thrown back in the air, my body hair sizzling before I hit the ground, leaving me smelling like an overcooked party piñata. The collision with the dirt was equally unpleasant.

"Thanks for trying that," said ShortThumb. "Let's try plan B."

"What's plan B?"

"Wait for— "

Before she finished her thought, plan B started without us. At first, gently: like a whisper in your ear, words carried on the wind, so soft you think you might be dreaming them.

We've been living under their rule for too long
Tentacles pulling our strings, where we belong
We were just finguies, caged in by their might
But now it's our turn, to take back what's right

Magnesar's anthem was beginning. Filling the air with the power of Rock, not that the Sters would ever understand a word of what was being sung: no, they were probably feeling the effects of powerful radio waves overwhelming their senses right around now.

Now we're rising, like a phoenix from the ashes
With music as our weapon, we'll smash their gases
With every chord we strum, we'll break their hold on us
Our music's a weapon, it's time to make a fuss!

"Huh," said ShortThumb. "You know, I was expecting worse for something composed at the last minute while under threat of annihilation."

"He went hard." I nodded. "He could have used any song and it would have worked."

The music was louder now and coming from all around, literally filling the air, or in this case, mist. The Sters in the compound ahead of us froze in place, the gas inside their bulbs swirling faster as the chorus hit.

We'll sing a song of freedom, a battle cry of might
With instruments a-blazing, we'll fight the good fight
We'll be the voice of humanity, we'll show them our might
With the power of music, we'll bring them down tonight

"Now that's an earworm," muttered ShortThumb.

"It's not bad, I'll give him that."

"You forget this is the first piece of music I've heard in twenty years." A smile drew itself across her face. "I don't care if it's a flop, I'll be singing it for the next twenty."

Rise up, rise up, the time has come
Our voices will be heard, our freedom won
With flux in our hands, we'll show them what we've got
We'll beat them at their own game, we'll rock, rock, rock!

"Frash yeah, let's do this thing!" ShortThumb rose to her feet, eyes wide and sparkling. Before I could say anything, she ran at the fence, screaming with her whole belly, *"we'll rock, rock, rock!"*

I watched, incapable of moving, as she assaulted a Ster, leaping into the air to punch the hypnotized creature. It flew into the shield, the air fizzling as they collided, its flux punching a hole into the force field. ShortThumb grabbed its tentacles and swung into the compound, landing softly on her feet like she'd been playing on a swing set.

"Take that, frashers!" She laughed, racing across the gravel. The Sters didn't register her presence: they remained frozen in place, overwhelmed by Magnesar's music as he swung into his second verse.

They think they're so powerful, with their flux so strong
But they don't know the power, of a rock and roll song
They've been holding us down, with their flux and their squirt
But now we're coming for them, with a chorus that'll hurt

I cringed—he was reaching there with some of his rhymes. Sure, the song was composed in less than a day, but he didn't need to write a new one from scratch. Honestly, I didn't know his music all that well: he could have been recycling from his lesser-known hits.

I raced towards the compound, hijacking a Ster like ShortThumb had, and breaking into the compound with a little less grace than she had. Not that she was watching, she was already far ahead of me, seemingly inspecting the gravel for human footsteps.

"They seem to be heading this way," she said, pointing towards one of the opaque buildings. "And lots of them."

Together we dashed across the open space, reaching what could be interpreted as a door as fast as we could. The trance couldn't last forever, and I didn't know much music Magnesar had composed for us. Thankfully we could hear his dulcet tones even inside the structure, which meant we had a little leeway for our infiltration.

We'll sing our battle cry, as we take to the skies
Our music a symphony, as we defy their lies
The Sters thought we were weak, but now they'll see
The power of humanity, and what we can be

Ok, I had to admit, it was growing on me. Nothing beats a good power ballad, and this was light-years better than his absurd *Wanderers* send-off song. Novalicious, this was going to hit the charts when we finally got off this planet.

The inside of the structure was darker than expected. The opaque walls let in little to no light, and the plants on the walls were dimmer than the ones out in the forest. As my eyes adjusted, the smell hit me: unwashed humans. Open cells lined the walls, their contents unidentifiable, but even in the near dark, it was clear there wasn't anyone inside.

ShortThumb and I shared a concerned look as we advanced down the corridor. We'd need to be careful in case any Sters had followed us in but, so far, we hadn't seen any sign of them. Magnesar's anthem was getting quieter by the second: was the building blocking out more sound, or were the Sters figuring out how to break through their trances and silence his singing?

We moved cautiously, scanning each room for danger as we passed. ShortThumb lifted her rifle and braced to shoot. I detected nothing, though at one point I could have sworn I saw something move just beyond my vision's range. My heart thudded against my rib cage as we edged closer to whatever it might be.

Deeper into the compound we went, descending ramps that led to more floors of empty cells. Where was everyone? I bit my lip: maybe we were too late. Maybe this was where the feral finguies had come from, and they were all out killing our troops.

I was more on edge as we descended even deeper. I could no longer hear Magnesar's anthem. If there were Sters down here, they could be on guard, waiting for us. But why would they be? There was nothing to find.

Until there was light.

"Shh." I gestured to ShortThumb. "Something's down there."

She nodded, bracing herself further. One more floor, one last ramp. We descended together, staying low, not that it would make any difference to the Ster below.

Hushed whispers filled the space, louder the lower we walked. Was that—a laugh?

"Want?" asked a voice. A squeaky one. The light significantly dimmed. "Don't you want to come home with me?"

"We want our families," said a voice—a familiar voice. My heart leapt in my chest—*Provis*? "Our Pods, as you call them. We want..."

We stepped down the ramp and I froze in shock. There in the hallway, a Ster glimmered. It hit me in an instant that this was the first time I had seen the enemy in the flesh.

Smaller than I expected, to be honest. Tentacle-y enough to give me the willies.

And the Ster wasn't alone. Behind it, dozens of *us*, all in different states of dazed and/or confused. We were late to the party.

"Another finguy!" the small Ster said excitedly. "And another one on top of that! More to rescue. Whoopee!"

I glanced back at ShortThumb, who held out her rifle like a promise. Her face was tight, stern—probably the same face I was meant to be making, if it hadn't been warped in confusion.

"What's your name, little one?" said the Ster. "I'm Gluuk, and these are my friends!"

A Ster, and one that could understand us at that. I opened my mouth, shut it again, then opened it again, all while ShortThumb kept her trembling arrow fixed on the creature. And out of the crowd came Provis, rushing up to cover her weapon with his hand.

"Don't shoot!" he said, lowering the arrow. "Gluuk is our friend!"

"I'm your friend?" Gluuk glowed an even brighter shade of pink. "This makes me so happy!"

Provis looked back at Gluuk, then at us. Without thinking, we threw our arms around each other: ShortThumb, Provis, and me, holding each other tight.

Party City, always together.

"What happened to you?" asked ShortThumb, as we pulled away. "We saw them take you, we didn't know… what…"

"They didn't have time to do anything." He smiled in a way that didn't quite reach his eyes. "They've all been distracted by something today. Gluuk here rescued me—rescued us—before they could do anything."

The figures surrounding Provis were from all different species. All wearing tight jumpsuits that showed way more than we needed to see.

Gluuk twirled in the air. "I'm going to take you all home," it said. "I have space in my room where I can hide you. My pod will have no idea!"

Provis looked up at Gluuk and sighed. "We talked about this, Gluuk." He turned back to me. "We came up with a plan! We have a Ster on our side, can you believe it?"

Gluuk twirled around again, which made all the former prisoners whoop and clap with glee. Was it... a child?

"Gluuk promised us their voice," Provis explained. "To speak to the Ster leaders on our behalf. To let them know we won't be their pets anymore."

I glanced up at Gluuk, still twirling for its uncomfortable audience, and back at Provis, who grinned, equally uncomfortable. ShortThumb bit her lip, saying nothing. I couldn't imagine how hard it was for her to stay so composed as she stood in front of the species that had taken so much from her.

"That is so kind of you, Gluuk! Is there a way you can speak to everyone at once?" I asked. "To project your voice into the cloud?"

Gluuk finally stopped twirling, to our collective relief. "I'm too young to be fully immersed in the mist."

"What about to send messages really long distances? Is there some kind of device like that?"

"There is, yeah," it said. "In my Sib-Parent's office, in the other building. But I'm not allowed in there. And —"

"You're not allowed *here*, either," said Provis, "Yet you rescued us."

"That's different," said Gluuk. "I didn't want Sib-Parent to hurt you."

"And if you do this, no one will hurt us ever again." ShortThumb stepped forward, dropping her bow and arrow to the ground with a clatter. "Can you do it for us, Gluuk?"

Gluuk bobbed up and down, somehow soberly. "I can."

TWENTY-THREE

WHEN LIFE GIVES YOU SQUABBLES, MAKE THEM YOUR LEVERAGE

Sally

IT'S NEVER A GOOD FEELING RUNNING INTO THE creep who bought you as their house pet. What makes it a tad worse is when he catches you trying to destroy their civilization.

Instead of saying anything, Vuzuk shrieked. Which is of course a difficult thing to do when you have no mouth, so instead, it felt like all the air in the room was about to drop a bottle of lightning on my head. Every one of my hairs stood on end, as though every oxygen molecule around me had donned a wool sweater and rubbed a balloon against it. Blayde, her hand in contact with the Ster corpse, backflipped elegantly off the former security guard, which promptly dropped into the bin of squirming insects. The lights, what few of them there were, shut off, plunging us into darkness, lit only by Vuzuk's shaky glow.

Well, that was easy.

"What have you done?" shouted Vuzuk. It fluxed us both into the air. Blayde and I rattled around like dolls in a poorly rendered AR experience.

It tossed us to the side. I pushed myself back up as Vuzuk tried to flux the corpse out of the bug pit generator. I saw what was coming, and trying not to think too hard about what I was getting myself into, I threw myself into the generator.

The millions of tiny legs skittered up my exposed flesh, but before I could let out a scream, I was pulled out by my ankle—Vuzuk. Its flux wasn't solid, but it was strong enough to lift me. The lights in the terrariums flickered.

I hadn't thought to look into backup generators.

"What do you think you're trying to do?" Vuzuk chucked the guard's corpse into the corner, lifting me higher. "My own finguy. I rescued you, gave you a home, shelter, food, someone who loved you and cared for your every whim, and this is how you repay me?"

I coughed: the static in the air was tickling my nostrils. Where was Blayde? Oh, there she was, dead in a corner. That wouldn't last too long, but I was alone for a bit, and it wasn't going to be pretty.

"I'm trying to get home, you entitled Squidward," I spat. "You should have seen since day one that I didn't need rescuing!"

"Watch who you call entitled."

My blood, which had until now been running down to my head and pooling in my fingertips, froze.

"Y-you could understand me?" I sputtered. "This whole time?"

The air skittered around it: a laugh.

"There wasn't much to understand. At least, not much that was interesting."

"But why?" I glanced over at Blayde again—still dead. I needed to kill time. Vuzuk's grip on my ankle ebbed and flowed: something was hurting its flux. Maybe it was the thing that infused the air, that made my heart thrum. "You knew we were intelligent this whole time, and you carried on making us your pets?"

"Intelligent?" it scoffed. "Please. Flapping your meat flaps to vibrate the air doesn't make you intelligent. You're about as intelligent as a plant or a tree. The way we care for you is a mercy."

"And yet, you are aware we are not from your world," I insisted. My head was getting hot now. There was something in the air for sure, and not just Vuzuk's anger. "That we come here on ships. That we're capable of traveling to places you cannot. That there are many other worlds out there."

"We are aware of where you come from. But up there? That is not the world. Our scientists have determined there are no clouds in the above realms."

I didn't have time for this kind of introspection: I had to shut it down. Save my people. Not… think about the implications of a species that needed a medium to interact with their environment. Not think of the ships the Sters would have to create if they wanted to travel the universe, blind and deaf to the wonders beyond.

Yeah. Definitely not the right time.

"We just want to go home," I said. "You understand me: Please, listen to me. Let us leave here, and we will never bother you again."

"You are not intelligent enough to make this kind of decision." Vuzuk's flux on me was… slipping now, for lack of a better word. I was getting lower… lower… not that I wanted back in the pit of bugs, but whatever I needed to do to shut this thing down, I would.

"Sib-Parent Granadam Vuzuk!"

The voice came from everywhere and nowhere at once, inside my head and out. I clamped my hands over my ears, for all the good that did me: I could still hear a buzz, like the feedback of a microphone.

"Who is that?" said Vuzuk. "Gluuk? Is that you?"

My jaw dropped—unfortunately, at the same time as Vuzuk dropped me. I fell headfirst back into the pit, bugs instantly taking up residence in my mouth. I snapped my jaw closed, spitting them out as I pushed myself through. The buggy quicksand was relentless, and I was sinking, and I…

Had I touched the bottom?

A squishy bottom.

I burst out of the pit, spitting out the disgusting bug bits, wiping off my face from where I could still feel them crawling. The corpse of the guard was gone, and so was Blayde—had she pushed it into the pit, before disappearing? If so, where was she? And how hadn't Vuzuk noticed that we'd already won?

Had we won?

"I am speaking now to you, Sib-Parent, but also to the entirety of Soil." Gluuk's voice was strong and proud in the darkness, filling up every corner of my mind. "I must tell you all that I have a gift. A rare gift from the ancestors: the ability to speak with finguies."

The room flashed hot with Vuzuk's annoyance. If it had eyes, I imagine it would be rolling them.

"And our finguies… They're not just random, silly creatures like we thought. They're actually super smart! They can talk! When they're messing with our stuff, it's not because they're wild. They're working together, trying to tell us something really important: they just want to go back home."

Way to go, Gluuk! Maybe it wasn't the only Ster to have whatever mutation allowed it to understand us, but to me, Gluuk was the chosen one. And I was happy to have been its E.T., even for a little while.

I take that back: Gluuk had dropped me and broke my arm. Gluuk was not a good pet parent.

"Oh, child," said Vuzuk. "What have you done?"

I couldn't help but laugh. Laugh the little buggy bits out of my mouth. Laugh Gluuk's voice out of my head. Laugh the sight of Vuzuk emotionally deflating in front of me.

"High and mighty Granadam Vuzuk," I said. "Decider of which species are intelligent or not. Even your own family can hear what we have to say. Even Gluuk knows our words have value."

"Enough!" it shouted. "Why can't I hear them? Where are they… where…"

"Oh Vuzuk." I stood back up. "You were so busy talking with little old me, questioning my intelligence, that you didn't even notice my friend had started shutting your little factory down."

"No!" it shouted. My arm lifted into the air by itself, only to collapse again, limp, at my side. Vuzuk couldn't flux me. "What have you done?"

"You need to start listening more, buddy."

Blayde appeared at my side, and next to her—*Marcy*. Immediately, three things were apparent:

One, that Blayde could jump again. It took everything in my power not to drop everything and jump to Zander's side.

Two, that Marcy was the most badass-looking rebel leader since Admiral Leah, and all that was wasted on Vuzuk's lack of sight.

And three—I was going to be an auntie.

I didn't know which part to squeal about first, so I just stared at them with the most uncomfortable grin on my face as possible.

But it wasn't Blayde who introduced the negotiations: it was Marcy.

"I take it you can hear me?" said Marcy, throwing me a wink before staring up at Vuzuk. "Good, because I need you to listen. We do not want to harm you. No matter what you have put us through, we are not here for revenge. Let us leave your planet, and we will give it back to you."

"You think you are in control?" Vuzuk sizzled, "We are all connected, all ready to fight back, all ready to…"

"And what for?" Marcy threw her arms wide. "Your entire world now knows we are not the idle house pets you've made us out to be. That the roving attacks are coordinated. What kind of pets would we make now?" She gestured at Vuzuk. "Right now, your people are safe inside their houses. Cut off from everyone else. How will you coordinate your defense? And you know what else is inside your houses? Finguies."

What was this new Marcy? I'd never seen her so… intense before. So in control. Even Blayde stood back and let her speak.

"What do you suggest?" said Vuzuk.

"A cease-fire," she replied. "My people leave your world. Then we return power over your clouds back to you. It's easy, and, if you agree, painless."

Vuzuk drifted lower and lower. "I… I agree to your conditions."

My phone lit up like a thousand suns: the notifications pouring in. How the phone managed to stay connected to Earth, I didn't know—I still hadn't seen my bill. But the fact it was online meant that connection had been established.

The clouds were coming down.

And I wasn't the only one getting notifications.

Marcy sighed, pulling out what looked like a phone from her pocket. A communicator? It too was vibrating. She held up a finger to the Ster—not that it could see, or would know what that meant even if it could.

A face appeared on the screen, a face of blinding beauty: Dany. Dany, who looked not like the strong Empress of the Universe we had come to know and love, but so terrified that her eyes took up most of the screen. If the message had come through so quickly, it meant she was nearby—perhaps on the *Traveler* itself.

"Dove," she said, her voice spilling crystal clear from the tiny communicator screen. "Are you all right? What have they done to you?"

I glanced up at Vuzuk. It didn't seem to be reacting to the call—could it feel it, through the cloud, or at least what was left of it, contained in this small room?

"I'm fine, darling, I'm fine," Marcy replied. "All things considered, I'm absolutely fine. Look, I've just negotiated a cease-fire. The Sters have agreed to let us leave their world, though we only have a small window to do it in. We need you to gather as many ships as you—"

"You negotiated a cease-fire?" Dany's eyes went impossibly wider. "You did what?"

"Is that so hard to believe?"

Choose your words wisely now, Dany. I smiled: it was honestly pretty dope to see the Empress of the Alliance cower before my bestie.

"Um… No, not really. I just thought you had been kidnapped, you know."

"Well, I wasn't." She took a deep breath. "I wanted this official liaison thing to work. I wanted it to work so badly, I came along, to force your hand. And now you're here. It was the right thing to do."

Dany's face retreated from the screen. Behind her was the glowing white of the *Traveler*'s bridge. Were the cameras rolling? How much of this was televised, for the whole Alliance to see? How much of this would go down in history, and how much in the bin?

"You're lying," she said, her face reverting to her empress-like neutral. "You think I've changed so much I can't tell when you're lying to me?"

"It's true." Marcy gripped the communicator with both hands. "I couldn't imagine Sally being stuck on this planet. I can't leave my friends behind, Dany. I can't. I…"

"Oh my stars." Dany's face lost all color. "You're pregnant."

My brows collapsed in on each other. She didn't know? Had Marcy not told her? Or had she come with us before she had any idea? No, it couldn't be, she was a few months along; she must have at least had an inkling before she stepped on our shuttle…

I bit my lip. Was this what this was all about? Was Marcy not running into the fight, but away from something bigger?

"I am. And I will not let you lock us away."

"Lock you…" Dany's pale face filled the screen again. "Dove, this is incredible! A miracle! Why didn't you tell me?" She paused for a second, glancing over both shoulders. "What do you mean, lock you away? When have I ever given you any kind of indication of—"

"You already have." Marcy dropped one of her hands, balling it into a fist. "Ever since you became empress, I have been relegated to the back of your life. I haven't even left the palace since we arrived here."

"But, Dove, Pyrina…"

"Is dangerous, I know! But it's also my new home. It's the world I'm supposed to help you care for. You're the hope of the Alliance, and I'm the pretty face that makes your hard decisions more palatable. And now, with this child? Your people would never let me leave my quarters if they knew, let alone the palace. I had to do something. I had to show you. I had to…"

I wrapped my arm around her waist, letting her collapse on me as she sobbed. Blayde pried the communicator from her hands, keeping Marcy in frame as she wept.

"I hope this means the negotiations are a success," said Vuzuk, hovering ominously in his corner.

"Just hashing out the minor details," said Blayde.

I rubbed Marcy's back, glaring at Dany on the screen. She had locked my Marcy up. Maybe not her directly, but her people had. The very people I was trying to prove myself to. Dany was supposed to make the Alliance a better place, but how could she when she was making life hell for her own spouse?

"I… I didn't know you felt this way." Dany pressed her face against her camera.

"How could you? We barely talk." Marcy pulled away from me, wiping the tears from her eyes. She pushed herself tall, standing straight again, never letting go of me entirely. "So I showed you. I showed you I was still the woman you married. I saved a planet, all while carrying your child. Is that enough for you to see me as an equal again?"

"I never stopped."

"Then tell that to your ministers," Marcy spat. "From now on, I am your Imperatrix. I am your right hand and your rock, as you are to me. I will be a part of your leadership and help make the Alliance a better place. And I will start with the abhorrent Child Hire 'program.' As of today, it no longer exists. Do you understand?"

"I do," said Dany. "With all my heart I do, Imperatrix."

"Good. And as for the cease-fire" —Marcy jutted her chin to Vuzuk— "send every hopper you have. The clouds are safe for the time being. We are evacuating this planet, and never coming back."

She hung up the call, turning now to me. "And you're throwing my baby shower."

I nodded as quickly and as vigorously as I could. "Anything for you, Imperatrix."

This was the Marcy I never knew she could be, and I was obsessed. She took her communicator back from Blayde, who kept her lips pressed shut, though her eyes were twinkling. I think she might have been as impressed as I was.

"Granadam Vuzuk," said Marcy, "Our ships are coming. We will return control of the clouds to you the second the last finguy has left your world. And you will never hear from us again."

"A shame, in a small way." It trembled its tentacles. "You are such a fascinating primitive species. It took you so long to agree on something so small. What an inefficient method of communication, your mechanical waves."

TWENTY-FOUR

REMEMBER WHEN? UNFORTUNATELY, YES.

Zander

WE COULDN'T SEE THE SUNLIGHT, BUT WE COULD feel it.

It was incredible how much had changed over the course of a few hours. Warmth filled every inch of airspace, toasting my fresh layer of skin, still baby smooth from its recent regrowth. All this, despite the fact the clouds were still there, slowly getting brighter: victory was all the heat we needed.

Shuttles were taking off—flying through the clouds, without crashing back down. Our radios crackled with the voices of our rescue ships, counting off each load of survivors that joined their hulls. Our people were smiling. They laughed. They piled into the space-worthy ships excitedly, happy despite cramped quarters, overjoyed as they left the atmosphere of the planet that had for so long kept them prisoner.

My feet felt like they were hovering an inch off the ground. We'd succeeded. We'd taken the scenic route, but we'd done what we'd set out to: we'd saved the world. Another one for the victory books. And this time, I'd just been along for the ride.

And now the field that charged the clouds was down, the planet was ours. We coordinated the rescue from city to city, getting the shuttles to the right place to ferry our people off world. Blayde had made her way to the cities to the east, offering quick transport back and from the ships. Sally had done the same to the west, ferrying people to the *Traveler* much more efficiently than shuttles could. More effectively than I could, my jumps bore the risk of me taking survivors through the time-space lottery.

Knowing Sally was here so close was burning me up inside. Being away from her now felt like an eternity. But she was safe: we just had to wait a little longer. And maybe take a second vacation; we sure deserved it.

Maybe then we could work out why Nimien had sent us here. Had it been a rescue mission, or was there more for us to find? We could jump to an earlier time in the labyrinth for our answers, but I wasn't sure I wanted to. Not when the last time I'd seen him had left my head… the way it had.

I returned to the mountain relay camp, and I was managing to do some good, helping to organize the crews for their trips to the *Traveler*. Everything was going perfectly, maybe due to the sense of victory that wafted over everyone present, the feeling of camaraderie in the wake of such a long war. I'd expected pushing and shoving for the shuttles, but our people rushed together, not against.

Which could not be said of those leaving the cities. Blayde had told me it was not going well on her planetary tour. Not all the Sters were giving up their finguies easily. But she had enough men to help her when trouble arose. And a catchy summer-pop hit to keep the Sters in line.

"ShortThumb, take over please," Provis ordered as he approached us, smiling more than I had ever seen him do before. The new scar that covered his face added some depth to his handsome features, though I wasn't sure if it made him look more, or less, familiar. The closer he got, the more I remembered the feeling of his lips against mine. Shame crawled up my throat.

"I'm fine, Provis," I said. My cheeks were warm, probably red. Now that we were illuminated by more than just glowing plants, it must have been plain to see. "I've got this, they need me here."

"You need a break." He brushed a hand through his hair. Not that he had enough hair left to warrant the move. "And you deserve that drink. Come on. We don't need to keep it any longer."

He held up his knapsack: the bottle he'd kept offering me at Party City stuck out of the top. He must have raided the ruins.

"They don't need us," said ShortThumb, gesturing at the shuttle as it departed with another batch of whooping survivors. "Enough to go around, General?"

"Plenty," said Provis, grinning wide. "And I think we're done with ranks for a while, ShortThumb."

"I don't think I even know your name. I'm Maryam."

"John," he said, and they bowed at each other before bursting out laughing. "God, I haven't used that name in years."

We found ourselves sitting on the edge of the bridge. In the darkness of the planet, it felt like we were out in the void of space, riding the ship as it tore through the universe.

"What's this?" I asked, as General Provis—John—handed me a bottle, still sealed. Not Alliance, that's for sure. He grinned, already tipsy from his first glugs of celebratory whiskey. I kept a safe distance away, trying to put the memory of the kiss out of my head. If I'd been single, would I have leaned in? Would I be here right now, would I be sitting closer, hoping for a sequel?

"I thought you were a fan of Earth drinks, *Luke Skywalker*," he said, laughing. The sound was electrifying. "It's the good stuff. That's what it is."

He was right. It was good stuff. Scotch, if the label was to be believed. Next time I was back on Earth, I'd stock up.

"You need to remember," a voice whispered in my ear. I spun around but saw nothing but air.

"You all right?" Maryam, formerly ShortThumb, asked. She rested with her back on the viewport, tapping the bottle on her chest.

"Yeah." I nodded. "Thought there was a fly. Thanks, Provis, this is a real treat."

"I've been saving it." He grinned. "I have no idea how it got to this planet, but when I saw it, I knew it was for me. I knew I would drink it today, on *this* day; but I expected all my enemies to be dead, not to let me just walk out."

I didn't answer. Maryam said nothing, either. It had been a long day. A long ordeal for the two of them, more than I'd ever understand. The thought of it chilled the warmth that ran through my veins.

"What happens now?" I took another swig, hoping it would soften me a little. I didn't get drunk, but it would at least warm my insides again.

John looked up, as if he had been in some kind of daze. "What?"

"Now," I repeated. "You're free to go home. What are your plans?"

"Well, that all depends on the Alliance remembering who I am." He let out a heavy sigh, a breath that wracked his entire body. "But then again, I am the highest ranked member of the *Wanderer* survivors. I think the glare of the public eye will force them to free me."

"Wait, what? Free you?" I sat up. "Free you from what?"

"I was an engineering grease monkey from the Alliance draftees," he said with a shrug. "It wasn't exactly my dream to be working on a ship. I miss my home, and my family. My parents, my little sister. God, what is she up to? Not like the Alliance will ever let me go back. But the least they can do is recognize my self-appointed battlefield rank."

"I'll make sure they do," I replied, finishing my glass. Frash, I'd had no idea he'd once been a child-hire. From one form of slavery to another. What a rough lot in life. If I had all my abilities at my disposal, I would have offered him a way off-world, a new life: but the best I could do was put in a good word with Dany, who would most likely owe me one for this.

Remember, the voice repeated. Sally's voice, inside my head. No, there she was, standing in the distance, a ghost floating in the dark, pointing at Provis…

I shook my head. Couldn't my subconscious leave me alone for more than five minutes? I wouldn't let myself feel guilty for how this man felt about me. I wasn't going to kiss him back, and I wasn't here for that. I wasn't going to *forget*.

"I've been meaning to ask." I cleared my throat. Maryam had her eyes closed now, dozing off after the events of the day. Safe. "We came here to find something that had been on the *Wanderer*."

"What?" John sat up straighter, putting the bottle down beside him. "You came for *us?*"

"It's what brought us here in the first place." I wanted to move back, but I had him hooked. He would tell me anything I wanted right now. His eyes met mine and waited expectantly, hanging on my every word. "The problem is, we don't know what else was on that ship."

He sighed heavily. He was so close right now, I could smell his breath, the sweetness of the scotch, taste the hope there.

"We weren't carrying anything," he said, "We were doing recon. No cargo. Unless you're looking for something that belonged to the upper crew members, I don't think our ship had anything of value. Though I wasn't privy to everything. Lower decks don't get the full briefing."

"To come all this way, to be stuck here, and not find what we came here for…" I shook my head.

"Maybe your friend meant something a little more… metaphorical?" John suggested. He was so close now, I could feel the heat off his chest. Just a few more seconds.

Remember! The voice was urgent now, screaming. I shook my head, trying to flush it out. My ears rang, downing it out. John didn't seem to notice, his eyes staring into mine, sparkling.

I couldn't hold it in any longer. "Where have I seen you before, John Provis?"

"What?" He laughed.

"Have we met before this planet?" I couldn't pull my eyes away. He had me entirely caught. I thought I was in control: now, I realized I was helpless. The situation was all his.

"You look terribly familiar."

"No way." John laughed again. "I think I would remember meeting you before, Zander. You're a little hard to forget."

His lips reached mine, and I couldn't pull away. I shattered, helpless, so taken by the gesture, by the overwhelming explosion of sensation.

"Remember!" Sally screamed, and in that instant, the floodgates opened.

A torrent of images rushed into my conscious mind. Thousands of years at once came flooding through, flickering before my eyes in seconds, before I could even grasp what they meant. Sounds, smells, feelings, all came to me at once, and I was washed away in thoughts from centuries ago.

The damn had broken. Everything I'd been trying to hold back was forced upon me. Lifetimes of memories filled my head, shoving into the places they had no room to be. Piling and cramming until I burst at the seams. Until I was exploding, screaming.

Every terrible thing I had ever done, or that had ever been done to me.

Every death. Every rebirth.

Every ending. Every heartbreak. Every loss.

And that's when I saw him.

Provis, at the bridge of a destroyer. Black uniform, gold trimmings. His face older, his hair greying. Provis all the same. His face bore the scar that was only beginning to heal on his face. Behind him flew an army of death, surrounded in fire.

They drifted above the ruins of what had once been a planet. A World. One of many.

The destroyer. The Butcher of Valndra, the reaper of Maarah. The man who killed billions, setting fire to entire planets. The man who brought death to hundreds of star systems. A man neither Blayde nor I could stop. Murder incarnate.

Before I knew what was happening, my hands were around his throat. I plucked his lips from mine and squeezed. Tight, quick. Painless. With a single twist he was gone. The evil never entered the world. The memory of his terror remained, but like a lingering dream. It would never happen now.

Maryam screamed, and something deeper inside me shattered.

I had killed Provis. I had killed… John. Not yet a butcher, not yet a reaper. A lost boy on a distant world who'd only just been freed from his despair.

"You should have listened to me," said Fake-Sally. "I told you that you could not hold them back forever."

My hands trembled before me. What had I done?

"You knew who he was." Was I speaking? My lips had gone numb. I looked down at his corpse. Seconds ago, I'd been kissing him. "You should have told me. You needed to tell me. You could have stopped me."

"You're insane!" Maryam rushed to Provis's side. "John? John!"

"I only know what you know," Fake-Sally said. "I didn't know Provis was the Devil's right hand. But if you had listened, actually taken in your memories, maybe you could have done something instead of, oh, I don't know, murdering him?"

"You should have warned me!" I shouted. "You should have told me!"

She was already gone. My mind was on fire. It was as if there were two of me: a man proud to have rid the world of an evil before it could consume it, and a man terrified of what he had just done. Murder.

Pure and simple murder.

New old memories shouted in my head. The old Zander was begging to get out. The new one shoved it back down. I needed help. I needed…

Sally.

She climbed up the maintenance ladder, smiling. She radiated beauty, her absence having made her grow more stunning; that and having traded her muddy clothes for a soft, clean Alliance uniform from the ship above. The real one? I didn't know.

"Hey, they told me I could find you here." She pushed herself up on the hull. "I—"

"Get help!" Maryam screamed. "He's not breathing!"

Sally's voice dwindled, her eyes widening when she saw the corpse at my feet. Her jaw dropped. And she screamed.

"John!" She choked as she said the name, rushing to the dead man's side, clasping his face in her hands, lifting it to look into his empty eyes. "John..."

She was sobbing now, her tears falling onto the man's hair, and she held him close to her, like a small girl clutching a parent, afraid. And I knew.

Nimien hadn't sent us here on some soul-searching expedition. He didn't want us to rescue this planet. He had found Sally's brother. The man who had died, years ago, in some forgotten place on Earth.

John had been abducted.

John had somehow ended up on board the *Wanderer*, an Alliance ship.

He was alive.

And I had just killed him.

Sally had done the math as well.

She stared at me with blank and empty eyes. The tears had ceased to fall, her face red, nostrils puffy, her stare filling with anger. I shuddered, taking a step back. I had never seen her like this before. Even in the plant-light, she was glowing, an ember at the heart of a bonfire.

"You." Her words were barely more than a whisper. "You killed him."

"He was going to destroy countless star systems!" I sputtered, but somehow the words sounded empty. "Wait!"

Sally took him up in her arms and vanished.

I stared at the sky, the darkness deepening with every passing second.

Sally was gone.

ACKNOWLEDGEMENTS

WRITING A BOOK IS NEVER EASY, BUT WRITING one while completing a thesis is like trying to navigate an asteroid field while being chased by space pirates. It's a bumpy ride, but somehow you manage to avoid crashing and burning, despite all the screaming along the way. But I couldn't have done it without the amazing people who helped make Wanderer a reality.

First, a huge shoutout to my publisher, Michelle Dunbar, who always had faith in me and pushed me to keep going even when I felt like giving up. And to my editors, Hilary Stokes and Anna Johnstone, thank you for your keen eye and expert editing skills. You made this book shine brighter than a supernova.

To my friend Cora Corrigall, thank you for being a constant source of support and love. Your enthusiasm for the characters and the story kept me going through the toughest times. And to my friend Crystal Duvall, thank you for being my hype woman and cheering me on every step of the way. You both are out of this world!

Last but not least, to my husband, thank you for being my partner in life and in writing. You are my moon and stars, and I couldn't have done this without you by my side.

ABOUT THE AUTHOR

S. E. ANDERSON is a galactic wizard who spends her days studying the stars and her nights spinning yarns of interstellar hilarity. With her trademark blend of humor and adventure, she's penned the wildly popular YA science fiction humor series STARSTRUCK SAGA, the zany SciFi Wizard of Oz retelling OVER THE MOON, and the YA contemporary novel AIX MARKS THE SPOT, based on her childhood adventures in Provence.

When she's not wrangling comets, her cats, or her freshly minted husband in Marseille, France, you can find her concocting new worlds and characters, or indulging in a good book with a cup of tea.

CONNECT WITH THE AUTHOR

www.seandersonauthor.com
facebook.com/seandersonauthor
instagram.com/seandersonauthor
tiktok.com/seandersonauthor
twitter.com/seandersonbooks

Ingram Content Group UK Ltd.
Milton Keynes UK
UKHW010852130723
425071UK00001B/7

9 781912 996384